Can Love Last?

Lauren walked a few steps away, then turned and paced back. "I can't do this," she said softly, then more loudly. "I can't do this! I love you, okay? I admit that. But I don't know if I'm ready for this. I mean… yes, I finally admitted something that's taken me this long to figure out. But that doesn't mean I'm ready to accept it. What if you decide we're not right for each other and we break up? What about our friendship then? We could ruin everything we have together!"

"Who says we're going to break up?" he asked softly, taking her hands in his. "Regardless of what you think, I'm not going anywhere. I've worked too hard to get to this point, and I'm not going to throw that all away. I love you, Lauren. I've loved you from the moment I saw you."

"But how do you know our love's going to last beyond tomorrow?" she asked desperately. "Or next week? Or even a year from now? Every guy I ever went out with either dumped me, cheated on me, or turned out to be a complete jerk. Something always came up in the relationships that made them end disastrously. How do I know the same thing's not going to happen with us?"

"No one knows what's going to happen in the future," he admitted gently. "Challenges always present themselves, but the trick is learning to work through those challenges and become stronger because of them. We have something special, Lauren, something I've never felt with *anybody* before. And that special friendship, that special bond… it's what's going to keep us together."

Praise for Love Beyond Tomorrow

In *Love Beyond Tomorrow*, Erin Klingler masterfully draws her readers into the lives of these likable characters. You can't help but laugh at their innocent foibles, feel empathy for their struggles, and cheer at their triumphs. As a writer and avid reader of LDS fiction, I was pulled right into this story, and enjoyed it through to the satisfying ending. For those of us who love to read about love, *Love Beyond Tomorrow* will capture your heart!
Tamra Norton
Best-selling author of *Molly Mormon?*

Love Beyond Tomorrow is a wonderful story that reflects the challenges of finding that special person. Erin Klingler does a fabulous job of taking the reader back to their college days, and reminding us of how difficult love can be, how hard it is to have faith, and just how sweet the rewards really are. A beautiful story about faith, love, trust, and perseverance, *Love Beyond Tomorrow* is a story with something for everyone. Whether you've found your Mr. Right or you're still looking, *Love Beyond Tomorrow* helps to show the true perspective of what it's all about.
Josi Kilpack
Author of *Surrounded by Strangers*

Love Beyond Tomorrow is a tender story of two people struggling with real issues who develop the courage to share what truly matters. Erin Klingler creates a heart-warming tale, a must read for any young woman eager for college and love.
Tara C. Allred
Author of *Sanders' Starfish*

Love Beyond Tomorrow

Erin Klingler

WindRiver Publishing
St. George, Utah

Queries, comments or correspondence concerning this work should be directed to the author and submitted to WindRiver Publishing at:

authors@windriverpublishing.com

Information regarding this work or other works published by WindRiver Publishing, Inc., and instructions for submitting manuscripts for review for publication, can be found at:

www.windriverpublishing.com

Love Beyond Tomorrow

Copyright © 2004 by Erin Klingler (www.erinklingler.com)
Cover design by Cathi Stevenson (www.bookcoverexpress.com)

All rights reserved. This book or any part thereof may not be reproduced in any form whatsoever, whether by graphic, visual, electronic, filming, microfilming, tape recording or any other means, without the prior written permission of the Publisher. Inquiries should be addressed to "Copyrights" at info@windriverpublishing.com.

WindRiver Publishing, the WindRiver Brand Logo and the WindRiver Windmill Logo are trademarks of WindRiver Publishing, Inc. All other brand, product or service names are the trademarks of their respective owners.

Library of Congress Control Number: 2003116756
ISBN 1-886249-12-1

First Printing 2004

Printed in the U.S.A. by Malloy, Inc. on acid-free paper

With love, I'd like to dedicate this book to the following people:

To my loving husband Dave, who is so very kind and patient, and supports me in all that I do.

To my mom and dad, who taught me to never let anyone tell me something couldn't be done.

To my online L&C buddies (you know who you are). You've taught me everything I know about writing and helped turn writing into a passion for me instead of just a hobby.

And to Barb, my very dearest friend. You always lift my spirits and brighten my day. If it weren't for all your hours of brainstorming and encouragement, I never would have finished this book.

Prologue

The pounding music reverberated through Ben's head making it impossible for him to think. Was the throbbing in his temples really matching the deep bass of the drums, or was it all in his mind?

Reaching up, he yanked the pillow from beneath his head and clamped it over his face, hoping to drown out the deafening music and drunken shouts from the party goers outside his bedroom door. It was only eight o'clock, but Steve and Josh's party was well on its way to becoming legendary. But then, their parties always were.

He shook his head in disgust. *What's happened to my friends, anyway?* he wondered. *All through high school they were fairly respectable, but the minute they entered college they turned into beer-guzzling party animals. I hardly know them anymore, let alone like them.*

Impossibly, the volume of the music seemed to rise yet another notch. Ben angrily threw the pillow off his head and sat up. "Forget this," he mumbled to himself as he got off his bed and reached for his backpack. "I'm going to the library where I can get some peace and quiet."

He quickly shoved a couple of textbooks into his backpack and struggled into his coat, wondering if Madge at the circulation desk might have some of her granddaughter's rum raisin cookies stashed under the counter to share with him. The possibility gave his spirits a little boost as he hurried from the room.

Negotiating the dark, crowded hallway of his apartment proved to be more difficult than he'd expected. He had to fight his way through the milling bodies, stumbling over half-empty pizza boxes and dozens of empty beer cans as he went. Just as he reached the living room, a stocky figure loomed out of the darkness and blocked his path.

"Hey Ben, where ya' goin'?" the man shouted above the din of the music.

Ben instantly recognized Josh's drunken voice. His friend threw a heavy arm around his shoulders and turned to the crowd of dancing couples that were laughing and talking loudly around them.

"Hey, everyone!" he yelled, holding up his beer can in an attempt to get their attention. It's my good friend Ben! Let's hear it for Ben!"

No one paid the slightest attention and Ben pushed his friend's arm away in disgust. The sudden motion caused Josh's beer to slosh out of its can and spill down Ben's jeans. Ben muttered a curse under his breath and bent over to brush what he could of the amber liquid from his clothes.

"*Sorry*, buddy," Josh half-slurred as he watched Ben's futile attempt to clean himself off. "Whynt'cha have a beer, man? You look a little tense."

Ben frowned and turned away, reaching up a hand to push his friend out of smelling distance. "Josh, go somewhere and dry up, will you?" he grumbled as he maneuvered past his roommate and practically ran out the front door.

The sounds of the party faded, then disappeared altogether as he reached the stairwell and made his way down to the ground floor. As he hurried out into the night, he was surprised to see that it was snowing, and from the looks of the snow-covered landscape, it had been snowing for quite a while. The weather had driven everyone inside, making him feel even more lost and alone than ever.

He stood there, unmoving, for several moments, letting the heavy, wet snowflakes tangle in his hair and wet his face. *When did my life take such a turn for the worse?* he asked himself miserably. *I'm studying pre-law at Harvard, something I absolutely love, I'm out on my own, with no parents to continually—and impossibly—try to please, and supposedly, the best years of my life are upon me. So why do I feel so miserable?*

With a troubled sigh, he shouldered his backpack and started walking, listening to the snow crunch under his feet as he walked the short distance to the campus. He waited at the corner for a car to pass, then stepped out into the street and hurried across. He shoved his hands deep into his coat pockets in an effort to ward off the chill in the air. To his surprise, his fingers encountered a stiff piece of paper.

Curious, he pulled the paper from his pocket and saw that it was a folded envelope. He looked at it more closely and saw his name written neatly and firmly across the front in a familiar script. He frowned. It was a letter from his father. He'd forgotten to open it yesterday after getting his mail. He was momentarily confused by the San Francisco return address until he remembered his father had been working with associates there for the past few weeks on a case.

Looking up from the envelope, Ben spotted a bench along the path up ahead. He walked over to it, dusted the light covering of snow off the slats, and sat down. Hesitantly, he looked back down at the letter. He debated for several moments whether to read it or not, but he finally gave in to curiosity and pulled the heavy linen sheets from the covering. Taking a deep breath, he started to read.

> *Ben,*
>
> *Your mother called and told me about that "B" you got on your midterms. Don't worry about it. Your professor, Stanley Winston, owes me a big favor for that case I won for him last spring, so I'll have a talk with him. Besides, the university wants our million dollars to help them build the new library. It won't take more than a phone call to let them know that if they don't see to it that you graduate at the top of your class, our money goes away. That's the one thing I*

hope you're learning there at law school. Everything and everyone in this world has their price.

Apparently, your sister refuses to stop going out with that chef from upstate New York, even though I've forbidden her to ever see him again. She's far better off with Charles Ingram's son. He's just graduated from Princeton and will be inheriting his father's millions before long, I suspect, since Charles isn't in the best of health. Call and talk to her and make her listen to reason, would you? She always listens to you more than me.

Let me know how the rest of your classes are going. If you need me to pull any strings for you, drop me a line.

Your father

Ben's jaw clenched as he finished reading the letter. Crumpling its pages into a tight ball, he resisted the urge to throw it out into the snow. He'd spent a lifetime watching his father use his power and position to intimidate, manipulate, and cajole people into doing things the way *he* wanted them to be done, and apparently, his father hadn't changed one bit. What he didn't seem to realize, though, was that Ben didn't want or need someone to pull strings for him. He refused to be his father's puppet in the play of life, to be danced around on stage as the main attraction, to be used to prove to his father's colleagues what a great father William J. Morrison was.

Ben shook his head. He loved studying law, but if being a lawyer meant becoming like his father, he didn't want any part of it. With a heavy sigh, he leaned back and stared out at the beautiful, snow-covered landscape, hoping to put his troubles aside, if only for a few minutes. Snow had draped everything in a velvety covering of white and the only noise he could hear was coming from the nearly deserted street he'd just crossed. It was a comforting contrast to the turmoil he felt inside. But the longer he sat there, the more his thoughts continued to force their way back into his mind.

Is this really what I want to be doing with my life? he asked himself seriously. *Do I really want to be here, living in a nightclub of an apartment with beer-guzzling, party animals for roommates, putting up with a father who thinks everyone in the world was put here specifically for him to buy and sell, and trying to live up to the expectations of law professors who think my father is so great, and who expect me to be like him?*

The answer was a resounding "No." But if this wasn't what he was supposed to be doing with his life, then what *was* he supposed to be doing? Surely there had to be more to life than this. There had to be. But he truthfully didn't know what it was.

Pushing a hand through his thick, dark brown hair dampened by the lightly falling snow, he sighed unhappily and leaned forward, putting his elbows on his knees and dropping his head into his hands in resignation. He didn't know how long he'd been sitting that way when a voice seemed to come out of nowhere.

"Are you okay, sir?"

Startled, he jerked his head up. He was surprised to see two guys about his age standing in front of him. They were dressed in long overcoats that hung open, revealing a glimpse of dark suits and ties underneath. His interest piqued by their appearance, he studied them more closely and noticed there was something different about them, something peaceful and confident in their countenance that instantly drew him in. With a start, he realized one of them had just spoken.

"I'm sorry, what did you say?" he asked, remembering his manners.

"We asked if you were okay. We didn't expect to see anyone out in this weather."

Ben smiled. "What, you don't think it's beautiful?"

The guy with the reddish-brown hair grinned broadly. "Beautiful? I'm from Idaho. I've seen enough snow to last me the rest of my life."

"Idaho, really?" Ben asked, raising an inquisitive eyebrow. "What are you doing all the way out here?"

"Actually, we're representatives for the Church of Jesus Christ of Latter-day Saints," he said eagerly, gesturing at himself and his blond friend. "We voluntarily serve missions when we turn nineteen, and we go wherever we're asked to share our message with those who want to hear it."

"Message?" Ben asked curiously. "What message?"

The blond guy opened his mouth to respond, but his obviously eager friend beat him to it. "It's about our purpose in life, what we're all here on earth to do."

Ben found himself intrigued. "Really?" he ventured. "Like what?"

The two young men turned to each other and smiled, then quickly hurried over to the bench and sat down beside him.

As Ben watched them pull a few items from a backpack, he had no idea that on that snowy December night on the outskirts of a Boston campus, those two young men in dark suits and overcoats were about to share a message with him that would change his life forever.

Chapter One

Eight Months Later

"Oh, *yeaaahhhh!* I'm new in town! How about showing me around?"

Lauren jumped at her friend's earsplitting yell and nearly swerved her late model, gold Honda Civic into the car driving in the lane next to them. She quickly straightened the steering wheel and turned to glare at her friend, only to see that Allison was leaning halfway out of the passenger side window and waving at two admittedly gorgeous guys about their age who were walking down the sidewalk.

Lauren rolled her eyes at her friend's antics and reached over to give her shirt a yank. "Come on, Allison, you're going to kill yourself hanging out of the window like that! Have some pride, would you? Besides, you nearly scared me half to death."

Allison just laughed as she plopped back into her seat and turned to smile broadly at Lauren, her blue eyes sparkling energetically. "Oh, lighten up, Lauren! We've been waiting forever for our college years, and now that they're finally here I'm going to make sure I enjoy every minute of them."

Lauren scowled at her before turning her attention back to her driving. "By shouting at every cute guy we drive past and making an idiot of yourself? Somehow I don't think that's going to get you a lot of dates."

"How do you know unless you try?" Allison asked with a mischievous grin.

Lauren simply smiled and shook her head in surrender. After all these years, she was used to her best friend's antics.

Out of the corner of her eye, she watched as Allison flipped open the tiny mirror on the visor to inspect her flawlessly-styled, short blond hair, newly cut in a cute and trendy style. She then ran a quick hand through the turned up ends at the nape of her neck and swiped away a fleck of stray mascara from her eyelid.

Lauren didn't know why Allison bothered. Her friend looked amazing as always, and with her curvy five-foot-five figure, her beautiful clear skin and her amazing sense of style, what guy wouldn't take a second look?

Feeling suddenly self-conscious in her cut-off jeans and oversized, navy T-shirt, Lauren glanced into the rearview mirror and noticed with disgust that as usual, she'd forgotten to put on any makeup that morning. She wrinkled her nose at her appearance. It was times like these, when she sat next to her perfectly groomed, well-dressed friend as they drove to their new apartment complex, that she wished she could have found time to at least look presentable.

Not that it would matter, Lauren thought with a sigh. She'd spent years watching guys flock around Allison and her other pretty, feminine friends, while she only went out on an occasional date. Her lack of dates wasn't because she wasn't pretty, though. She was. At five-foot-ten she was tall and willowy with a trim, athletic figure, eyes the color of a bright copper penny and long, reddish-brown hair.

But first impressions had never been her problem. It was when the guys learned more about her that they lost interest. They just didn't want to go out with someone who could outplay them on a ball field, maintain a 4.0 grade average, and score in the ninetieth percentile on the SATs. She'd realized long ago that guys didn't go for girls like her who were smart, athletic and who generally threatened their egos.

But then, she'd learned that the hard way.

Giving herself a mental shake, she managed to push aside her painful memories and reached up to resignedly smooth back a few reddish-brown wisps of hair that had escaped from her long ponytail. As she turned her attention back to the road, the driver in front of her suddenly slammed on his brakes and turned into a driveway. Lauren had to swerve to avoid a collision. She didn't realize she'd been gripping the steering wheel so hard until Allison reached over to squeeze her hand comfortingly.

"Lauren, relax," she said. "We made it. We're in Rexburg, Idaho, the thriving Metropolis of the west."

Lauren grinned, her bitterness of a moment ago eased. "Yeah, right," she replied, looking around at the buildings of the surprisingly small town that was home to BYU-Idaho. "To tell you the truth, though, I kind of like it. It seems peaceful."

"A college town? Peaceful? Not if I have anything to say about it," she quipped, once again flashing her energetic smile. Then, as if to prove what she meant, she turned and let out an earth-shattering wolf whistle at a group of guys playing Frisbee in the parking lot of a nearby apartment complex.

"Oh, look," Lauren pointed out teasingly. "A whole apartment complex full of guys. Are you sure you wouldn't like me to just drop you off right here so you can make the rounds?"

Allison laughed and smacked Lauren on the arm indignantly. "All right, all right, I'll stop embarrassing you." Her eyes shifted from the guys in the parking lot to the buildings ahead. One caught her eye and she gestured excitedly toward it. "Hey, isn't that our apartment complex over there?"

Lauren glanced in the direction Allison was pointing and spotted a tall, white building on the right. "I think so," she answered uncertainly, squinting to study the building more closely since she'd only driven past it once a couple of months ago.

As they drew closer, Allison spotted the sign out front and started thumping Lauren's arm enthusiastically. "Yeah, this is it! Turn in that driveway right there!"

"Ow, quit pounding on me!" Lauren complained, though inwardly she was as excited as Allison. She'd been looking forward to college for a long time, and now that they were finally here, she felt her stomach start to dance with nervous anticipation.

Steering her car into an empty parking space near the front of the complex, she turned off the ignition. For several moments they sat in silence, studying the tall, three-story building. The first level sat a few feet below ground, with the doors of its apartments only half visible above the top of the cement retaining wall that rose a few inches above the ground and ran the length of the building. But clearly visible through the second and third floor's wrought-iron railings were the dozens of apartment doors that lined the cement walkways. It was on the second floor that they spotted a sign on the door of the end apartment that read "Office."

Allison pushed open the door and jumped out of the car. "Well, what are we waiting for?" she exclaimed eagerly. "Let's go check in!"

A few minutes later they had their welcome packets and keys in hand and were walking down the long, cement walkway toward their second floor apartment. "Hey, here it is—205!" Allison exclaimed, picking up her pace. "And it looks like somebody's already moved in."

Lauren followed Allison's gaze and saw that the curtains were open and a few pictures had already been hung on the white living room walls. Allison threw open their apartment door and bounded in, announcing their presence in her usual, energetic way.

With a sweeping glance, Lauren took in the apartment that would be her home for the school year. It wasn't bad. The decent-sized living room contained a neutral brown couch, a matching loveseat and armchair, and an older end table with a lamp. At the far end of the living room, the kitchen was clearly visible from the front door, with only a partial wall to separate it from the living room.

"Helloooo!" Allison called out eagerly. "Anybody here?"

Allison's greeting was followed by sounds coming from the back of the apartment and a moment later, a tall, pretty girl with long blond hair and emerald green eyes emerged from the hallway wearing faded jeans, a white T-shirt with the words "Santa Cruz" printed across the front in blue lettering, and a bright, cheerful smile.

"Hi!" she exclaimed as she tossed her blond hair over her shoulder and extended a slender hand to Allison, then to Lauren. "I'm Breanna, but you can call me Bree. You must be my new roommates!"

Allison nodded and gave her a cheerful smile of her own. "I'm Allison, and this is Lauren. We're from Idaho Falls, which is just a half hour from here."

A look of recognition crossed Bree's face. "Oh, I know where that is! I remember driving past it a couple of days ago on my way up here from California with my parents."

"Are your parents still here?" Lauren asked politely.

Bree waved a hand dismissively as if shooing away some annoying insect. "Oh, no, they're long gone. They left the day after we got here. I wanted to fly, but my parents insisted on driving me. They're a little bit overprotective." She rolled her pretty green eyes dramatically.

Lauren smiled understandingly, then turned to glance around the room. "Looks like you've been busy," she commented, gesturing to the stack of dish towels on the kitchen counter, a plastic drainer next to the sink with drying dishes resting in it, and the several pictures hung carefully on the living room walls.

"Well, I've been alone here for a couple of days, so it wasn't like there was a lot to do," she confessed. "Besides, I have a friend who went to college here last year who warned me to bring some pictures and stuff to decorate the apartment to make it feel more like home. She said it would cut back on the homesickness."

"That's the nice thing about living so close," Allison admitted. "Lauren and I can just drive home if we get homesick—although I can't imagine *that* happening. Not with all these good looking guys around campus to distract us."

"Oh, I know!" Bree immediately chimed in, her green eyes sparkling with excitement. "I've already scoped out the guy's dorms, and there's a really big guy's complex just across the street. I say they're both definitely worth checking out!"

Allison's face lit up, her smile making it clear that she was thrilled to find out that her newest roommate was as neurotically boy-crazy as she was. "I like the way you think," she told Bree happily. "Especially since Lauren here avoids guys like the plague."

Bree lifted her eyebrows at Lauren in surprise. "What, you don't like guys?"

"Only if they're related to me," she responded dryly.

"Ah-ha," Bree replied as if she'd just uncovered the secret of the universe. "Let me guess. You've been seriously burned in a previous relationship."

Lauren frowned. "You could say that. Trust me, guys are highly overrated. They just want some shallow, good-looking girl to hang on their arm at social events and make them popular with their friends. The second they find out a girl has a mind of her own and knows who she is and what she wants out of life, they take off running in the opposite direction. Their fragile male egos just can't take feeling threatened. So before you two start getting any ideas about setting me up on some disastrous blind date, let me make something clear—count me out."

Bree looked at Allison and whistled. "It's not going to be easy to change her opinion of the male gender, is it?"

"Nope," Allison answered. "But I told her that this year I'm going to prove to her once and for all that not all guys are bent on making a girl's life miserable. If it's the last thing I do, I'm going to help her find her knight in shining armor. Want to help?"

Bree's eyes lit up. "You bet! I'm all for playing cupid."

"Forget it, you two." Lauren shook her head, causing her long ponytail to bounce around her shoulders. "Save your dating games for the guys *you* want to go out with, okay? I've got better things to do. Like unpacking. What do you say, Allison? Should we get started?"

Allison sighed. "I guess we should. The sooner we get it over with, the better."

"Do you need any help?" Bree asked.

Lauren nodded gratefully. "Sure, we'd love some help carrying things up from the car, if you don't mind."

"Not at all." Bree gestured to the hallway. "Let me show you where everything is, and then I'll come help you."

They followed Bree through the door separating the living room from the hall and sleeping quarters. As they walked down the hall, Lauren noticed that the bathroom was bigger than she'd expected, with a long counter containing double sinks, and a large vanity area. They continued on down to the end of the hall where there were two bedrooms.

Bree gestured to the door on their left. "I'm sharing this bedroom with Melia. She's originally from Hawaii, but she's lived in southern California for the past ten years. She's really great. You'll like her." Then she pushed open the door on their right. "This room doesn't have anyone in it. I'm assuming you two want to share."

As Lauren walked into the vacant bedroom, her eyes swept the room's contents, taking in the desk, the two twin-sized beds, the four-drawer dresser, and the large closet occupying one of the walls. The room wasn't anything fancy, but it was neat and clean and had ample space for their needs.

Lauren dropped her duffle bag and welcome folder onto the bed next to the window and said to Allison, "Since you'll probably never be here anyway, I'm sure you won't mind if I take this bed."

Allison shrugged. "Fine by me. But now that we know where to bring our stuff, let's start unloading. I don't want to be stuck here all afternoon."

For the next twenty minutes, the three of them talked and laughed as they brought up their things from the car and started to unpack. By the time they were more or less finished, Lauren knew they were all well on their way to becoming fast friends.

"Lauren and I were planning on going to the campus to look around," Allison told Bree. "Do you want to come with us?"

Bree nodded happily. "I'd love to."

Just then they heard the front door open, and moments later a slim girl about five-foot-seven, with a pretty, oval face and the most gorgeous, waist length, jet black hair Lauren had ever seen appeared in the hall, balancing a rather large stack of books in her arms. Even if Bree hadn't told them that Melia was Hawaiian, Lauren would've had no trouble guessing. Her exotic features and slender form were absolutely stunning.

"Hey, Melia," Bree greeted her cheerfully. "Geez, did you just clean out the bookstore or what?"

"Just about." Melia laughed. "I had no idea how many books my classes were going to require. I had nowhere near this many books for my classes here last year." Melia put her books on her bed, then came back to stand next to Bree in the hall. She offered a friendly smile to Lauren and Allison. "I don't believe we've met."

Bree quickly made the introductions, and Lauren found herself immediately liking Melia. She was as friendly as Bree, but there was something different about her, an air of maturity and an amazing amount of confidence and grace that Lauren instantly admired.

"We were just heading up to the campus to check things out," Allison told Melia. "You're welcome to join us, but it looks like you just came from there."

Melia smiled graciously. "I did. Thanks for the offer, but I wore myself out carrying all those books back from the bookstore. I think I'll just catch up on a few things around here instead. You guys go on ahead."

"Next time you have an armful, give me a holler and I'll drive you," Lauren offered.

Melia cocked an eyebrow. "Hmmm. A roommate with a car, huh? That's a definite plus." She winked. "I'll take you up on that ride in the future."

"Do," Lauren told her sincerely. Then she turned to her other two roommates. "Are you guys ready to go?"

Allison and Bree nodded, and soon they were on their way to the campus.

• • •

An hour later, Bree ended their tour at the student union building, the Manwaring Center, and Lauren gestured to the bookstore's entrance.

"Do you guys mind if we go in?" Lauren asked. "I'm supposed to check in with the manager to find out what my work schedule's going to be."

Bree raised her eyebrows in surprise. "You're going to be working at the bookstore?"

Lauren nodded. "Since my parents weren't really planning on paying tuition and housing costs for me, I thought it'd be nice to get a job so they wouldn't have to shoulder all the costs."

"How very responsible of you," Bree teased lightly as they walked through the tiled lobby toward the bookstore's entrance. "How come they weren't planning on paying tuition? Weren't you planning on going to college?"

"It's not that," Lauren told her. "It's just that I could've gotten free tuition at the junior college where my dad teaches, or I could've taken one of the full-ride scholarships I was offered from a couple of other colleges."

Bree's eyes widened. "Why on earth didn't you take them?"

"The scholarships were to play softball, and I wanted to concentrate on my classes instead. It's not easy to do that when you're at practice for hours a day, and on the road, traveling to games."

"So, why not go to school where your dad teaches and get the free tuition?"

Lauren scrunched up her nose. "That's exactly what my dad wanted me to do, but I figured it wouldn't have been the same as going away to college and being on my own."

"Makes sense," Bree answered with a nod. "I didn't want to stay at home, either. It's not nearly as much fun. Besides, I knew most of the Mormon guys at home. Here, there's a whole campus of cute ones I don't know."

She winked, and Lauren rolled her eyes teasingly. She and Allison were simply incorrigible.

When they made it through the crowds of students standing in lines at the front of the bookstore with armloads of textbooks and supplies, Allison and Bree went to browse the store's shelves while Lauren asked one of the employees whom she was supposed to check in with. A few minutes later she found herself talking with the manager, Brother Jenks, a slightly plump, cheerful man in his late forties. He gave her a brief tour of the store and explained what her job entailed.

They were just setting up a time for her to come in for training the next day when Brother Jenks spotted one of his employees walking past with an armload of books and waved him over. When the guy turned their direction, Lauren couldn't help noticing how handsome he was with his sandy blond hair, deep blue eyes, and the longest lashes she'd ever seen.

Brother Jenks quickly introduced them. "Lauren Holt, this is Dan Barker. It's his second year working here, so he can answer any questions you might have over the next few days."

"New blood, huh?" Dan asked with obvious delight as he set his stack of books down and flashed his brilliant, toothpaste-commercial smile her direction. He turned to Brother Jenks and spoke with a casualness that suggested he knew him well. "I think you've done well hiring this one. She's sure to make an impression on the customers. The male ones, anyway," he added, including her in his broad wink.

Brother Jenks gave him a fatherly look of warning, then turned a reassuring smile Lauren's direction. "Don't worry. Dan here's my nephew, and I know him well enough to assure you that he's harmless. He thinks he's working here to have a great social life, but the truth of the matter is, his dad wants him working here where I can keep an eye on him." Dan laughed.

"Okay, you got me. But I'll have you know that working here definitely has its advantages. For example, who would've known that my reward for coming in to work today would be meeting the prettiest girl on campus?"

Lauren raised her eyebrows in surprise. Who did this guy think he was? He obviously knew he was drop dead gorgeous and extremely charming. But that was proof enough that he couldn't be trusted. Any guy so charming and witty had to have practiced on somebody. Or a hundred somebodies. She, however, refused to be taken in by Dan's smooth words and perfect smile. She'd fallen for such a guy once before and it had only brought her heartache. So much, in fact, that she knew there was no way she was ever going to let it happen again.

Brother Jenks was suddenly called to the phone and hurried away. Dan turned to Lauren and flashed her a pleased smile. "Finally, alone with the woman of my dreams," he said in his smooth, rich voice.

Coolly, Lauren glanced around the bustling aisles, then cocked a condescending eyebrow at him. "In a store full of people? I'd hardly call that alone."

Dan chuckled. "You've got a point." He glanced momentarily around the aisle, then leaned forward conspiratorially and lowered his voice to a husky whisper. "So, what are you doing later tonight? I'm sure I can find somewhere for us to go where we can really be alone. Maybe I could give you a late night tour of the campus?"

Lauren nearly laughed out loud at his obvious come-on. Instead, she smiled coyly, leaned forward, and whispered in his ear, "Not a chance."

When she pulled away, she caught a quick flash of disappointment in his eyes, but then it was gone, and his toothpaste-commercial smile was back. "Well, you can't blame a guy for trying."

In spite of herself, Lauren allowed a little smile of her own to slip out. "I'm flattered, really, but I'll tell you right off—I'm not into the dating scene. I'm here to work my way through school and get good grades. That's it."

Dan shook his head and made a disapproving clicking sound with his tongue. "Doesn't sound like much of a life. Didn't anyone ever tell you that college was supposed to be fun?"

She straightened up defensively. "I have fun. Just not the way you obviously do."

"Hey, don't knock it 'til you try it," he quipped easily.

Before Lauren could reply, Allison and Bree descended upon them in a whirlwind of activity. "Ooh, Lauren, who's your new friend?" they cooed. "Aren't you going to introduce us?"

As Dan's brilliant smile and hopelessly long eyelashes turned to his new, more appreciative audience, Lauren slipped away to check her work schedule. The last thing she wanted to do was hang around and watch her friends flirt shamelessly with her new coworker. She carefully wrote down her schedule, then collected Allison and Bree and left the bookstore.

"Man, is he ever cute!" Bree raved breathlessly as they walked out of the building and headed for Lauren's car. "I can't believe you're going to be working with him! You're so lucky."

"If you say so," Lauren replied indifferently.

Allison gave Lauren an exasperated look. "Come on, Lauren, give him a chance. He's gorgeous! What if he's your knight in shining armor?"

"You've got to be kidding!" Lauren scoffed. "Sure, he's good looking and charming, but my idea of a knight in shining armor doesn't consist of some commitment-shy guy with a hundred different girls' phone numbers in his pocket."

"Well, if you aren't interested," Bree chimed in, "then you won't mind if I give it a shot. I'd be more than happy to have a commitment-free date with him. Or several, for that matter."

Lauren rolled her eyes. "Fine by me."

As Bree and Allison argued playfully over who should go out with him first, Lauren found herself tuning out. If her friends wanted to chase after every cute guy they came across, that was up to them. But she didn't want any part of it. Opening herself up to someone only meant opening herself up to being hurt in the process. She'd learned the hard way that it wasn't worth it.

They all climbed into the car and Lauren followed Bree's directions to a grocery store so they could pick up a few things. When they finally returned home and put their purchases away, Lauren retreated to her bedroom, relieved to have a few minutes to herself.

She saw that one small box still remained unpacked on her bed so she crossed over to it and opened the lid, smiling when she saw it contained the framed pictures she'd brought from home. Her smile widened as she looked at each picture in turn.

In the first picture, she was sitting with her family in a large raft, completely drenched and smiling triumphantly after whitewater rafting down their favorite section of the Snake River. The second picture was one that had been taken of her four months ago as she stood on the pitcher's mound, smiling broadly, mitt and ball still in hand after pitching a no-hitter and leading her high school softball team to the state championship title. Her dad stood next to her, smiling just as broadly, with his arm slung proudly around her shoulders.

Putting it on the dresser next to the first, she turned and lifted the last picture from the box. When she did, a sudden rush of love and warmth flooded through her. This picture was her very favorite. It had been taken of her and her brother Jack the day her family had driven him down to the MTC to send him off on his mission. She couldn't help noticing how much they looked alike with their reddish-brown hair and shining brown eyes as they stood, cheeks pressed together and arms around each other's shoulders, mugging for the camera.

She smiled. Of all her brothers, Jack was her favorite. Whenever things had gotten tough or she'd needed an encouraging word, a sympathetic ear, or just a friend to do something with, Jack had always been there for her. The last two years had been really tough, not having him around, but he'd always written such encouraging letters full of what he was going through that it had helped make the time go a little faster. Just seeing his open, friendly face in the picture made her feel a little better.

"What are you doing?"

The voice startled Lauren and she looked up to see Bree standing in the doorway. "Hey," Lauren greeted her with a smile. "What's going on?"

"I'm just letting you know that we're going to order pizza. It's too crazy to try to cook tonight. Do you want to chip in?"

Lauren nodded. "Absolutely."

Bree spotted the picture Lauren was holding and came in to investigate. "Hey, who's the gorgeous guy? You holding out on us, Holt?"

Lauren shook her head and laughed. "No, this is my brother Jack. He's in New York on a mission, but he should be home in about a month. I can hardly wait."

"Does he have a girlfriend?" Bree asked, only half teasing.

Lauren glared at her playfully. "Is that all you think about? Finding a cute guy to go out with?"

"Not all the time," Bree defended herself. Then she winked. "Just most of the time."

Lauren shook her head and grinned as she set the picture on her dresser next to the others. When she turned back to Bree, she saw that her new roommate had a thoughtful look on her face. "What?" she asked cautiously.

Bree deliberated for a moment, then forged ahead. "Did you really mean what you said earlier? About not wanting anything to do with guys?"

Lauren's expression clouded over. "The last time I let myself get involved I got destroyed. It still hurts to think about it. I don't know if I ever want to go through that again, you know?" At the sympathy in Bree's eyes, she looked down at the hem of her shirt and fingered a loose thread. "Anyway, I'd love to believe that there's one special man out there who's just waiting to sweep me off my feet and promise that we'll live happily ever after; but after everything I've been through, I'm not sure I believe in 'happily ever after.'"

"Well, I do," Bree said quietly but firmly. "And I hope that Mr. Right comes along this year and proves you wrong. In the meantime, we've got a pizza to order." Then, with a quick wink and a reassuring smile, Bree turned and headed out of the room.

When she was alone again, Lauren turned to look out her window at the looming darkness beyond, as if it alone held the answers she sought. As she did, Bree's words echoed over and over again in her mind. Her new roommate seemed so certain that not all relationships were doomed to fail. Could she be right? Could there really be a "happily ever after" guy out there waiting for her somewhere, staring out at the same night sky she was?

For a moment Lauren felt a glimmer of hope. But then she remembered Dan Barker at the bookstore, and that glimmer was quickly dashed. He was exactly like every other womanizing flirt she'd known in high school who only cared if a girl was a perfect size six and totally gorgeous. He didn't care one bit about who she was, or about her goals and aspirations. In fact, he was so much like Matt that the resemblance was uncanny.

Her heart clenched painfully at the memory.

Matt Nelson had been one of the most popular guys in school—and definitely the best looking guy in her stake. He was witty and charming, and it had surprised her when he'd started flirting with her near the end of her junior year.

She'd been skeptical of his obvious interest in her at first, since she'd been hurt more times than she cared to admit by guys who only dated her long enough to realize they felt threatened by her drive, her athletic ability, and her scholastic success, and would quickly dump her for one of her more feminine friends. But when Matt continued to pursue her, she found herself falling for him and was soon head over heels in love. But then the night of her junior prom, her world had come crashing down around her.

Unwilling to dredge up painful memories, Lauren pulled her thoughts from her past—only to have the pain return when she again thought of her encounter with Dan at the bookstore. She frowned and shook her head.

She'd secretly hoped that she'd see more of a maturity level in the guys she met at college, but obviously that wasn't going to happen. Apparently guys were guys, no matter how old they were or what stage of life they were in. There were no knights in shining armor, no gallant and chivalrous men waiting to sweep her off her feet.

And, surprisingly enough, she realized she was disappointed.

With a sigh, Lauren turned away from her window and went to join her roommates for dinner.

Chapter Two

Ben tore his gaze away from the darkening night sky outside his bedroom window and forced his attention back to his unpacking. *What am I doing here?* he asked himself for what seemed like the hundredth time. *I'm 2,000 miles from home, enrolled at a college that I didn't even know existed six months ago and other than Craig, I don't know a soul in town. I must be completely crazy.*

When his friend Craig had first suggested he head out west with him to go to school at BYU-Idaho, he'd thought he was crazy. Ben didn't know a thing about Idaho, other than the fact that it was famous for its potatoes. It made more sense for him to keep working to try to save enough money for his tuition now that he was on his own, without any monetary support from his family. But something about heading out west with Craig kept nagging at him, and the idea simply wouldn't leave him alone. Finally, he decided to pray about it, and when he did, his answer came immediately.

Heavenly Father wanted him at BYU-Idaho.

For whatever reason, he was supposed to be there. He knew it without a shadow of a doubt. He wasn't exactly sure why his Heavenly Father wanted him there, but at this point in his life he was used to going on faith. Sometimes it seemed like faith was all he had.

Putting away the last of his clothes, he zipped his suitcase and carefully slid it under his bed. Finally, he turned to inspect his room. A smile crept across his face. His own side of the room was neat and orderly while Craig's side looked like several suitcases had exploded. Clothes and personal items were strewn haphazardly across the unmade bed and recently purchased textbooks, folders, and school supplies littered the desk and floor. If he hadn't been used to his best friend's mess, it might have made him crazy. But he wasn't about to complain. Craig had come into his life right when he'd needed someone the most, and he was eternally grateful.

With a mixture of happiness and heartache, he thought back to when he was taking the missionary discussions. He'd been so excited to learn about the gospel. Everything about life suddenly made sense. He was a child of God and had an eternal purpose. He felt wonderful. He felt invincible.

Until he told his parents about his decision to be baptized.

He could still remember that day vividly. He'd never seen his father so angry. His father had always been an atheist and he couldn't believe his son would want to spend his days worshipping a God that didn't exist. He'd used his best prosecuting skills to destroy the Mormon Church's credibility in his son's eyes and when that didn't work, he threatened to disown him if he followed through with his plans to be baptized.

Thinking his father was bluffing, he went ahead and got baptized… and immediately found himself out on the street, penniless. Church members had taken him into their homes until he'd been able to find a job and an apartment, but he'd faced a completely different lifestyle than the one he'd known. He had felt discouraged and alone. If it hadn't been for his testimony of the gospel's truthfulness and his faith that he was doing what the Lord wanted him to do, he might have called it quits.

But then he'd met Craig. Craig had just returned from his mission a few months before and had been assigned as Ben's home teaching companion. They'd clicked instantly. Maybe it had to do with Craig's having been a missionary for the past two years and Ben being newly baptized, but they'd formed a fast friendship and been inseparable ever since. Ben found himself thanking Heavenly Father every day for Craig's friendship and for the particularly inspired timing. He doubted he would have made it without him.

The sound of laughter outside his main floor window brought him back to the present. It made him realize how quiet his apartment was. Craig had left a couple of hours earlier to visit some of his friends in a neighboring apartment complex, and Ben had no idea where the rest of his roommates had gone. Regardless, in the stillness of his surroundings, he couldn't help feeling a little lost and alone.

A familiar still, small voice in the back of his head whispered to him to pray, something he'd found himself doing a lot since he left Boston—and his family—after he'd joined the Church. So, struggling in spirit, he knelt humbly beside his bed and closed his eyes.

Heavenly Father, I'm here in Rexburg. This is where you wanted me to be, isn't it? I'm still not sure why I'm supposed to be here, but I have faith you'll tell me when the time is right. In the meantime, I'm feeling a little lost. Please help restore my spirits, and help me not to feel so alone.

Then, after giving thanks for all the blessings he did have, including his membership in the Church, he closed his prayer and stood up, feeling a little better.

Just then a knock sounded at the front door. Surprised, Ben hurried from his room and opened the door. Three men in church attire were standing there. "Yes?" he asked tentatively.

The largest of the three broke into a ready smile and eagerly extended his hand. "Hello! I'm Bishop Warner, and this is Brother Peeples and Brother Greene. We're just making the rounds tonight, introducing ourselves to everyone in the ward."

Ben smiled back in greeting, shaking each of the men's hands as they were extended to him. "I'm Ben Morrison. Would you like to come in?"

Bishop Warner beamed. "We'd love to."

When everyone was settled onto the worn couch and loveseat in the living room, Bishop Warner leaned forward, resting his large elbows on his knees. "So tell me about yourself, Ben. Where are you from?"

Ben's smile faded. It still hurt to talk about his home and family. Subconsciously, he pushed a hand through his thick brown hair before dropping it back into his lap. "Umm, Boston, actually."

"How wonderful!" the bishop exclaimed. "Beautiful area. What made you decide to come all the way out here to BYU-Idaho?"

"My friend—roommate, actually—Craig. I met him in my ward there, and he convinced me to come out here with him," Ben admitted.

"Craig Stewart?" Brother Peebles inquired.

Ben stared at him in surprise. "Yeah. How'd you know?"

Brother Peeples smiled and held up the stapled packet in his hand. "We've been given a list of everyone in each apartment as a sort of ward roster. We're trying to match names with faces."

"Sounds like you have your work cut out for you." Ben smiled. "So, everyone in our complex is in the ward?"

"Yes, plus there are a couple of other complexes in our ward boundaries, as well."

"Wow. I guess I didn't think about that. I sort of thought we'd be integrated into an established Rexburg ward or something."

"Oh, heavens no," Bishop Warner exclaimed. "There are so many students each semester that they're put into student wards."

Ben felt his cheeks redden. "Sorry. I guess I have a lot to learn."

"Oh?" Bishop Warner prompted.

"Yeah, well..." Ben pushed his hand through his hair again. "It's not something I go around telling everyone, but I've only been a member of the Church since early this year."

Bishop Warner's face lit up. "Really? That's wonderful! I'm a convert myself," he said, sitting up proudly. "But if it's not too personal, may I ask why you're hesitant to admit that?"

Ben squirmed under the bishop's intent gaze. "I guess I just feel a little...inadequate, surrounded by all these people who've been members their whole lives," he admitted sheepishly.

"Nonsense!" Bishop Warner protested. "When I joined the Church I had similar fears, but I promise you, nobody's going to think you're a social outcast just because you're a recent convert. In fact, most will probably think it's pretty terrific. What about your family? Were they baptized, too?"

Ben looked down at his hands. When he responded, his voice was low and sad. "No, I'm the only member in my family. As a matter of fact..." he paused to steady his voice, "...they disowned me when I got baptized. I'm pretty much on my own."

A heavy silence filled the small room. Finally, Bishop Warner spoke up, his voice filled with compassion. "Ben, I'm so sorry to hear that. Is there anything we can do for you?"

"No, I'm okay," Ben hurried to reassure them, feeling embarrassed about having them think he needed to be their first service project. "It's a change that I've had to get used to, but I know the Church is true. I wasn't going to pretend that I didn't have a testimony of it."

The men seemed impressed. Bishop Warner stood up and walked over to clap Ben on his shoulder. "You're an extraordinary young man, Ben. We're glad you're going to be in our ward."

Ben felt a slow blush color his cheeks. "Thank you."

"Well, we'd better get moving if we want to finish our visits," Brother Peeples admitted.

"You're right," Bishop Warner agreed. "But before we go, we wanted to let you know that we're having our first ward activity—sort of a welcome party—tomorrow night at six o'clock at Smith Park. We're barbequing hot dogs and hamburgers, and my wife's promised to make a huge bowl of her potato salad." He winked. "It's fabulous. You and your roommates wouldn't want to miss it."

Ben smiled and took the bright blue paper with a map to the park that Brother Peebles handed him. "I'll be there."

"Great! We'll see you then." With a final wave, the men went on their way.

When they were gone, Ben couldn't help breathing a sigh of relief. He'd been secretly worried about his new ward, but now he knew that he had nothing to fear. His bishopric was great and it sounded like they had fun things planned. Maybe he was going to be glad he came here with Craig after all.

Walking into the kitchen, he opened the fridge and pulled out a package of lunchmeat and a jar of mayonnaise. He was in the process of making a sandwich for an improvised dinner when he heard the front door open. Moments later, Craig walked into the kitchen, whistling cheerfully.

"Hey," Craig said as he spotted Ben. "You gonna make me one of those?"

Ben grinned. "Forget it. You're on your own."

"That's gratefulness for you," Craig told him as he snatched the loaf of bread and drew out two slices of his own. "I bring you all the way across the country to the wonderful state of Idaho and to this great university, and you won't even make me a sandwich."

"Well, maybe I would if you could tell me exactly why I'm here," Ben replied, only half joking. "That's something I still haven't figured out." He added a few slices of lunchmeat to his bread, put the sandwich together, then went to sit down at the table. As he watched, Craig fumbled with the knife and then dropped it onto the counter, leaving a long streak of mayonnaise on the surface. Ben laughed as his friend growled in frustration.

"I hate to think how you fed yourself on your mission for two years," Ben joked as he tossed his friend a couple of napkins from the table. "I know you couldn't have afforded fast food or pizza every night."

"Hey, I had companions who took pity on me, what can I say?"

Ben took a bite of his sandwich. "So, how were your friends?"

"Great," Craig told him as he finished cleaning up his mess and managed to make his sandwich without any further mishaps. "It was good to see them again. I served with Andrew on my mission. He's still the same. Neurotic, but nice." He grinned at his own analysis of his friend, then sat down next to Ben. "What'd you do?"

"Just hung around here and finished unpacking. Oh, I almost forgot." He reached out for the bright blue paper that was sitting on the table and pushed it toward Craig. "Our new bishopric stopped by and invited us to this."

"Mmm, a welcoming party at the park, huh? Barbeque, volleyball, softball..." he read through a mouthful of sandwich. "Sounds like fun. You planning on going?"

"Definitely," Ben answered with a nod. "You?"

Craig grinned. "Wouldn't miss it. Just think of the girls we'll meet."

"Yeah, all sorts of girls who don't know you're useless in the kitchen and a complete slob," Ben joked.

Craig laughed and nearly choked on his sandwich. After thumping himself on the chest a couple of times, he eyed Ben warningly. "That's right, so don't go spoiling everything by telling them."

"Hey, I wouldn't say a word! Besides, they'll learn all that soon enough." He grinned and jumped aside as his friend took a swing at him.

Just then the front door opened and Scott, one of their roommates, walked in. They all hung out for a while and talked as one by one, his other three roommates started filing in. The apartment got a bit chaotic as the evening wore on, but Ben found it refreshing, especially after his experience with his so-called "friends" at Harvard. Not only was the mood different—no drunken, passed-out friends to step over or avoid, no loud, pulsating music, no depressing atmosphere—but the way he felt inside was different. He felt at peace, secure in the knowledge that he was among friends who shared a common belief in their Heavenly Father and in His eternal plan. The Spirit prevailed, and it was truly an amazing contrast.

I may not know exactly why I'm supposed to be here, Ben thought, *but I don't think I'd want to be anywhere else.*

A short time later Ben headed for his bedroom, intent on gathering what he needed for his classes the next day. He pulled his class schedule from his top dresser drawer and sat down on the bed to study it carefully. Even his schedule was different from the one he'd had at Harvard. Instead of the rigorous, stress-inducing classes he'd previously had, he found himself actually looking forward to his diversified schedule: Chemistry, Psychology, Fine Arts—even a Book of Mormon class that he was so excited about taking. He could hardly wait to get started.

Yes, coming here was definitely the right move to make. But his prayers had been answered with such intensity that it seemed to indicate there was an important reason Heavenly Father wanted him here, one more important than anything else. Just what that was he didn't know.

With a sigh, he realized he would have to be patient. Heavenly Father would tell him what that reason was in His own good time.

Chapter Three

The incessant beeping of Lauren's alarm clock drew her out of her slumber, and she pulled her pillow over her head to dampen the noise. She fumbled blindly for the alarm clock's snooze button, silenced the alarm, then sank back beneath the covers. She'd almost drifted off to sleep again when she remembered. Today was the first day of classes!

Suddenly wide awake, she sat up, threw off her covers, and climbed out of bed. She glanced over at the still form in the bed across the room before walking over and yanking the covers off her sleeping friend. "Allison, wake up! We've got classes this morning!"

Allison grabbed the covers and pulled them back up over her head in protest. "You've got to be kidding. I feel like I just went to bed three hours ago."

"It was four hours ago and nope, I'm not kidding." Lauren grinned as she went over and flipped on the light switch, flooding the room with light. "Come on, get up. You've got your first class in an hour and a half." She stopped when she saw her friend had no intentions of moving, and she knew she was going to have to pull out the heavy artillery.

Leaning closer to her friend, she sing-songed, "Just think of all the cute guys you'll meet."

Allison groaned and slowly pulled the covers off her face. "You would have to resort to that, wouldn't you?"

Lauren grinned. "Hey, I do what it takes. Did it work?"

"Maybe," Allison mumbled as she sat up slowly and let her feet dangle above the floor. She squinted at Lauren, who was pulling clothes out of her dresser drawer and humming. "How can you possibly be so cheerful at this hour?" she grumbled. "I've always hated that about you."

"Well, get used to it," Lauren answered cheerfully, undeterred by her friend's usual morning grumpiness, "because we're going to be rooming together for the next seven months. So are you getting up or what?"

Allison nodded half-heartedly. "Go take your shower. By the time you're done, I'll be coherent."

"You'd better be," Lauren told her in a stern, mother-like voice, then took her clothes with her into the bathroom and climbed into the shower. She decided to make it a quick one since she knew Allison would be useless until she had a hot shower of her own. Especially after a late night like the one they'd had the night before.

After their pizza had been delivered, Bree, Melia, Lauren, and Allison had devoured slice after slice until they were too stuffed to even move. Then they'd lounged around and had a full-blown session of girl-talk that lasted late into the night. No one went to sleep before two a.m.

Lauren shook her head. No wonder she felt groggy. She wasn't used to staying up so late, but it had been an exhilarating experience not to have hovering parents telling her to go to bed. She could tell that there were many things about college life—including her newly found freedom—that she was going to like.

Hurrying through her shower, she got out and dressed. As soon as she opened the bathroom door, Allison rushed in, and she could hear Bree calling out that she was next. Lauren returned to her bedroom and plugged in her blow dryer, deciding to use the mirror over the desk as a vanity area.

Several minutes later, her long, thick hair was finally dry. She ran a brush quickly through the tangled ends, then gathered it into one hand and reached for the black scrunchie she'd worn the day before. With a quick flip of her wrist she secured it into a simple ponytail, then put on a touch of makeup, just enough to look like she hadn't just climbed out of bed. Finally, she slipped into her lightweight, navy jacket, slung her backpack over one shoulder and headed into the kitchen. She was just spreading some jam onto a piece of toast when Allison walked in combing her damp hair.

She eyed Lauren critically. "Is that what you're wearing today?"

Lauren glanced down at her new jeans and hunter green, ribbed knit T-shirt. She looked back up at Allison and cocked an eyebrow. "What's wrong with what I'm wearing?"

Allison rolled her eyes and sighed in exasperation. "Lauren, it's the first day of college! Don't you want to make an impression?"

Lauren smiled easily as she turned back to spreading jam on her toast. "Well, gosh, if you think all my teachers are going to flunk me because I'm not wearing just the right outfit, then by all means, I'll rush back in and change into something of yours." She winked at her friend, then put the jam away. Taking a bite of her toast, she adjusted her backpack on her shoulder and waggled her fingers at Allison. "See you later."

The morning sun felt warm on Lauren's face as she left her complex behind and made her way up the street toward the campus, eating her toast as she went. As she neared the Manwaring Center, the sidewalks became more crowded. She was relieved to see that most of the other students were dressed as she was, in nice jeans and simple shirts. Everyone seemed to be in good spirits as they made their way to classes, talking and laughing as they went.

Even though Lauren knew she should be hurrying, she found herself taking her time. It was a glorious morning. The sun was shining brightly from a brilliant, cloudless blue sky and the air was cool and crisp. Rainbird sprinklers chugged along rhythmically in their circular patterns over the well-kept lawns, and the sweet fragrance of honeysuckle and other bright, cheerful flowers wafted up from the carefully planted flower beds that bordered the path. Lauren closed her eyes and breathed deeply. She loved Idaho mornings. Everything always smelled so fresh and clean. She was certain there was nothing else like it in the world.

Forcing herself to focus on where she was going, she found her eight o'clock "Intro to Physical Therapy" class with minutes to spare and sat down in a desk near the back. She thumbed through her textbook until their professor, a stern-looking, middle-aged man, walked in and set his books down on his desk.

"Welcome, everyone," he called out when he saw that he had everyone's attention. "As you may know, getting into a Physical Therapy program is incredibly tough. In some universities, it's tougher than getting into a medical program. That's why I plan to work you incredibly hard this semester, to make sure you're up to the challenge. Now, get out your textbooks. We're going to briefly go over the four chapters that you'll be reading tonight for your homework."

Lauren groaned along with the students around her. Four chapters on the first day of class? He had to be kidding! With a sigh, she opened her book and prepared to follow along. She had a feeling it was going to be a very long day.

By the end of the afternoon, Lauren knew her prediction had been right. It had indeed been a very long day. In addition to her four chapters of reading homework in her first class, she'd been assigned written assignments in her math and English classes. And if she hadn't been stressed out enough at the prospect of all that homework, she would've been after the two hours she'd just spent in training at the bookstore. Between learning where everything belonged, how to use the registers, and all the ins and outs that her job entailed, she was feeling more than a little overwhelmed.

You'll be fine, she told herself in an improvised pep talk as she trudged home, feeling both physically and mentally exhausted. *Your whole routine is just new. Besides, you've always heard that the first week of college is the hardest. Things will get better when you've had a little time to adjust.*

Hoping the little voice in her head was right, she dragged herself up the stairs to her second floor apartment, still not thrilled about the prospect of a long evening of homework. But then she remembered the ward activity scheduled for that evening, and her spirits quickly rose. When the bishopric had stopped by the evening before to say hello and invite them to the ward activity, she'd been excited. They had seemed so genuinely nice that she was eager to get to know them and the other people in her ward. Tonight's ward activity seemed like the perfect way to do that. Besides, it was exactly the diversion from schoolwork she needed.

As she was nearing her apartment, one of the apartment doors close to her flew open and she nearly crashed into the person coming out. She opened her mouth to apologize, but when she saw who it was, her eyes widened in disbelief.

Elena Wilkinson!

Lauren groaned inwardly. Of all the people she'd known in high school, no one had been more bent on making her life miserable than Elena. They'd grown up in the same stake, so they'd spent years of Girls' Camp and countless Young Women activities together. At every opportunity, Elena had spread rumors about her, gotten her blamed for pranks Elena herself had played on others at camp, and seemed to delight in teasing and tormenting her endlessly. Lauren had no idea why Elena had always had it in for her, but she seemed to derive pleasure from making Lauren miserable.

Lauren hadn't seen much of Elena over the summer, but she had to admit that Elena still looked as beautiful as ever. With her fashion-magazine looks and her long, brown hair that tapered prettily around her face, emphasizing her hazel eyes and perfect features, she always had a trail of guys following her practically everywhere she went. Lauren knew, though, that for all of Elena's good looks, she wasn't all peaches and cream.

Before Lauren could recover enough to speak, Elena tossed her long, blond hair over her shoulder haughtily. "Well, well, if it isn't Ms. Perfect. What are you doing here? I thought you would've taken one of those full-ride scholarships everybody at home was bragging about. What's the matter? Did you decide none of them were good enough for you?"

Lauren flinched. Obviously, Elena hadn't changed one single bit over the summer. "I decided to go to school here instead," she responded, trying to bite back her defensiveness. "But what about you? I thought someone said you were going to beauty school or something."

Elena shrugged. "I'd planned to, but my father had some pull in admissions here, so I'm in." She smiled smugly. "See, unlike you, I didn't have to spend all my waking hours studying and being Ms. Straight Arrow. I managed to have fun in high school and still get into college."

Her patience already wearing, she grumbled, "Yeah, go figure." But before she could walk away, Elena's voice stopped her short.

"Well, I guess this means we'll be seeing a lot of each other, with me living on the same floor as you. That means we'll be in the same ward. Won't that be great?" Elena drawled in false enthusiasm.

Lauren cringed. She knew Elena well enough to understand the underlying meaning in her words. What Elena really meant was that she thought it was going to be great to have a familiar target around to torment. Lauren shook her head dismally. *Perfect. Just perfect.*

Before Lauren could compose herself enough to respond, Elena gave Lauren a big, false smile and backed slowly away. "Be seeing you," she called as she disappeared down the stairs.

Her discouragement of a few minutes before returning, Lauren trudged the rest of the way to her apartment and walked in. When she did, Allison looked up from where she and Bree were sitting on the couch talking.

"Laur, what's wrong? You look down."

Lauren sighed as she dropped her backpack to the floor and slumped onto the couch next to her friend. "You'll never guess who I just ran into."

"Who?"

"Elena Wilkinson."

Allison's eyebrows shot up. "Elena Wilkinson? You can't be serious!"

Bree stared at them blankly. "Who's Elena Wilkinson?"

Allison's look of surprise turned to one of contempt. "Someone from our stake back home who's always had it in for Lauren. Don't ask me why. She's never been happy unless she's succeeded in making Lauren feel miserable."

"You're kidding," Bree said in surprise. "What'd you ever do to her?"

"I wish I knew." Lauren frowned. "Mostly, I've just tried to ignore her whenever she's on one of her nasty streaks, but it doesn't look like it's going to be that easy to do this time around. As fate would have it, she lives just a few apartments down and is in our ward."

"Terrific," Allison grumbled.

Lauren sighed. "Yeah, I know."

A moment later, Allison gave Lauren's arm a sympathetic squeeze, then stood up. "Well, it's not going to do any good to sit around and mope about this. We have a ward activity to get ready for. Are you going?"

Lauren nodded. "Of course. After the day I've had, it'll be a nice distraction."

She followed Allison into the bedroom to change for the party. She was planning to change into her relaxed fit jeans and a T-shirt, but Allison put her foot down, telling her there was no way she was going to let her go to their first ward activity dressed like that. So she and Bree joined forces to clothe her properly.

Within minutes, she found herself wearing Bree's faded, straight-legged designer jeans with Allison's favorite snug-fitting, dark-blue top. Then to complete the outfit, Bree loaned her a wide, leather belt with a silver buckle, and her big-soled, white tennis shoes. When she saw Allison open her jewelry box, though, Lauren finally drew the line.

"Forget it, Al, I'm not wearing jewelry," she protested. "I don't feel like myself as it is." She reached for her scrunchie, but Allison quickly stepped in.

"Lauren, don't you dare pull your hair back into the same old ponytail! You always do that and it makes me crazy."

"Yeah, Lauren, your hair is gorgeous!" Bree chimed in. "If I had your hair, I'd leave it down all the time for everyone to admire."

Lauren rolled her eyes. "Guys, come on, it's just hair. Besides, I hate it when it gets in my face. It's just so much easier to pull it back."

But Allison reached out and snatched the scrunchie from Lauren's hand and looked at her sternly. "Humor me this once, okay?"

"Fine," Lauren grumbled in surrender, then made a point of glancing at her watch. "But if we don't hurry we're going to miss dinner."

That did the trick. Allison and Bree scrambled to finish getting themselves ready, and before long, Bree, Melia, Allison, and Lauren were piling into Lauren's Honda and following the bishopric's map to Smith Park. When they arrived, Lauren concentrated on parallel parking while Bree and Allison checked out the guys who'd beaten them there.

"Man, look at that cute, dark-haired guy over by the tables!" Bree exclaimed, practically drooling. "I really go for the big, stocky guys."

Allison wrinkled her nose. "Not me. I prefer mine lean and muscular. Hey, like that blond guy right over there!" She reached over to thump Lauren's shoulder. "Stop, Lauren, let me out! I've got to go introduce myself to the love of my life."

Lauren rolled her eyes when Allison and Bree practically flew out of the car the second she put it in park. Lauren turned to Melia. "What are we going to do with them?"

Melia laughed, her beautiful, exotic eyes crinkling into thin lines as she did. "My sister's the same way. You just deal with it. Come on, let's go make sure they don't make total fools of themselves."

Lauren climbed out of the car with Melia, and together they surveyed the scene. There were already dozens of people milling around, and she spotted a member of the bishopric carrying a large, rolled up volleyball net toward the volleyball pit. A short distance away, several guys were hauling baseball equipment toward the baseball diamond, and everywhere she looked there were people hanging around, talking and laughing and getting to know one another.

Melia nudged her and gestured to their right. Lauren turned to see that several tables had been covered with tablecloths, and the other members of their bishopric were manning the barbeque pits. Lauren could smell the hamburgers cooking even from where she and Melia stood.

"Smells great," Melia commented. "Should we see if the bishopric needs any help?"

They wandered over to say hi and asked what they could do to help. Obviously grateful for the offer, Bishop Warner directed them to a box containing paper plates, napkins, and plastic utensils, and had them set the items out on the table. As she did, Lauren couldn't help eyeing the spread. There were large bowls of potato salad, green salads, Jell-O salads, plates of cut-up vegetables, and huge packages of rolls. Everything looked incredible.

As her stomach started to grumble in anticipation, Lauren chuckled softly to herself. *Two days away from home and you're already missing a good, home-cooked meal*, she thought. *That's not a good sign.* She'd just snatched a carrot stick from the vegetable tray and taken a bite when Allison came rushing up behind her, grabbed her arm, and whirled her around.

"Lauren, quick, we need you!"

Lauren nearly choked on the mouthful of carrot. "Geez, Allison, way to nearly kill me," she complained when she managed to clear her throat. "What are you so worked up about?"

Allison's eyes were alive with excitement as she dragged Lauren away from the table. "The guys are setting up for a quick baseball game before the hamburgers are ready, and they need a pitcher."

Lauren's heart leaped into her throat. "Oh, no, Allison, no way!" she protested as she tried to free her arm from her friend's grip. "There's no way on this earth that I'm going to pitch here! Forget it. Uh-uh."

But her protests fell on deaf ears as Allison refused to relinquish her grip on Lauren's arm, and before Lauren could ramble on any further, she was dragged over to a group of guys and girls standing near the dugout. When they were within hearing range, Allison waved her free arm at the good-looking blond guy she'd first spotted when they'd arrived and called out, "Hey, Craig! I have a pitcher here for you!"

Lauren heard a couple of the guys beside Craig start to snicker, and she wished the earth would open up and swallow her whole. The guys who'd snickered made a point of eyeing her up and down critically, obviously wondering what kind of joke was being played on them. But Craig smiled warmly at her, the corners of his green eyes crinkling pleasantly as he reached into a large, cardboard box at his feet and tossed her a mitt.

"All right, guys, we have a pitcher!" he called out before walking over to her. "We don't have enough time before dinner's ready to play innings, so we're just going to set up an infield and an outfield and make some plays. Have you ever pitched before, Lauren? Do you know what to do?"

After the snickering she'd just endured, Lauren couldn't help feeling defensive. "Yeah, I think I can figure it out," she retorted, unable to keep the sarcasm out of her voice. But when Craig only gave her an encouraging smile and turned to join the others, Lauren felt guilty for her outburst. He didn't seem like one of the guys she'd come to know over the years who scoffed at the idea of a girl being able to play well. She shook her head. She'd make it up to him later.

As several guys and girls started taking their places on bases and in the outfield, she slid her left hand into the glove and forced herself to take a deep breath. She walked to the pitcher's mound and looked down at the sand under her feet, suddenly experiencing a sense of peace. No matter what else happened in her life, this was a place where she felt comfortable, confident. She loved the feeling of being in control, of knowing she was good at something.

But this isn't the state championships, she reminded herself. *This is just a ward picnic. You're not here to impress anyone. Just take things easy.*

Feeling a little calmer, she circled her arm around her shoulder to loosen it up and looked at Craig, who had taken up the catcher's position behind the plate. Then she glanced at the cocky, dark-haired guy who was approaching the batter's box and immediately recognized him as one of the guys who'd snickered at her.

"So what kind of pitching are we doing?" she asked Craig as she easily caught the softball he threw to her. "Slow or fast pitch?"

Craig cocked an eyebrow at her in surprise. "Um, whatever Travis here wants, I guess."

Travis laughed as he stepped up to the plate and banged the bat cockily against the sole of his shoe. "Oh, you think you're good enough to give me a choice, huh? Well then, give me a fast pitch. Let's see what you've got."

Fine, Lauren thought as Travis stepped into position and waved the tip of the bat over his shoulder. *If he wants something challenging, that's what he's going to get.*

She glanced around at the players on bases and in the outfield to make sure everyone was ready, then turned back to Travis. A slow grin tugged at the corners of her mouth. She couldn't wait to knock that arrogant smile off Travis's face. She shook her arm out one more time, clasped the ball in her hand, and closed her eyes, just as she'd done thousands of times before. She twisted the ball in her hand until she could feel the seam pressing against her fingertips, then took a deep, calming breath and opened her eyes.

Shutting out everything except the feel of the ball in her hand and the catcher's mitt held up in anticipation behind the plate, she wound up, moved her weight forward, and let the ball fly.

Chapter Four

Ben pulled up to the park and noticed that his parking space of ten minutes ago was gone, and there wasn't another parking space in sight. He groaned. He was going to have to park further up and walk a little.

He drove past the long line of cars and parked near the far corner of the park, then collected the two plastic grocery bags, climbed out of the truck, and headed toward the large gathering of people at the park's west end. He had to admit, he'd been feeling anxious about the ward activity all afternoon. He'd been a member less than a year, and he still felt self-conscious at large ward gatherings. There was still so much he didn't know about the gospel, and he couldn't help feeling inadequate around those who had been members their entire lives. He was always afraid of opening his mouth and saying something stupid and having his new "family" look down on him.

When Ben and Craig had arrived at the park for the ward activity, they were a little early. Ben had spotted Bishop Warner unloading boxes of food and picnic supplies from his car and had gone over to help. Bishop Warner had greeted him like an old friend and clapped him on the shoulder, telling him how pleased he was to see him there. Ben's anxiety at feeling like he didn't belong had vanished completely, and he wanted more than anything to repay this man's kindness. So when the bishop discovered he was short on hamburger buns, Ben had quickly offered to take Craig's old truck and run to the store for more.

Shifting the grocery bags from one hand to the other, he finally reached the gathering and headed for Bishop Warner, who was standing at one of the barbeque grills flipping sizzling hamburger patties. At the sight of his stocky, six-foot-four-inch bishop wearing a dark blue apron with the words "Kiss the Cook" printed across the front, he couldn't help smiling. He set the bags down on the table nearest the bishop's grill.

"Here you go, Bishop. We're all set."

"Ah, thank you, Ben. You're heaven sent." Bishop Warner paused long enough in his task to turn and flash him a grateful smile. "So how did your first day of classes go?"

"Not bad," Ben admitted. He reached for a handful of olives from the vegetable tray, then leaned back against the picnic table to munch on them as he talked. "The classes are more relaxed than the ones I had in Massachusetts, and the spirit here is completely different. I really love that. I think my Book of Mormon class is going to be my favorite."

"It was always mine," Bishop Warner responded with a smile. "I'm glad to hear you're holding your own. I can't imagine what it must be like for you, after everything you've been through."

Feeling the all-too-familiar sadness creep in, Ben looked down at the ground and shrugged. "Yeah, well... I try not to think too much about it. Sometimes it's hard, but it helps to know that this was what the Lord wanted me to do."

The bishop shook his head slowly. "You're an amazing young man, Ben. But sometimes I wonder if you're fighting too much of this battle on your own. You let me know if you need help, and don't be afraid to ask, okay? I mean that. Heavenly Father wants us to bear one another's burdens. That's what we're all here for."

A deep sense of gratitude warmed Ben's heart. "Thanks, Bishop, I appreciate that. I'm fine for now, though."

"Glad to hear it." Bishop Warner's jovial tone was back, and he turned to point toward the gathering crowds with his spatula. "Now get out of here and go socialize with someone your own age until the hamburgers are ready." Then, with a final wink, he turned back to the barbeque grill.

Ben smiled and nodded as he popped the last of his olives into his mouth, then he turned to look for Craig. As he did, he couldn't help replaying the bishop's words of encouragement in his mind. It certainly seemed that Heavenly Father had called caring leaders to watch out for him at this time in his life, and he said a silent prayer of thanks. Right now he could use all the divine help he could get.

As he continued walking through the park in search of Craig, he heard a loud cheer erupt from a crowd that was gathering at the baseball diamond. Since it seemed like that was where most of the ward members were congregating, he headed that direction.

Another roar erupted, arousing Ben's curiosity. *What's going on?* he wondered. Trying to figure out what all the excitement was about, he walked the rest of the distance to the baseball diamond in quick strides and joined the crowd gathering behind the dugout. He spotted Craig squatting down in his catcher's pose behind home plate, and he noticed that his next-door neighbor, Travis, a cocky freshman he'd met last night, was at bat, looking both aggravated and determined as he waited for a pitch. Interested in what was upsetting Travis, he shifted his gaze to the pitcher's mound.

That's when he saw her.

The most gorgeous girl he'd ever seen was standing on the mound in a classic pitcher's pose, ball in hand, her eyes closed in deep concentration. She had rich, reddish-brown hair that spilled down her back in thick waves and danced in the sunlight every time she moved. She was slender and tall (about five-foot-ten, he guessed) and she looked incredibly well toned and athletic.

As he continued to stare at her, completely captivated by her every movement, a warm, tingling sensation flooded through him and a sweet sense of peace permeated his soul. It was undeniably the same feeling he'd had almost a year ago when the missionaries had testified to him of the gospel's truthfulness. Someone had been trying to tell him something then, and someone was trying to tell him something now. He wasn't exactly sure what, but he knew it had something to do with this beautiful girl standing on the pitcher's mound.

Unable to tear his eyes away from her, he watched in utter fascination as she opened her eyes, let out a slow, deep breath, then wound up and let loose a screaming-fast underhand pitch. The ball hurtled toward home plate, rocketed past Travis's swinging bat, and landed with an alarmingly loud *thump* in Craig's catcher's mitt. Another roar went up from the crowd and Ben lifted his eyebrows in surprise. Wow!

Instead of acting embarrassed by the attention, the girl smiled confidently, obviously not one to coddle a guy and tell him how big and strong and brave he was like so many other girls he'd known. He didn't know about anyone else, but he was impressed.

Moving closer to the chain link fence, he watched as she caught the ball Craig threw back to her, then rolled it in her hand briefly before setting up in her pose. She wound up a moment later and threw yet another impressive fast pitch. Once again, Travis's bat met with only air.

Craig let out a whoop as the ball landed in his glove, and he stood up and shook his gloved hand out as if the pitch had stung. Maybe it had. A cheer immediately went up from the crowd, and Travis let out an aggravated growl when he realized a girl had just struck him out.

Ben watched the girl try to smother a smile as Travis stomped away, clearly humiliated. The next batter stepped up, this time a girl, and the girl on the mound slowed her pitch and gave it a bit more arc, giving the batter a better chance to make contact. The batter hit it on the second pitch, and the infielders scrambled to retrieve the ball. As the next couple of batters stepped up, some good-naturedly asked for her fast pitch and made their best efforts to hit it. Some did, while others didn't fare as well. Ben was relieved to see that most of those who missed simply laughed and shook their heads as they retreated back into the dugout.

After a brief lull, Craig turned and looked around for the next batter. "Hey, we need a batter! Someone get up here!"

When no one made a move to step forward, Ben knew this was his big chance. He simply had to meet her. And if that meant swallowing a little pride in the batter's box, that was a sacrifice he was willing to make. As if guided forward by some unseen force, he found himself stepping around the edge of the fence.

Craig saw him and grinned. "All right, Ben! Get on up here and see if you can hold your own."

With a sheepish smile, Ben picked up the bat and made his way to the plate.

How did I get roped into this? Lauren found herself wondering as she stood on the pitcher's mound and heard Craig call for another batter. She glanced down at her borrowed white tennis shoes and noticed they were coated with sand. *Great,* she thought. *Bree's gonna kill me when she sees what I've done to her shoes.*

Just then she heard Craig call out to someone and she looked up. When she did, her heart betrayed her by doing a little flip. The guy stepping up to the plate was tall, at least six-foot-two, with broad shoulders and a muscular build. He wore form-fitting jeans and a plain white T-shirt that contrasted sharply against his deeply tanned, olive complexion. His thick brown hair was so dark it almost looked black, and even from where she stood, she could make out his rich, chocolate-brown eyes framed by thick, sweeping lashes. She watched as he grinned at something Craig said and when he turned his dazzling smile her direction, she suddenly wasn't sure she could remember how to throw a softball, let alone strike someone out.

"Give him your best fastball," Craig called out to her with a smile as he crouched down behind the plate. "I think Ben here could use a little humbling."

Ben turned to Craig and laughed. It was a deep, rumbling sound that she instantly liked. "That's easy for you to say," he told Craig easily. "You don't have to worry about hitting it." But to prove he was a good sport, he turned to her and grinned, causing her stomach to fill with butterflies. "Give me that fastball of yours. I'm game."

Lauren couldn't stop herself from grinning back. "Whatever you say."

She watched as he backed away from the box and took a couple of practice swings before returning to the plate and getting into position. Judging from his stance, grip, and practice swings, she could tell he was a pretty good player, in spite of him joking with Craig about his ability. Deciding to treat him as such, she wound up and threw him the same fastball she'd thrown to Travis. He swung and missed.

"She's making you look ba-ad!" Craig sing-songed as he caught the ball and threw it back to Lauren.

"Nah, I'm just warming up," he said, giving Craig a good-natured grin.

When he got back into his stance, Lauren decided to take a little off her second pitch. But when she did, he surprised her by making good, solid contact, even though the ball went foul down the third base line. She turned back to him and raised her eyebrows in surprise. He grinned and lifted his eyebrows back at her in response, then raised the bat back up over his shoulder.

Knowing that she'd better not go soft on him or else he might send the ball down her throat, she decided to give him her fast pitch again. She took an extra moment to visualize, then wound up and gave her final pitch everything she had. Luckily, it was enough, and the ball sailed past Ben's swinging bat and landed safely in Craig's glove.

The crowd let out another cheer just as Craig stood up and yelled, "You're outta here!" Lauren couldn't help grinning as she watched Craig taunt Ben a little more and then thump him good-naturedly on the shoulder, evidence that they were good friends. For a moment, Lauren worried that he might resent her for showing him up, but as he set the bat down and started back to the dugout, he caught her eye and gave her a wonderful wink. She felt like melting.

Just then someone hollered that the food was ready, and everyone started heading for the tables. Lauren followed along, accepting people's praise as she went. She felt a little awkward being the center of attention, but she was relieved to see how many people seemed so genuinely nice. She'd almost reached the food tables when someone shouldered her, nearly causing her to trip over her feet. When she turned, she saw the culprit was Elena.

"I see you're already working on alienating the boys," Elena said snidely.

Lauren sighed and rolled her eyes as Elena fell into step with her. "Not that I care, but... what are you talking about?"

"Well, striking out the cutest guy in the ward is hardly the way to get him to ask you out," Elena drawled. "We're supposed to be starting a whole new chapter in our lives here at college, but you're still the same old Lauren. Do I have to remind you that guys don't like to be shown up by girls?" She paused and shook her head. "Not that it would matter, I guess. Who'd want to go out with a tomboy like you?"

Lauren winced. She was used to Elena's put-downs, but this one really stung. Before she could recover, Elena flashed her a triumphant smile. She knew her barb had hit its mark.

"See you later," Elena sing-songed, fluttering her perfectly manicured nails at Lauren before stepping up her pace and disappearing into the crowd.

Lauren stared after her for several moments, trying to calm herself down. She knew she shouldn't let Elena get to her. After all, she was used to her put-downs. For whatever reason, Elena simply delighted in being mean. But still, her last comment had definitely been a low blow.

Come on, don't let her spoil your night, Lauren told herself as she approached the tables. *She's not worth getting upset about.*

By the time she reached the food table, she'd managed to pull herself together. She moved to the end of the long line and looked around for her roommates. When they were nowhere to be seen, Lauren sighed. With her luck, they were near the front of the line and would be finished eating by the time she found them.

It seemed like forever until she finally got close enough to pick up a plate and as she did, she heard a trill of laughter. She looked up to see Elena standing a short distance away, flirting shamelessly with no less than four guys. Lauren wrinkled her nose. *Gross. Talk about having no pride.*

Just then someone brushed up against her and a deep voice murmured in her ear, "That's quite an arm you have there."

Whirling around, Lauren came face to face with its owner, and her breath caught in her throat. *Ben.* He was standing there smiling at her, his rich, chocolate-brown eyes warm and friendly. If possible, he was even better looking up close. There were tiny gold flecks in his eyes that she hadn't noticed from a distance and a slight dimple in his right cheek. And as his gaze held hers, she couldn't help noticing that there was a quiet gentleness in his eyes that tugged at the carefully constructed walls around her heart.

Feeling oddly vulnerable, she gave him what she hoped was a friendly smile. "Thanks. You're Ben, right?"

He nodded. "Ben Morrison. And you are…?"

"Lauren Holt. It's nice to meet you."

"The pleasure is mine," he answered sincerely, his beautiful brown eyes sparkling. He picked up two plates and handed one to her. "So, where did you learn to pitch like that?"

Lauren accepted the plate and started to dish up as she explained. "My dad coaches football and baseball at a junior college, and I have four older brothers who play. When I came along, it was pretty much expected of me to play, too."

"Kind of like a family tradition?"

She smiled. "Something like that." As they waited for the line to progress, Lauren asked, "Where are you from?"

"Boston, actually."

She raised an eyebrow. "Wow. What brings you all the way out here?"

"You know Craig, the guy who was playing catcher?" When she nodded, he continued. "Well, he and I met there last spring. I wasn't happy at the university I was attending so he convinced me to come to school with him here. We're rooming together."

"It's nice when you already know one of your roommates going in," she replied. "My roommate is my best friend from home, so I'm speaking from experience." She grinned at him and felt an unexpected rush of pleasure when he grinned back. "What university were you attending before coming here?"

His smile slipped a little and he tried to cover it up by reaching out to spoon some potato salad onto his plate. "I was studying pre-law at Harvard."

"Ivy league," Lauren replied with a whistle. "Pretty impressive."

"Well, I don't know about impressive," he responded humbly. "It was a lot of hard work. I love studying law, but I wasn't enjoying it there. Too much pressure."

Lauren nodded sympathetically. "I can imagine."

They continued to the end of the table, but as Lauren reached for one of the Styrofoam cups of soda, her plate nearly toppled from her hands. Thinking quickly, Ben reached out to steady it.

"Here," he said, chuckling. "Let me help."

An unsolicited blush started to creep across her cheeks as she stammered, "No, I'm fine, really. I can get it."

"It's no trouble at all," he insisted, taking her plate into his free hand. "How about you get the drinks, and I'll carry the plates."

"Deal," Lauren replied with a grateful smile.

When she picked up a cup for each of them, Ben turned to give their surroundings a cursory glance. "Where are you sitting?"

"Um," she began, scanning the sea of people sitting on the lawn nearby. "I was planning to sit with my roommates, but I kind of lost track of them."

"Hey, Ben!"

They both turned toward the voice and spotted Craig sitting a short distance away, his arm raised to catch their attention. Lauren saw that he was sitting with Allison, Bree, and Melia. "Looks like your roommate is sitting with my roommates," she told Ben as she nodded their direction. Then she surprised herself by asking, "Would you like to join us?"

His eyes sparkled at her offer. "I'd love to."

As they started toward her roommates, Lauren caught a glimpse of Elena standing nearby with her group of admirers.

With a sudden rush of satisfaction, Lauren noticed that she and Ben had caught Elena's attention. Lauren felt like cheering when she realized that Elena actually looked jealous. But then Elena's scolding words rushed to her mind, and she felt a momentary stab of concern. Ben wasn't really angry she'd struck him out, was he? Was giving her his attention just some cruel joke he was playing to get back at her? But as she studied Ben's features for any sign of animosity, she was relieved to see only warmth and sincerity in his eyes.

"So, where are *you* from?" Ben asked, his soft eyes on hers as they walked.

Letting the concern of a moment before dissipate, she relaxed under his gaze and answered, "Idaho Falls. It's just a half hour from here. Far enough away to feel like I'm on my own, but close enough to take my laundry home on the weekends." She grinned wryly.

Ben laughed, then nodded toward her friends. "And how are you getting along with your roommates?"

"Good so far," she answered as they reached her friends and sat down. She smiled at her roommates. "We like each other, don't we guys?"

"Depends on how clean my shoes are when you return 'em," Bree joked through a mouthful of her hamburger as she nodded at Lauren's sand-covered shoes.

Lauren sat down and took the plate Ben was handing her before he sat down himself. Settling her plate on the grass in front of her, she told her roommates, "I thought I'd lost you guys."

Allison shook her head. "Nah, we were just staking out a place. By the way, this is Craig."

Lauren gave him a friendly smile. "We've met. Nice catching back there."

"Nice *pitching* back there," he said sincerely. "Pretty impressive."

Lauren blushed for the second time that evening. "Thanks." She took a bite of her burger, but then noticed that her roommates were eyeing Ben curiously. "Oh, I'm sorry," she spoke up quickly. "Guys, this is Ben. Ben, this is Melia, Bree, and Allison." She pointed to each in turn. "Oh, and Allison's the friend from home that I'm rooming with."

Ben flashed them his dazzling smile. "Nice to meet all of you."

"So, what about you?" Lauren asked Ben. "How are you getting along with your roommates?"

"Good, I think. Craig and I already knew each other, so I already know *his* shortcomings." He laughed as he ducked the olive Craig threw at him in retaliation. "But the other guys in our apartment seem pretty cool, too."

"Is this your first year here?" Craig asked, directing the question at the four girls.

Allison nodded. "Except for Melia. She was here last year. She'll have to show us the ropes."

Melia smiled. "I'd be happy to. My parents were encouraging me to go to BYU-Hawaii this year and live with my uncle, but I wanted to come back here."

"And turn down a chance to live in Hawaii?" Bree asked incredulously.

Melia laughed. "I grew up there, remember? It's nothing I haven't experienced before. Besides, I kind of like the snow. There's not much of it in Hawaii or California." She winked at Bree.

Just then they heard someone call, "Hey, Craig! Is that you?"

Craig looked up to see the owner of the voice and his eyes lit up. "Hey, Steve! I'll be right there." He picked up his empty plate and gave them an apologetic look. "Sorry to eat and run, but Steve and I roomed together my freshman year. I think I'll go say hello." He stood up, but turned to smile at Allison before leaving. "I'll catch up with you in a few minutes?" When Allison nodded he gave her a smile, then he was gone.

Lauren couldn't help watching their exchange, and—judging from the looks passing between them—she had no doubt Craig would follow through with his promise. He and Allison really seemed to be hitting it off.

51

When he was gone, Ben turned to Melia. "So, where in Hawaii did you grow up? I've been there quite a few times myself."

He and Melia started talking about their favorite places on the Islands, and Lauren found herself content to sit back and study Ben while she ate. There was an ease with which he talked to people, and she noted with pleasure the way he carefully watched each person's face as they spoke, indicating that he was listening intently to what each person had to say. Not once did she see the glazed look come into his eyes that usually came when a guy was engaged in a conversation that wasn't entirely about him. Grudgingly, she had to admit she was impressed.

As Ben and Melia's conversation wound down, Melia excused herself to go for seconds and Bree left to socialize with some of her new friends. While Allison was busy finishing up what remained on her plate, Ben turned to Lauren and asked, "So, what about you? Have you ever been to Hawaii?"

Lauren shook her head. "No, most of our family vacations entailed backpacking, camping, or whitewater rafting."

Ben's eyes widened. "Really?"

"Well, you have to understand," Allison jumped in, "Lauren's the only girl in her family, and she has four older brothers. Her vote for luxurious vacation spots was usually vetoed."

Ben laughed. "I see. I'm not sure that's entirely fair, though."

"Sometimes I didn't think it was either," Lauren admitted sheepishly. "But growing up in a family of boys, I didn't have much choice. That's the kind of stuff they wanted to do."

"What about your parents?" Ben asked. "Did they like doing those things, too?"

Lauren nodded. "My parents are both athletic and love the outdoors, so hiking, camping, and whitewater rafting were the vacations of choice. It's a good thing they had four boys to do all that with. But then I came along, and I had no choice but to do what everyone else was doing."

"Hmmm," Ben mumbled through his last mouthful of food as he pushed away his empty plate and leaned back casually on one elbow. "So, what was it like, growing up with four older brothers?"

Lauren wrinkled her nose. "The problem with older brothers is that you get forced to do all sorts of things because they're bigger than you and won't take no for an answer."

"What kinds of things did they make you do?"

She laughed. "Oh, where do I start?"

Allison nudged Lauren's leg with the toe of her shoe. "Tell him about the time they used you for a tackling dummy."

Ben's eyes widened in disbelief. "You're kidding."

Lauren grimaced playfully. "Unfortunately, she's not. My brothers were really getting into football when I was about eight or nine and they were short of practice partners one night, so they dressed me up in their pads, told me where to stand, and then flattened me. You should've seen my mom come flying out of the house yelling at them. They were grounded for weeks."

Ben laughed and Lauren's heart lifted. She'd only met him a short time ago, but already she loved the deep, carefree sound of his laughter. "Anyway," she continued, "I remember being bruised for a few days, but I think in the long run they helped toughen me up."

A few moments later, Allison stood up with her empty plate and brushed the grass off her pants. "Well, I'm done. I'm going to go mingle," she said casually. "See you guys later?"

Lauren nodded at her as Ben politely said goodbye, then Allison turned and disappeared into the crowd. Feeling strangely nervous at being alone with Ben, Lauren turned back to him and smiled tentatively.

"So, what about you?" she finally asked. "Other than the fact that you were previously an Ivy-Leaguer and are smart enough to study pre-law, I don't know anything about you."

He laughed again and sat up, brushing a few pieces of grass from his elbow. "I don't know about the 'smart enough to study pre-law' part, but what do you want to know?"

"Well, I know you're from Boston," she began, "but what about your family? Do you have any brothers or sisters?"

Ben's smile faded and a dark cloud of emotion crossed his face. Startled by the abrupt change in his mood, she wondered what she'd said to upset him. Finally, he smiled a little sadly and nodded. "I have a younger sister. Emily. We've always been really close."

"Is she still back east?" Lauren asked, more cautiously this time.

"Yes, she's finishing her senior year in high school."

Lauren could see the sadness in his eyes. "You must miss her."

Ben nodded slowly and pushed a hand through his thick, dark hair. "Yeah, I guess I do," he answered quietly. He lifted his eyes and stared off into the distance. He looked so lost and vulnerable that Lauren desperately wanted to say something—anything—that would bring back his carefree, easy laughter of just a few minutes before.

"Hey, Ben, come here! You have to meet a friend of mine."

Together, they looked over to see Craig standing near the volleyball pit, waving Ben over. Ben lifted his hand in acknowledgement to his friend, then turned back to Lauren. As he did, she thought she caught a glimpse of disappointment in his eyes.

"I guess I should go," he said reluctantly, getting to his feet. "Thanks for letting me eat with you guys."

"No problem," she answered as she stood up beside him and walked with him to the nearest garbage can so they could throw away their plates. "Maybe I'll see you later."

"You can count on it."

When she looked up at him, she saw a slow smile dance across his eyes. Then, before Lauren could respond, he gave her a broad wink and disappeared into the crowd.

Lauren remained rooted in place for several moments, a smile working its way up from her heart and spreading across her face. He wanted to see her again! He seemed like such a nice guy, and she couldn't help feeling flattered by his attention. But then the memory of other "nice guys" came into her mind, and when she remembered how devastating her relationship with those "nice guys" had been, it brought her back to earth with a thump.

Nope. Forget it, she told herself sternly. Love was tricky, unpredictable, and full of surprises... and not all of them good. And she, for one, didn't like surprises.

I don't care how nice you think this Ben is, you've got to keep your distance, she reminded herself. *He may seem wonderful now, but you've only known him, what... fifteen minutes? How much can you really know about him in such a short time? If you really got to know him, you'd probably learn he's not as wonderful as he seems. He'd show you he's just like every other guy you've ever met—as fickle in love as he is in life. What would be the point of getting involved?*

No, the problem here, as always, was that getting involved meant getting hurt. And there was no way she was ever going to let that happen again.

Deciding to find her roommates, Lauren wandered around for a few minutes before finally spotting Allison and Bree seated on the bleachers behind the baseball diamond. A bunch of their ward members were gathering to start a post-dinner game, so she climbed up onto the bleachers next to them.

"Hey," Bree greeted her as they scooted over to make room for her. "You should go offer to pitch again."

Lauren shook her head. "I think I'll sit this one out." A warm breeze kicked up, blowing her long hair across her face. Annoyed, she reached up to smooth her hair back from her face and gathered it into one hand at the nape of her neck. The breeze felt good on her hot neck, and she dropped her chin to let the breeze sweep across her moist skin. "One of you wouldn't happen to have a ponytail holder or a clip, would you? Having my hair down is driving me nuts."

Allison turned and gave her a scolding look. "Don't you dare pull it back. It's gorgeous down like that."

With a sigh, Lauren released her hair and let it cascade down her back. She watched the start of the game for a few moments, then turned to her friends. "So, what are you guys doing over here? You're not exactly baseball fans."

Allison's eyes sparkled as she gestured toward home plate. "Craig's playing."

Lauren looked over to see Craig crouching behind home plate. "Ahhh," she said with sudden understanding, "now it all makes sense."

Allison grinned, then glanced around pointedly. "So, where's Ben? When I left, you guys were still eating."

Lauren's heartbeat quickened at the mention of his name, but she tossed her hair over her shoulder and forced herself to shrug indifferently. "He went to meet one of Craig's friends or something."

"He's pretty cute, huh?" Allison prompted mischievously.

"I guess."

Allison rolled her eyes and nudged Bree. "'I guess,' she says. Listen to her."

Bree laughed. "I know. Lauren, I think you're totally playing Ben down. If you ask me, there was some definite chemistry going on between you guys back there."

When Allison nodded in agreement, Lauren let out an aggravated growl. "Will you guys give it a rest? Okay, he's nice. And cute. But we were just talking! There's nothing going on between us, nor will there ever be. I'm going guy-free, remember?"

Allison exchanged a look with Bree, then gave Lauren a placating smile. "If you say so," she said, obviously unconvinced. Then she turned her attention back to the baseball game—and Craig.

As the game got underway, Lauren realized how good it felt to be a spectator for once and not have the pressure of a team counting on her to help them win. She leaned back and propped her elbows on the bleacher behind her as she watched. Everyone seemed to be having a good time; even Bishop Warner got talked into playing. When he stepped up to bat he hit a home run on his very first pitch, causing everyone to cheer wildly. He ran around the bases as fast as his large, stocky frame would allow, and when he reached home plate, he accepted the high-fives of those nearby. Lauren couldn't help grinning at his youthful energy. He obviously had a knack for relating to people their age, and she had no doubt he was going to be a devoted, caring bishop.

As the game continued, Lauren let her attention drift to the classes she'd attended that day. She was mentally reviewing the pages of reading she had to do that night when Allison suddenly elbowed her painfully in the side.

"Ow!" Lauren protested as she turned to scowl at her friend. "What was that for?"

Allison nodded toward the baseball diamond. "Check it out."

Lauren followed her gaze and saw Ben walking toward home plate. Instantly, her heart started tapping out an erratic rhythm. He was stepping up to bat, and Lauren couldn't help noticing that the chatter of the girls seated in the bleachers around her suddenly quieted.

Can't say that I blame them for being interested, she thought grudgingly. *He's definitely easy on the eyes.*

She watched as he lifted the bat over his shoulder, then swung at the pitch. There was a loud crack as he made contact with the ball and took off running. Lauren found herself cheering with the others as he rounded the bases and managed to make it back to home plate, just moments before the ball did. The cheers followed him all the way back to the dugout and he flashed his megawatt smile in appreciation. Lauren could tell that his brilliant smile had the same effect on the other girls as it did on her since a swarm of female admirers swooped down on him as soon as he was within reach, all clamoring for his undivided attention.

Lauren watched in disgust as Elena worked her way to his side, threaded her arm through his, and nestled up against him. "Oh, Ben, that was so wonderful, the way you hit that ball and ran so fast like that!" she gushed, her words drifting up to Lauren. "I bet you're good at everything you do, aren't you?"

Lauren's stomach tightened into a knot. How could he just stand there and let her go on like that? She was so obviously fake that Lauren felt like throwing something at Ben for being so dense. But even so, she was unable to tear her gaze away as she watched Elena stand on her tiptoes so she could whisper something in his ear. Ben smiled in response to whatever it was she said, and Lauren felt a sudden, unexpected stab of jealousy.

Jealous? How can you possibly be jealous? she asked herself indignantly. *You hardly know him! Just because he ate dinner with you and your roommates doesn't mean you have any claim to him. Besides, you're not getting involved, remember?*

Allison's hand on her arm and reassuring voice pulled her from her thoughts. "Don't worry, he's just being polite. There's no possible way he could be interested in Elena. She's so totally fake."

Lauren tore her eyes from Ben and Elena and turned to Allison. "I don't care who he talks to," she told Allison, shrugging off her friend's reassurances. "I don't even know him. Besides, it's obvious his taste in women is completely lacking. If that's the kind of girl he likes, more power to him." She stood up abruptly and climbed down from her spot on the bleachers. "Do you want to come with me to grab some dessert? I'm suddenly craving a couple of scoops of chocolate ice cream."

As daylight started to fade, the ward activity wound down and everyone started heading home. Lauren walked with her roommates to the car, but as she opened the door to let them climb in, she suddenly realized Allison was no longer with them. Puzzled, she turned to look for her. She scanned the area behind her, but her friend was nowhere in sight. She finally spotted her over near the picnic tables, talking and laughing with Craig.

"Come on, Allison, let's go!" she called out to her.

Allison gave her a quick wave to let her know she'd heard and then started talking with Craig again. Lauren groaned inwardly. At this rate, she'd never get her homework done.

"Heading home, huh?"

Lauren jumped at the sound of the unexpected voice and turned to see Ben walking up to her. His bright smile made her heart do a series of flips, and unable to stop herself, she felt herself smiling back. "Hi, Ben. Yeah, I've got a ton of homework to do, but I can't seem to round up my roommate."

Ben's gaze followed Lauren's and he chuckled when he spotted his roommate with Allison. "Looks like you have your work cut out for you."

Lauren grinned. "Do you think she'll notice if I just get in the car and leave?"

He laughed. "You could always try and find out."

Lauren stared in frustration at her flirting roommate for another few moments, then turned back to Ben. When she did, their eyes met, and something almost tangible passed between them, making Lauren's skin tingle and her heart pound. Suddenly feeling self-conscious, she averted her gaze. Refusing to let her heart rule her head, she nervously tucked a stray strand of hair behind her ear and commanded herself to pull it together.

Ben cleared his throat quietly as he leaned back against the fender of her car and slid his hands casually into the pockets of his jeans. "I had fun tonight," he finally said in an attempt to break the silence. "Even if I did get struck out by a girl." He gave her a broad wink.

Lauren's mouth quirked into a smile. "Well, anytime you want to be struck out by a girl, just say the word."

"I will." As their gazes met and held, his smile softened. After another moment of comfortable silence, he shifted his weight on the car and crossed one foot over the other. "Hey, I was wondering... what are you doing Friday night? If you're not busy, maybe we could get together and do something."

Lauren stiffened. Painful memories of her past relationships flashed through her mind, causing her throat to constrict. Trying to control the shake in her voice, she asked, "You mean... like on a date?"

"Yeah, like on a date," he answered with an amused grin. "You know, like when two people who want to get to know each other better arrange to meet, then go someplace where they can talk, maybe get something to eat or go to a movie... Lauren? Are you okay?" His brow furrowed in concern when he noticed she looked decidedly pale.

Lauren swallowed hard as she tried to control the momentary, completely irrational desire to panic. *Lauren, calm down, this is no big deal*, she reassured herself. *It's not like you're going to be condemned for turning him down. He doesn't know anything about you, and he doesn't need to know why you're not willing to ever go through the 'falling in love' thing again. Just tell him you're too busy.*

Once she got a grip on her emotions, she realized that was the perfect thing to do. It would let him down easy, and best of all, it would be the truth. Well... mostly.

"Oh, um, it's really nice of you to ask me, Ben, and I'm flattered, really," she began awkwardly, "but it's only the first day of school, and already I'm overwhelmed by schoolwork. By this weekend I'm going to need every spare minute just to catch up. But really... thanks, anyway."

Ben's face fell momentarily and she felt horrible. But then he made a valiant effort to refresh his smile and nodded understandingly. "Yeah, I know how hard it can be, trying to adjust to class loads. Maybe some other time."

Just then Allison arrived, much to Lauren's relief, and Lauren said a hasty goodbye to Ben before getting in the car and pulling into traffic. Lauren forced herself to keep her eyes away from the rearview mirror to see if Ben was still standing there, watching them drive away.

You did the right thing, Lauren assured herself. *It's better this way. You'll see.*

As Lauren stopped at a red light, Allison grinned at her, obviously unaware of Lauren's inner turmoil. "Craig's pretty great, huh?"

Lauren forced a smile and nodded. "Yeah, he seems really nice."

"Nice is hardly the word. He's gorgeous, funny, *and* he's a returned missionary. My mom would be thrilled." She grinned, and Lauren had to laugh. The rest of the short drive home, Bree and Melia chatted in the back seat while Allison gushed over Craig until Lauren had heard more than enough.

When they got home, Lauren made a beeline for her bedroom, grateful for a few minutes alone. She changed into an oversized T-shirt and her favorite blue plaid flannel boxers, then climbed into bed with her textbooks and spent the next two hours reading. She was just closing her textbook and planning to call it a night when Allison came in.

"I wondered where you'd disappeared to," she said as she opened her dresser drawer and pulled out her pajamas. "Why did you hole yourself up in here? We were having fun talking in the front room."

Lauren moved her textbooks to the desktop next to her bed and slid down under her blankets. "I had too much homework."

"Did you get it all done?" Allison asked as she chucked her shoes through the open closet door, causing a resounding *thump* as they hit the back wall.

"Yeah, I did." Lauren made a face. "You're going to put a hole in the wall doing that."

Allison made a face at her. "Did anyone ever tell you that you worry too much?"

Lauren cocked an eyebrow at her. "Besides you?"

Allison laughed. "Okay, you got me." She finished changing, then turned off the bedroom light and climbed into bed. "So, what were you and Ben talking about at the car? You two looked pretty chummy."

"Nothing important," she answered vaguely. "Just stuff."

"Oh, really?" Allison teased. "Well, you may not want to believe this, but I think he has a thing for you."

Lauren felt a momentary twinge of hope, but then forced it away, knowing that even if he did, nothing could ever come of it. She wouldn't let it.

Giving a short laugh to mask her emotions, Lauren rolled over and propped her head up with her hand as she managed to meet Allison's gaze through the darkness. "Allison, I love you, but you have the wildest imagination of anyone I know. Just because he talked to me tonight doesn't mean he has a thing for me. Besides, he's a guy... you know, cute on the surface, but deep down, scum of the earth."

Allison laughed. "Oh, come on, Lauren! Besides being totally gorgeous, he seems like a completely likeable guy. There's got to be *something* about him you like."

Lauren thought for a moment. "Well, I guess he was a pretty good sport when I struck him out," she admitted reluctantly.

"See? That's something," Allison pointed out with satisfaction.

"And I certainly wouldn't dispute the fact that he's totally gorgeous," Lauren conceded, a slow grin playing across her lips. "He did seem pretty nice, too. None of that really matters, though, because I'm *not* getting involved with him. With anyone," she quickly amended. "But I guess if I were to get involved with someone, he wouldn't be the worst choice possible…"

"Ah-ha!" Allison exclaimed, sitting up in bed so suddenly that it made Lauren jump. "So you *are* interested!"

"No, I'm not! I'm just saying that a girl could do worse than Ben. Well… maybe." She made a face. "Who knows? I don't even know him. Maybe he's a total jerk like every other guy in the world."

"Except Craig," Allison amended.

"Oh, of course. Except for Craig." Lauren grinned. It was quiet for several moments, then Lauren spoke again, this time hesitantly. "Allison, can I ask you something?"

"Shoot."

"You don't think I purposely try to show up guys, do you?"

Allison propped herself up on her elbow, and Lauren could see the look of confusion on her friend's face. "What makes you say that?"

Lauren sighed. "It was just something Elena said tonight." Haltingly, she told Allison about her run-in with Elena.

"Forget about Elena," Allison demanded. "She's a world-class jerk. She doesn't have any idea what she's talking about. Look at Ben. Was he scared off by you?"

"No, I guess not," Lauren admitted. "He seemed to think it was kind of funny, actually."

"See? Not all guys are jerks and have huge ego issues." She paused for a moment, obviously considering something. Finally, she forged on. "Do something for me, would you?"

"Sure. What?"

"I know you have all these issues about guys, but there's something about Ben... he just seems like a really great guy. I'm not saying you have to agree to go out with him or anything, but... just give him a chance, okay?"

Lauren rolled her eyes. "Goodnight, Allison."

Sensing that she'd already said too much, Allison said goodnight, then rolled over and went to sleep. The sound of quiet snoring a few minutes later told Lauren that her friend was asleep, but sleep continued to evade her as she stared up at the darkened ceiling and mulled over Allison's request.

Allison was right about one thing. There was definitely something about Ben that had caught her interest. How far she pursued that interest, though, was a different matter. Too much had happened in her past with relationships that made her gun shy about ever wanting to share her heart again. It seemed easier to simply dismiss Allison's request and go on with her life. But whenever she closed her eyes, images of Ben's warm smile and beautiful, gentle eyes kept forcing their way into her mind, and she wondered how easy that would actually be.

She sighed as she rolled over in bed and pulled the covers up around her shoulders. One thing was certain—sleep was going to be a long time in coming tonight.

Chapter Five

"You're still awake? What are you doing up?"

Ben looked up from where he sat on the couch reading his scriptures to see Craig coming into the apartment. "I couldn't sleep," he explained, setting his battered scriptures aside and glancing up at the clock on the wall. It was nearly midnight.

Craig wandered into the kitchen to grab a couple of cookies from a bag on the counter, then came back into the living room and plopped down into the armchair next to the couch. He nodded at Ben's scriptures as he took a bite of one of his cookies. "Doing some reading?"

"A little." He sighed. "Mostly thinking, actually."

Craig cocked a sandy blond eyebrow at him. "Uh-oh."

"Nothing earth-shattering," Ben said with a smile as he raised his arms above his head and stretched. "I was just thinking about tonight."

"Yeah, that ward party was pretty great, huh?" Craig enthused. "Could you believe all the gorgeous girls in our ward? I see some definite dating possibilities." He took another bite, then waved his cookie at Ben. "Oh, and speaking of which, I have a date with Allison tomorrow night."

Ben chuckled. "Why am I not surprised?"

"Well, she does seem pretty cool. Anyway, what about you? I couldn't help noticing that you were practically drooling over that girl Lauren. Man, she's got an arm on her," he said, referring to her pitching. "And she's pretty darned hot, if you ask me."

"Yeah, I thought she was pretty great, too."

"So, are you going to ask her out or what?"

Ben sighed. "Actually, I did. She kind of freaked. I've been trying to figure out what that means."

Craig's brows furrowed. "What do you mean, 'freaked'?"

Ben's mind flashed back to the abrupt change in Lauren's demeanor when he'd asked her out and he grimaced. He didn't understand it. From the moment he'd seen her on the pitcher's mound, he knew she was something special. There was just something about her that made her irresistible to him, and it had been all he could do not to ask her out the second he'd approached her in the food line. He'd been thrilled when she asked him to eat with her and her roommates since it gave him the perfect opportunity to get to know her better.

And what he saw, he'd liked. She was kind, funny, and easy to talk to, and she tugged at his heartstrings in a way no other girl ever had. He wanted more than anything to find out what it was about her that touched his soul so deeply. But all hopes of learning what that was vanished when he'd asked her out. It was impossible to forget the way her expression had changed from a look of comfortable ease to one of utter panic. And that confused him more than anything.

Ben finally looked at Craig and shrugged. "Well, everything was going well," he began, hoping his friend would be able to give him some insight on the matter. "We were really hitting it off… or at least, I thought we were. We were joking around and talking, then I asked her if she wanted to do something on Friday. The next thing I knew, she got this completely panicked look on her face and spouted off something about spending the weekend catching up on her school work."

"That is weird," Craig agreed. A look of deliberation crossed his face as he polished off the last of his cookie. "Maybe she's doesn't like dating," he finally suggested, "or maybe she thought you were a complete jerk." He grinned as Ben tossed a throw pillow at him. But then Craig sobered and he continued. "Who knows, maybe she really *is* having a hard time adjusting. The best advice I can give you is to give it some time and see what happens."

"Yeah, you're probably right," Ben admitted, picking up his scriptures and standing up. "Well, I guess I'll get some sleep. Maybe I'll get hit with inspiration during the night."

Ben said goodnight and went into his bedroom. He quickly changed into a T-shirt and boxers, then dropped to his knees beside his bed to pray. He bowed his head humbly, thanking his Heavenly Father for his blessings, and once again asked to be blessed with the answers he sought regarding this new phase of his life. When he finished, he climbed into bed and closed his eyes, willing the familiar, soothing darkness of sleep to creep across his mind.

But hard as he tried to make his mind and body rest, a single image remained steadfast in his head, refusing to be crowded out by the comfort of sleep. It was the image of a young woman with long auburn hair and light brown, gold-flecked eyes; an image of a young woman who, in the space of just one evening, had had the ability to reach clear into the depths of his soul. He had no idea what it was about Lauren that gave her so much power over his heart in such a short amount of time; he only knew that power was real.

Giving in to the persistent images in his mind, he tucked his hands beneath his head and stared up at the dark ceiling. A slow smile tugged at the corners of his mouth. Lauren was simply incredible. He loved the lilt in her voice as she spoke, the sweet sound of her easy laughter, and the way her eyes lit up and sparkled as she told him something about her family—her brothers in particular.

But then he remembered her expression when he'd asked her out, and his smile faded. He'd definitely liked what he'd seen of her that evening, but he had to admit, she was still a bit of a mystery. Why had she acted so strangely when he'd asked her out?

Maybe Craig was right. Maybe she wasn't into the dating scene. But then, that didn't make much sense either. If that were the case, she would have just told him no, that she wasn't interested in going out with anybody. Instead, the look in her eyes when he'd asked her out flashed into his mind, and one thing became clear. That look wasn't indifference. It was fear.

He shook his head. So what was she so afraid of? There was more to this than classes and workloads and he was determined to get to the bottom of it. But how?

Rolling over in bed, he finally succeeded in pushing the images of her and his unanswered questions into the back of his mind, and he slowly drifted off to sleep. There would be time enough tomorrow to try to find his elusive answers.

The sun was almost directly overhead the next day when Ben made his way across the crowded campus and into the building where his third and final class of the morning was to be held. He'd just turned down the hall and was about to go into his classroom when he heard someone calling his name.

"Hey, Ben! Is that you?"

Turning, he recognized Lauren's roommate from the ward activity the night before. "Allison, right?" he asked with a smile. When she nodded, he jabbed his thumb over his shoulder at the classroom behind him. "Psychology 111?"

She made a face. "Unfortunately, yes. But at least I know someone in the class now. Come on, let's go grab those two empty desks in the back corner."

They walked together to the seats in the back, then shrugged out of their backpacks and sat down. "So, how'd you like the ward activity last night?" Allison asked when they were settled.

"It was fun," Ben answered cheerfully. "I think our ward's going to be great."

Allison nodded. "I think so too. Bishop Warner seems really nice."

"Yeah, he does. I have to admit, though, I was a little apprehensive about what our ward was going to be like."

Allison's brows furrowed. "Really? How come?"

Realizing he'd just revealed more than he'd intended, Ben groaned inwardly. The very last thing he wanted to do was share his miserable past with everyone he met. For whatever reason, though, he found Allison surprisingly easy to talk to. Still, he knew he'd better be more careful in the future if he didn't want to reveal more pieces of his past that were better left forgotten.

Seeing that Allison was waiting for an answer, he gave a little shrug. "No reason. Didn't you worry about what your ward and roommates were going to be like?"

Allison laughed and leaned back in her chair. "Nah, that's Lauren's department. She worries enough for the both of us."

Ben cocked an eyebrow. "Really? She worries about things?"

Allison nodded as she ran her painted fingernails through the turned up ends of her blond hair. "You could say that. She's always been a worrier, ever since I've known her."

Ben filed away that little piece of information, then fished for more. "How long have you two been friends?"

"Just this side of forever. For years I've been trying to get her to lighten up, and she's been trying to straighten me out. We sort of balance each other out."

Ben laughed. "Sounds like it."

Allison leaned over to pull her psychology textbook from her backpack, and Ben had a moment to consider Allison's words. If Lauren really was a worrier, as Allison said, then the concerns Lauren had expressed last night about falling behind in her schoolwork might actually be valid. But that didn't explain the look of fear in her eyes. There simply had to be a different reason for her turning him down.

Deciding to pry for a little information, he asked, "Allison, you said Lauren was worried about things. Do you know if she's worried about her schoolwork? She seemed a little keyed up about it last night."

"I don't know that she's worried about her classes, really," Allison told him as she opened her notebook and uncapped her pen. "She's always been a good student. She does seem a little worried about juggling her classes and her job, though."

Ben cocked an eyebrow in surprise. "She has a job?"

Allison nodded. "She's working part-time at the college bookstore to help pay her tuition."

"Really? I didn't know that," Ben said with interest. "When does she work?"

"Mondays, Wednesdays, and Fridays, from noon to five," Allison recited. "But I think she'll also fill in on other shifts if they need her."

Ben's heart leapt. Today was Wednesday. Lauren's shift started at noon. His Psych class ended at noon. Hmm. He had a feeling that after class, he was going to get a sudden, irresistible urge to go and buy a book.

Just then the professor came into the room, effectively cutting off any further conversation between them. But that didn't stop Ben's mind from whirling at the possibility of seeing Lauren again in less than an hour. He was relieved that the hour was spent going over the class synopsis, and not on anything of earth shattering importance since his mind was elsewhere.

It seemed like an eternity before class was finally over, and when it was, Ben was out of his seat in a flash. It was only Allison's voice behind him that stopped his mad dash out the door.

"Where are you off to in such a rush?" she asked as she shrugged into her backpack.

He slowed his pace and walked beside her out into the beautiful, fall sunshine. "I thought I'd go meet a friend," he answered with an evasive smile.

"Speaking of meeting friends," Allison said coyly, a slow smile working its way across her face, "you and Craig are roommates; you wouldn't happen to know his schedule, would you?"

Ben chuckled. "Ahh, the old 'prying information out of the roommate' trick, huh? That's pretty sneaky."

"Okay, you caught me," Allison said with a sheepish grin. "So, is that a yes or a no?"

With another laugh and a shake of his head, he recited what he knew about Craig's schedule while Allison jotted down the information in her notebook. When she was finished, she studied his schedule thoughtfully.

"So he's getting out of Communications right now, which is just a couple of buildings away. If I hurry I can catch him." With new enthusiasm, she flashed him a brilliant smile and thumped him lightly on the arm. "Ben, you are just the best. I owe you one!"

An image of Lauren flashed into his mind. "I'm going to take you up on that!" he called after her retreating figure.

As Allison disappeared into the crowd of students, Ben smiled and shook his head. She was definitely a bundle of energy and enthusiasm, and it wasn't hard to see why Craig was interested in her. He, on the other hand, preferred someone with a slightly less keyed-up personality—someone with gorgeous auburn hair and a smile that made his heart melt; someone who was sure to brighten his day each and every time he saw her. With a heartbeat that matched his quickening steps, he turned and headed for the bookstore.

Lauren looked up from the box of textbooks she was unpacking in time to see Dan hitting on yet another girl. The girl was tall and slender, with long, silky blond hair, ocean blue eyes, and flawless skin. Lauren rolled her eyes. One more demonstration of the hopeless chauvinism in men. Who cared what her mind was like, as long as she had a perfect figure and a pretty face.

After one more quiet exchange, the girl wrote something down on a piece of paper and slipped it into Dan's hand. Then she flashed him a winning smile before turning to leave. When she was gone, Dan turned to Lauren, pumped his fist, and exclaimed, "Yes! Am I good or what?"

Lauren rolled her eyes again as she turned back to her unpacking. "Another number to add to your little black book?"

Dan tucked the piece of paper carefully into his pocket and smiled as he strutted down the aisle toward her. "As a matter of fact, yes. We're going out tonight."

"Well, have fun. Now if you don't mind," she said, her voice dripping with sarcasm, "could you help me out by actually doing some work? I'm getting a little behind."

Dan picked up several books from the box and stacked them on the shelf. "Lighten up, Lauren," he teased. "You know what you need? You need a charming, good-looking guy to take you out and show you how to have a good time." His grin broadened. "Oh, hey... I think that's me."

This time she couldn't help smiling. "Yeah, right, Dan," she teased back. "Keep dreaming. You're not my type."

"Oh really," he retorted, phrasing it more as a comment than a question. "Then who *is* your type? No, wait... don't tell me... someone *responsible*." He let the word roll off his tongue sourly.

"Maybe, or maybe not," Lauren defended herself. "I can tell you one thing, though—my type definitely wouldn't be some pushy womanizer who only goes out with a girl once or twice and is never heard from again." She smiled tauntingly. "In other words, not you."

Dan gasped and thumped a hand over his heart. "Ouch! That was pretty harsh, Holt. And... okay... one hundred percent accurate." He grinned. "But let's let that be our little secret, shall we? I have a feeling that little piece of information would seriously kill my dating status."

Lauren's eyebrows lifted and her smile turned mischievous. "I sense some serious blackmail coming on."

"Don't you dare," Dan replied with a laugh. He lifted the remaining books from the box and stacked them on the shelf with the others. "Well, that's the last of 'em."

"Thank goodness," Lauren sighed as she bent over to pick up the empty box. When she straightened, she was surprised to see Ben standing just a few feet away.

He was the picture of casualness as he stood there watching her, leaning up against the bookshelf with his shoulder, his arms crossed comfortably across his chest. When their eyes met, a slow, beautiful smile worked its way across his face, causing Lauren's heart rate to quicken. She felt a momentary rush of pleasure at seeing him again, but then quickly reminded herself of the consequences that came from letting one's heart rule one's head.

"Hi, Ben," she greeted, making a conscious effort to sound friendly, yet maintain her emotional distance at the same time. "What are you doing here?"

He pushed off from the bookshelf and sauntered toward her in slow, easy strides. "I came by to pick up a couple of textbooks and saw you over here. You didn't tell me you were working here."

She nodded. "It helps pay my tuition, plus I get a discount on my textbooks and stuff."

"Sounds perfect."

He stopped a stride away from her and she caught the faint, musky scent of his cologne, so familiar from the night before. For a moment, her resolve to maintain her emotional distance wavered. She couldn't remember the last time—if ever—anyone's closeness had had such an effect on her.

Before she could give herself another talking to, Dan stepped up and nudged Lauren with his elbow. "Aren't you going to introduce me to your... friend?" he asked, an unmistakable teasing note in his voice.

Lauren tried to ignore it as she introduced Ben as a friend from her ward, but Dan lifted his eyebrows in playful challenge. He looked Ben up and down, then turned back to Lauren in time to see the slight blush creeping across her cheeks. A look of understanding flickered in his eyes and he turned to Ben, a broad grin hovering at the corners of his mouth. "I bet you're responsible, aren't you?"

"Dan!" Lauren gasped, whirling around and giving him a withering stare. "Don't you have something to do? Like... I don't know, flirting with some female customers or something?"

Unaffected, Dan just smiled triumphantly and backed away. "Sure, I get it. You want to be alone with Mr. Responsible." When Lauren took a menacing step toward him, he laughed and darted away.

When he disappeared around the corner, Ben looked at Lauren in confusion. "What was that all about?"

Lauren waved her hand dismissively in the direction Dan had disappeared. "Forget it. He's like a pesky little brother teasing everyone about everything. So, you said you needed a couple of textbooks?" she asked, making a point of changing the subject.

Ben nodded. "Trig and Bio."

"No problem. Let me show you where they are."

As she led the way down the aisle, Lauren could almost sense Ben's gaze boring into the back of her neck. It was all she could do to force her mind away from the image of those beautiful brown eyes and focus on the task at hand. When they finally turned down the aisle she was looking for, she found herself breathing an inward sigh of relief.

"Here they are," she said with a casualness she didn't feel. "The trigonometry texts are here, and the biology ones are in this section over here. Is there anything else I can help you find?"

He picked up the trigonometry textbook and started to flip through it. "How about a book to help me understand the trigonometry book?"

She laughed. "What, didn't they teach you trig at Harvard?"

His brown eyes sparkled as they met hers. "Nope. I was lucky and avoided it my first year. Math's never been my strong suit."

"Well, sorry, but we don't have any trig Cliffnotes," she joked. "You'll just have to study hard like the rest of us."

Ben laughed. "Great. And I thought college out west was going to be easy."

When their laughter faded, Lauren saw something unreadable flicker in Ben's eyes, and for a moment she thought he was about to ask her something. But then the look was gone and his easygoing smile returned.

"Well, thanks for helping me locate the books," he told her cheerfully. "I guess I should let you get back to work."

"Yes, I guess I should," Lauren admitted with a sigh. "It's been really busy today."

"I'll bet. Anyway, it was good to see you again," he said sincerely.

Lauren was surprised to realize she felt the same way. "It was good to see you, too."

He smiled one last time as he backed up a few steps, then turned and disappeared around the end of the aisle. Lauren watched him go, a myriad of emotions filling her heart. The attraction she felt toward him was completely irrational; she knew that. And she knew she had to stay away from him. But could she? Maybe that was the question she should be asking herself.

With a heavy sigh, she set off for the back room where she was sure there were more boxes of textbooks waiting to be unpacked.

Chapter Six

Ben's steps were light as he trotted down the stairs from the bookstore. Seeing Lauren again had been incredible, and in only those few short minutes, he'd found himself falling for her all over again. What made his heart feel as light as his feet was the way Lauren's eyes had lit up with pleasure when she'd seen him standing there. That alone made his trip to the bookstore worth it.

The thing that stuck out in his mind, though, was how different she'd seemed just now as compared to the night before. Not *bad* different, just different. Other than the brief time he'd seen her on the pitching mound at the ward activity, she seemed so much more in her element there in the bookstore, dressed in nice but casual jeans, medium-blue collared shirt, and her beautiful reddish brown hair smoothed back neatly into a ponytail. He loved the way it danced around her shoulders when she shook her head and when she'd whirled around to chase Dan away. And in the thirty seconds or so that he'd been watching her before she'd noticed him, he'd seen the ease with which she'd been interacting with Dan. He hadn't overheard much of their conversation, but she was clearly at ease in Dan's company.

For a few moments, he'd been jealous as he'd watched their easy interaction. But then he'd realized that their interaction seemed more like the way one would talk with a brother or a friend, not a potential boyfriend. Even so, he knew that more than anything, *he* wanted to be the person she verbally sparred with, the one she talked, laughed, and had fun with.

He'd almost pressed the issue and asked her out again as they were standing there discussing his textbooks, but just as he'd gathered up the nerve to ask the question, something deep inside of him, some little voice of caution and reason, had told him not to push. There was much more to her rejection the night before than she was letting on, and he had to admit that pushing too hard would probably only push her farther away. So, with a frustrated, inward sigh, he'd listened to the little voice of warning, knowing it was right. He would just have to bide his time.

Not that being patient was going to be easy. The attraction he felt toward her was unlike anything he'd ever experienced, and he didn't *want* to wait. More than anything, he wanted to get to know her, to simply be *with* her. But before he could figure out a way to do that, he knew he was going to have to get to the bottom of the mystery that was Lauren.

The thought made him smile. He had the sneaking suspicion that that was going to be half the fun.

The rest of Wednesday passed in a flurry of activity. After seeing Lauren at the bookstore, Ben went to the library to sign up for a tutoring job. It didn't pay much, but it was enough to cover the expenses his grants and scholarships didn't cover. Then, before he left, he established an email account and sat down to write an email.

He typed in his sister's email address, the one only he knew about. It was their secret way of staying in touch, even though their father had insisted on severing all family ties with Ben after he was baptized. Ben was certain that if their father ever found out he and his sister were communicating against his wishes, he would hit the roof. That didn't deter him, though. He and Emily had always been so close that he couldn't bear not to at least drop her a line occasionally to let her know he was okay, and to hear the same from her.

Even though he knew it was risky, that's what he did now. He assured Emily that he was fine and settling in, and that things were going well for him in Idaho. Then he sent the email off and headed for home.

Wednesday blended into Thursday and Ben went through the motions of going to his classes and trying to concentrate, but thoughts of Lauren kept invading his mind. In an effort to catch up on what he'd missed, he went to the library after his classes to read through his notes and study for the psychology quiz he knew he had the next morning. The sound of his stomach rumbling reminded him of the approaching dinner hour, and he finally decided to call it a night and head for home.

He walked the short distance from the campus to his apartment, and when he opened the door, he was surprised to see Allison sitting in the front room, talking with Craig.

"Hey, Allison," he said as he shut the door behind him.

"Ben!" she responded cheerfully. "Where've you been off to?"

He dropped his backpack on the floor near the couch and sat down. "I was up at the library studying."

Allison rolled her eyes. "You're just like Lauren. She's spent half her life studying in a library. You two really ought to get out more. So, what were you studying?"

"Psych. Are you ready for our quiz tomorrow?"

She groaned. "Oh, no, I forgot all about it! Craig, I gotta go," she told him apologetically as she climbed to her feet. "Are we still on for pizza tomorrow night?"

He nodded. "You bet. Your place? Six?"

She flashed him a grin. "You got it. Why don't you come, too, Ben? We're just hanging out with my roommates, eating pizza, and talking. It should be fun."

"Will Lauren be there?" he asked hopefully, trying to keep the excitement he felt at the prospect of seeing Lauren again out of his voice. He knew he hadn't been entirely successful, however, when Craig and Allison exchanged a quick, knowing look.

Allison nodded as she tried to wipe the smile off her face. "I'm sure she will be. She does live there, and she has no real life to speak of." She gave him a friendly wink, then turned to Craig. "See ya later, Craig. Bye, Ben."

After she was gone, Ben told Craig, "Pizza sounds like fun. I just wonder if Lauren will really want me there. She's so hard to figure out. I wish I knew what her story was."

"So, ask one of her roommates," Craig said matter-of-factly. "If they're anything like my sisters, they tell each other everything."

Ben mulled the suggestion over in his mind. He'd already thought of quizzing Allison, but normally he wouldn't think of trying to pry information from someone he'd known less than a week. But Allison was so friendly and easy to talk to that he didn't feel uncomfortable broaching the topic. In the short time that he'd known her, he already thought of her as a friend.

Besides, he thought, *she already said she owed me one for giving her Craig's class schedule. If she feels like something is too personal to answer, she'll say so, and that'll be that.*

At any rate, he figured it was worth a try.

Ben walked out of the Clark building the next afternoon in a daze. The psych quiz had been brutal. Their professor had seemed bent on putting everyone in their place and forcing them to work harder by giving them bad grades on the first quiz of the semester.

At least I hope that was his intent, Ben thought dismally, *or I'm going to be in big trouble.*

He was halfway down the building's steps when a voice shook him out of his daze. "You still coming over tonight with Craig?"

He turned and saw Allison falling into step with him. He immediately wanted to kick himself. He'd been so preoccupied with thoughts of his disastrous quiz that he'd completely forgotten his intentions to talk with Allison about Lauren.

"Hey, Allison," he greeted her cheerfully. "Yeah, I'm looking forward to tonight. Lauren's not going out on a date or anything, is she?"

Allison laughed loudly, causing several people to turn and look at them. "With a guy?" she managed. "You've got to be kidding."

Ben's brow furrowed in confusion. "What do you mean?"

They reached the bottom of the steps and Allison paused to adjust her backpack on her shoulder. "Lauren thinks all guys are shallow, cheating womanizers. I don't think I'll live long enough to see her agree to go out with anybody."

"Oh. Well, that would explain her reaction when I asked her out Tuesday night."

Allison's jaw practically hit the sidewalk. "You asked her out?"

"Yeah," he admitted sheepishly, "but she shot me down."

"Hmm." Allison looked thoughtful as they started walking slowly down the sidewalk. "Somehow Lauren managed to leave out that little detail when she was talking to me about you."

Ben's heart skipped a beat. "She was talking about me?"

Allison grinned. "Yeah. She said she thought you were pretty cool. And coming from Lauren, that's saying a lot."

Maybe there's hope for me after all, he thought happily. Then, deciding this was the perfect opportunity to ask his question, he took a deep breath and forged ahead.

"Remember the other day when you said you owed me one for giving you Craig's schedule? 'Prying the information out of the roommate,' and all that?" When she nodded, he continued. "Okay, then, I'm collecting. What's the story with Lauren? Why does she think all guys are scum?"

Allison shook her head grimly. "It's a long story. Besides, she'd lynch me if she ever found out I told you."

"Please, Allison? I really want to know."

Allison studied the longing expression in his eyes for a moment. "You really like her, don't you?" she said softly.

Ben hesitated. Finally, he nodded. "Yeah, I do. I can't stop thinking about her. But I don't want to blow my chances with her before I can find a way to convince her I'm not scum."

Allison laughed. "Yeah, that wouldn't be good." Finally, she let out her breath in a rush and rolled her eyes. "Fine. But if you ever breathe a word of this to anyone...."

He quickly held up three fingers in a Boy Scout gesture like he'd seen people do in the movies. "Scout's honor."

She looked at him dubiously. "Were you ever a Boy Scout?"

He laughed. "Okay, you caught me. But what do you want me to do? Slit my palm open and seal my promise with blood?"

Allison looked momentarily queasy. "No, that's okay. I'll take your word for it." They walked for a short distance in silence, then she sighed. "I don't know how much I can tell you without betraying a confidence, but let's just say that she's had a series of not-so-great relationships that have left her feeling a little... disillusioned."

He frowned. "That bad, huh?"

Allison nodded. "She's gotten pretty burned. Guys have used her to get good grades on finals, cheated on her... things like that. But Matt was the worst. He really devastated her."

"Who was Matt?" Ben asked, not entirely sure he wanted to know.

She sighed and looked a little uncertain about whether or not to proceed. Finally, she gestured to a low brick wall nearby and they went over and sat down on it. Ben waited for several moments as Allison collected her thoughts.

"This is where you need to promise never to reveal what I'm about to tell you... to *anybody*," she emphasized. "Understand?"

When Ben nodded, Allison went on. "Being an only girl with five older brothers, Lauren learned different things than, say, I did, growing up with sisters. Instead of spending time doing girl things, like experimenting with makeup and hairstyles, she spent all her time going to ballgames with her dad and brothers, and learning to play ball and hike and stuff like that.

"The trouble was, she was so smart and athletic and driven that guys tended to be intimidated by her. After a date or two, they'd move on to somebody else who was more interested in hanging on their arm and telling them how big and strong and wonderful they were—and Lauren would be crushed.

"Her confidence started to suffer, so she built up this emotional wall to keep herself from being hurt any more than she already had. When the rest of us kept getting asked out and she didn't, she pretended she didn't care, but I know she did. Then, toward the end of our junior year, Matt Nelson came along. He was popular and charming and good looking...."

She paused and made a face. "I never liked him, to be honest. And at first, Lauren was wary of his attention. But he *was* charming, and before long, he'd somehow managed to break through her defenses and win her over. They started dating pretty regularly, and it wasn't hard to see that he'd swept her off her feet. She fell for him hard. She thought she'd finally found somebody who wasn't intimidated by her and could love her for who she was."

"But it didn't work out?" Ben prompted.

Allison shook her head grimly. "You could say that. The night of our junior prom, Matt went to get some punch, and when he didn't come back, Lauren went looking for him. She finally found him outside in a lip-lock with his ex-girlfriend."

Ben cringed. "Ouch."

"Yeah. Ouch." Allison frowned at the memory, then went on. "Lauren was devastated. It had been hard enough for her to open up her heart and trust somebody after all the rejections she'd had, and then Matt repaid her efforts by cheating on her. His betrayal was kind of the final nail in the coffin. She was so hurt that she swore she was never going to open up her heart to anybody ever again."

Ben nodded, suddenly understanding why she'd reacted the way she had the other night when he'd asked her out. She was perfectly willing to talk to him as a guy *friend*, but as soon as he'd asked to see her in a more "relationship" type of situation, she'd panicked. He could hardly blame her.

"So, where does that leave me?" Ben asked quietly. "I want to get to know her better, but if she's not even going to give me the time of day...."

"Well, I know she likes you," she told him with a quick wink. "She hasn't said as much, but I know her well enough to know she does. My advice to you is to take things slow. Don't pressure her into anything or you'll definitely scare her off. Be her friend and build her trust. Prove to her that you're not like all those other guys who've hurt her in the past. After that, who knows what might happen."

"Be her friend, huh?" Ben echoed thoughtfully. "I think I can manage that."

Allison grinned. "Good. Well, I've got to get home and grab some lunch before my next class. I'll see you tonight?"

He nodded. "I'll be there."

With a friendly wink, Allison turned and walked away, leaving Ben alone with his thoughts. Now that he knew what had happened to make Lauren so guarded, her reaction to being asked out made sense. She was understandably wary. Not only had her fragile trust been betrayed, but she was having to recover from a broken heart. He'd never had it happen to him personally, but he'd seen it happen to some of his friends, and he remembered that it wasn't pretty.

What Allison had suggested, though, certainly made sense, Ben thought. If he was Lauren's friend first, and he could prove to her that he really was a genuinely nice guy with no ulterior motives, then maybe he stood a chance with her. It gave him a glimmer of hope, anyway.

As he walked to the library, his heart felt a little lighter knowing there was something he could do. He'd be Lauren's friend. And if it took fifty years to convince her to give him a chance, he was sure it would be worth the wait.

Chapter Seven

Lauren trudged up her apartment steps Friday evening, completely exhausted. For a reason she couldn't even begin to fathom, she thought working at the bookstore was going to be easy. But now she was beginning to see just how wrong she was.

She'd picked up on things quickly, but the high pressure and constant stream of students needing this and looking for that had left her feeling frazzled and frustrated. And as if that hadn't been enough, she'd had to put up with Dan's infuriating flirting—not only with her, but with every pretty girl who came into the bookstore. She couldn't believe the number of girls who'd fallen for his practiced charms and readily handed over their phone numbers to him. She felt like smacking them for being so easily taken in by a handsome face and a bit of charm.

Then to top off an already frustrating week, she'd been assigned enough homework in her classes during the first four days to last her an entire month. She loved her classes, especially her sports medicine class, but she had a sinking feeling that her anatomy/physiology class was going to give her fits. Her professor was a stickler and had let them know right up front that he expected one hundred and fifty percent from his students. He seemed to have the impression that his was the only class his students had, and gave homework accordingly. She shuddered at the thought of the hours of homework that lay ahead of her for the weekend.

With heavy steps, Lauren finally made it to her apartment and pushed the door open. Allison looked up from the couch where she was relaxing and flipping through a fashion magazine.

"Man, Lauren, you look beat," she observed, taking in her friend's tired and rumpled appearance.

Lauren nodded and collapsed into the armchair. "You've got that right. I'm thinking that a long, hot bath would be wonderful."

"Sorry, not gonna happen," Allison told her cheerfully as she stood up and headed into the bathroom. "We have company coming over in about five minutes."

Lauren lifted her eyebrow curiously. "We?" she called loud enough that Allison could hear her in the bathroom. "Don't you mean 'you'?"

Allison leaned out of the open bathroom door and grinned at her mischievously. "Nope. We."

Lauren let her head fall back against the chair and groaned. "Come on, Al, I'm too tired for twenty questions. What are you trying to say?"

"Oh, I just invited a couple of people over for pizza tonight, that's all."

A slow, uneasy feeling crept into her stomach. She stood up slowly and made her way to the bathroom where Allison was touching up her makeup. Lauren folded her arms and looked at her friend suspiciously. "Who's coming over?"

Just then a loud knock sounded on the door, and Allison caught Lauren's eye in the mirror. "That'll be Craig and Ben. Will you answer that?"

Lauren's eyes widened and she stared at her friend in shock. "Allison, you didn't! How could you do this? You know I don't want to be set up!"

"Who said anything about setting you up?" Allison replied innocently. "All I did was invite a couple of my friends over for pizza. What's wrong with that?" She pushed past Lauren and headed into the living room. "So, are you coming or what?"

Catching a glimpse of her rumpled appearance in the mirror, Lauren quickly shook her head and rushed into her bedroom. "You go ahead. I've got to change into something presentable."

Ignoring the amused look on Allison's face, Lauren hurried into her bedroom and shut the door behind her. She looked around her room frantically. What should she wear? She didn't want to look like she went to a lot of trouble, but then she didn't want to look like she'd just rolled out of bed, either. She rushed to the closet and started rifling through her handful of clothes. Making a quick decision, she pulled her favorite white, long-sleeved, ribbed knit T-shirt off its hanger and started to reach for her nice tan slacks.

But then she gave herself a mental shake. Why on earth should she have to go to so much trouble? It wasn't like she was trying to impress anyone. Besides, it was Friday night. She wanted to be comfortable, not dressy.

Her mind made up, she reached instead for her denim Old Navy overalls and pulled them on over a white shirt. Then she buckled the straps, stepped into her comfortable white canvas mules, and finally turned to study her reflection in the mirror. She grimaced. Her hair was a mess, and what little makeup she'd applied that morning had long since disappeared.

Working quickly, she released her hair from the ponytail and let it cascade down her back. She grabbed her brush from her dresser and quickly ran it through her thick hair, then touched up her blush and eyeliner. Giving her reflection one last glance, she hurried out to join Allison.

Ben sat on the couch next to Craig and Allison, trying not to look as anxious as he felt. As soon as Allison had ushered him and Craig inside, Bree and Melia magically appeared, and everyone started talking and laughing. The only person missing from their little impromptu party of sorts was the one he'd specifically come to see. He tried to look interested as he talked with Bree about their first week of college, but he found his gaze continually shifting to the hall doorway, hoping that Lauren would soon appear.

It seemed like an eternity before he finally heard Allison say, "Hey, Lauren. It's about time you joined us."

Ben looked up in time to see Lauren emerging from the hall, and his heart did a little flip. She looked amazing. The white shirt she was wearing set off her lightly tanned skin, and her denim overalls did little to detract from her slim, curvy figure. Her hair hung around her shoulders and down her back in pretty auburn waves, and her eyes sparkled as her gaze met and held his.

He smiled, trying to appear calmer than he felt. "Hi, Lauren."

A chorus of greetings followed, and she greeted everyone with a smile... although Ben couldn't help noticing that her smile didn't reach all the way into her eyes. She seemed nervous. His eyes followed her as she walked the rest of the way into the room where she stood for a moment, looking around for somewhere to sit. Melia was in the armchair, Bree was lying on the loveseat with her legs stretched out across the cushions, and Ben, Craig, and Allison were sharing the couch. Looking uncertain, Lauren started to lower herself to the floor near the couch, but Ben quickly stopped her.

"Oh, don't sit on the floor," he objected. "We'll make room for you here, won't we guys?"

Craig and Allison seemed more than happy to move closer together, and within moments, there was an empty space beside Ben on the couch. He patted the cushion encouragingly. "Come on, sit."

She smiled gratefully. "Thanks. The floor would've been fine, though."

Ben feigned offense and put a hand to his heart, hoping that a little joking might put her at ease. "What kind of gentleman would I be if I let you sit on the floor?"

This time a genuine smile broke through and she visibly relaxed. "I guess you have a point there."

"So, how's your job going?" he asked, hoping to keep the conversation rolling.

Lauren sighed. "I'm never going to get the hang of it," she told him with a discouraged shake of her head. "I understand about stocking the books and merchandise, but working the register is really confusing. Just today I rang up somebody and ended up charging him twice for everything, and then I couldn't remember how to void the items. He was furious because I was making him late to class. Luckily, my boss showed up and helped me, but it was a mess! I swear I'm going to be fired by the end of the week."

Allison overheard and started to laugh. "You're not going to get fired," she consoled. "It might take you a few days to get the hang of things, but you'll get it. In the meantime, don't get so worked up about it. Have a brownie or something."

Ben lifted an eyebrow questioningly. "A brownie?"

Lauren shot Allison a threatening look, but Allison completely ignored her and grinned at Ben.

"Lauren's a chocolate freak," she explained. "Chocolate always calms her down when she's upset or stressed out, and brownies work better than anything else."

Ben started to laugh. "Oh really? And why's that?" He turned to look at Lauren, who suddenly looked as if she wished she could disappear.

"Who knows?" Allison answered when Lauren didn't. "But the gooier and fudgier, the better. Trust me. It works wonders."

Ben's grin widened. "I'll have to remember that."

"So, what about you?" Lauren asked him, finally finding her voice and trying to change the subject. "Are you working?"

Ben nodded. "I signed up to do some tutoring. It doesn't pay much, but it's enough. I've already got a couple of sessions lined up for next week."

"That sounds great," Lauren agreed. "Your schedule will be flexible, and you don't have a boss hovering around, seeing every mistake you make." She grimaced.

Ben laughed. "I guess there is that."

"At least I have the weekend off so I won't be humiliating myself for a few days."

"You're not working tomorrow?" he asked, thinking it might be the perfect opportunity to spend some time with her. But as soon as he spoke the words, he couldn't help cringing at the hopefulness he heard in his own voice.

If she noticed, though, she didn't let on. "I'm work free," she informed him with a smile. "I'll probably spend most of the weekend catching up on my homework, but at least I can go jogging in the morning. It's my favorite stress reliever."

"You jog?" Ben asked, somehow unsurprised.

"Well, sure. My softball coach believed that 'a fit player is a good player.'" She smiled at the quote her coach used often. "She had us run two miles a day after practice. Do you jog?"

"Sure, all the time," Ben exaggerated, hoping he'd be forgiven for a little white lie told for the sake of love.

Lauren's eyes lit up. "Great! We should go together some time. No one around here wants to go with me."

Allison snorted. "Can you blame us? Who wants to get up at six a.m. on a Saturday to go jogging?"

Everyone laughed, and Lauren pouted playfully. "Hey, I like being up early," she said in her own defense.

The beginnings of an idea started to creep into Ben's mind, but before he could consider it further, Allison jumped to her feet. "I don't know about any of you, but I'm starved. Who wants pizza?"

The next few minutes were crazy as everyone argued and debated over the best toppings to add to the pizzas, then Allison went to call in their orders. A few minutes later, the sound of the receiver being slammed down and Allison's aggravated growl caught everyone's attention.

"What's wrong?" Craig asked.

"It's going to be forty-five minutes!" she complained as she dropped onto the couch beside Craig. "They're so busy that all their delivery people are backlogged."

"I can pick it up," Lauren volunteered. "I don't mind."

Allison's eyes lit up. "Really, would you? Oh, Lauren, you're a saint! I'm so starved I don't think I could wait forty-five minutes."

"No problem." Lauren stood up to get her jacket from the front closet and Ben was instantly on his feet.

"I'll go with you," he offered. "You won't be able to carry all those pizzas by yourself."

Surprised, Lauren turned to him and smiled gratefully. "Thanks. Let me just grab my keys and I'll be ready to go."

Ben waited at the front door as she disappeared down the hallway, then returned moments later with the keys in hand. "Ready?" he asked. When she nodded, he opened the front door for her, which elicited another look of surprise from her. *Obviously, this girl's not used to chivalry,* he decided.

They walked to Lauren's car and drove to the pizza parlor in relative silence. By the time they parked and climbed out of the car, Ben knew he had to say something. He was going to waste his chance to be alone with her if he didn't.

He held the pizza parlor door open for her, and the smell of freshly cooked pizza and garlic wafted out around them. "Mmm, I love the smell of pizza," he said in an attempt to start some kind of conversation.

"I do, too," she answered, breathing in deeply as they walked in and got in line. "We never went out for pizza much when I was growing up, though. Having four brothers, it got too expensive to order enough pizzas to feed everybody."

Ben laughed. "I can imagine."

When they got up to the counter, the man at the pickup window told them it would be another five minutes until the pizzas were ready. "If you just take a seat, I'll call you when they're ready."

"No problem," Ben assured him, then turned to Lauren. "Do you want a root beer or something while we wait?"

"Sure, that'd be great."

Ben got one for each of them and they slipped into a vacant booth near the front. As they sipped their drinks, Ben asked, "How are your classes so far?"

"Good, I think. I have the sinking suspicion that I'm going to have to work extra hard in my anatomy/physiology class, though."

Ben's eyebrows lifted. "Anatomy/physiology, huh? That's a tough class. What are you majoring in?"

"Well, I want to major in physical therapy, but they don't have that program here. For now I'm a Sports Medicine major while I get my GE requirements out of the way, then I'll switch to a school with a good physical therapy program."

"I'm impressed," Ben admitted. "What made you decide on physical therapy?"

She averted her eyes as she started to blush and concentrated on swirling her straw in her root beer. "It would just bore you."

"No, really, I want to hear it," he insisted, leaning forward and resting his forearms on the table.

Lauren studied him for a moment, trying to decide whether or not he was being sincere. Finally, she shrugged. "Well, don't say I didn't warn you." She took a sip of her root beer, then began.

"Back in my junior year in high school, I tore my rotator cuff while pitching, and I had to have surgery to repair it. The surgery went fine and about a week later, I started going to physical therapy for rehab. It was one of the hardest things I've ever had to do." She grimaced at the memory.

"Anyway, recovery was slow, and there were a lot of times when I got discouraged and wanted to quit, but the therapist was great. He was kind and encouraging, and he never let me give up. By the time I finished I was as good as new, but the whole experience really had an effect on me. That's when I decided I wanted to be a physical therapist. I think it would be really rewarding to help others come back from injuries and get them back to doing the activities they love."

Ben listened in fascination, more impressed than ever. "Wow," he said when she finished. "I think it's great that you know what you want to do. Not many people do."

"You did, Mr. Harvard Pre-Law," she pointed out with a teasing smile.

At the reminder, Ben's smile faded a little. "Yeah, well, following in my father's footsteps was all I was ever expected to do."

Lauren picked up on the hint of bitterness in his voice. "You didn't want to be a lawyer?"

"Oh, it's not that," he quickly amended. "I love studying law, and maybe I'll go back to law school someday, but I want to do it because *I* want to, not because I'm expected to." When he saw the look of sympathy in her eyes, he realized he'd spoken more vehemently than he'd intended. He smiled at her sheepishly. "Sorry. I didn't mean to come off sounding bitter."

"No, that's okay," Lauren reassured him, her eyes caring. "It doesn't sound like you and your father get along very well."

Ben's expression hardened as the familiar feelings of heartache and loneliness started to resurface. "No, we don't."

Impulsively, Lauren reached across the table and placed her hand on his. "I'm sorry to hear that."

Ben lifted his eyes to hers, and the look of genuine sympathy in her eyes chased away his sadness. He smiled softly and tightened his fingers around hers for a moment before releasing them. "Thanks."

As Lauren dropped her hand back into her lap, she asked haltingly, "Do you talk to him much?"

Ben raised his eyebrows. "My father?" When she nodded, he looked down at his hands and rubbed at a pencil mark on his palm. "No," he said sadly. "I haven't talked to him in almost a year."

"You're kidding. How come?"

Ben's lips tightened into a thin line. "We had a bit of a falling out last December. He told me that if I got baptized, I shouldn't plan on speaking to him or anyone else in my family ever again."

Lauren's mouth fell open. Then her shock dissipated and a sudden surge of anger flashed across her face. "And he disowned you? Just like that?"

Ben nodded miserably. "Just like that."

"But—" Lauren stammered, at an apparent loss for words. "But what did you do? How did you live?"

Ben shrugged. "I quit school, got a job... lived hand to mouth for a while. The members in my new ward were really great, and that helped. That's where I met Craig; he was in my ward. He'd just gotten off his mission and we became good friends. I'm glad, too, because I don't think I would've made it through without him."

"I can't imagine having to do something like that," Lauren replied, still obviously shell shocked by his revelation. "I don't think I would have had the courage to leave my family."

He smiled slightly, but his expression remained sad. "Don't sell yourself short. I'm not going to say it wasn't hard, because it was. But for the longest time, I felt like I was missing something really important in my life. I felt misplaced in my group of friends and in the society circles my family surrounded themselves with. Then last winter, I'd finally reached the end of my rope. I hated school, I hated my friends... I hated my life." His voice trailed off, and he quickly averted his eyes when he felt the familiar sting of tears that always seemed to surface whenever he thought of his past.

When he managed to regain control of his emotions, he cleared his throat softly. "Anyway, that's when the missionaries found me. I know they were sent into my life at just that moment, when there was no way I could deny the truthfulness of the gospel. It was exactly what I'd been looking for all those years, and I couldn't deny the whisperings of the Holy Ghost. I knew that joining the Church was what I needed to do, so I committed to being baptized and ever since, my testimony has kept me going, even when times got tough."

Lauren's eyes were moist when he finished. "What you did took a lot of courage," she said quietly.

"I don't know about that," he answered modestly, taking a sip of his drink. "Anyone would have done what I did under the circumstances."

Lauren shook her head slowly. "I'm not so sure. I don't think many people would be brave enough to give up their family and their life for the gospel. And knowing that you did—that says an awful lot about you, Ben Morrison."

A slow smile tugged at the corners of her mouth and as their eyes met, something special passed between them. Ben's heart soared. Maybe there was hope for him yet.

"Order up! Number thirty-seven!"

Tearing his gaze away from hers, Ben looked up and spotted the man behind the counter waving at them. "I guess that's us."

Lauren glanced over her shoulder at the counter, then turned back to Ben. "Yeah, I guess so."

For one heart-stopping moment, Ben thought he saw something that looked like disappointment in her eyes. Had she really been enjoying their conversation as much as he had? His past wasn't something he usually shared with people because he didn't want to be pitied, but for whatever reason, it just felt right sharing it with Lauren. And maybe, just maybe, it might help her to see that he wasn't like all those guys she loved to hate.

As he stood up to follow her to the counter, his heart felt lighter than it had in a long time.

Chapter Eight

Lauren was jarred awake when her alarm clock rang at 5:45 the next morning. For several long minutes, she seriously debated about whether or not she really wanted to get up to go running. Normally a morning person, she was finding it hard to gather the willpower to pull herself out of bed after her long, busy week; but after a few minutes of debate, she gave in to the voice of reason and got up.

Sliding out of bed quietly, she dressed in her navy running pants, a comfortable white T-shirt, and an oversized gray sweatshirt. Then she grabbed a pair of athletic socks and her running shoes and tiptoed out of the room. She stopped in the bathroom just long enough to brush her teeth and pull her hair back into her usual ponytail, then went into the living room to put on her socks and shoes. As she tied her shoelaces, her mind started to wake up, and images of the night before crept into her mind.

She smiled. Pizza with her roommates and Craig and Ben had been so much fun. The guys had stayed until the Resident Assistant kicked them out at ten, but in those few hours, Lauren had found herself warming up to Ben a lot more than she'd intended.

As much as she hated to admit it, she couldn't stop thinking about what an amazing guy he seemed to be. She was impressed by his maturity, and even more impressed by the strength of conviction he'd shown in deciding that the gospel was worth risking everything he knew and loved. She'd never known anyone to be so emotionally strong, so set on doing what was right. If she'd been in his situation, she wasn't sure she would have been able to do the same thing. But he had, and that impressed her. Maybe more than she'd ever been impressed in her life.

With a start, she realized she was going to have to be careful. Ben was definitely someone she could fall for. But she knew she couldn't risk being hurt again, not after everything she'd been through.

He may seem like this really amazing guy, she told herself firmly, *but sooner or later you'll see that he's like every other guy you ever met. You wait and see.*

Feeling more confident of her ability to stay emotionally detached, she finished tying her shoes, grabbed a quick glass of orange juice, and headed out the door. The cool, refreshing morning air hit her, and she breathed in deeply. She loved being out early and jogging down quiet streets in the soft pre-dawn light. If anything could get her mind off a familiar pair of warm, brown eyes and a gentle smile, it would be....

"Ben!"

The name hung on Lauren's lips moments after she spoke it, and she had to blink twice to make sure she wasn't seeing things. It didn't take her long to realize she wasn't. It really was Ben standing down there in the parking lot, not ten feet from the balcony, leaning against the hood of her car with his arms folded across his chest and a grin lighting up his features.

Stepping up to the wrought iron railing, her voice reflected both surprise and confusion as she stage whispered, "What are you doing here?"

His grin widened. "I'm waiting for you. Didn't you say you wanted a jogging partner?"

For the first time, Lauren noticed he was dressed for jogging. He was wearing black sweats and a gray sweatshirt with "Harvard" printed across the front in burgundy block letters. She had to admit, even in sweats he looked pretty amazing.

"But it's barely six a.m. I thought you said that was too early for you."

"No," he clarified, walking closer to the balcony. "*Allison* said it was too early. I didn't say anything."

A warm feeling started in her heart and spread out from there. He'd actually shown up at six o'clock on a Saturday morning to go jogging with her. Who was this guy?

When she remained rooted to her spot, Ben put his hands on his hips and scowled playfully. "So, are you coming down here or what? I've got a plate of double fudge brownies that says you won't last two miles with me."

She laughed softly, then pushed away from the balcony. "You're on."

***

Twenty minutes later, Ben's side ached and his lungs felt like they were going to explode. He watched Lauren jogging a few steps ahead of him, her long, thick ponytail bouncing around her shoulders, and he groaned inwardly. She wasn't even winded.

Deciding he couldn't run even one more step, he slowed to a walk, then stopped altogether. He bent over and put his hands on his knees, trying desperately to catch his breath.

Lauren turned in confusion when she realized Ben wasn't with her any longer. When she spotted him leaning over and breathing heavily, she grinned and walked back to him. "I thought you said you did this all the time," she teased.

He straightened only slightly and managed between breaths, "Okay, so I fudged a bit. I *used* to jog all the time, but it was a few years ago. I guess I'm a little out of shape."

She laughed. "A little, huh? Are you sure I don't need to use what I'm learning in my first aid class on you?"

Ben was tempted to make a remark about being a willing mouth-to-mouth recipient, but quickly decided against it. Instead, he stood up and put his hands on his hips. "Nah, I'll be fine as soon as I catch my breath." He gave her a sheepish smile. "I guess I owe you those brownies, huh?"

"You'd better believe it, mister," she answered with mock firmness. "And don't think I won't try to collect."

He chuckled. Any chance he got to see her was fine by him. "I'll have them ready for you. But for now," he breathed, "do me a favor. If we run across anyone on the way home, don't let on that you're in better shape than I am. I have a reputation to protect."

She laughed. "You got it. Should I be the one hunched over and holding my side?"

He gave her a playful glare. "Don't start with me, Holt."

"Or what?" she challenged. "All I'd have to do is run. You'd never catch up to me in your condition." Then, with a maddening grin, Lauren flipped her ponytail triumphantly over her shoulder and started off down the street.

Ben watched her walk away for a moment before hurrying to catch up with her, all the while trying to resist the unfamiliar stirrings of his heart. There was something undeniably wonderful, almost magical, between them. He'd never felt so drawn to anyone in his entire life, and it scared him. It made him feel vulnerable in a way he never had before, yet so strong and alive. How was it possible to feel so many things at once?

When he fell into step beside her and she gave him that beautiful smile, he knew he was fighting a losing battle. There was just no way he was going to be able to stay away from Lauren Holt.

Chapter Nine

"I still can't believe Ben showed up yesterday morning to go jogging with you," Allison said as she and Lauren stood in front of the bathroom mirror doing their hair and makeup for church.

Lauren unrolled one of the hot rollers from her hair, leaving a long, curly strand dangling next to the others. "I know," she answered, smiling at the memory. "But I have to say, his fitness level leaves something to be desired."

Allison smiled. "Then I'd say he definitely went above and beyond the call of duty."

Lauren glanced over at her friend. "What do you mean by that?"

"Just that the guy sacrificed probably his only morning to sleep in and got up to go be humiliated by you," she answered while applying her eyeliner. "If that's not true love, I don't know what is."

Lauren laughed as she pulled the last hot roller from her hair. "Allison, stop! You know where I stand as far as relationships are concerned. Nothing's going to happen between Ben and me. I won't let it. Besides, he's not in love with me. He's just a really nice guy, and we're friends. That's all there is to it."

"If you say so," Allison retorted, obviously unconvinced. She watched Lauren run a pick through her long auburn mane of fresh curls. "You're going to an awful lot of trouble this morning, aren't you?"

Before Lauren could defend herself, Bree pushed her way into the bathroom and into a spot in front of the mirror. "I can't believe I overslept," she breathed, scrambling for her makeup bag. "I've got exactly fifteen minutes to make myself irresistible."

"Irresistible for whom?" Lauren asked.

"For whomever." Bree gave her a mischievous, sideways grin. "I could be asking you the same thing. What's with the curls and makeup? You trying to impress someone?"

Allison let out a burst of laughter. "See? I'm not the only one noticing."

"Noticing what?" Lauren asked indignantly. "All I'm doing is dressing up for church. Since when is that a crime?"

Allison and Bree exchanged a look, and Lauren rolled her eyes in exasperation. "I don't know why I put up with you guys," she grumbled as she finished brushing out her curls. "Are you two coming or what?"

Fifteen minutes later, Allison, Bree, Melia, and Lauren were walking to the Romney building where their ward was holding church. It was a bright, clear Sabbath morning, and Lauren felt at peace as she walked across the campus. She couldn't help feeling a twinge of anticipation, though, as she wondered what church would be like in a new ward and in a classroom instead of a church building. But by the time she and her roommates walked into the Romney building, she realized she shouldn't have worried.

Everyone was dressed in his or her Sunday best, and Bishop Warner was standing outside one of the large auditorium classrooms greeting everyone as they entered. As they neared the room, Lauren got a glimpse of one of the young women playing prelude music at a portable keyboard.

"It's great to see you," Bishop Warner's jovial voice greeted them as he shook each of their hands enthusiastically. "Go on in and have a seat. Sacrament meeting will start in just a few minutes."

As he moved to greet the ward members behind them, Lauren and her roommates went on into the room and sat in a row of empty seats about halfway down. Lauren looked around with interest, noting the long table draped with a white tablecloth off to one side at the front of the room to be used for the sacrament. She felt the familiar sense of peace as she listened to the prelude music, and it occurred to her that it was the gospel and the gathering of church members that brought the Spirit, not the building they met in. The realization touched her and gave her testimony a little boost.

"Don't I know you from somewhere?" a voice asked in her ear.

Turning, she found herself staring into Ben's smiling eyes, and her heart immediately started tapping out an erratic rhythm. He looked more incredible than ever. He was wearing an olive green suit that brought out the tiny hazel flecks in his brown eyes, a crisp white shirt, and a printed silk tie in muted shades of greens and browns.

"Hey, Ben," she greeted him with a smile. "Recovered yet from our little run yesterday?"

Ben glanced around in mock dismay. "Sssh!" he whispered. "You're supposed to be helping me maintain my dignity, remember?"

She laughed. "Oh, yeah, sorry. Hi, Craig," she added when she spotted Craig standing behind Ben.

From beside her, Allison beamed at Craig, then motioned for them to sit down. "Come on, you two, sit with us. We'll make room." She proceeded to scoot everybody down and shift people around. She directed Craig to the seat on the aisle and sat down beside him, then gestured for Ben to sit on her other side. That left only one vacant seat for Lauren—the one beside Ben.

Lauren wanted to lynch Allison for being so obvious. But as she lowered herself into the seat cautiously, she was relieved to see that Ben didn't seem to notice Allison's meddling. A moment later, Bishop Warner's voice came across the microphone at the podium, and all attention turned to him as he welcomed everyone to the ward's first sacrament meeting.

As he conducted a little business, Lauren tried her best to listen, but it was no easy task with Ben's shoulder brushing against hers, causing her skin to tingle beneath the thin fabric of her dress. She glanced at him out of the corner of her eye, taking in his firm jawline and rugged good looks. She was surprised by the sudden rush of tenderness she felt toward him, knowing that an amazing amount of strength and conviction lay hidden beneath those warm brown eyes and gentle smile. He was certainly more than a handsome face.

As quickly as the feeling came, though, she tried to force it away. She couldn't allow herself to fall for Ben, or for anyone else for that matter. It simply wasn't an option.

For the rest of the meeting, Lauren forced herself to keep her mind on the speakers, and when the meeting was over, everyone separated to attend their Sunday School, Relief Society, and Priesthood meetings. The next two hours flew by, and soon it was time to go home.

Lauren and her roommates walked out of the room where Relief Society had been held and saw that Priesthood meeting was letting out across the hall. Everyone was congregating in the hallway, and Lauren found herself scanning the crowd for a familiar handsome face. It didn't take her long to spot Ben near the far wall, and she felt a flutter of excitement. She watched as he glanced around the crowd for a moment, as if looking for someone. Suddenly, his eyes found hers, and his heart-stopping smile lit up his face.

He started her direction, making his way through the crowd, and finally stopped beside her. "Hi," he exclaimed cheerfully, glancing around at the bustling lobby. "It's a madhouse out here."

"Yeah, I know. How did your meetings go?"

"Pretty good," Ben admitted, nodding. "I was a little apprehensive, but everything turned out okay."

Lauren regarded him curiously. "Why were you apprehensive?"

His smile lost some of its brilliance, and he shrugged as he shoved his hands into his pockets. "I guess I just didn't know what to expect," he confessed quietly, moving closer so only she would hear. "I mean, I've only been a member for nine months, and I was worried that I would open my mouth and ask some really stupid question that everyone had known the answer to since they were ten."

Lauren leaned toward him and lowered her voice, as well. "Ben, half the things *I* hear in classes I don't remember ever learning before, and I've been a member my whole life. It's not that I wasn't taught some particular aspect of the gospel, I just wasn't ready to apply it, so it blew right past me. That's the really great thing about the gospel; there's always something new to learn."

Lauren noticed a glimmer of hope in Ben's eyes and felt the need to reasurre him further. She smiled conspiringly and said, "If you're worried about sounding like an idiot, do what I do and wait until class is over to ask your questions, one-on-one with the teacher. That way only one person thinks you're an idiot." She winked.

A look of relief washed over his face, and his easygoing smile returned. He placed his hand on her forearm and gave it a quick squeeze. "Thanks, Lauren. I appreciate it."

Her arm tingled where his hand lay, and she found herself surprisingly short of breath. When his hand dropped back to his side, she felt oddly disappointed. She gave him a little smile and shrugged. "No problem. I'm happy to oblige."

Just then a strong hand reached over and clapped Ben on the shoulder, causing them both to look up. Bishop Warner was standing there, smiling. "Hello, Lauren, Ben," he said, nodding at each of them in turn. "How are you two doing?"

Lauren was surprised that he remembered her name, but Ben didn't skip a beat. "Hi, Bishop," Ben greeted the large man with a friendly handshake. "We're fine. This was a great meeting."

Bishop Warner beamed. "Glad to hear you enjoyed it." Then his countenance became more serious as he asked, "Ben, do you have a second?"

A concerned look flashed momentarily across Ben's face. He glanced at Lauren apprehensively, then turned back to the bishop and said, "Sure, no problem." Then he followed Bishop Warner into the room where Priesthood meeting had been held.

Lauren watched, concerned. *I hope nothing is wrong*, she thought. Not knowing if she should wait for Ben or go, she glanced around, looking for her roommates. They were nowhere to be seen. She was just about to go look for them when she heard someone call her name. She turned, then grimaced inwardly when she saw Elena approaching.

"Hi, Lauren," Elena said in a sickeningly sweet voice. "I couldn't help noticing you were sitting with Ben during Sacrament meeting."

Lauren eyed her warily. "So?"

"Well, I just hope this isn't some pathetic effort to try to win him over."

Lauren bristled. "What's that supposed to mean?"

"I'm just saying, I understand where you're coming from. He's the cutest guy in the ward. But just so you don't get your hopes up, I plan on going after him. That being the case, who do you think will win? Some tomboy like you, or someone pretty and glamorous like me?"

Lauren forced herself to count to ten. She knew Elena was just trying to get a rise out of her, but still, Ben was a nice guy, and he definitely deserved something better than superficial, two-faced Elena stalking him.

Trying to keep her voice steady, she responded, "Elena, Ben's a nice guy, *and* he's my friend. I don't want to see him get hurt. Why don't you leave him alone and find someone else to sink your claws into?"

Elena cocked an eyebrow, and a smug smile spread across her face. "Afraid that I might pose a little unfair competition?"

Lauren glared at Elena. "Elena, what's your deal? Why do you go out of your way to be so mean? I've never done anything to you."

Elena's eyes narrowed and the pretty smile she'd pasted on her face became an angry frown. "Forget it," she grumbled. "Just know that you're not going to come out on top this time. Ben's mine. Just you wait and see." And with that, Elena spun on her heels and stalked away into the crowd.

Lauren stared after her for a long moment, both angry and confused. She didn't know what Elena's problem was, but one thing was for sure. She was going to make sure Elena stayed away from Ben. Far, far away.

"So, how are things going for you, Ben?" Bishop Warner asked after they sat down inside the empty classroom.

Ben eyed the man sitting across from him warily. "Fine, Bishop. Umm... did I do something wrong?"

Bishop Warner laughed. "No, not at all. I'm sorry if I gave you the wrong impression. I asked to talk to you because I wanted to touch base with you to see how you were doing."

Ben sighed in relief and felt his tense muscles relax. "Whew," he replied with a sheepish grin. "I was worried there for a minute. Honestly, Bishop, I'm fine."

"Are you settling in? Getting along with your roommates?"

"Yes to both." Ben nodded. "And so far I really like my classes."

"And how about your finances?" he asked seriously. "Are you making ends meet?"

"Yeah, I'm okay," Ben admitted. "Money's tight, but I have enough for the essentials. Plus I signed up to be a tutor, so that will help."

"That's great." Bishop Warner nodded enthusiastically. Then he sobered. "Ben, if you run into any trouble at all, I'd like you to come to me. I remember how tough that first year is for a convert, and I can imagine it would be even tougher for you, considering your circumstances. I don't want you to feel like you're alone in this."

Ben smiled reassuringly. "I will, Bishop... and I don't," he said, answering his questions respectively.

Satisfied, Bishop Warner stood up to shake his hand. "Glad to hear it, Ben. Then I guess I'll see you next week."

Ben left the room and walked down the hall, keeping his eyes open for Lauren. He couldn't help hoping she was still around somewhere, waiting for him. A moment later, he spotted her standing over by the doors and hurried over to her. He was surprised to see that she looked a little upset.

"Lauren?" he asked, putting a hand on her arm. "Is everything okay?"

She jumped at his touch, then relaxed when she saw it was him. "Oh, I'm fine; you just startled me, that's all. So?" she asked, obviously trying to change the subject. "What did Bishop Warner want? Are you in trouble?"

Ben laughed and shook his head. "Nope, he just wanted to see how I was doing."

A hint of her old self emerged as she joked, "I thought maybe he was going to call you to the Elder's quorum presidency or something."

"Yeah, right," Ben snorted. "That would be the day."

Lauren scowled at him playfully. "Ben Morrison, you don't give yourself nearly enough credit," she scolded, sliding her arm through his and walking with him down the hall. "I can assure you that you are twice the man most of the guys around here are, and don't you forget it." She emphasized her last demand by giving his arm a friendly tug.

His heart swelled at her reassurance, and he gave her a grateful smile as he tightened his arm on hers. "Yes, *Mom*," he teased, delighting in the sound of her answering laughter.

As they neared the doors, Lauren spotted her roommates and let her arm slip from his as they hurried over. He wondered momentarily if that meant anything, but as they all walked out of the building together and headed for home, talking and laughing, he let it slip from his mind.

Melia stretched her arms and tilted her face up toward the sun. "Don't you guys just love Sunday afternoons? They're so peaceful and relaxing."

Lauren wrinkled her nose. "Yeah, but Sunday means that tomorrow is Monday, and *that* means more humiliation and frustration at work."

Ben laughed. "Now *you're* the one being too hard on yourself. Quit worrying about it. You've only been working there a week, and everyone knows that the first week is the hardest. I promise it'll get better."

Lauren sighed, unconvinced. "I hope you're right."

By the end of the next week, Lauren realized Ben *had* been right. Her tasks at the bookstore were beginning to feel like second nature, and she was starting to really enjoy working there. Even Dan was someone she was beginning to call a friend now that they'd accepted each other's differences, and she found herself enjoying the easy camaraderie they shared. He was fun to talk to and joke around with, and having a friend there made her shifts go by faster. On top of work, she was relieved to discover that she was finally settling into a class and study routine. Juggling her new life didn't necessarily seem easier, but she felt better able to manage it.

She jogged up the steps to her apartment and walked in the door. She spotted Allison on the phone, and her friend gestured at her and pointed to the phone as she said into it, "Oh, hold on a sec, Lauren just walked in. Here she is."

Lauren raised her eyebrows questioningly as Allison smiled and handed her the phone. "It's your mom."

Lauren took the phone from her and put it to her ear. "Hi, Mom. ...Yeah, I'm fine. I just got off work. Yes, I'm making sure I have plenty of time to study." She rolled her eyes at Allison, who laughed quietly and began to rummage around the kitchen for a snack.

Ben walked out of the library into a beautiful fall evening. He'd spent the afternoon studying, and now he felt relaxed and contented. He breathed in deeply, enjoying the clean, fall air that was so different from the smoggy, stale atmosphere of cities in the east.

Now that he wasn't concentrating on his studies, he allowed his suppressed thoughts of Lauren to surface. He found it impossible not to think about her. He'd be studying or listening to one of his professors, and an image of her would conjure itself up in his mind.

There were so many things about her he loved—the caring and kindness clearly evident in her beautiful, light-brown eyes, the way the corners of her mouth twitched before she laughed, as if she was harboring some deep, dark secret, and the way her eyes lit up when she was excited about something. But more than anything, he loved the way she made him feel when he was around her. The kindness and sympathy she'd shown him at the pizza parlor when he'd poured out his painful history, and then again on Sunday when she'd reassured him that no one was going to look down on him just because he hadn't been a member of the Church as long as they had, really stuck with him. One thing was for sure, she was definitely one in a million.

With a start, he suddenly realized it had been almost a week since he'd seen her. It hadn't been easy to stay away, but with his professors assigning homework more freely and prepping them for tests, life had gotten crazy. But now that the school week was over, he decided to stop by and see how she was doing. His heart fluttered in anticipation as he altered his course and headed for Lauren's apartment.

When he arrived a few minutes later, Allison answered the door. "Hey, Ben," she said, giving him a friendly smile. "Come on in. I'm assuming you came by to see Lauren." When he nodded, she jammed a thumb over her shoulder in the direction of the kitchen. "She's on the phone."

He looked in the direction Allison indicated and spotted Lauren leaning against the wall, her back to him as she talked on the phone, as yet unaware of his presence. Allison discreetly left the room, and Ben let his backpack slip off his shoulder and fall to the floor beside the couch. Lauren heard the *thunk* and turned. His heartbeat quickened when he watched her eyes light up when she saw him. She waved him in. Ben walked quietly into the kitchen and sat down at the table to wait for her to finish talking.

"I know, Mom," she said into the phone, twisting her fingers around the cord distractedly. "Yes, I'm eating healthy. No, I'm not getting behind on my schoolwork. Mom, my laundry's fine!" She rolled her eyes at Ben, and he chuckled softly. "Mom... MOM! Yeah, I've got to go. I will. Yeah, I love you too. Bye."

She hung up the phone and let out an aggravated growl. "In case you couldn't tell, that was my mom."

He grinned. "Yeah, I heard."

"Don't get me wrong, I love her and all," she told him truthfully. "I just wish she didn't feel the urge to check up on me so much. It's not long distance to call from Idaho Falls, so she definitely takes advantage of that."

He laughed. "Well, don't let her get to you. To be honest, I'd love to have a mom like yours. She sounds pretty great."

"She is," Lauren admitted tenderly. "But sometimes I feel suffocated, you know? It's like she thinks I need a little protecting or something."

"Maybe she treats you like that because you're her only daughter," Ben pointed out. "And since you're here and she's there, maybe she's a little lonely without another girl in the family to talk to."

Lauren blinked. "I never thought about it that way. I wish she'd stop babying me, though. Growing up with four brothers, I learned plenty about taking care of myself."

"I'm sure you did. It must've been nice, having all those brothers looking out for you. I bet you never got picked on while you were growing up."

She snorted and rolled her eyes. "Yeah, but because of them, I didn't worry about being asked out much, either."

He looked confused. "Why's that?"

"Would you want to ask out a girl who had four older brothers?" she asked. "They got so good at scaring guys off that I never really had to worry about dating. I remember one time in particular when all four of my brothers converged on my date when he came to pick me up. I don't know what they told him before I came downstairs, but when I did, the guy's face was as white as a sheet, and he didn't so much as hold my hand all night."

Ben cracked up. "I can imagine. The poor guy."

"Yeah, he never did ask me out again."

"Well, then I'd say it was his loss." Their eyes met and he smiled softly.

It was quiet for a moment, then Lauren reached back to tighten her ponytail and asked, "So, what are you doing here? Not that I'm not happy to see you," she clarified with a smile.

"No reason." He shrugged. "I just haven't seen you since Sunday and wondered what you were up to."

"Not much," she admitted. "Classes are keeping me busy, and so is work. But I'm holding my own."

"And anatomy/physiology? Last time we talked you were worried you were in over your head."

She grimaced. "It's still hard, but I'm going to spend the weekend studying. We have a test on the entire skeletal structure on Monday."

"Do you want me to help you study for it?" he offered. "I don't know much about anatomy, but I'd be the one looking at the textbook, so that wouldn't matter." He grinned at her, and a hopeful look crossed her face.

"Would you really?" she asked. But then she sobered. "Nah, I'm sure you have better things to do on a Friday night."

He leaned back in his chair with a grin and folded his arms across his chest. "Nope. I'm all yours."

The rest of the evening went by in a happy blur. Before hitting the books, Lauren and Ben decided to make something for dinner, and Lauren was pleasantly surprised to see what a natural Ben was in the kitchen. He made a mouthwatering omelet for them with only a few ingredients from the fridge, and she spent the entire meal oohing and ahhing over his concoction. When dinner was over, they retired to the couch with a bag of microwave popcorn and Lauren's anatomy/physiology textbook.

Then for the next two hours, Ben quizzed Lauren on the skeletal structure, and he kept making her laugh by coming up with funny ways to remember parts of the skeleton. She couldn't remember the last time she'd enjoyed an evening more. It had been a long time since she'd been able to relax and be herself with a guy, and not have to worry about his motives. But with Ben, she felt completely comfortable and content in a way she'd never felt before.

When ten o'clock finally came, Lauren realized she was actually sad to see the evening end. She walked Ben to the door and he smiled at her softly. "Be sure to let me know how you do on the test. I'll be anxious to hear."

She nodded. "I will. Thanks for coming over tonight. I can't remember the last time I had this much fun studying."

Ben's eyes twinkled in response. "I'm glad. To tell you the truth, I had fun, too. The best night I've had in a long time, actually."

Then, before she could respond, Ben stepped out the door and lifted his hand in a half wave. "Goodnight, Lauren. See you soon." He shut the door behind him and was gone.

Lauren stood motionless for several moments, smiling for what felt like the hundredth time that evening. She just couldn't get over what a great guy he was. He was kind, thoughtful, and funny, and there was just something about him that made her want to trust him, to let him through the carefully constructed walls around her heart. He was quickly becoming a good friend, and that surprised her. It had been ages since she'd had a guy whom she trusted enough to call a friend.

As she turned out the living room light and headed for her bedroom, she realized, strangely enough, that she could hardly wait to see him again.

Chapter Ten

Ben packed up his textbooks and notepads after spending hours in the library, first with someone he was tutoring in chemistry, then studying and doing his own homework. When everything was in his backpack, he decided to find a computer and check his email. He hadn't heard from his sister yet, and he was beginning to get anxious.

He found an empty terminal and sat down. He quickly called up his email and waited apprehensively for several long moments before the program notified him that he had a message. His heart leapt when he saw it was from Emily. With shaking hands, he clicked on the email and opened it, eager to devour every word.

> *Hey Bro!*
>
> *Sorry it's taken me so long to respond to your email. I'm so relieved to hear that you're doing well, and that you're enjoying your classes. You deserve to be happy.*
>
> *Things are pretty tense here right now. Dad's really on the warpath lately, with things so stressful at the firm. They're handling some huge case, and from his mood, I take it things aren't going well. I wish you were here. You always seemed to be able to reason with him. Well, most of the time, anyway.*
>
> *I'm still seeing Jason secretively, and things are pretty good between us. I hate sneaking around behind Dad's back,*

but he doesn't understand about being in love. He can't control my life forever, so we're just keeping our relationship quiet for now. Maybe one of these days he'll come around.

I just realized how depressing this email must sound. Sorry about that. But don't worry, everything's fine. I'm fine. I just miss having you around to talk to and hang with, you know? Anyway, keep working hard in school, and I'll be looking forward to hearing from you again soon!

Love always,

Emily

Ben's stomach tightened as he finished reading the email. She didn't sound happy. More than anything, he wanted to be there for her to help her through the tough times as they'd done for each other when they were growing up. But this time he couldn't. And that hurt more than anything.

Trying not to let the familiar cloud of darkness settle over him, he printed the email and slid the paper into his notebook to read again later. Then he brought up a blank email and started to type.

Emily,

I'm sorry to hear things aren't going that great. I only wish I could be there to cheer you up in person. It's too bad Dad can't see what a great person Jason is. Just because his family isn't enormously wealthy is no reason to ostracize him. I'm glad you haven't. Hang in there.

As for me—yes, school's fine. Rooming with Craig is working out great, and I'm making new friends as well. One of them is a girl named Lauren. She's incredible. If only I could get her to feel the same way about me as I'm beginning to feel about her. Anyway, I'll keep you posted. Remember, I love you.

Ben

With a heavy heart, Ben logged off and headed out of the library. He had an hour before his next class, so he figured it would be a good time to grab some lunch. Unable to resist the sun spilling across the quad near the entrance to the library, he picked a vacant spot on the warm grass and sat down. Then he reached into his backpack for the lunch he'd packed earlier that morning.

As he did, his fingers brushed the well-worn cover of his triple combination that he still had in his backpack from his Book of Mormon class that morning. He paused. Whenever life had left him feeling low this past year, reading his scriptures had never failed to lift his spirits. Realizing that he needed the comfort the scriptures provided now more than ever, he pulled out his triple combination, set it on the grass beside him, and began to read as he ate. He was so entranced in the words of 2 Nephi that he didn't notice someone sitting down in front of him.

"Hey. What are you doing?"

Startled, he looked up at the owner of the voice and froze. *Lauren*. She looked even better than usual in a long-sleeved, navy shirt that was tucked into the waistband of her form-fitting jeans, and her long, auburn hair was spilling down around her shoulders—the sunshine making it seem even redder than usual.

"Hey yourself," he said with a smile. "Where'd you come from?"

"Anatomy. I was on my way to work when I saw you sitting here by yourself. Taking a lunch break?" she asked, nodding at the sandwich in his hand.

"Yeah. I have an hour before my next class, so it seemed like a good time to grab a bite. So?" he asked, changing the subject and looking at her expectantly. "How'd your test go?"

A huge smile broke out across her face. "Aced it, thanks to you."

"Hey, that's great! I knew you could do it," he exclaimed happily. "I'd say that deserves a reward." He took the bag of grapes from his lunch bag and handed them to her. "Have some."

"Thanks." She took several from the bag and popped one into her mouth. As she did, she noticed the battered book lying open beside him. "What are you reading?" she asked, leaning forward to get a better look. He flipped the cover closed so she could see, and she lifted her eyebrows in surprise. "Wow, reading your scriptures? I'm impressed. You have no idea how attractive it is to a girl to see a guy reading his scriptures in public." She gave him a quick wink.

He laughed. "Really? I'll have to remember that."

Lauren eyed him critically for a moment, noticing that his smile didn't reach all the way into his eyes. "Other than your heartfelt congratulations, you don't seem like your usual sunny self today. Is something wrong?"

His smile faded and he shrugged. "I don't know. I got an email from my sister, and it wasn't the happiest one I've ever received."

Lauren's expression clouded in concern. "Bad news?"

"No, she just sounded down, that's all. I wish I could be there to cheer her up, you know?"

Lauren nodded. "What did she say?"

He set his sandwich down and flipped open his backpack. Then he pulled the paper from his notebook and handed it to her. "Here. You can read it."

Lauren took the paper from him and started to read. When she finished, she frowned and handed it back to him. "You're right. It sounds like she's having a rough time right now." She watched him return the paper to his notebook. "It must be hard, not being able to be there for her like you want to be."

Ben avoided her gaze as he nodded. "I think that's the hardest part. We were so close growing up. She always knew me better than anyone else did, and could make me laugh when I was down, or could talk some sense into me when I got impetuous." He smiled sadly. "We were pretty much inseparable."

Lauren smiled understandingly. "Your relationship with her sounds like the one I have with my brother Jack."

"Remind me, which brother is Jack again?" Ben asked, his brow furrowing in concentration.

"He's older than me by a couple of years," Lauren explained. "Of all my brothers, we're the closest. He's a lot like your sister in that he's always been there for me when I needed him. I've really missed him the past two years while he's been on his mission, but he'll be home in just a few weeks. I can hardly wait."

"I bet."

"Yeah, it'll be great to have him home," she said on a sigh. A memory from her childhood surfaced, and she smiled nostalgically. "I remember when I was nine, I was climbing the big maple tree behind my house. I fell and sliced open my knee, but Jack picked me up and carried me into the house, cleaned me up, and put a butterfly bandage on my knee. In that instant he became my hero. I started following him around everywhere he went, and never once did he chase me away or tell me to get lost."

"Sounds like quite a guy."

"Yeah," Lauren replied, her smile softening. "He's pretty great. I always felt safe when he was around, and I knew exactly where I stood with him. He's kind and funny and thoughtful.... Actually, he's a lot like you."

As if suddenly realizing what she'd just said, she stopped, and Ben thought she looked startled for a moment, as if she'd never considered that before. Then her expression changed to one of confusion, and she looked pensive.

Sensing the sudden awkwardness, Ben decided to cover for her. He cleared his throat and leaned back on one hand casually. With a mischievous smile, he teased, "So, if he's a lot like me, he must be handsome and charming and a real catch...."

His words had the desired effect, and Lauren started to laugh. She threw a grape at him. "Yeah, but at least he's humble."

When their laughter faded away a moment later, Lauren glanced down at her watch and grimaced. "I guess I'd better get going," she told him, getting to her feet. "My shift starts in five minutes."

Ben squinted up at her in the sunlight. "Well, have fun at work, and congrats on your test. I'm glad it went well."

She slid her backpack onto her shoulder and adjusted the straps. "Thanks. I hope you feel better about your sister. I just wish there was something I could do to help."

"You've already done more than you know," he told her sincerely. "Just talking to you about it has made me feel better. Thanks for listening."

She smiled softly. "Anytime. I'll talk to you later?" When he nodded, she turned and hurried off toward the bookstore.

Ben watched her go, feeling incredibly lucky to have Lauren for a friend. She'd single-handedly managed to restore his good mood simply by being with him. He shook his head in amazement. She was definitely one in a million.

Ben's good mood lasted for the remainder of the week, and as soon as his classes were over on Friday afternoon, he headed over to the bookstore to see if Lauren was off work. He'd just entered the Manwaring Center when he saw her leaving the bookstore, struggling into the straps of her backpack as she walked.

"Hey, Lauren, wait up!"

She turned at the sound of his voice and her face creased into a happy smile when she saw him jogging toward her. "Ben! What are you doing here?"

He slowed to a stop beside her and returned her smile with one of his own. "I just got done with my classes and thought I'd walk you home."

She nodded happily. "Great! I'd love some company."

They headed out of the building and were walking toward her apartment when Lauren spoke, breaking their companionable silence. "So, how are you? Are you feeling any better about the situation with your sister since we talked?"

He nodded slowly. "Yeah, I think I do. It's not ever going to be easy, having to sneak around behind my father's back to talk to her, but at least we're able to stay in touch."

"Yeah, that's something," she agreed sympathetically. Seeing that the topic wasn't exactly the easiest for him to discuss, she decided to change the subject. "How's everything else going?"

They talked about classes and professors the rest of the way home, and when they finally walked into Lauren's apartment, she sniffed the air in surprise. "Yum. What smells so good?" she called out.

Melia was bending over the open oven door and pulling a steaming dish out of the oven. "Lasagna," she called out as she set it on the stovetop. "Hungry? I figured I'd make something home-cooked for everyone for once."

Lauren unceremoniously dumped her backpack onto the floor next to the couch and hurried into the kitchen. "Melia, you cooked for us? You're unbelievable!" She cautiously lifted a corner of the aluminum top to peer at the ingredients bubbling inside. "How did you manage this?"

Melia laughed as Ben came into the kitchen to investigate as well. "You'd think I'd just cooked a five-star, four-course meal," she teased. "I just bought one of those prepared lasagnas from the grocery store and stuck it in the oven for a couple of hours. No big deal."

"Yes, it's a big deal!" Lauren gushed. "I can't remember the last time I had something for dinner that required more than ten minutes in the microwave."

Ben laughed. "You sound as bad as me."

Lauren laughed, too. "Well, with classes and studying and my job, when do I have time to cook? Melia, we're definitely going to owe you one."

Melia smiled and shrugged. "If you really feel like doing something in return, you can do the dishes after dinner."

Lauren nodded eagerly. "Done."

Just then Allison came into the room and spotted Lauren and Ben. "Hey, guys. Isn't Melia the greatest?" When Melia only laughed in grateful acceptance of their accolades, Allison turned back to Lauren and said, "I've got something for you that's going to make you love me as much as Melia."

"Not possible," Lauren teased as Allison disappeared back into the bedroom, then returned a moment later with an envelope.

Allison gave her a smug smile and waved the envelope in her face. "How about this? It's a letter from Jack."

Lauren let out an excited gasp and eagerly snatched the letter from her friend's hand.

"Jack, your brother?" Ben asked as Lauren sat down on the couch and started opening the envelope.

Lauren nodded. "Yeah. Any day we're expecting to find out what day he's flying home." She finally managed to pull out the letter containing Jack's familiar scrawl and quickly devoured every word.

> Dear Lauren,
>
> So you're a college student now, huh? You poor girl. How's that going? I remember you saying you were going to room with Allison, but do you like your other roommates? I'm sure you're working hard to get good grades, but knowing you, that's all you're doing. Remember to have some fun, too, okay?
>
> It's hard to believe I only have a month left on my mission. Thinking about it mostly makes me sad, because I've never felt a greater love for the Lord than when I've been teaching the gospel. I've seen the difference it's made in the lives of those we've baptized, and it gives me great joy to think my companions and I have had some part in that. I've always had a testimony of the gospel's truthfulness, but being out here in the mission field and teaching others about the gospel has made that testimony grow even more. My work here hasn't been easy, but it's been more rewarding than anything I've ever done.
>
> While I hate to leave here, I've missed all of you terribly, and it will be wonderful to see you all again. I'll mail you with my travel details as soon as I get them. In the meantime, remember... have some fun! I'll talk to you soon!
>
> Love you!
>
> Jack

Lauren grinned happily as she finished reading the letter and slid it back into its envelope. She could hardly wait for Jack to come home. She was so thrilled that he was enjoying his mission, but she'd felt a little misplaced the last two years without him. He'd always been the one she sought out at home to talk to or hang out with, and he was the one she'd always turned to when she had a problem. Having him home again would definitely be the highlight of her year.

"So?" Allison pried. "Does he say when he's coming home?"

Lauren shook her head. "No, just that he'll get us the travel details as soon as he has them. He says he's doing well and is excited to come home, but that he'll be sad to leave at the same time."

"I can imagine," Allison replied.

"I think it's awesome that your brother's serving a mission," Ben chimed in. "I don't know what I would've done if the missionaries hadn't approached me with their message. They definitely changed my life."

Lauren smiled understandingly. "I know they did."

Ben looked down at his hands and started to chuckle. "Yeah, I'll never forget those two missionaries, the way they were stumbling all over themselves and interrupting each other, eager to teach me the gospel. Elder Simmons and Elder H—"

Ben stopped abruptly, his heart pounding and a tingle creeping up his spine. He'd never even considered the possibility before. His gaze flew to Lauren's face and his voice was a bare whisper when he asked, "Where's your brother serving his mission?"

Lauren's brow furrowed in confusion. "He's in Vermont."

Ben's eyes widened. "Isn't that part of the Massachusetts Boston mission?"

"Yes," Lauren answered slowly, still confused about why this was affecting Ben as it was. "He spent the first part of his mission in Boston, then got transferred to…" Lauren's voice suddenly trailed off as her eyes widened in shock.

Allison looked from Ben to Lauren and then back again. "What? What's going on?"

Ben's eyes never left Lauren's as he asked, "Do you have a picture of him?"

Lauren nodded silently, then stood up and hurried from the room, with Allison's confused gaze following her movements.

Lauren returned a moment later with the framed picture of herself and her brother at the MTC. With shaking hands, she handed it wordlessly to Ben.

When he looked at it, his face went ashen and his jaw dropped open. In that instant, Lauren knew.

"Okay, that's it!" Allison demanded, drawing their attention. "*What* is going on?"

Lauren tried to speak, but nothing came out. She tried again. This time she found her voice. "Jack... Jack is the one who baptized Ben."

Allison let out an excited squeal. "No way!" she exclaimed. "That is so cool! Does he know? I mean, does Jack know that you know Ben?"

Ben glanced at Lauren questioningly, but Lauren shook her head. "I haven't even written him since school started a couple of weeks ago. I've been too busy."

"Well, you guys should tell him!" Allison insisted. "He'd be so excited! I bet he—" Her voice trailed off as Lauren reached out to grasp her forearm. "What?"

"I just had an idea," Lauren began, her eyes widening with excitement. "Let's *not* tell him; let's just surprise him by having Ben show up at his homecoming." She glanced over at Ben to see what he thought of the idea and was rewarded by his bright, eager smile.

"Perfect!" he agreed. Then he shook his head in disbelief and leaned back against the couch, trying to let this new piece of information sink in. "I can't believe this. Your brother is Elder Holt. I mean, he told me he was from Idaho, and then I met you, and your last name was Holt, too, but I guess I just never considered the possibility. This is so incredible!"

"I know," Lauren breathed. "What a small world. I can imagine that a missionary would always wonder what happened to the people he baptized, but to actually have one run across one of your family members... what a coincidence!"

Ben stared at Lauren, suddenly realizing he hadn't even thought about it that way. But that *was* weird. *Could it be just a coincidence?* he wondered. Somehow, he had a hard time believing it was. But if it wasn't, what exactly was it?

Before he could think about it further, Melia walked in, interrupting them. "Okay, guys, dinner's ready. Bree had an early date, so she can eat when she gets home, but the rest of us can get started... hey, what's going on?" she asked, looking from one dazed and excited expression to another.

Lauren grinned as she stood up and pulled Ben up by his arm to stand beside her. "Something unbelievable. Come on. We'll tell you while we eat."

Dinner turned out to be fabulous, and Lauren enjoyed spending time with Ben and her roommates as much as she enjoyed the great meal. They all talked and laughed and had a great time together, and Lauren wasn't surprised when the discussion kept turning back to the fact that Ben had been baptized by Lauren's brother.

Lauren was eager to hear every last detail Ben shared with them about her brother as a missionary. It was exciting to hear about Jack from a newly baptized Church member's perspective. She felt a new appreciation and love for Jack as she listened to Ben explain how her brother had found him, taught him, baptized him, and in the process, developed a relationship with him as a young man seeking to change his life through the gospel. It brought tears to her eyes to think of her brother befriending and bringing the gospel to someone who's past had been as troubled as Ben's.

At the end of the evening, after Ben had gone home, Lauren lay awake in bed for a long time, thinking. There were lots of times when she wanted to leap up, grab a pen and a piece of paper, and write to Jack right then about the new, exciting discovery they'd made tonight. But each time she stopped herself, knowing it would be even more fun to keep it a surprise. She could hardly wait to see Jack's face when he saw Ben standing there with her when he came home.

The following Sunday morning, Ben was sitting with Lauren and her roommates during sacrament meeting when Bishop

119

Warner stood and started to conduct the meeting. One particular matter of business he announced caused Ben to sit up straighter and listen with rapt attention.

"We have a ward temple trip scheduled for a week from Thursday to do baptisms for the dead, and we'd love to have as many of you as possible attend. For those of you who'll need temple recommends, we'll be conducting interviews this afternoon. This is a special opportunity to do the work for those who need it done, so I hope all of you will try to attend."

Bishop Warner went on to other matters of business, but Ben was no longer listening. All he could think about was the prospect of doing baptisms for the dead. More than anything, he wanted to go. But was it possible? He'd only been a member for several months. Was there a certain length of time he had to be a member before he could consider getting a recommend to do temple baptisms? He didn't know.

The rest of church went by in a blur as Ben's mind churned with the possibility. When Priesthood meeting was over, he made a beeline for Bishop Warner. "Bishop, can I talk to you for a minute?"

Bishop Warner gave him a puzzled look, then nodded. "Sure. Let's go down the hall."

They maneuvered through the crowds and went into an empty classroom. When Bishop Warner shut the door behind them and gestured for Ben to sit, he asked, "What can I do for you, Ben?"

Feeling a little anxious, Ben explained how he would love to join them on the temple trip, but voiced his concern that he had not been a member long enough to get a temple recommend. Bishop Warner quickly allayed his fears, however, and before he knew it, Ben received his first temple recommend interview and was pronounced worthy to join the ward members to do baptisms for the dead.

As Ben walked out of the room, he realized he could hardly wait. He was sure the next eleven days until the temple trip would last forever.

• • •

When the day of the ward's temple trip finally arrived, Ben found himself standing in the parking lot of the girls' apartment complex where everyone was meeting. Lauren was standing beside him, and he could hardly contain his excitement as everyone loaded their things into the trunks of the four vehicles they were to be traveling in.

As people started climbing into cars, Ben grabbed Lauren's hand and pulled her toward the Bishop's suburban. "Come on, let's sit together. You can show me the sights on the way to Idaho Falls."

Lauren laughed as she climbed into the back seat next to him. "What sights? Between here and Idaho Falls, it's just fields and stuff. Certainly nothing for a Boston boy to be excited about."

Allison and Craig climbed into the middle seat ahead of them, and they all talked and laughed as they traveled. When they finally turned off the highway and could see the temple looming ahead of them, Ben felt a lump in his throat. Seeing the beautiful, gleaming temple with the shining statue of Moroni on top touched him in a way no other building ever had before.

Lauren nudged him with her elbow after they'd climbed out of the car and were waiting to get their bags. "Are you okay?" she asked. "You seem quiet all of a sudden."

He pulled his eyes from the tall, white building and smiled at her. "I'm just excited, I guess. This is my first time doing baptisms for the dead, and going to the temple is something I've been looking forward to ever since I was baptized."

Lauren looked up at the temple, trying to see it through a new convert's eyes. "I guess I kind of take the temple for granted, having one so close to home," she admitted. "I've done baptisms for the dead a few times. I have to say, though, the peace you feel here will make you want to come back again and again."

Ben knew she was right. The feeling of peace that filled the temple touched his soul, and he couldn't wait for the day when he could get his regular recommend and return often to enjoy its blessings. He had the feeling that no matter what might be wrong in his life, the temple would give him the peace and clarity he needed to deal with whatever trials came his way.

Almost two hours later Ben was once again in the waiting room, enjoying the Spirit and waiting for the others to finish changing. He smiled when Lauren finally reappeared and sat down next to him.

"Good grief, it took you that long and you're still not finished?" he teased, watching her pull her long hair over her shoulder and comb her fingers though the damp ends.

"Hey, my long hair takes forever to dry," she defended herself. "So don't start in with that whole girls-take-forever-to-get-ready spiel."

He grinned. "Well, it's a well-known fact that girls take longer than boys to get ready."

"Not true!" she argued. "I've seen my brothers get ready for dates, and they're not always fast."

With her hair pulled away from her neck, he noticed that the tag of her dress was sticking up. "You've got a little tag problem happening," he told her, reaching out to tuck it into the collar of her dress without thinking. As he did, his fingers involuntarily lingered at the base of her neck, and he saw her cheeks flush.

"Sorry," he said, pulling his hand back quickly. "I just didn't want you walking around with people staring at your back, thinking you never learned how to properly dress yourself."

She laughed, the easy mood between them restored. "Then I guess I should thank you."

"Hey, since your brothers aren't around, someone has to look out for you—you know, making sure you're prepared for tests, that your shoes are on the right feet...." To demonstrate, he leaned forward and checked her shoes. "Yep. You're good."

She laughed again and swatted his shoulder playfully. "You're terrible."

"Am I?" he asked as he stood up to follow Bishop Warner and the others out the doors to the parking lot.

She stood up beside him and nodded. "Yes, you are. But still..." she continued, her voice softening, "I kind of like having you around. It's nice to have someone looking out for me."

And then, to Ben's surprise and delight, she threaded her arm through his and smiled up at him as they walked to the car.

Chapter Eleven

The first week in October, Lauren found herself engaged in a silent debate as she headed off campus after a long day of classes. She couldn't decide whether to stop by Ben's apartment to say hi, or head home to grab a bite to eat before heading back up to the library to study. With midterms rapidly approaching and with all the time she'd spent hanging out with Ben in her spare time lately, she realized that, for the first time ever, she didn't feel quite as prepared for them as she knew she could be. She loved dropping by Ben's apartment to hang out and talk, but she knew she'd never forgive herself if she got anything less than an A on her midterms.

With a sigh of resignation, she headed for her apartment. She'd just walked in and opened the fridge to examine its contents when Allison sauntered into the kitchen.

"Hey," Allison said casually. "What's up?"

"Not much," Lauren replied without taking her eyes off the fridge's contents. "I'm going to grab some dinner, then head back up to study at the library. I've got a big test in the morning. What about you?"

Allison shook her head and grinned as she pulled out a chair from the table and dropped into it. "No studying for me. I have a date."

"With Craig?"

"Nope. With Brad."

That got Lauren's attention. "What happened with Craig?" she asked curiously

"Nothing. We talked a little, and we agreed that we're not ready for an exclusive relationship yet, so we're going to see other people for a while, too."

"I see," Lauren responded uncertainly. "So, who's Brad?"

Allison grinned mischievously. "Only the cutest guy in my communications class."

Lauren rolled her eyes. "And how long's this one going to last?"

"Who cares?" Allison shrugged. "Half the fun is going out with someone new. You should try it sometime."

Lauren wrinkled her nose in disgust. "No thanks." Surveying the fridge's contents one last time, she pulled out a few slices of lunchmeat and an apple.

"Oh, I have something for you," Allison said suddenly, handing her an envelope that was sitting on the table. "It's a letter from Jack."

Lauren snatched the letter eagerly from Allison's hands. "You didn't read it before I got a chance to, did you?"

Allison clutched at her heart, feigning shock. "How could you even think that? Besides, I'm pretty sure I know what's in it. Your mom's already called about a dozen times, and she said the letter she got today had Jack's travel arrangements in it."

"Really?" Lauren squealed. She tore open the envelope and quickly scanned the information inside. When she finished, she grabbed Allison by the shoulders and started jumping up and down. "He's going to be home in three weeks!" she exclaimed. "Three weeks! Can you believe it?"

"That's only part of the news," Allison told her when she'd calmed down enough to listen. "Your mom said his mission president is letting him phone home tonight at seven to finalize travel arrangements. She wanted me to tell you that in case you wanted to be there when he called."

"You bet I do!" Lauren exclaimed eagerly. The last time she'd talked to Jack was Christmas almost a year ago, and even thirty seconds on the phone with him would make her entire year. She quickly scrambled for her car keys, then turned to

Allison. "Want to come to Idaho Falls with me? We'd probably make it in time to get a good, home-cooked meal."

Allison shook her head. "Can't. My date, remember?"

"You'd rather go out with a guy than have a home-cooked meal? Your priorities *are* screwed up," she teased. She grabbed her purse and headed for the door, her food forgotten on the counter. "Bye!"

"What about studying?" Allison called after her.

"It'll have to wait until I get back. See you in a while!"

When Lauren finally got back to her apartment that night with only minutes to spare before curfew, she was on an emotional high. Talking with Jack even for the few short minutes she'd been allowed had been incredible. She could tell he'd grown a lot spiritually and emotionally in the past year, but beneath all that, he was still the same big brother she'd loved and admired all her life. And he would be home in three weeks. She could hardly wait.

She fell right to sleep that night, the excitement of the evening having worn her out. But the next morning she was brought back to earth with a thump when she walked into her anatomy/physiology class and remembered they were having a test. She groaned. With all the excitement of the night before, she'd completely forgotten to study.

Shuffling to her desk, she slid into it dejectedly and awaited her fate. She was sure it wasn't going to be pretty.

Ben walked into his apartment after his morning classes and was surprised to find it empty. In the past few weeks, the apartment had become a gathering place for many of his roommates' friends, and without a crowd of people, the place seemed strangely quiet.

Deciding to take advantage of it and enjoy a few minutes of peace, he grabbed an apple from the kitchen and dropped into the armchair in the front room. He'd barely taken his first bite when he heard a pounding at the door.

So much for my peace and quiet, he thought with a sigh. He got up to open the door, expecting to see one of his roommate's friends. Instead, Lauren stood there with a quivering lip and tear-filled eyes.

"Lauren!" he exclaimed, his heart in his throat. "What's wrong? What happened?"

She rushed past him into the apartment and started to pace back and forth across the small living room, her hand gestures becoming more and more agitated with every word she spoke.

"I went to Idaho Falls last night because my brother was calling and I wanted to talk to him," she started to explain, "but after talking to Jack we were all excited, and I stayed too long because by the time I got back last night it was late, and I was tired, and not thinking clearly, and then I woke up this morning and went to my anatomy class, and now I wish I hadn't, because now I know what a complete failure I am!"

Ben watched helplessly as her ranting picked up steam, but his confusion grew by the second. Finally, he reached out and captured her shoulders in his hands to prevent her from wearing a hole in the carpet.

"Lauren, stop!" he exclaimed, the firmness in his voice bringing her babbling to a sudden halt. When she looked at him expectantly, he released her shoulders and breathed a sigh of relief. "Thank you. Now, just take a deep breath and calm down. None of this can be as bad as you're making it out to be, whatever it is. Why don't we just sit down, and you can tell me what on earth you're babbling about." He led her over to the couch and pulled her down beside him. "Now, tell me what's wrong."

Her composure crumbled as she said, "My test. I got a 'D' on my test." Then, as Ben watched in shocked silence, she leaned forward, buried her face in her hands, and started to cry.

Ben's heart twisted painfully. He was used to seeing a wide variety of emotions from her, but this one was new to him. Without hesitation, he pulled her into his embrace, holding her tightly as she cried. He still wasn't sure why one bad test grade would make her react like this, but he knew questioning that right now wasn't the thing to do.

As if it was the most natural thing in the world, he dropped his head to hers and kissed the top of her head lightly. "Lauren, I'm sorry," he whispered. "I wish I knew what to do or say to make you feel better."

When she was finally able to compose herself, she pulled away and wiped the tears from her cheeks. "No, *I'm* sorry," she apologized quietly. "I shouldn't have fallen apart like that."

"Hey, it's okay," he told her sincerely. "Everybody falls apart at one time or another. But I have to admit, I'm not sure I understand why you're so upset about this. Contrary to what you think, one bad grade isn't the end of the world. Just study a little harder for the next one and it will even out in the end."

"But you don't understand," she argued, pushing herself up from the couch and starting to pace again. "You have no idea how hard it is to get into a good physical therapy program. They only take those people with the very best grades and transcripts, and we have midterms in two weeks, for crying out loud! What if I do lousy on them, too? Being a physical therapist is all I've wanted to do. If I get bad grades on my midterms, too, would that mean I'm not cut out for this, that I'm not good enough to be doing what I'm doing? Maybe—"

Ben rolled his eyes in exasperation. "Lauren, it's one grade! It doesn't mean that you're not cut out to be a physical therapist. If anyone can do it, you can. You have more drive and determination than anybody I know."

Her arguments went silent and she stared down at the floor for several long moments. Finally, she sighed. "I don't know. I guess I just feel so much pressure to do everything right. If my dad ever hears about this...."

"I'm sure he'll understand."

"No, he won't." Lauren shook her head. "You have no idea what he's like."

Ben's brows furrowed in confusion. "What do you mean?"

Lauren shook her head, as if realizing she'd just said too much. "It's nothing, really," she amended. "Forget I said anything."

But Ben wasn't about to let it go. He got up and went to stand beside her, taking her hands in his. "Lauren, we're friends. You know I'd never betray a confidence, or make you tell me something you don't want to. But if you want to tell me what's *really* bothering you about this, I have two ears... no waiting." He smiled gently, and when he caught her gaze, she smiled back hesitantly.

Finally, she let her breath out in a rush. She pulled her hands out of his and turned away, wrapping her arms around herself as she strolled over to the window and stared unseeingly outside. When she spoke, her voice was low and halting. "My dad's always had a special bond with my older brothers. They're naturally athletic like he is, and he taught them to play football and baseball, and took them camping and hiking and stuff. Then I came along, and I guess my parents figured they'd finally gotten their girl, so our family was complete.

"I think Mom was more excited about having a girl than Dad was. There are all these pictures in our family album of me dressed in cute, frilly dresses, with my hair in ringlets and bows." She smiled nostalgically. "But the more I grew up, the more the pictures changed—me wearing my brothers' football pads, me pitching in little league games, me baiting my own fishing hooks.... With all that testosterone in my family, it was inevitable that I'd be more like the guys than the little dainty girl my mom probably wanted me to be."

She smiled, this time a little sadly. "Anyway, the more I tagged along with my dad and brothers, the more I saw how proud he was of them every time they threw a game-winning touchdown, made an all-star team, or broke a record of some sort. And I wanted that. I wanted him to be as proud of me as he was of them. So I started doing everything my brothers did. I played on little league teams, begged him to teach me how to throw a baseball and football... stuff like that. But even though there were brief flashes when I felt like I'd finally won his approval, I still never felt like I measured up."

She stopped and stared out the window again before she continued. "Then I made the decision to go to school here instead of one of the schools that offered me an athletic scholarship, and he wasn't happy, to say the least. But I didn't want to deal with classes and traveling with a team at the same time. Becoming a physical therapist is important to me, and he just doesn't understand that. If he finds out I got a bad grade on a test, he'll start in with his speech about how he's spending all this money to pay for my tuition here, and how, if I'm not going to take my schoolwork seriously, I could've saved him the money and gone to school at the junior college where he teaches and had free tuition. That's why it's important for me to do well here. Even if I can't make him as proud of me as he is of my brothers, at least I can prove to him that he's not wasting his money."

Ben stared at her in shocked silence. Outwardly, he knew her to be strong, determined, and self-sufficient, but he was beginning to see that inwardly, she was insecure and vulnerable, and desperately yearning for her father's approval. And the strange thing was, he knew exactly how she felt.

Taking a step toward her, he put a sympathetic hand on her shoulder and said gently, "I don't know what to say. I had no idea...."

"Well, it's not exactly something I go around telling everyone," she told him, wiping a stray tear from her cheek. But then she looked up at him, her eyes pleading. "Promise me you won't ever tell anyone I told you this, okay? I don't want to sound like I'm ungrateful for everything my parents have done for me, I just sometimes wish my dad loved me for *me*, you know?"

Ben nodded solemnly, knowing all too well how she felt. "I know. And I promise you can trust me."

A tentative smile worked its way across her face. "Yeah, I can tell that about you." Then, without warning, she stepped into his arms and gave him a hug. "Thanks, Ben."

He drew her closer and closed his eyes, savoring the heavenly feeling of holding her. "Anytime," he murmured.

When Lauren finally stepped out of his embrace, she glanced around her, looking for the backpack she knew she'd brought with her. At last she spotted it by the far wall and went to pick it up. "I guess I should get going."

"Are you sure?" he asked, wishing she could stay forever. "I'm not doing anything. You're welcome to stay a while."

A tiny smile broke through, but she shook her head. "Thanks, but I really should hit the books. I don't think I could handle a repeat performance of today's disaster." She grimaced, then went to open the door.

He followed her, and when she was standing in the open doorway, she turned back to smile at him gratefully. "Thanks again, Ben. You're such a good friend."

His face fell momentarily at her words. "Good friend," he muttered, trying not to let the discouragement he felt seep into his voice. Then he forced himself to pull it together long enough to smile at her, though it felt like his cheeks would crack from the effort. "Call me later, okay?"

She nodded. "I will." And then she was gone.

He stood staring at the door after he closed it behind her. *Good friend*, he thought dismally. *Would she ever think of him as anything else?*

Chapter Twelve

For the next two weeks, Lauren threw herself into her schoolwork. Every time she thought of that big, red "D" on the top of her anatomy test, she drove herself even harder. It remained the solitary driving force for the amount of hours she put into studying for midterms. The fact that Jack would be home the weekend following midterms gave her something to look forward to, and it kept her from burning out entirely from having pushed herself so hard.

Somehow she managed to stay focused through her first midterms, and she was pleasantly surprised when they went even better than she expected.

By Friday morning, Lauren only had her English midterm to go, and it was all she could do to keep from dancing out of her seat as she waited to take it. She knew Jack's plane would be landing in Idaho Falls any minute.

She wished she could be there with her parents to greet Jack, but she hadn't even bothered to try to reschedule her last test because she knew airport and church regulations wouldn't allow a big gathering of people anyway. Instead, she was going to pick up Allison and Ben after she finished her last midterm, and then head for home.

Lauren smiled as she thought about Ben going home with her. Her parents had been ecstatic when she'd told them about Ben and how Jack had baptized him in Boston. Just as she'd hoped they would, they'd insisted she bring him home with her to stay for the weekend.

Ben, however, hadn't been as easy to convince when she'd given him the news. He worried that he'd be intruding on a private family celebration, but Lauren had quickly assured him that her parents were as happy to have him with them as she was, and he'd finally acquiesced. Lauren could hardly wait—not only to see Jack, but for Jack to see Ben. She'd made her parents promise not to say anything, and she was sure it would be a wonderful surprise.

Trying to put all that out of her mind, Lauren glanced down at her English midterm and forced herself to concentrate. It wouldn't be long before she was done and heading for home.

When Lauren's English midterm was finally over, she practically flew back to her apartment. She hurried into her bedroom and found Allison almost finished with her packing.

"Hey," Allison greeted her. "How'd your English midterm go?"

"Aced it." Lauren beamed. "It's a good thing I didn't have one of my tougher midterms today, though, or I might not have. I'm so excited I can hardly think."

Allison laughed. "I know what you mean. Jack's plane should've landed about half an hour ago, so they'll probably be getting home about the same time we do."

"Perfect." Lauren grabbed the suitcase she'd packed the night before. "What about you? Are you ready to go?"

Allison nodded. "Pretty much. I've got a couple more things to throw in, then I'll be ready. Oh, Ben called about twenty minutes ago. He said he was all packed, so he's ready whenever we are."

"Great. Then let's get a move on." Lauren put a few last minute items into a shoulder bag, then carried it and her suitcase down to her car. Allison joined her a few minutes later, and they were on their way.

They drove the short distance to Ben's apartment and pulled into a parking space. Before either of them could get out to go knock on Ben's door, he was hurrying toward them with a duffle bag in one hand and a garment bag in the other. "Hey, guys," he greeted them cheerfully as he climbed into the back seat.

"Holy cow, you packed more stuff than I did," Lauren teased as he set his duffle bag on the seat next to him and hung the garment bag from the coat hook over the door.

Ben grinned good-naturedly. "I did not. It just looks like I did because my suit is bulkier than your stuff."

The three of them continued to tease and joke with each other during the twenty minute drive to Idaho Falls, but when they turned off the highway, Ben watched in fascination as farmlands quickly yielded to subdivisions and shopping plazas. Even as they did, however, he could tell from the occasional tractor and farm implement stores they passed that the city had maintained the relatively quiet, rural feel it had had when it was established many years ago.

He continued to stare out his window as Lauren drove through the city and then finally turned onto a quiet, secluded lane in a subdivision on the outskirts of town. Ben had to admit, he liked what he saw. Each house sat on at least an acre of land, so the homes were spaced comfortably apart, and large evergreen and deciduous trees lined both sides of the street. The houses weren't mansions like the ones in the prestigious neighborhood he'd grown up in, but they were comfortably large and well kept.

What impressed him the most, though, were the motor homes, camp trailers, and other recreational vehicles he spotted parked alongside the homes or inside open garages, suggesting that the families they belonged to actually did things together. It was just another testament of the different lifestyles in which he and Lauren had been raised—one based on money and prestige, the other full of warmth, love, and family togetherness.

For a moment, he felt a twinge of sadness and longing. While he'd spent most of his years at expensive private schools, seeing only brief flashes of his parents when they'd taken him and his sister along to exclusive vacation retreats, Lauren and Allison had been camping and doing outdoorsy things with their families.

He didn't have long to dwell on what he'd missed out on since Lauren was pulling into the driveway of a cheerful looking yellow two-story home with blue shutters, a steeply angled roof, large dormer windows, and a white front porch that ran the entire length of the house. A large, computer-printed banner announcing "Welcome Home, Jack!" had been tacked up across the garage door, and cars lined both sides of the street in front of the house.

"Judging from the number of cars, I'd say he's already home and attracting a crowd," Lauren surmised as she turned off the ignition. The three of them climbed out of the car and hurried up the front walk.

The second they opened the door, they were inundated with the sounds of laughter and happy, excited chatter. Lauren stood on her tiptoes, eagerly searching for a glimpse of her brother above the large crowd of people milling about in the living room.

As she did, Ben took the opportunity to look around. He loved the living room's lived-in cheeriness, with its yellow walls and warm blue accents. A cozy brick fireplace rose up along the far wall, its mantel adorned with dozens of family pictures. In the corner of the room next to the fireplace, a large, fluffy gray and white cat lay curled up on an overstuffed, blue armchair as it eyed the crowd warily, obviously worrying that someone might move it from its coveted spot.

Ben couldn't help smiling. The warmth he felt from his surroundings was nothing like the cold, impersonal feeling he always got from the stuffy social events his parents frequently held at their immaculate mansion during his childhood.

Just as he was turning back to Lauren, he caught sight of an attractive, middle-aged woman hurrying through the crowd toward them. Without even being introduced, Ben could tell she was Lauren's mom. The resemblance between them was unmistakable. They had the same pretty auburn hair, though Sister Holt's hair was cut short in a no-nonsense style, and both mother and daughter had the same striking light brown eyes and bright smile.

"You made it!" Sister Holt exclaimed happily as she gave Lauren a big hug. "It's so good to see you. I'm glad you're home for a few days."

Lauren hugged her mom back, then turned to gesture at Ben standing beside her. "Mom, this is Ben, the one I told you about."

Sister Holt's eyes twinkled with excitement as she surprised Ben by giving him a warm hug. "Ben! It's so wonderful to have you here."

Ben smiled, liking her immediately. "Hello, Sister Holt. It's a pleasure to meet you. And thank you so much for having me. I hope I won't be an imposition."

Her eyes widened in response. "You most certainly won't be!" she insisted. "We're thrilled to have you. When Lauren told us you'd been baptized by Jack, I was delighted to have a chance to meet you! What a wonderful coincidence. I'm sure it'll be a wonderful surprise for Jack, as well."

"Speaking of Jack..." Lauren interrupted.

Sister Holt turned back to her daughter, her eyes lighting up. "Oh, Lauren, he looks so great! He's grown at least a couple of inches, and he's changed so much."

"And in other ways, he's the same old Jack," a new voice chimed in, causing them to turn.

Ben saw that the new voice belonged to a tall, stocky man with dark brown hair, a hard-set jaw, and steely green eyes. The man's eyes softened when they fell on Lauren.

"Hi, sweetie. It's good to have you home."

Lauren stepped into his embrace and Ben realized this was her father. A moment later, Brother Holt released her and smiled at the look of excitement lighting up her eyes. "You're not eager to see your brother, are you?"

Allison smiled at Lauren's parents, who she'd come to know as her second family. "Brother Holt, you have no idea. She's been bouncing off the walls all day."

Lauren's dad chuckled deeply. "I hope your excitement to see Jack didn't hamper your ability to do well on your midterms."

Lauren's smile slipped a little, but she recovered quickly. "Of course not. I aced 'em," she said proudly.

"That's my girl," he said, reaching out to give his daughter's shoulder a squeeze.

Deciding to change the subject, Lauren turned to her mom and asked, "So, where's Jack?"

"In the family room," Sister Holt answered, gesturing to the crowd that had overflowed from the family room and into the kitchen behind her. "He's been asking about you since the minute he stepped off the plane. He's not the only one, though. Your other brothers were wondering when you were getting home. Tom and Jennifer are already here with their gang," her mom informed her, referring to Lauren's oldest brother, his wife, and their four young children. "They made the 'Welcome Home' banner that's out on the garage. And Rick's here with Melissa," she continued, referring this time to Lauren's second oldest brother and his wife of just eighteen months, "but she's so close to having her baby that she feels miserable. Connor couldn't make it today, though. His plane was delayed in Seattle due to bad weather."

Lauren felt bad that Connor, her third oldest brother, couldn't be there, but she knew a weather delay wouldn't keep him away forever. She was sure he'd be home in time for Jack's homecoming on Sunday.

Her mother's voice interrupted her thoughts. "Why don't you go say hello to Jack and surprise him with Ben?"

Lauren smiled and nodded. "I think I will." She turned to Allison and Ben. "Come on, guys. I'm sure we'll find him in the middle of the chaos." She led the way through the crowd, and when they finally stood in the family room entrance, she eagerly searched the faces in the crowd.

It wasn't long before she finally caught a glimpse of someone near the sliding glass door who had a familiar shock of reddish brown hair and was wearing a dark blue suit. Her breath caught in her throat.

He looked so incredible—so much the same, yet different, too. His countenance radiated the gospel that he'd just spent the last twenty-four months of his life teaching, and in that instant, she'd never been more proud of him for choosing to serve the Lord.

Unable to contain her excitement even one moment longer, she pushed through the crowd, leaving Allison and Ben several paces behind her. Realizing who was vaulting across the room only moments before she was upon him, Jack's happy laughter rang out as Lauren launched herself into his arms. She squealed as he returned her energetic embrace with one of his own.

When he finally released her, he took a step back and lifted his eyebrows in surprise. He slowly looked her up and down. "Someone's gone and grown up while I was gone," he announced with mixed emotions. "You look great! Any boys I need to be fighting off now that I'm back?"

Lauren laughed through happy tears and gave him a playful shove. "You scared them all off years ago. I think I'm safe."

"Good to know," he joked, draping his arm around her shoulders and pulling her close once again. "I'm not ready to have my little sister grow up any faster than she already has."

Just then Allison appeared at his side, and Jack released Lauren to give Allison a brotherly hug. "Allison! It's so good to see you again."

He was about to say more, but his gaze shifted to the young man emerging from the crowd. As the young man stopped next to Allison, Jack gasped in amazement. His expression turned to one of astonishment and disbelief as he stared at Ben for what seemed like an eternity. Then, after several moments of shocked silence, Jack's face creased into a grin that nearly split his face.

"Ben Morrison!" he exclaimed excitedly as he stepped forward and hugged Ben as tightly as he had Lauren only moments before. "Oh my gosh, I can't believe it! What are you doing here?"

Ben laughed as he returned Jack's hug. Then they clapped each other on the back and began talking at the same time, their words coming fast and furiously.

"How've you been? When I got transferred out of the area, I lost track of you," Jack admitted.

Ben grinned at Jack and nodded. "I know. Things got a little crazy. And when I tried to contact you they said you'd been transferred, and I never found out where." He paused and shook his head incredulously. "You have no idea how great it is to see you again. When Lauren and I met at school, I didn't put two and two together that you were related until she mentioned you were coming home from your mission in Boston. I couldn't believe it."

Jack laughed happily and clapped Ben on the shoulder. "I can't believe it, either. So, tell me how things are going for you. I guess you decided not to stay at Harvard."

The memory left a hollow feeling in Ben's chest, and Jack instantly caught the change in his demeanor. He frowned. "I take it things didn't go well with your parents."

Ben shook his head. "No, they didn't."

Jack's expression saddened. "I'm sorry to hear that."

"Yeah, well, I had to do what I felt was right, even if it meant going it alone," he said with a shrug that didn't quite mask the sadness in his heart.

"You know, in my entire mission I never met another person who had your strength of conviction," Jack said with a shake of his head. "I think that's awesome."

Just then someone else came up to talk to Jack, and Lauren realized this was a crazy time to have a lengthy talk. She gave Ben's arm a squeeze, then smiled up at Jack. "We're going to grab something to eat. You finish greeting your legions of fans," she winked, "and when all this chaos is over, we'll sit down and talk. I can't wait to hear how you guys came across each other."

Jack and Ben both smiled and nodded their agreement, and Lauren led Ben and Allison to the kitchen for a snack.

The rest of the evening went by in a whirlwind of activity. A steady stream of ward members and friends kept arriving at the house, and the atmosphere was one of happy rejoicing. Lauren didn't see much of Jack, other than brief glimpses across the room, but she knew there would be plenty of time for heart-to-heart talks over the weekend. Just knowing that he was finally home and that she was able to see his broad smile and hear his deep laughter was enough for now.

Lauren made certain that she introduced Ben to her brothers and their wives, and when she explained that he'd been baptized by Jack, he became a mini celebrity of sorts. They all wanted to hear how it had happened and were excited to hear, firsthand, what Jack had been like as a missionary. Sister Holt seemed especially excited to hear about it, and as she and Ben talked, they seemed to develop an instant rapport. She asked him about his background and listened raptly as he told her how Jack's service as a missionary had changed his life.

Lauren could tell by the tears in her mom's eyes that he'd officially won her over at that point. Not that her mom was hard to win over, but hearing that her son had made such a difference in someone's life had obviously touched her deeply.

Things finally wound down around nine-thirty that night, and Lauren couldn't help feeling relieved. It had been a long day—a long week, what with midterms and all—and she was tired. She couldn't even imagine how Jack must be feeling. His body was still on Eastern Standard time.

Eager to get the cleanup done and maybe talk a little with Jack, Lauren picked up a handful of paper plates that were lying around the house and carried them into the kitchen. Her mom was putting Saran Wrap on several dessert dishes they'd had out for their guests. As Lauren tossed the plates in the overflowing garbage can, she heard the sound of male voices and looked up. Jack and Ben were coming into the kitchen with a garbage sack they'd been using to pick up the family room, and were talking and laughing together.

Lauren glared at them playfully. "You two didn't go and have a long talk that I missed out on, did you? I still want to hear all the details about how you guys met and stuff."

"Nah, we just barely ran into each other during garbage duty," Jack assured her, holding the garbage bag up as proof. "But speaking of Ben," he continued, turning to Ben as they worked at emptying the kitchen trash, "I'm dying to hear how things have been going for you since you joined the Church. Care to fill me in?"

Allison joined them as they finished straightening up the kitchen, and they all listened to Ben tell Jack how he'd survived his first few months after being disowned by his family, how he and Craig had become friends, and how they'd come out to BYU-Idaho together. Jack also asked about Ben's sister since he knew they'd been close, and Ben admitted that they emailed each other secretively from time to time.

"And things are going better for you now?" Jack asked sympathetically as they finally all sat down around the table to talk some more. "You're managing school and stuff okay?"

Ben nodded. "Yeah, things are good. But even when my classes get tough, I don't stress out like Lauren does." He grinned teasingly at Lauren.

"Hey, don't start with me," Lauren threatened Ben playfully. "I have all those tough classes, and each and every teacher treats their class like it's the only one we have. I'm talking hours and hours of homework! How can you not get occasionally stressed out by that?"

Ben looked around the room in mock panic. "Oh, no, we have an emergency! Get her some chocolate, quick!"

Jack seemed to think that was absolutely hysterical, and both he and Ben cracked up.

"What?" Lauren asked, pouting playfully.

When Jack was finally able to compose himself, he said, "I'd say Ben knows you pretty well."

Ben smiled triumphantly. "I guess you could say that."

Before Lauren could defend herself, Sister Holt laughed and walked over to Ben, putting a motherly hand on his shoulder. "Before this conversation turns into something ugly," she grinned, "I think I'll step in here and change the subject. Ben, just so you know, whenever you're ready to turn in, I have everything set up for you in the guest room. I've seen to it that you have clean sheets and extra blankets in case you get cold during the night. Lauren, will you please show him where the guest room is?"

When Lauren nodded, Sister Holt went back to putting desserts in the fridge, and Lauren led Ben toward the stairs. She smiled at him over her shoulder as they started to climb the steps. "Knowing my mom, she probably put mints on your pillow, too," she joked. "She loves having company."

Ben laughed softly as they reached the top of the stairs and started down a long hallway. When Lauren gestured to a door on their left and said, "That's my room there," he couldn't help sneaking a glance. The walls were adorned with posters of athletes and various motivational quotes, and the long shelf along the far wall was jammed with sports trophies. He smiled. It looked just like he'd imagined it would.

They continued on down the hall and Lauren pushed open the last door on the right. "Here's the guest room. When you get your bags from the car, you'll know where to put them."

Ben looked around the small room and was impressed by the coziness the warm, sage green walls and denim quilt on the bed lent to the room. It was neat and homey, and he was sure he'd enjoy his stay there.

They headed back down the stairs, and Ben slipped outside to get his things from the car. When Lauren returned to the kitchen alone, Allison looked at her in surprise. "Where's Ben?"

"Getting his things," she explained as she took the wet rag her mother handed her and started wiping down the counters.

"So, how are your classes?" Jack asked. He stood up and walked over to lean against the stove. "Good, I hope."

Lauren nodded as she scrubbed at a spot on the counter. "Yeah. I was a little stressed out about midterms, but they're over now, so I can relax."

Jack turned to Allison. "And am I correct in assuming that studying is all she does?" he asked dryly.

Allison laughed. "You know Lauren. Studying is her life. Unless she's doing something with Ben, of course."

Jack lifted his eyebrows in surprise and a slow smile worked its way across his face. "Doing things with Ben, huh?"

"He's just a friend," Lauren clarified, giving Allison a playful glare.

His interest suddenly piqued, Jack folded his arms across his chest and smirked at Lauren. "Oh, really? Just a friend, huh?"

Lauren threw the wet rag at her brother. "Don't give me that look. Honestly, Ben and I *are* just friends. He helps me study, gives me pep talks, goes running with me sometimes... you know, stuff like that."

Jack's smile widened maddeningly. "Uh-huh."

Lauren rolled her eyes indignantly. "I can't believe you two! I have a boy who's a friend that I do things with, and suddenly you two are jumping to all kinds of conclusions. If you don't believe me, that's your problem."

Just then Ben came back into the house, effectively putting an end to their conversation, but Lauren could sense everyone's eyes on her as she finished wiping the counters. She could tell from the looks they exchanged that they weren't buying her story, but she didn't know what else to say to convince them. She and Ben were friends. And that was all there was to it.

Chapter Thirteen

Monday evening, Ben cleaned up his books and papers after his tutoring session and tucked everything into his backpack. Ever since he'd gone home with Lauren for Elder Holt's—Jack's—homecoming over the weekend, he'd been on an emotional high. It had been such an incredible experience to see and talk with Jack again, to get to know him as a person, instead of just as the missionary who'd taught him the gospel. He knew that even if he were to express his thanks a hundred times over to the missionary who'd changed his life forever, it wouldn't even begin to express his gratitude.

Eager to share his experience with somebody, he finished packing up his stuff and found an empty computer terminal. He sat down, opened the email program, inserted his sister's email address in the "to" field, and started typing.

Hey Emily!

You'll never guess what happened this weekend. Remember the girl I told you about that I met—Lauren? I was recently shocked to discover that her brother is the missionary who baptized me in Boston! Small world, huh? I went home with her for the weekend (she lives half an hour away) to attend her brother's homecoming (that's what we Mormons call it when missionaries come home and talk in church about how their mission went). It was SO great to see and talk to him again. I owe him so much.

I know you probably won't understand this, but seeing him again brought back all the wonderful, indescribable emotions that I felt when I listened to the missionaries teach me about the gospel of Jesus Christ for the very first time. I remember how skeptical you were when I first told you I was taking the missionary discussions, but never once did you react with the anger that Dad did. And I appreciate that. It helped so much to know that I had your support, even if you weren't convinced I was doing the right thing.

But I assure you, Em—I did do the right thing. You have no idea how much the gospel has changed my life for the better. It's taught me about who I am, where I came from, and where I'm going. It has given my life purpose and direction, and an incredible sense of peace in spite of the chaos of the world. I have a testimony of the gospel, and I know that Heavenly Father was mindful of me and all the struggles I was going through, and sent the missionaries into my life right at the time I needed the gospel the most. And for that, I'll be forever thankful.

I hope I haven't sounded too preachy, but I was so excited that I just had to share my feelings with somebody. I immediately thought of you.

I love you, Em, and I'll talk to you soon,

Ben

Ben sent the email, then logged off the computer and headed down to the main floor of the library. He was just crossing through the lobby when he heard someone calling his name. Turning, he saw a slender, pretty girl with hazel eyes and silky, waist-length, brown hair hurrying to catch up with him. As she neared, he recognized her as one of the girls from his ward.

"Ben, hi!" she exclaimed, stopping next to him and giving him a dazzling smile. "I was looking for you."

"It's Elena, right?" he asked uncertainly.

Her smile brightened even further and she tossed her long hair back over one shoulder. "I'm flattered you remembered."

"Well, uh—" he stammered, not sure how to respond to that. Then he remembered her greeting. "You said you were looking for me?"

"Oh, yeah," she replied easily. "I was just up at the tutoring center, asking about hiring a tutor, and they said you were available. So now you're officially my tutor. Isn't that great?" Her eyes danced as she placed a perfectly manicured hand on his arm. "It's fate, that's what this is."

Ben blinked and glanced down at her hand in confusion. Was she really flirting with him, or was it just his imagination? Deciding to play it safe, he asked, "What classes do you need help with?"

Elena sighed dramatically, a frown marring her otherwise perfect features. "Well, they're *all* so hard, but I just hate that awful algebra. I get so confused by all those numbers."

"Well, algebra's not that hard once you understand the basics," Ben told her diplomatically. "I'm sure you'll be understanding it in no time."

"Oh, that is so great! I just knew you'd be the perfect tutor. You're so smart and helpful... not to mention cute." She threaded her arm through his and looked up at him from beneath lowered lashes.

Ben almost laughed. *Yep. Definitely flirting.* While he was flattered, he really didn't think this girl was his type. Trying not to appear too obvious, he lifted his arm to adjust his backpack strap, which inconspicuously dislodged her arm. "Um... what's your schedule like? Is there a day or time that works better for you to meet?"

When they'd agreed upon a day and time, Elena gave him a flirtatious grin. "Friday it is, then. I'll look forward to it." Then, with one last sidelong look, she turned and walked out of the library.

Ben hung back until she was gone, still trying to gather his thoughts. Elena seemed to be using tutoring as an excuse to flirt with him. He certainly hoped that wasn't the case. He knew he'd be getting paid regardless, but he really didn't want to waste his time tutoring someone who wasn't serious about learning. And there was something else about Elena, something he couldn't quite put his finger on... but it hinted at trouble.

Unable to come to any conclusions, Ben pushed the thoughts aside as he stepped out into the beautiful autumn evening and headed for home.

"Has anyone seen my chemistry book?" Lauren heard Melia ask as she walked into her apartment after work on Wednesday evening.

Lauren shut the apartment door behind her and shrugged out of her backpack. "Uh-oh. Did you lose it?"

Melia nodded as she rushed into the kitchen. "Yeah, and I've got study group in ten minutes."

Lauren unzipped her backpack and pulled out her own chemistry textbook. "Here, you can borrow mine," she offered, handing her roommate the book. "I'm sure yours will turn up somewhere around here."

"Lauren, you're a life saver," Melia breathed as she put the book into her own backpack and pulled on her jacket. Then she made a dash for the door. "Bye!"

She yanked the door open and very nearly collided with Ben, who was standing there with his hand raised to knock. Quick "hellos" were exchanged, and Lauren laughed as she watched Ben and her roommate do some fancy footwork trying to maneuver past each other in the doorway.

When Melia was finally gone, Ben came through the door and spotted Lauren. "That was close." He chuckled. "Where's she off to in such a hurry?"

"Study date," Lauren answered, slipping out of her jacket and tossing it onto the couch. "By the way, your timing is perfect. I just walked in the door."

"What makes you think I came by to see you?" he taunted.

Lauren picked up a pillow from the couch and threw it at him. "You're such a creep. I don't know why I put up with you."

"Because I put up with *you*," he shot back, his grin widening.

Lauren rolled her eyes and sauntered into the kitchen. "What'd you do, wake up this morning and decide you missed teasing your sister, so you came here to practice on me?" She opened the fridge and started searching for something to eat.

Ben followed her into the kitchen and leaned up against the counter. "You got it. How am I doing?"

"Not very well," she said without turning away from the fridge. "I grew up with four brothers, remember? You're going to have to do better than that."

"Mmm, I must be rusty," he commented thoughtfully. He watched her search the fridge for another minute, then she sighed and shut the door.

"I seriously have to go grocery shopping tomorrow," she mumbled. "We have no good food in this place." Shaking her head, she went over to one of the cupboards and pulled out a can of green beans.

Curious, Ben watched her extract a can opener from a drawer, open the can, then pop one of the green beans into her mouth. Ben raised his eyebrows in alarm. "What on earth are you doing?"

"Eating some beans," she answered matter-of-factly. "You have a problem with that?"

He snorted. "Ye-ah," he emphasized, drawing out the word to make it sound like two. "You're not going to add butter to them and warm them up or something?"

She let a slow smile creep across her face. "What? Is this grossing you out?"

"Ye-ah," he repeated, eyeing the open can in her hand as if it contained worms instead of vegetables. Her smile only broadened as she popped another green bean into her mouth. He rolled his eyes and groaned in disgust. "Give me that," he demanded, grabbing the can out of her hand and reaching for a bowl in the cupboard.

"Hey!" she protested. "What are you doing?"

"I'm going to put them in a bowl and warm them up for you, since you're obviously not going to do it yourself."

"I don't want them warmed up!" she insisted, trying to reach around him to grab the can back as he tried to dump the beans into the bowl he'd set on the counter. "I like eating them cold!"

Ben shifted his hip in an effort to block her attempts to reach the can. "Well, you're not going to while I'm around," he told her with a laugh. "Talk about disgusting!"

Lauren couldn't help giggling as she maneuvered around his block and made another grab for the beans. "It's not disgusting! Give me back my beans."

"No!" he insisted, starting to laugh harder. He realized keeping her away was no easy task. She'd obviously had a lot of practice sticking up for herself with all those brothers around. He grabbed the bowl full of green beans and turned his back to her, keeping his body between her and her vegetables as he fought his way to the microwave.

"You're not going to microwave those!" she told him, barely managing to get the words out from between giggles.

He continued to laugh as she threw herself across his back in another attempt to stop him. "Oh yeah? Who's going to stop me?" he taunted, managing to dislodge her with a twist of his torso and quickly getting the bowl into the microwave.

"I am!" she choked out through her laughter. She made a desperate grab for his hand and managed to pull it away before he could start the microwave. He fought to get back to it, and it was all she could do to keep him away. With each of them laughing too hard to talk, a wrestling match ensued.

Ben put a hand on her head and stiff-armed her, keeping her at a distance, but she took advantage of her lowered position and wrapped her arms around his leg to keep him from going anywhere. Trying to free himself, he slipped his arm around her neck in a half-nelson as they continued to battle for the upper hand.

They were laughing so hard that they didn't hear the knock on the door, or hear Bree open it to let the visitor in. It wasn't until Lauren heard a familiar booming voice that she stopped laughing and looked up in surprise.

Her brother Jack was standing just inside the door, his eyes wide with surprise at finding his sister and Ben tangled up in a wrestling move. As Ben and Lauren stood frozen in position, an amused smile slowly crept across Jack's face. "Hi guys," he said maddeningly. "Am I interrupting something?"

Lauren quickly released Ben's leg and felt Ben's arm loosen from around her neck. She straightened and adjusted her twisted shirt. "Jack!" she exclaimed in a mixture of surprise and dismay at being caught in such a state with the guy her brother had baptized. Then, by way of explanation, she announced, "He was going to microwave my beans."

Jack's smile widened and he held up his hands in a placating gesture. "I don't want to know."

Lauren groaned inwardly. This was all she needed. Now her brother was definitely going to think there was something going on between them. Trying to play down the moment, she went over to Jack and gave him a hug. "So, what are you doing here?"

"Well, other than wanting to come by and see firsthand how my little sister was faring at college," Jack grinned at Lauren, "Mom insisted that I take you out for something to eat. She even sent me with money." He pulled several bills from his pocket and waved them at her. "Apparently, she thinks you're starving yourself. You know, too busy studying to eat, and all that."

Ben laughed as he came to stand beside them. "You're not far off, unless you count a can of green beans as a good dinner."

Lauren glared at Ben and elbowed him in the ribs. Then she turned back to her brother. "Dinner out sounds wonderful."

Jack nodded, then turned to Ben. "Why don't you come with us?"

Ben shook his head regretfully. "I wish I could, but I've got a tutoring session in half an hour. I just popped in for a few minutes. Another time, though?"

"You can count on it," Jack told him. "And don't be surprised if I pop in to see you from time to time now that I know you're around these parts."

Ben smiled and said sincerely, "I'd love it. See you two later?"

When they said their goodbyes, Ben headed back to the campus while Jack drove Lauren to a restaurant not far away. Lauren tried to convince him to settle for fast food, but Jack wouldn't listen.

"Can't a brother take his starving college-student sister out for a healthy meal?" he asked teasingly.

As they were seated and were left to look over their menus, Jack lifted his eyebrows at Lauren and a mischievous smile lit up his face. "So, what's going on between you and Ben? And don't feed me some 'we're just friends' story. I wouldn't believe you."

Lauren met his gaze steadily. "Why not? That's what we are."

"Mmm-hmm," he mumbled, unconvinced. "Then how do you explain that little scene I witnessed when I walked in?"

Lauren snorted with laughter. "We were just goofing around! As usual, you're jumping to conclusions."

He raised his glass of water to his lips, his eyes twinkling merrily. "Am I?"

"Yes, you are."

He set his glass back down on the table and fixed her with a brotherly stare. "I don't think I am. Maybe you're not seeing it, but to me, it's obvious. You're crazy about him."

Lauren gasped indignantly. "I am not!"

"Are too."

"Am not," she argued back, suddenly feeling like she was back in the days of their childhood when they argued in just such a fashion. "Yes, I like Ben, but only *as a friend*," she emphasized forcefully.

Jack was quiet for a long minute. Finally, he said, "You know, there's nothing wrong with admitting you like someone, Laur. Just because you had some bad experiences and got your heart broken in the past doesn't mean you should always be afraid to give your heart to someone else. Ben's a really great guy. I saw firsthand what he had to go through to join the Church, and believe me, he's as good as they come. I'd hate to see you blow off what you two obviously have just because you're afraid of being hurt. Sometimes love's a risk. But in my opinion, it's a risk worth taking."

Their waitress came over to take their order, effectively putting an end to their conversation. Jack never brought up the subject of Ben again, and Lauren was glad. She had no idea what to say. She'd always valued Jack's opinion more than anyone else's, but this time....

Jack doesn't know what he's talking about, Lauren told herself silently. *He may think he sees something between me and Ben, but I just don't care about Ben that way... romantically, I mean.*

She shook her head. He was just good old reliable Ben, the friend she could talk to and laugh with, and who was always there for her when she needed somebody. And even if she did feel that way about him—which she didn't—it wouldn't matter because he didn't feel that way about her. She was sure of it. If he had, she would have picked up on it by now. All he'd offered her was friendship.

Regardless of what Jack said, opening her heart up to somebody was not a risk she thought worth taking again—now or ever.

Chapter Fourteen

November arrived with a surge of cold weather. When Lauren awoke that first Friday, she was excited to see that snow had fallen overnight, covering the landscape with a gleaming blanket of white.

"Allison, wake up!" Lauren exclaimed, throwing her pillow onto her sleeping friend.

Allison groaned and rolled over to face her, struggling to crack an eyelid. "What?"

"It snowed! Check it out."

"You gotta be kidding," Allison grumbled, pulling the blankets over her head. "What, you've never seen snow before? You grew up in Idaho, for cryin' out loud."

Lauren laughed. "I know, but I love the snow. Everything looks so beautiful and peaceful. Aren't you going to get up?"

"Uh-uh," came the muted reply. "I don't have class until ten."

Lauren shrugged and jumped out of bed. "Suit yourself. But you won't get to throw the first snowball of the season."

"Throw it for me," Allison mumbled before drifting back to sleep.

Smiling, Lauren shook her head and went into the bathroom to brush her hair and teeth. With practiced fingers, she pulled her hair back into a French braid, then dabbed on a touch of base and eyeliner before hurrying into the kitchen for a glass of orange juice. She glanced at the clock. Five minutes to eight. If she didn't hurry, she was going to be late.

Downing her juice, she grabbed her backpack, shrugged into her coat, and hurried out into the brisk morning air.

A few hours later, Lauren skipped lightly down the steps of the Clark building after her morning classes and breathed deeply. She savored the fresh, cold air filling her nostrils and the feel of a brisk breeze on her face. It brought back wonderful memories of winters past—bundling up in warm coats and gloves, going cross-country skiing, snowshoeing, and tubing with her dad and brothers, and drinking hot chocolate afterward by a roaring fire.

She had ten minutes until her shift at the bookstore started, so she took her time walking to the Manwaring Center, enjoying the sound of the snow crunching under her feet. Everything was dusted with a light covering of snow, and the sunlight sneaking through the clouds glinted off the coating of white like a mirror.

Lauren smiled. She'd always loved the snow, but today, somehow, it seemed even more glorious that usual. As she neared the Manwaring Center, she saw Ben standing on the steps of the building, talking to a couple of guys she recognized from their ward. Her heart feeling as light as her feet, she skipped over and came to an abrupt stop beside him, shouldering him playfully.

"Hey!" she exclaimed cheerfully. "What are you doing?"

Saying a quick goodbye to his friends, he laughed and shouldered her back. "Getting knocked down by someone who's entirely too cheerful on a snowy November day. What's with you?"

"What do you mean, what's with me? It's Friday, classes are over for the week, the snow's made everything beautiful," she said, gesturing dramatically at the snow-covered landscape, "and classes are over for the week."

He grinned. "You just said that."

She grinned back. "So I did." She flipped her long braid back over her shoulder and nodded at the books in his arms. "So, where are you off to?"

"The library. I've got three different tutoring sessions this afternoon. You heading to work?"

She nodded. "Yep. But it's Friday night, and with midterms over, I've decided to rebel and not study tonight. Do you want to do something?"

"Sure, sounds great," he answered happily. "What do you have in mind?"

She shrugged. "As long as it doesn't involve studying, I'm up for anything. We could just hang out and I'd be thrilled."

Ben laughed. "Me too. If you want, why don't you meet me at the library when you get off work? Then we can decide what we want to do tonight."

"Sounds great!"

"Good, I'll see you then." With one last smile, he turned and started for the library.

On an impulse, Lauren bent over, picked up a handful of snow, formed it into a hasty snowball, took aim, and let it fly. She watched in delight as it hit Ben smack dab between the shoulder blades. Ben let out a surprised gasp, then started to laugh. He made a quick snowball of his own and threw it at her in retaliation, but it missed her by a mile.

"Nice, Ben," she taunted when she was able to stop laughing. "Did anybody ever tell you that you throw like a girl?"

"You better watch out, Holt," he called in warning, his eyes twinkling mischievously, "because when you least expect it, I'm going to get you back!"

"Dream on, Morrison!"

Ben was still grinning as he shook his head and continued on his way to the library, brushing snow off his coat as he went. When he was out of sight, Lauren glanced down at her watch. She'd better hurry if she didn't want to be late for work. Turning on her heel, she took the steps two at a time and went to clock in.

Ben glanced up at the clock on the wall. Never had he been so grateful to see an hour end. His tutoring session with Elena had been a total waste. No matter how hard he tried to help her with her class work, all she seemed interested in was flirting. And she was good at it; he had to give her credit. But nothing he said or did seemed to deter her—the harder he tried to ward off her advances, the more she flirted. He knew he should feel flattered, but he only felt frustrated instead. When their hour was finally up, Ben closed his books pointedly and stood up. "Our time's up, I guess."

Elena sighed dramatically and stood up beside him. "I guess so. You've been *such* a big help," she gushed, arranging her books neatly in the crook of her arm and sidling up to him. "You just *have* to let me repay you for all you've done. Maybe let me take you out for dinner soon? I know this great little restaurant along the riverbank in Idaho Falls...."

Ben grimaced inwardly. That was all he needed—an entire evening of pretending to be flattered by her attention. He smiled gracefully and shook his head. "Thanks, but you're already paying me for the tutoring."

"If you say so," Elena said, pouting. "At least we can spend time together studying. Same time next week?"

Ben was tempted to tell her to forget it, that if she wasn't serious about learning, she could take a hike. But money was money, and it was definitely getting a little scarce lately. With a sigh, he nodded. "Yeah, I'll be here."

"Great! But just in case you change your mind about getting together to do something," she said, carefully pulling out a half sheet of paper that was sticking out of her notebook and handing it to him, "here's my phone number. Call me anytime." Then with one last flirtatious smile, she turned and walked away.

Ben glanced down at the paper in his hand and shook his head. Taking a step toward the table to gather up his books, he caught a sudden movement out of the corner of his eye. He glanced up and saw Lauren standing a short distance away, her arms crossed petulantly and an uncharacteristic scowl on her face.

"Hi, Lauren."

"Don't 'hi Lauren' me," she shot back in an angry whisper. "What were you doing with Elena?"

Ben stared at Lauren, not sure what to make of her tone. "Well... I'm tutoring her," he replied cautiously.

"And what's this, her phone number?" she demanded, marching over and snatching the paper out of his hand. She glanced at it, then crumpled it up and chucked it angrily into a nearby garbage can, muttering, "I can't believe her!"

Ben let out a surprised laugh. "Lauren, what has gotten into you?"

Lauren whirled around to face him, her eyes flashing. "Nothing's gotten into me!" she snapped. The librarian at the front desk shushed her, and Lauren fixed her with a scathing glare before turning back to Ben. Eyeing him coldly, she stepped closer and hissed, "Maybe I should be asking what's gotten into you!"

More confused than ever, Ben whispered back, "What are you talking about?"

"Elena, that's what I'm talking about!" Lauren countered, gesturing in the direction Elena had gone. "How can you even talk to her? Don't you know what a malicious, two-faced person she is?"

"Oh, come on," Ben pacified. "She can be a little pushy, but she's okay."

"How can you say that?" Lauren demanded, stomping her foot in anger. "You don't know thing one about her!"

Ben held up his hands in a placating gesture. "Lauren, calm down. I'm just tutoring her, for crying out loud. Don't get so upset."

"I'm not upset!"

"Oh yes, you are," Ben contended. "I can always tell when you're upset. Your cheeks get all flushed and you get these little wrinkles at the corners of your eyes."

Lauren's frown deepened. "Okay, so what if I am? You don't know Elena like I do. You can't honestly think she wants tutoring, do you? How can you be so naïve?"

Ben stiffened. "I'm not naïve!"

"Oh, really? You've already fallen for her little act! She comes to you all innocent and pleading for help, saying she's too dumb to pass her classes on her own. Then you go feeling sorry for her and offer to help, and voilà! The next thing you know, she's robbed you of your good senses and you're following her around like some lost little puppy."

"I am not some lost little—" he began, but then stopped when something suddenly occurred to him. A slow smile started to spread across his face. "Wait… are you jealous?"

Lauren's eyes widened and she stared at him incredulously. "What? No, I'm not jealous! We're friends, and maybe I just don't want to see you get hurt. Did you ever think of that?"

Realizing he'd struck a nerve, Ben's grin widened. He leaned back against the table and crossed his arms over his chest. "You're jealous. You saw Elena up here flirting with me, and you couldn't handle it. Admit it."

"I will not!" Lauren argued vehemently. When he continued to stare at her with that maddening grin, she fixed him with a smoldering stare. "Forget it. If you don't want to believe me, fine. I'm outta here." She turned and stormed toward the doors.

Ben's smile quickly vanished. "But wait! What about tonight? We had plans!"

Lauren glared at him over her shoulder without slowing her stride. "Call Elena. I'm sure she's free." And with that, she marched out the door, leaving him staring after her in shocked silence.

Lauren stormed into her apartment a short time later, drawing curious stares from Bree, Allison, and Melia, who were sitting in the living room, talking. Unfazed, Lauren marched past them and into her bedroom, slamming the door behind her with such force that the windows rattled. Then she dropkicked her backpack into the closet, feeling a brief flash of pain in her toes. With tears of anger and pain in her eyes, she limped over to her bed and dropped down onto it.

Just then Allison opened the bedroom door and walked in, shutting the door behind her. She sat down calmly on her bed and stared at Lauren expectantly. "So? What happened?"

"Nothing," Lauren grumbled. "Can't I be angry in peace?"

Allison shook her head. "Nope. Now spill."

"Ben's just the biggest jerk that ever lived, that's all."

Allison raised her eyebrows curiously. "Uh-oh. What'd he do?"

Lauren sighed heavily. "We were going to do something tonight, so after work I went to the library to meet him because he was tutoring. When I got there, guess who he was tutoring? Elena."

"Elena Wilkinson?" Allison squeaked.

Lauren nodded. "And you should've seen how she was flirting with him! She was practically throwing herself at him!"

"What happened then?" Allison prodded.

"Oh, I blew up at him and told him how naïve he was being. Then he accuses me of being jealous! Me! Can you believe that? I told him I was just trying to protect him since he obviously didn't know Elena as well as I did."

"So, were you?"

Lauren looked at her blankly. "Was I what?"

"Jealous."

"Not you, too!" Lauren exclaimed, leaping to her feet. "What is this, a conspiracy?"

Allison shook her head calmly. "No, but you have to admit, you're pretty upset about this. Don't you think that means something?"

"It means I don't want to see him get hurt! You know what Elena's like! Ben's a nice guy, and he's my friend. He deserves better than Elena."

"Don't worry, he's got more common sense than to go out with her," Allison reassured her. "Besides, you're obviously the one he wants to spend time with. Didn't you say you guys were doing something tonight?"

Lauren made a face. "Not anymore."

"Oh, come on, Laur, it's Friday night. You should be out doing something fun instead of being stuck at home."

"No thanks. I just want to stay home and be mad."

Allison shrugged and stood up. "Suit yourself."

When she left, Lauren flopped back onto her bed and stared up at the ceiling. Going out would've been fun, but there was no way she was going to call Ben. She was too angry. She'd tried to warn him about Elena, and all he did was laugh and tell her in so many words that she was being ridiculous.

Well, he's the one being ridiculous if he thinks Elena's being sincere in wanting him to help her with her schoolwork! she thought indignantly. *And what was that about accusing me of being jealous? That's a laugh! Nothing could be further from the truth.*

Lauren rolled over onto her side and fingered a loose thread on her comforter. He didn't seem to believe her when she'd denied it, though. Even Allison seemed to think she was jealous. How could they think that? She and Ben were friends. *Friends.* So, why did everyone keep thinking there was more to their relationship than that?

Still....

Lauren couldn't erase the feeling she'd had when she went through those library doors and saw Elena flirting with Ben. It was as if somebody had kicked her in the stomach. That didn't mean anything, did it?

No way, she argued vehemently. *Why would I be jealous? It's not as if I own him, or have some prior claim to him or something. There's been nothing in our relationship to indicate we're anything more than friends.*

Lauren pulled her pillow over her head and groaned. Why was she even thinking about this? The whole idea of her being jealous was simply ludicrous. It was just easier being mad. And right now, that's all she wanted to be.

Ben woke up for church on Sunday feeling miserable. Ever since Lauren had stormed out of the library Friday night, he'd wanted to talk to her, to apologize for being such a jerk. But each time he'd tried to call her, she hadn't been there. She seemed to be effectively ditching him.

Obviously, there was something going on between Lauren and Elena that made Lauren react the way she did, but instead of being sensitive and talking things out with her, he'd laughed, and even accused her of being jealous. For that fleeting moment when he'd stood before her in the library listening to her tirade, he honestly thought she was jealous. His hopes had soared. He'd been waiting and waiting for any sign that she was beginning to feel about him the way he felt about her, and it seemed he finally had one. But then she'd stormed off and had refused to speak with him since. If this irrevocably damaged their relationship, he was never going to forgive himself.

As he dressed for church, he hoped that he'd see Lauren there so he could talk to her. He wasn't sure what he was going to say, but he knew some kind of groveling would be involved.

He got to church a few minutes early and was surprised to see Lauren and her roommates already there. Bree and Allison were talking and laughing with a couple of the guys near the doors, but Lauren was sitting by herself about halfway down the room, her head bowed over her scriptures as she read.

Gathering his courage, he walked up to her and said quietly, "Hey."

Her head jerked up, and when she saw him, a myriad of emotions flickered across her face. "Hey," she responded cautiously.

He studied her carefully for any signs of lingering anger, but when her expression remained neutral, he gestured hopefully at the empty seat beside her. "Saving this for anyone?" When she shook her head wordlessly, he slipped out of his overcoat and sat down. He swallowed his pride and decided it was now or never. Quietly and sincerely, he began, "Lauren, I owe you an apology."

Her eyes widened at this unexpected opening. "No, I owe you one," she amended sheepishly. "I shouldn't have lost my temper like that."

"But you had every reason to be angry," he insisted. "You were upset and I just laughed off your concerns. It was completely insensitive, and I wouldn't blame you if you never wanted to speak to me again."

The hint of a smile tugged at the corners of her mouth. "Well, that's a little harsh. I was mad, but it's not like you were the only one to blame. In case you haven't noticed, I tend to overreact at times."

He laughed softly. "It's one of the things I like most about you." Their eyes met and held, and he asked hopefully, "So am I forgiven? Are we still friends?"

Lauren rolled her eyes and then leaned over to bump her shoulder gently against his. "Of course we're still friends."

Ben let his breath out in a rush. "You have no idea how glad I am to hear that. But that still leaves one thing unresolved."

"Oh?"

"We had plans on Friday night that didn't get met. What do you say I make up for it by cooking you the most amazing Sunday dinner you've ever had?"

Lauren's eyes lit up. "You've got yourself a deal! Man, if this is how we make up after a fight, I say we do it more often."

"No way," he scolded her playfully. "The turmoil isn't worth it."

Her grin softened, and she slid her arm through his. "Fair enough. So, tell me. What are you going to cook me for dinner?"

Before he could respond, Bishop Warner stood up to conduct the meeting, and they both turned their attention to him. But as Ben sat with Lauren's arm still looped through his, causing his skin to dance with excitement, he found it hard to concentrate on anything that was being said. All he could think about was the fact that he hadn't completely ruined things with Lauren.

With a sigh of relief, Ben tightened his arm on Lauren's. At least for now, all seemed right with the world.

Chapter Fifteen

"Oh, come on! You didn't see that coming?" Allison shouted at the woman on the movie screen, who screamed when her pursuer jumped out at her from behind a tree.

Several people turned to shush her, and Lauren slid further down in her seat. She knew this was a bad idea. It was Monday night, and her family home evening brothers had convinced her and her roommates that seeing the popular action/suspense movie that was playing up on campus would be fun. She should've known, though, that Allison would never keep quiet in a movie like this, where the characters often made stupid, irrational decisions. She only hoped that the other patrons didn't have them kicked out before it was over.

When they finally made it to the end of the movie, Lauren found herself breathing a sigh of relief. She stood up to follow her roommates and family home evening brothers out of the building. Darkness had fallen, but the moon overhead reflected off the newly fallen snow, making it seem as light as day.

"I can't believe you did that!" Lauren said, elbowing Allison and laughing as they made their way down the sidewalk. "Everybody was staring at us. I thought that guy up front was going to have us thrown out."

"Well, why do they make the characters so *dumb*?" Allison protested. "It ruins the movie."

Before Lauren could respond, she felt something thump her between her shoulder blades, and she cried out in surprise as something cold and wet trickled down her back. Just then snowballs started splattering all around them, and there was a chorus of squeals as her roommates scrambled for cover.

Lauren whirled around to see who was behind the sudden attack and caught sight of Ben's familiar form a dozen or so yards away. But he wasn't alone. Four of his five roommates were with him, and judging from their laughter and shouts as they chased the girls across the snow covered lawn, they were in on the attack.

"Didn't I tell you I was going to get you back when you least expected it?" Ben yelled tauntingly.

A wild snowball fight ensued, and Lauren made a valiant effort to defend herself and her roommates as they took cover behind a row of shrubs. Together they continued to defend their position with hastily made snowballs, but before long, the guys were upon them, and her roommates squealed and scattered. Lauren, however, held her ground, throwing one missile after another until her arm started to ache. When she knew she couldn't hold them off a moment longer, she turned and tried to run, but the near knee-deep snow made a hasty retreat virtually impossible.

She'd only gone a few steps before a muscular arm caught her around the waist and threw her on her back in the deep snow. Laughing too hard to breathe, she looked up to see that it was Ben who was straddling her legs, keeping her arms pinned harmlessly on either side of her head.

"Okay, okay, I give!" she shouted through her laughter.

Smiling triumphantly, Ben released her hands and sat up, unknowingly giving her just the opportunity she needed. She twisted sideways in the snow, bringing her leg up at the same time and sending him rolling off into a drift. She scrambled to her knees, surprising him with her quickness, and made a hasty grab for him. For several minutes they wrestled in the snow, each trying to get the upper hand. When it became apparent that neither had an edge over the other, they finally flopped down in the snow, laughing and completely out of breath.

When Ben finally caught his breath, he propped himself up on his hand and stared down at her, his eyes twinkling. "Where did you learn to wrestle like that?"

She laughed. "I have four brothers, remember? Wrestling was a life skill when I was growing up."

"Well, I'd say it's one you've mastered."

They fell into a comfortable silence, and Lauren closed her eyes for a moment, too tired to get up from her wet resting place. When she reopened them, she was surprised to find Ben staring down at her in a way that made her heart start to pound. His handsome face was silhouetted by the snow-gray sky, and she found herself mesmerized as she took in his long lashes, sparkling with snow, his dark, tousled hair, and his flushed cheeks.

An eternity seemed to pass as they stared into each other's eyes. Then slowly, almost imperceptibly, he lowered his face to hers. Lauren's heart started to thud wildly in her chest, and she found herself unable to move, unable to breathe. His lips parted slightly as they neared hers, and she closed her eyes, willing the inevitable to happen. Only a breath separated them when suddenly....

Whack!

Something cold and wet dribbled down onto Lauren's face, and her eyes flew open in shock. Ben quickly jerked his head up and started to grumble and laugh at the same time.

"Take that, Morrison!" one of the girls yelled, followed by a round of laughter.

Lauren whipped her head around to see Bree, Allison, and Melia standing a dozen or so yards away, whooping and hollering as they threw their arms above their heads in a gesture of victory.

"Oh, they are so dead," Ben muttered, but a sporting smile proved that he wasn't really angry. He scrambled to his feet and shouted, "You guys had better run because when I get hold of you, you're going to wish you'd never done that!"

They squealed and scattered, their loud laughter carrying on the breeze as they retreated. Turning back to Lauren, he flashed her a smile and helped her to her feet, the intimacy of the moment gone. "I think we should let 'em have it," he said, winking conspiratorially and trying to goad her into retaliation.

Lauren laughed as she brushed the snow off her damp jeans. "Don't look at me! You're the one who started this!"

"Yeah, Morrison!" one of Ben's roommates called out. "Whose side do you think she's on, anyway?"

Ben started to laugh. "Okay, okay, I give. But next time, she's on my team." He reached up and rubbed the shoulder she'd pelted with a snowball. "Without her throwing arm on my side, I'm doomed."

Everybody was laughing as they started back down the street, brushing snow from their clothes and hair. One of Lauren's family home evening brothers clapped Ben on the back and said, "That'll teach you to take one of our family home evening sisters hostage!"

"Oh, I don't know," Bree chimed in. "It didn't look to me like she was all that interested in being rescued."

Lauren flushed a bright shade of red, and Ben glanced at her, looking slightly embarrassed as well. But then a smile broke out across his handsome face and he gave her a wonderful wink.

When Lauren got back to her apartment, she flopped down on her bed, her mind whirling. *Did Ben really almost kiss me?* she asked herself. If they hadn't been interrupted at just that moment, she was sure he would have.

But that doesn't make any sense, she thought. *We're friends, and friends don't kiss each other. A fluke, that's what it was. I'm sure it'll never happen again.*

But if that were true, why did she feel so disappointed?

As Ben walked up the stairs to Lauren's apartment a few days later, he couldn't help feeling apprehensive about how she was going to react after Monday night's encounter. For what seemed like the millionth time since that night, he asked himself, *What were you thinking?*

He shook his head. He couldn't believe he'd almost kissed her. He knew what her previous relationships had been like, and he knew that if he rushed this, he could scare her off for good. But she'd looked so irresistible lying there in the snow, her lips were so close, and things had been going so well between them. He'd never felt this way about anybody before, and the closer they got, the harder it was to keep his feelings in check.

But he knew he had to. She was too important to him to do something foolish now. For one wonderful moment, he'd sensed she wanted to kiss him as much as he wanted to kiss her. Or had he simply misinterpreted? Either way, he knew he had to tread lightly and not slip up again—not before she gave him some indication that she was ready to take the next step in their relationship. He had to let her be in control or this simply wouldn't work.

With a determined set to his jaw, he walked up to her apartment and knocked. Melia answered the door and invited him in where he found Lauren sitting at the table, eating a bowl of soup. She greeted him cheerfully, giving no sign that she was upset over their encounter on Monday evening. Breathing a sigh of relief, he went over and sat at the table with her.

They'd only been chatting for a few minutes when the front door flew open and Allison rushed in looking frazzled. She caught sight of Lauren sitting at the table and ran over.

"Oh, Lauren, you *have* to help me!"

Lauren eyed her warily. "What's wrong?"

"There's this really cute guy that I want to go to the Thanksgiving semiformal with and I really like him and don't want to scare him off. You have to double date with me and keep me from saying or doing the wrong things. Pleeeease?"

Lauren stared at her, dumbfounded. "What happened to the guy in your communications class?"

Allison waved her hand dismissively. "Ancient history." Then she leaned forward to grab Lauren's hands tightly. "Pleeease, Lauren? I promise you'll have a good time, and I'll even pay for your ticket."

Lauren snorted. "Yeah, right. Who am I going to go with?"

Allison turned pleading eyes in Ben's direction. "Ben will go with you, won't you, Ben?"

Ben glanced at Lauren. Of course he'd be thrilled to go. But how did he tell Lauren that without sending her fleeing?

When Ben didn't respond right away, Allison rushed on in an effort to convince them. "Oh come on, you guys have got to help me! I honestly think Trevor might be the one."

"The one what?" Lauren asked dryly.

But Allison only continued to plead with her until Lauren groaned and rolled her eyes. "Okay, fine," she gave in, completely surprising Ben. She turned to him and sighed. "I don't mind going if you don't."

"Fine with me," he replied nonchalantly, belaying the growing excitement he felt inside. He couldn't think of anything better than going to a semiformal dance with Lauren.

Allison let out a whoop and threw her arms around Lauren, then around Ben. "Oh, you guys are just the best!" she squealed, dancing around the room.

Lauren rolled her eyes again and looked at Ben. "What have we done?" she whispered.

Ben shook his head at her and smiled. He didn't know what he'd done, but he was certain he was going to love it.

Chapter Sixteen

That weekend, Lauren drove into Idaho Falls with Allison to go dress shopping. It was something she'd insisted she couldn't afford—until her mom had gotten wind of the fact that she was going to a semiformal dance. Since Lauren had only gone to one formal dance in high school, her mom had quickly put up the money for a dress. Lauren felt a little guilty about accepting it, but she sensed this was her mom's way of sharing some of the excitement of a big dance with her only daughter. Lauren didn't have the heart to tell her that she was only going to the dance with a friend, but it didn't matter. Her mom's enthusiasm had won out in the end.

Allison and Lauren spent the morning cruising the mall, and Allison was lucky enough to find the perfect dress—an ankle-length royal blue dress that complimented her petite frame perfectly. But by lunchtime, Lauren still hadn't found anything she liked. They grabbed a bite to eat, then left the mall to hit a few of the smaller boutiques around town. Lauren was losing hope of finding anything she liked until they walked into a bridal shop. Allison let out a gasp as she rushed over to lift a dark burgundy dress from the rack and held it up for Lauren's approval.

When Lauren tried it on in the fitting room, she had to admit, it was perfect. The silky, burgundy material hung almost to the floor, and not only did it make her skin look creamier and her eyes sparkle and dance with life, but the color was the perfect complement to her auburn tresses. She loved its straight, clean lines and the way it emphasized her slender curves and slim waist.

She walked out to model it for Allison, and her friend let out a low whistle. "If that doesn't knock Ben's socks off, nothing will."

Lauren rolled her eyes. "I'm not trying to knock Ben's socks off. We're only going as friends, remember?"

"Maybe so, but it'll still knock his socks off," Allison said with a wink. Then she turned to the clerk. "We'll take it."

The next two weeks sailed by, and Lauren couldn't help looking forward to the Thanksgiving break. Ben, on the other hand, seemed to avoid the topic of Thanksgiving altogether. After much prodding, Lauren finally managed to get him to open up about it.

"It's never been a holiday I looked forward to," he admitted hesitantly. "None of my relatives were into the family gathering thing, so if we weren't spending the holiday skiing in the Alps or vacationing in the Bahamas, we mostly went to my father's colleagues' houses for dinner parties." He grimaced. "It was just a bunch of overworked, pompous lawyers patting themselves on the back."

"Well, why don't you come home with me and spend Thanksgiving with my family?" she suggested. "My mom would love to have you, and I'm sure Jack would be thrilled too. It would give me a chance to show you what a real Thanksgiving is all about."

Ben hesitated. "Well, if you're sure your parents wouldn't mind…."

"They won't," she insisted. "Besides, all my brothers and their wives and kids come over for the holiday, and it's pandemonium anyway. One more mouth to feed would not be an imposition. Trust me, you'll love it."

When he agreed to come, Lauren was thrilled. She couldn't bear the thought of Ben staying in his college apartment alone during the holiday. He deserved better than that. Inviting him to share Thanksgiving with her family was the least she could do. Besides, she had to admit it sounded like fun, having Ben there to talk to and joke with.

As Thanksgiving approached, Ben emailed his sister to let her know what he was doing for Thanksgiving because he knew she'd be worrying about him spending the holiday alone. His assurances that he was going to be enjoying the holiday with Lauren's family brought a cheery email from her.

"*Lauren, huh?*" she'd typed. "*Sounds serious! Have fun, and keep me posted.*"

He'd smiled at that, not yet able to open his heart and tell anyone—including his sister—just how much it meant to him to be invited by Lauren to spend Thanksgiving with her family. It may not have seemed like much to her, but to him, it meant she trusted him and felt comfortable enough with him to, in a sense, invite him into her family.

But spending Thanksgiving with Lauren wasn't the only thing he was excited about. When the day of the Thanksgiving semiformal finally arrived, spending a night out at a semiformal dance with her was all he could think about. He knew that they were only going together under the pretense of supporting Allison, but even so, he could hardly wait to enjoy the evening with Lauren, and have the chance to hold her in his arms as they danced.

As he showered and dressed in his Sunday best, he found himself hoping that, in a setting such as this, maybe, just maybe, Lauren might finally be able to see him as more than a friend. He wasn't exactly sure how that would happen, but when he'd prayed fervently about it the night before, pleading for some divine intervention, a calm assurance had filled his soul, telling him that things would work out. He only hoped the reassurances he was feeling were truly an answer to prayer, and not just his own feelings manifesting themselves as such.

With one final glance in the mirror, he said yet another quick prayer, then headed out the door to pick up Lauren.

"Lauren, would you please hold still?" Allison complained in frustration. "I can't zip this thing if you keep moving around."

"Sorry," Lauren mumbled, trying her best to stop fidgeting. But it wasn't easy. For some unfathomable reason, she was nervous.

You're only going to the dance with Ben, she told herself for the hundredth time. *He's a friend. It's not like this is a date or anything.*

Even so, she felt jumpy and jittery, and when a knock sounded at the front door, she nearly jumped out of her skin.

Allison grinned. "For someone who's going to the dance with 'just a friend,' you're sure a basket case." A moment later they heard Melia call from the front room that Trevor was there, and Allison glanced down at herself. "He's right on time. How do I look?"

Lauren eyed her friend critically, but Allison looked incredible in her flowing blue dress with her makeup and hair done to perfection. "You look great."

Allison beamed. "Thanks. So do you, by the way. Ben's gonna bust something when he sees you."

"Yeah, right," Lauren drawled, rolling her eyes. But she felt pleased by the compliment just the same.

"Well, I guess I'd better not keep Trevor waiting. We'll meet you there, okay?"

When Lauren nodded, Allison hurried into the front room to greet her date. Once she was alone, Lauren took several deep breaths, trying to calm the butterflies in her stomach. She didn't understand why it was so important to her that she look her best, but she wandered over to her bedroom mirror to make sure she did.

Staring at her reflection, Lauren shook her head in amazement. She hardly recognized herself. Her full-length burgundy dress complemented her slender form and creamy complexion, and the makeup Allison had applied drew attention to her light brown eyes and high cheekbones. But what she loved the most was her hair. Allison had swept it up into an elegant French twist, and had left a couple of long strands curled into loose ringlets around her face. The effect was stunning. She only hoped Ben would appreciate the change.

Trying not to wipe her damp hands on her dress, she paced anxiously around her room, waiting for Ben to arrive. The minutes passed, and when she finally heard a knock at the front door, her heart leaped into her throat. She heard Melia open the door and greet somebody, then the sound of Ben's voice and the deep, rich sound of his easy laughter reached her ears, causing a swarm of butterflies to take up permanent residence in her stomach.

He's just a friend, she reminded herself over and over again in an attempt to maintain some control. Taking one last deep breath, she smoothed the front of her dress, then headed for the living room.

As she emerged from the hall and saw Ben standing in the living room, her breath caught in her throat. He looked more handsome than ever. He was wearing a charcoal gray suit that made his shoulders look even broader than usual, and his crisp, white shirt really set off his olive complexion. She had to smile, though, at his flashy red tie with a collage of bold yellow geometric shapes on it. One thing he didn't have was boring taste in ties.

She cleared her throat softly, causing him to turn. When he did, his smile froze and his eyes widened in a look of open admiration. For several long moments he didn't say a word. Then a smile flashed across his face and he quickly closed the distance between them.

"Wow, Lauren, you look amazing!" he exclaimed, his beautiful brown eyes sparkling as he continued to take in her appearance. "I can hardly believe it's you."

Any trace of nervousness vanished and she started to grin. "Wow, you really know how to compliment a girl," she retorted, planting her hands on her hips and scowling at him playfully.

His face turned a dark crimson as he realized his faux pas. "Oh, I didn't mean... I mean, you always look great... it's just...."

Lauren laughed as she threaded her arm through his and gave him a tug toward the door. "Ben, do yourself a favor. Shut up."

The comfortable familiarity returned as Ben helped her on with her coat and they walked the short distance through the cool night air to the Manwaring Center. When they arrived, they hung up their coats and followed the music upstairs. As they stepped into the ballroom, Lauren let out a little gasp.

The place had been transformed. In the dim light, slowly dancing couples formed moving silhouettes against the hundreds of tiny white lights that twinkled merrily from the walls. Dozens of small round tables swathed in silky, silver tablecloths had been set up around the edge of the dance floor, their elegant candle-filled centerpieces glowing softly upon the faces of couples either resting or enjoying the refreshments being served from a long, cloth-covered table near the back of the hall.

Lauren stared, mesmerized for several long moments, soaking in the atmosphere. Now that she was here, she felt jittery with excitement.

"Wow, it's packed," Ben observed, nodding toward the crowded dance floor. "Where are we supposed to meet Allison and her date?"

Lauren looked around the room slowly. "I don't see them, but in this crowd, they could be anywhere."

"Well, how do you feel about getting out on the dance floor?" he asked with a smile. "Maybe if we get out there and move around, we'll stumble across them."

Lauren grinned at him eagerly. "You're on."

To her surprise, Lauren discovered that Ben was a great dancer. She wasn't as good as he was, but she felt fairly competent on the dance floor, and together they had a great time. Several fast dances later, they decided they were ready for something to drink. They made their way to the refreshment table where Ben picked up two cups of punch and handed one to Lauren.

She'd almost finished hers when she caught sight of her roommate. "Hey, there's Allison and Trevor," she said, gesturing off to their right.

Ben followed her gaze and spotted Allison and Trevor sitting at a table near the back of the room. They were holding hands and smiling at each other as they talked. "It looks like Allison didn't have anything to worry about. They look like they're having a great time."

Lauren nodded. "Yeah, it does. Let's go say hi."

They skirted the edge of the dance floor, and as they approached her table, Allison looked up and gave them a bright smile. Introductions were made, and for the next little while they talked and laughed as they enjoyed the music. A short time later, the DJ cued up an upbeat, fast song, and they all decided to dance. They spent the song trying to one-up each other with fancy steps, and improvised to the beat as they danced. By the time the song was over, they were all laughing and out of breath.

They remained on the dance floor as they waited for the next song to begin, and when it did, Lauren's smile froze. It was a slow song. She'd never been in Ben's arms other than an occasional comforting hug now and then, and the idea of being so close to him was doing funny things to her insides.

Ben sensed her uneasiness, but he just smiled softly and held out his arms invitingly. When she looked up at his face, his warm brown eyes were reassuring. "I promise, I won't bite," he whispered.

Lauren laughed nervously. She stepped self-consciously into his arms, slipping her hand into his as his right arm encircled her waist. She felt a strange, tingling sensation where his hand rested warmly on the small of her back, and her breathing felt shallow as they started to sway to the music.

Leaning forward, Ben whispered into her ear, "Relax. This is supposed to be fun."

She shivered slightly as his breath warmed her cheek, and she forced herself to take a deep breath. *This is just Ben,* she reminded herself reassuringly. *You don't have to worry about any romantic entanglements, so just relax and enjoy yourself for once.*

With a bit of effort, she forced herself to relax in his arms, and it wasn't long before she found herself enjoying his closeness. When the song ended, Lauren felt strangely disappointed as loud, upbeat music started to play.

The next two hours flew by in a sort of magical daze as Lauren danced song after song with Ben, sometimes with Trevor and Allison nearby, sometimes not. As the last half hour of the dance came, they decided to take a break from dancing and step out into the lobby where it was cooler. They walked over to the floor-to-ceiling windows overlooking the darkened quad and stood in companionable silence for several moments.

"So, are you having a good time?" Ben asked, leaning one shoulder against the wall and slipping his hands into his pockets.

"The time of my life," she admitted with a smile. "The only dance like this I've ever been to was a complete disaster, so I've always wondered what all the hype was about. Now I know."

Ben's brow furrowed. "You've only been to one prom?"

She nodded her head. "Yeah."

He stared at her in disbelief. "I find that hard to believe," he said quietly. "Those guys in your high school must've been blind."

Feeling a flush creep across her cheeks, she looked down at her feet and smiled sheepishly. "Well, I don't know about that, but... thank you."

As Ben stood there looking at her, it occurred to him that she obviously didn't know how truly amazing she was. She'd been hurt so much in the past that she had no clue about the devastating effect she could have on his heart.

Just then the strains of a popular romantic ballad came from the ballroom, and Lauren let out a little gasp. "Oh, I love this song!" she exclaimed excitedly. "Come on, let's go dance."

He smiled at her enthusiasm as he followed her back into the ballroom and onto the dance floor. Then, as if it were the most natural thing in the world, he took her into his arms and pulled her close. To his surprise, she nestled her face against his chest, and he wondered if she could hear the furious pounding of his heart.

Closing his eyes, he dropped his head to hers and breathed deeply, savoring the lingering scent of her perfume. Everything about her seemed so familiar to him, so comforting, and he was suddenly overcome by the incredible sensation of having her in his arms. It felt unbelievably right to be with her like this, with her head tucked beneath his chin as they swayed slowly to the music. For a few blissful moments, he let himself imagine they were in love, and that she felt as much for him as he did for her.

When the last strains of the music started to fade, he lifted his head from hers and reluctantly loosened his arm from around her waist. As if sensing his gaze, Lauren hesitantly raised her face to his. He was surprised to see a hint of the same happiness he was feeling reflected in her eyes.

He lifted a tentative hand and swept back a long ringlet from her face, tucking it gently behind her ear. "Lauren..." he said quietly, his voice a mere whisper. Words failed him as his fingers lingered on her cheek. He slowly studied her face, taking in the beautiful light brown eyes, the smooth curve of her jaw… her full, red lips.

His gaze was drawn back to her eyes and they stared at each other for a long moment, the world around them gently fading into the background. Ben's heart started to pound wildly as he closed the distance between them almost imperceptibly. When their lips were only a breath apart, he paused. He searched her eyes intently, as if gauging her reaction. But then she tipped her face up to his, and that was all the encouragement he needed.

Giving in to the intense desire to kiss her, he closed the remaining distance between them. Then, as if in slow motion, he leaned down and tentatively touched his lips to hers. An electric shock jolted through him as their lips met, and his arms involuntarily tightened around her, drawing her closer. He closed his eyes, savoring the intoxicating sensation of his lips on hers. He half expected her to pull away but instead, she slipped her arms around his neck and responded to his kiss until he was breathless.

When they finally parted, Ben opened his eyes slowly, taking in Lauren's kiss-reddened lips and the slight flush to her cheeks. Something deep inside him knew that what had just passed between them was something truly special.

A moment later, Lauren's lids slowly fluttered open. As they stared deeply into each other's eyes, the expression in hers told him she'd been as moved by their kiss as he was. But then, before he could comprehend what was happening, Lauren's eyes widened in shock and she jerked backward, dropping her arms from around his neck. She stared at him for a moment in shocked silence; then, lifting a shaking hand to her lips, she backed away slowly for a step or two before she turned and bolted for the door.

"Lauren!" he called after her, his heart in his throat. He tried to hurry after her, but with the crowd of couples blocking his path, he could only watch in horror as she ran through the ballroom doors and disappeared into the lobby.

• • •

Lauren didn't stop running until she was outside and could no longer hear the music from the upstairs ballroom. She stood at the top of the steps, sucking in long, gasping breaths as the tears streamed down her face. Expecting Ben to come bursting out of the building after her at any second, she hurried down the steps and around the corner of the building. She spotted a bench along the path and sank down onto its cold surface in desolation.

What did you just do? she accused silently. *How could you have kissed Ben? You're supposed to be friends—best friends, as a matter of fact. What were you thinking?*

Trying to command her brain to work, she tried to remember exactly what had happened. Had he initiated the kiss or had she? She wasn't entirely sure, and she was even less sure about how to classify the myriad of emotions flooding through her. The only thing she was sure about was that his kiss had awakened something deep inside of her, something she had locked away long ago and had refused to let herself feel again.

The sound of approaching footsteps made her heart stop, and she looked up to see Ben coming around the corner of the building, out of breath and looking scared. "Lauren! I've been looking everywhere for you! What are you doing out here without your coat? It's freezing."

Without hesitation, he slipped out of his suit jacket and draped it around her shoulders. When she didn't throw it to the ground and stomp on it, he took it as a good sign and sat down beside her. He studied her carefully, and what he saw made his heart plummet. Her eyes were red and puffy and she looked as miserable as he felt.

"Lauren, I'm *so* sorry," he insisted emphatically. "I don't know what came over me. I must've gotten carried away by the music and the atmosphere—"

"Ben, please," she cut him off, getting shakily to her feet. "I just—I can't talk about this right now."

"Lauren, we have to," he pleaded, standing up beside her. "I know I hurt you, and I'm sorry. Please don't run away from this. You mean too much to me to let our friendship be hurt by this...."

Lauren saw the grief-stricken look in his eyes and heard the pleading in his voice, and suddenly she felt more miserable than ever. Feeling fresh tears start to spill down her cheeks, she quickly turned away and shook her head. "I'm sorry, Ben, I just can't deal with this right now. Please... take me home."

Ben stared at her forlornly for several long, silent moments, then finally nodded. "I'll go get your coat."

The walk back to her apartment was a solemn one, and Ben spent the entire time wading through a sea of guilt. This was all his fault. He'd moved too fast, even after he'd promised to let her set the pace in their relationship, and now he'd ruined everything. He knew that if he couldn't repair the damage he'd done, he was never going to forgive himself.

When they finally reached her apartment, he gathered what little courage he had left and stepped in front of her, blocking the door. "Lauren, wait. There's got to be something I can do or say that will convince you not to shut me out of your life. Please. Our friendship means too much to me to let it end this way."

Lauren looked into the gentle, pleading brown eyes she'd come to know so well over the past few months, and she felt herself waiver. But the feeling quickly vanished when the memories of their kiss surfaced... the way his eyes had sparkled when they were only inches from hers, the warm, soft touch of his lips, the feel of his arms as they tightened around her waist... and the confusion and guilt she felt afterward, knowing she'd just kissed one of her very best friends.

"I'm—I'm sorry," she managed, struggling to contain her unstable emotions. "I've got to go." And with that, she pushed past Ben and rushed into the apartment, slamming the door behind her.

When she was safely shut in her bedroom, she collapsed on her bed and let the tears flow. As much as she longed to have things as they were, she knew that everything was different. And she had no idea how she was ever going to make things right again.

By the time Allison came home, humming happily, Lauren's sobs had decreased, but the ache was still painfully fresh.

"Oh, I had the most *amazing* evening," Allison sung, spinning around excitedly. "Trevor is so...." She let her sentence trail off when she noticed her friend's tear-streaked cheeks. "Lauren, what's wrong? Did something happen between you and Ben?"

Lauren fought back a fresh round of tears as she told her friend about the kiss. "After it happened, I guess I kind of freaked," she admitted. "I mean... he's one of my very best friends. How could this have happened?"

"Lauren, let me ask you something," Allison began seriously. "When he kissed you, did you kiss him back?"

"Yes, I kissed him back!" Lauren exclaimed, wringing her hands anxiously. "Didn't you listen to a word I said?"

Ignoring her friend's growing agitation, Allison continued, "And what happened *after* he kissed you?"

Lauren sobered. "I—I took off. I just had to get out of there. I felt guilty and confused.... Oh, Allison, what am I going to do? Our friendship's never going to be the same again. I'm supposed to be writing off guys forever, but I go and do something like this. And with Ben! What was I thinking?"

Allison reached out to squeeze her friend's hands comfortingly. "It sounds to me like you were just following your heart. There's no shame in that. Besides, Ben's a really great guy. You should feel lucky to have someone as great as him in love with you."

Lauren's heart skipped a beat as she looked up at her friend in shock. "In—in love with me?"

Allison let out her breath in a rush and rolled her eyes skyward. "You've got to be kidding! How could you not know that he loves you? Geez, girl, how blind can you be? *I* can see it, everyone who knows you can see it. What's it going to take to make *you* see it?"

Lauren shook her head slowly. "Well, I... I guess I knew that he liked me, but I had no idea...."

"Lauren, he doesn't just *like* you. He's head over heels in love with you. But you've been so dead set on not having your heart broken that you haven't been able to see what's right in front of you."

"But—" Lauren stammered, feeling shell-shocked. "But I can't feel that way about Ben! He's just my friend...."

"A friend who loves you," Allison emphasized, looking at her sternly. "Come on, Lauren, you're perfect for each other. Don't push him away because you're afraid of being hurt."

The hint of a smile tugged at Lauren's lips. "Jack said something like that not long ago."

"Well, Jack's a smart guy," Allison responded lightly. Then her smile softened and she gave Lauren's hands another squeeze. "Lauren, listen to Jack—and me. Ben's too good a guy to lose. He loves you more than anything, and I know he'd move heaven and earth to make you happy. Don't you think that kind of love's worth the risk?"

Lauren hesitated. "I—I don't know what to think right now. So much has happened, and I'm kind of having a hard time processing everything, you know?"

She nodded. "Yeah, I know. But promise me you'll at least think about it, okay?"

Lauren nodded reluctantly and Allison gave her a supportive hug before going out to the kitchen for a snack, leaving her alone.

Lauren changed into her pajamas and climbed into bed, her mind going over and over everything that had happened. So Ben loved her. She could hardly believe it. But then she realized she shouldn't have been too shocked; there'd been lots of signs over the past few months that should have tipped her off... if only she'd opened her eyes to them. But the big question was, did she love him?

Lauren had automatically pushed this thought out of her head for months, but now she tried to coax her repressed thoughts and feelings to the surface. *Did* she think about Ben that way? *Did* she love him?

She shook her head silently. What difference would it make even if she did? Every guy she'd thought she loved had ended up breaking her heart. And this time, she knew that things were even more risky. She and Ben were practically best friends. She turned to him for everything, *depended* on him for everything. If she were crazy enough to let herself become involved, what would happen if their newfound love went awry? She'd be lost, devastated, heartbroken. She didn't think she could handle that.

Come on, Lauren, the little voice in her head persisted. *Stop being so rational and just answer the question. Do you love him?*

Lauren forced herself to think long and hard. She was used to treating Ben as a friend—a great friend—and she loved being with him more than anyone else in the world. Whenever something good or bad happened, he was the first one she thought of to run and tell about it. He was gentle, kind, and patient, and he was always there for her when she needed him. He listened, consoled, offered words of comfort, and never once pushed her to be somebody she wasn't. Most importantly, she felt safe with him in a way she'd never known. The thought of *not* having him around to run to, to share things with, or to just talk and laugh with… it scared her.

She thought back to the scene in the library when she'd seen Elena flirting with Ben. She'd gotten angry with him, and he'd accused her of being jealous, and later, so had Allison. She'd quickly denied it, but now as she thought about Ben with another girl, she realized they'd been right. She *had* been jealous.

And that's when it finally hit her. She *did* love Ben—*had* loved him for quite some time. Somehow, when she hadn't been paying attention, he'd crept his way into her heart and made it impossible for her to think of a future without him. Why hadn't she realized it before? Had she simply stifled those feelings, afraid of where they might lead?

The possibility of what could be scared her. The idea of opening herself up and loving someone was scary. She'd done it before and had been burned in the process. Was she willing to risk it again?

Okay, she thought, *say you don't open up, yet somehow manage to remain friends—sooner or later he would start dating. Would you be able to stand seeing him with someone else?* The answer was a resounding *no.*

So where did that leave her?

With a heavy sigh, Lauren rolled over in bed and pulled the covers more firmly up around her. Neither choice was going to be an easy one to make.

Chapter Seventeen

Lauren spent the next few days avoiding Ben as she struggled to come to terms with everything that had happened. She still had no idea what she was going to do, and making up her mind was proving to be no easy task. She went through her classes in a daze, unable to concentrate, unable to do anything but think about the decisions she had to make. But by Wednesday morning, the day before Thanksgiving—and the first official day of Thanksgiving break—she still hadn't come to any conclusions.

With no classes to use as a distraction, Lauren paced the apartment anxiously, knowing that in just a few short hours, she and Allison would be going home to Idaho Falls for the holiday... and Ben would be joining them.

Her stomach tied itself up in knots every time she thought about having to spend the next four days with him. It wasn't that she didn't want to see him, she just didn't know what to say to him or how to act around him now that she recognized her true feelings. But she knew it wasn't fair to renege on her invitation to have Ben spend Thanksgiving with her family, especially since he had no place else to go.

As the time drew closer for them to pick him up, she found her apprehension growing. She went into her bedroom where Allison was packing a couple of bags and asked, "Are you sure Ben said he still wanted to go with us? He hasn't changed his mind or anything?"

"Yeah, when I talked to him a couple of days ago, I reassured him that we both still wanted him to come." Allison looked up from her packing. "Lauren, what is with you? Ever since the dance you've been acting weird. Granted, acting weird after what happened is normal, but this is too weird. What's going on?"

Lauren leaned up against the doorframe and sighed. "I don't think I can face Ben this afternoon, let alone for the next four days."

"Because he kissed you at the dance? Lauren, we've already been over this. He—"

"No," Lauren interrupted, unable to look Allison in the eyes, "because I love him."

Allison's jaw dropped. When she recovered from the shock, she let out a squeal and threw her arms around her friend. "Lauren, that's so great!" she exclaimed ecstatically, hugging her tightly.

But Lauren pulled back and shook her head, the familiar feeling of panic starting to rise in her throat. "No, Allison, it's *not* great! I can't love him! He'll just end up breaking my heart, and then where will I be? We're best friends. I couldn't stand to lose him."

"You're not going to lose him," Allison insisted, "*because* you were friends first. Most people in a relationship never start off with a foundation like that." When Lauren remained quiet, Allison sighed in frustration. "Come on, Lauren, I know you haven't exactly had the best of luck in relationships, but Ben's different. He's totally and completely amazing, *and* he loves you. You owe it to him—and to yourself—to tell him how you feel."

Lauren felt a tiny sliver of hope work its way into her heart. "And what then?"

"Well, he'd start off by telling you what a lunkhead you were for not realizing how he felt about you sooner," she said, a slow, teasing smile spreading across her face, "then he'd totally sweep you off your feet with the most romantic kiss of all time, and you two would get married and live happily ever after."

Lauren contemplated Allison's words. It sounded so easy, but she knew it wasn't. The fairy tale happily-ever-after thing hardly ever happened. But could it happen to her?

With a sigh, she pulled her bags out of the closet and started to pack. She had a feeling she was going to find out soon enough if there was a fairy tale ending in her future.

Lauren was a basket case by the time she pulled up in front of Ben's apartment. How was she supposed to act around him? What was she supposed to say? She didn't have much time to figure it out before they spotted him coming out of his apartment with his garment bag and a small suitcase.

He slid into the back seat with his bags and glanced warily at Lauren, then at Allison. "Hi," he said tentatively.

Allison greeted him cheerfully, but Lauren only muttered "Hello" from the driver's seat before pulling out of the lot and concentrating on the road.

Ben's heart sank. This was the first time he'd actually seen her since the semiformal, and it hurt to see her acting so cool and aloof. With a heavy sigh, he realized he wasn't sure if he could handle spending the next few days with her giving him the cold shoulder. It would hurt too much to be around her, knowing that he'd blown his chances with her for good.

Trying to maintain a cheerfulness he didn't feel, he chatted with Allison for most of the twenty-minute drive, all the while sneaking looks at Lauren. They were almost to Idaho Falls when Allison had apparently had enough of Lauren's silence.

"So, Lauren. Who all's going to be at your house?"

Lauren shrugged. "Pretty much everyone. Jack's already there, and Connor should be in tonight, but everyone else will probably come over in the morning."

When she didn't say anything else, Ben and Allison exchanged a quick glance, then fell into silence for the remainder of the ride.

It seemed like an eternity before Lauren pulled into Allison's driveway to drop her off. She thought she had her emotions under control, but as Allison opened the door to climb out, Lauren felt a sudden urge to panic. Allison was her moral support. Her presence was enough to force Ben to keep the conversation on safe topics. When she and Ben were finally alone, what was going to keep him from wanting to talk to her about what had happened? She wasn't ready to do that. Not yet.

Setting the emergency brake, Lauren jumped out of the car and hurried to the trunk to help Allison get her things. "Allison, you can't leave," she whispered frantically, giving her friend a panicked look. "What am I going to say to Ben?"

Allison chuckled softly and whispered, "Lauren, you're going to be fine. Just remember, the sooner you tell him how you feel and talk this out with him, the better. Trust me."

Lauren sighed heavily as she shut the trunk. "Yeah, I guess. I just don't know how to do it."

"It's easy. You start with 'I love you' and go from there." Allison smiled, then gave Lauren a supportive hug. "Let me know how it goes." And with that, she turned and hurried into the house, leaving Lauren standing alone beside the car.

It was several moments before Lauren could make her feet move. When she finally did, she walked back to the driver's side and climbed back behind the wheel, her heart pounding so loud she was sure Ben could hear it. She pretended not to notice the curious look Ben gave her as she fumbled with her seatbelt, but knowing he was studying her intently only flustered her further. When she tried to put the car in reverse, she ended up grinding the gears.

Ben suppressed a smile. "Everything okay?" he asked, noting the sudden coloring to her cheeks.

"Yeah, everything's fine," she bit back as she finally managed to put the car into reverse and back out of the driveway.

In spite of her aggravated response, Ben could tell she was flustered, and he wasn't sure what to make out of it. Did she really hate him so much that she didn't even want to be in the same car with him? Or was she just feeling as awkward about what had happened as he was?

Unable to come up with an answer, he stared out his window as they drove back toward Lauren's house. When they pulled into the driveway, neither spoke as they got out and walked into the living room. A wonderful aroma of freshly baked bread filled the air, and Ben breathed in deeply. It was definitely a smell he could get used to.

Just then they heard the sound of approaching footsteps, and a moment later, Lauren's mom, wearing a flour-dusted apron that covered her pretty, tan pantsuit, came into the room.

"You two made it," she exclaimed happily as she hurried over to give each of them a hug. "How was the drive?"

"Uneventful," Lauren answered casually. "It's so quiet. Where is everybody?"

"I sent your dad and Jack to run some errands for me, but they should be back by dinner." Then Sister Holt turned to Ben and smiled warmly. "We're so thrilled you could spend Thanksgiving with us."

Ben smiled back. "Thanks so much for having me. I hope I won't be an imposition."

Sister Holt laughed. "Not a chance. Any extra pair of hands to help with the pies is greatly appreciated." She winked at him, then turned to her daughter. "Why don't you guys get your bags and put them away. Then when your father and brother get back, you won't have anything left to do but visit. If you want, you can help me fill the dozen or so pie crusts I just finished making."

Ben's stomach grumbled at the thought. He'd always heard about Thanksgivings with homemade pies and other great, homemade food, but he'd never had a chance to experience them. Now was his chance. Everything would be perfect, if only….

He glanced over at Lauren's carefully masked expression and sighed. Somehow he suspected that not everything about the holiday was going to be perfect.

As Sister Holt bustled back into the kitchen, Lauren turned wordlessly back to the door and headed for the car. Ben had no choice but to follow. He collected his bags, then went back into the house and followed Lauren silently up the stairs. When they reached the landing, Lauren lost her grip on her bag and scrambled to keep it from falling back down the steps.

Ben quickly made a grab for it. "Why don't you let me carry this for you?" he offered quietly.

For a brief moment Ben thought she might tell him she could carry her own bag, but then she gave a little shrug and handed it to him. They walked down the hall and into Lauren's room, but she kept her gaze averted as she reached for her suitcase. As she did, their hands touched, and Ben felt an electrical current pass between them. Lauren obviously felt it, too, because she jumped back and quickly let go, causing the bag to thump to the floor.

She glanced up at him nervously, then averted her gaze once again and said quietly, "Um, thanks." She was silent for a moment, then gestured to the doorway. "My mom's set up the guest room for you again. You remember where it is?"

When he nodded, she walked past him out into the hall. "Good. Then I'll see you downstairs."

As she disappeared around the corner, Ben sighed. *Oh yeah, this is going to be fun*, he thought dismally. *She won't talk to me, won't look at me, and acts like she's been bitten by a snake when I touch her. I can tell this is going to be a great vacation.*

He set his bags on the bed in the guest room, then went down to the kitchen to try to make the best out of his four days there.

For the next couple of hours, Ben, Lauren, and her mom filled the pies in preparation for tomorrow's feast. Sister Holt happily carried on a conversation with him about his courses at school, his experience with the gospel in the past year, and everything else she could think of. He was glad to see that she didn't seem to notice Lauren's unusual silence.

At one point, Ben had finished filling a pie and went to place it on the table at the same time Lauren was walking back from the table. They nearly collided, and for a moment, their eyes met. In that second he thought he saw a flash of something in her eyes that he hadn't seen there before, a softness and a vulnerability that seemed so out of place when compared with the relatively cool exterior she'd shown him all day. But as quickly as it had come, it was gone, and as she turned away, he had to wonder if he'd really seen it at all.

Before Ben could dwell on it further, Jack and Brother Holt returned home, and the reunion between Jack and Ben was energetic. Then Lauren's next oldest brother, Connor, arrived, and introductions were made. He was as nice and as outgoing as Jack, and Ben liked him immediately.

As Lauren's brothers and Ben continued to talk and laugh together, Lauren couldn't help noticing how accepting everyone was being of Ben. It was clear that everyone was eager to welcome him into their home, and Lauren wasn't sure how she felt about that. It was almost as if her parents and brothers were accepting Ben into their family, and that only increased Lauren's nervousness.

Several times she felt like shouting, *Stop treating him like a member of the family! You all assume he and I are an item. What if things go horribly wrong and I have to explain why the guy you all like is no longer around? Do you think I can handle that kind of pressure?*

No one seemed to notice her mounting tension—except Ben. When dinner was finally ready, Sister Holt assigned Lauren and Ben to set the table. Ben went to help Lauren get the plates from the cupboard, and he saw it as a rare opportunity to catch a moment with her alone.

As she pulled down a stack of plates and handed them to him, he gathered his courage and told her quietly, "I know my being here is awkward for you after what happened, and I'm sorry. Maybe I shouldn't have come."

Surprised he'd think that, she turned to him. For the first time since they'd arrived, she saw the strain in his eyes that he'd obviously hid so well from her family. She immediately felt horrible. "No, I'm sorry," she said, softening. "I didn't mean to give you the impression that I didn't want you here, or that I'm angry with you, because I'm not." She paused, and he looked at her, his eyes suddenly hopeful. Unable to meet his gaze, she said, "I'm just… I don't know what I am. Maybe confused… or maybe…." But before she could finish, Jack came over to help them carry dishes, and any further attempt at conversation was halted. Ben cast an apologetic look at Lauren, and she turned back to her task with a sigh, discouraged that the opportunity to talk had passed them by.

At dinner, she sat quietly and listened as everyone talked and laughed. She pushed her food around on her plate, her appetite practically non-existent as she listened to Ben answer questions about school and professors and his tutoring job. She found herself tuning out after a while, and was surprised when she heard someone calling her name.

She looked up and found everyone looking at her expectantly. "I'm sorry, what?"

Her dad laughed. "Lauren, you're off in your own little world. Don't you know it's rude to have a guest and not even participate in the conversation?"

Lauren felt her cheeks flush. "Sorry," she said quietly. "I had some big tests this week, and I guess I'm a little tired."

Brother Holt nodded. "Understandable, I guess. So, tell me. How *are* your classes going? Are you holding your own?"

"Yeah, I'm doing good. I love my classes, and I got 'A's' on my midterms," she told him proudly. "Except for a 'B' in my anatomy class. That one's been really tough."

Instead of the praise she'd been expecting, her dad frowned. "Struggling a little, huh? Well, don't worry. I'm sure you can pull that grade up by the end of the term. Remember, if you're serious about wanting to be a physical therapist, those are the classes a big school's really going to look at."

Unexpected tears filled Lauren's eyes, and she lowered her gaze to her plate, hoping to hide them by pretending to be occupied with her dinner. She felt Ben's eyes on her, but she didn't dare look up. If she did, and she saw any sympathy in them from his knowing how hard she'd worked for that B, she knew she was going to lose it.

The conversation drifted to other things, and Lauren quietly excused herself. She carried her plate to the sink, then grabbed her coat from the closet and slipped, unnoticed, out the back door. She barely made it outside before the tears began to fall. Taking the steps down from the back porch in one giant leap, she started half-walking, half-running across the back field, eager to put some distance between her and the house.

How can he be so callous? she wondered. *And in front of a roomful of people like that. Does he really think so little of me that he has to degrade me every chance he gets?*

She stumbled blindly in the knee-deep snow as her tears blurred her vision, but she kept going. Even the sound of the back door slamming shut, or the sound of feet crunching in the snow behind her didn't slow her down.

"Lauren, wait!"

She recognized Ben's voice, but more than anything, she just wanted to be left alone. "Go away!" she choked out, unable to say anything more.

But the sound of footsteps in the snow grew closer, and a moment later, Ben's hand was on her shoulder. He turned her around to face him. Lauren took one look at the sympathetic expression on his face and a sob escaped her throat.

"Why does he do that?" she demanded tearfully. "Why does he have to be so cold hearted? Doesn't he know how hard I worked to get that 'B'? And what about all my 'A's'? Did he even congratulate me on those? All he cares about is that I got one lousy 'B,' like that makes me some kind of failure or something. Nothing I do is ever good enough for him!"

Ben reached up to brush the glistening tears from her cheek. "I think fathers *do* want what's best for us, but somewhere along the line their good intentions become hurtful. They probably don't even realize they're doing it. Believe me, I know."

The sincerity in his voice caught her attention, and as she looked into his eyes, she realized he did know how she felt. He'd never talked much about his father, but she suspected that their relationship had been strained even before his father had disowned him.

"Maybe," she admitted tearfully, "but it doesn't make it hurt any less."

"I know it doesn't," he agreed. "But Lauren, you've got to talk to him; tell him how you feel. You've obviously harbored this resentment toward him for a long time, and it's beginning to eat you up inside."

Lauren turned away from him and dropped her gaze. "I can't," she whispered.

"Why not? What's the worst that can happen? To hear him say you don't measure up to your brothers in his eyes? Well, you already feel like that, so why not give him the benefit of the doubt? There could be a completely different explanation for his behavior. It might surprise you."

A flicker of hope danced across her eyes. "You think so?"

Ben shrugged. "You won't know until you ask him."

She sniffled, then finally nodded. "Okay, I think I will."

"Good. I think a talk between you two has been a long time in coming."

"Yeah, you're probably right," she admitted quietly. "Thanks."

Ben felt his heart contract as she timidly met his gaze. It seemed like an eternity since she'd actually looked willingly into his eyes. As she did, he realized just how much he'd missed the easy camaraderie they'd shared.

He was unable to tear his gaze away from her as he watched her brush away a few stray tears, then turn her gaze to the open expanse of field behind her house. The winter breeze blew a strand of her hair across her face and Ben reached out to brush it back, his fingers lingering on her cheek.

For a second he thought she was going to pull away, but when she didn't, he felt an enormous sense of relief. "I've missed you," he ventured quietly. "I've been so worried—worried that you'd never forgive me, worried that I'd ruined everything between us. You have no idea how sorry I am that I hurt you."

Lauren shook her head slowly. "You didn't hurt me," she returned quietly. "I'm sorry I made you think you did, and that I didn't talk to you sooner about what happened, but I couldn't." She paused, then averted her eyes and started scuffing at the snow with her foot. "Allison said something that really made me think, and I've been so confused...."

"I know, and I'm so sorry—"

"Will you stop saying that?" she said in exasperation, finally looking up at him. "This isn't entirely your fault. I mean, I was there, too...."

"But I overstepped my bounds, and that was completely unforgivable," he told her, pushing a hand roughly through his hair. "If you feel like you can never trust me again, I'd understand, but—"

"Ben!"

He stopped. When he looked at her expectantly, she took a deep breath. If she didn't do it now, she might lose her nerve and never have a chance like this again.

In a scared whisper, she said simply, "I love you."

Ben blinked. He stared at her in silence, and for one heart-wrenching moment, Lauren wondered if Allison had been completely wrong about Ben's feelings for her; maybe he didn't feel anything for her beyond friendship. When his silence continued, she wished she could take back her declaration of love, and just drop off the face of the earth.

After what seemed like an eternity, Ben finally found his voice. "Did you just say you loved me?"

She shifted her feet anxiously. What was she supposed to say? Did she quickly retract her words and pretend she was suffering from a momentary delusion brought on by a severe and unusual case of pre-hypothermia? Did she plead temporary insanity?

She swallowed hard, then decided to go for it. She'd come this far. What did she have to lose?

Well... everything, she thought.

She started to tremble, and she wasn't sure if it was from the cold winter air, or the snow seeping into her shoes, or if she was just afraid. "Um... yeah?" she replied, saying it more as a tentative question than as an answer.

Tears started to gather in Ben's eyes, and for a second, Lauren honestly thought he might cry. Then he let out a whoop and grabbed her in his arms, spinning her around crazily and laughing with pure joy.

When he finally put her down, he cupped her face gently in his hands. "Oh, Lauren," he murmured huskily. "You have no idea how amazing it is to hear you say that. I have loved you for so long, and I was beginning to wonder if you were ever going to feel the same way about me."

His eyes were filled with tenderness as he continued to stare at her, and Lauren marveled that she could have overlooked the fact that he loved her. Then, before another word was said, Ben leaned down and gently touched his lips to hers. His kiss was tender and sweet, and she found herself responding.

But then the reality of it all hit her, and the confusion she'd been feeling flooded back into her consciousness. She quickly pulled away, causing Ben to stare at her in confusion. "Lauren? What's wrong?"

She walked a few steps away, then turned and paced back. "I can't do this," she said softly, then more loudly. "I can't do this! I love you, okay? I admit that. But I don't know if I'm ready for this. I mean... yes, I finally admitted something that's taken me this long to figure out. But that doesn't mean I'm ready to accept it. What if you decide we're not right for each other and we break up? What about our friendship then? We could ruin everything we have together!"

"Who says we're going to break up?" he asked softly, taking her hands in his. "Regardless of what you think, I'm not going anywhere. I've worked too hard to get to this point, and I'm not going to throw that all away. I love you, Lauren. I've loved you from the moment I saw you."

"But how do you know our love's going to last beyond tomorrow?" she asked desperately. "Or next week? Or even a year from now? Every guy I ever went out with either dumped me, cheated on me, or turned out to be a complete jerk. Something always came up in the relationships that made them end disastrously. How do I know the same thing's not going to happen with us?"

"No one knows what's going to happen in the future," he admitted gently. "Challenges always present themselves, but the trick is learning to work through those challenges and become stronger because of them. We have something special, Lauren, something I've never felt with *anybody* before. And that special friendship, that special bond... it's what's going to keep us together."

Lauren felt torn. She wanted so badly to believe that Ben was right, that they could surrender themselves to love and end up living happily ever after. But her more rational side reminded her that she'd entrusted her heart to someone once before—and had it crushed.

Ben sensed her struggling with her emotions, and he tightened his grip on her hands. "Lauren, every reason you've given me for why this can't work just adds up to you being afraid. Stop worrying about what your head is saying and start listening to your heart. What is it telling you?"

She knew her answer without even thinking about it. "It says that I love you."

"Then go with it," he told her gently but firmly. "Don't be afraid of it. And if you need a little time to get used to the idea, that's fine. I'll let you set the pace." He lifted her hands to his lips and kissed them softly. "Please, Lauren? Say you'll give us a chance."

Lauren stared into his soulful brown eyes and felt herself start to waiver. He was the most wonderful guy she'd ever met—kind, patient, thoughtful…. Didn't she deserve the kind of happiness that loving somebody like Ben could bring? Finally, she felt herself nodding. "I'll give us a chance," she agreed softly.

Ben let out the breath he hadn't known he'd been holding and pulled her gently into his embrace. "Thank you," he whispered emotionally. He tightened his arms around her and pressed a kiss into her hair. "I promise, you won't regret it."

Lauren lay in bed that night watching the shadows from the old maple tree outside her window dance across her ceiling. A slow smile spread across her face as she thought about Ben sleeping in the guest room just down the hall.

She'd finally done it. She'd told Ben she loved him. And even better, he'd told her he loved her in return. True, she was still scared, but she'd promised to give their new relationship a chance, and she would. She only hoped he would be patient with her.

She rolled over in bed again, trying to find a comfortable position. After several restless minutes, however, she knew it was hopeless. Sleep wasn't going to come.

She threw off her blanket and climbed out of bed, then stood on the cold floor gazing out the window at the frosted, moonlit landscape for a long time. Finally, she slipped into her robe and wandered downstairs to the kitchen for a midnight snack. She opened her door quietly and tiptoed down the stairs. As she turned the corner into the kitchen, she was surprised to see the light was already on, and her dad was sitting at the table eating a small helping of leftovers. He looked just as surprised to see her as she was to see him.

"What are you doing up so late?" he asked quietly.

She smiled. "The same thing you are, it appears. I couldn't sleep, so I decided to get a snack." She moved past him to open the fridge door, then peered inside. She was still trying to decide what she was in the mood for when her dad spoke again.

"Is everything okay, Lauren? You seemed really quiet at dinner tonight."

Lauren flinched. *At least he noticed something was wrong*, she thought with a silent note of sarcasm. *I guess that's something.*

She was prepared to give her usual response that everything was fine, but then Ben's words echoed in her mind: *Why not give him the opportunity to explain his behavior?* After a moment of deliberation, she decided to do just that.

Feeling suddenly nervous, she shut the fridge and walked over to the table. "Well, since you asked..." she began hesitantly. She sat down in the chair next to him and took a deep breath. "Dad, can I ask you something?"

"Sure, honey."

She paused, trying to work up the courage to say what she was thinking. "Am I a disappointment to you?"

Her dad looked up at her, his eyes wide with disbelief. "What?"

She squirmed under the intensity of his gaze. "It's just... no matter what I do or how hard I try, it doesn't seem to be good enough for you. Like tonight at dinner, for example. I was so proud of the grades I got on my midterms because I worked so hard for them, especially that 'B' in Anatomy. But instead of being proud of me, you told me to work harder and do better next time. Do you have any idea how much that hurt? How much it always hurts to work hard to accomplish something, only to have you act like no matter what I do, it still isn't good enough?"

Her dad continued to stare at her in disbelief. "Is that honestly what you think? How can you think that?"

"How can I not?" Lauren shot back painfully. "All these years I've worked so hard to impress you, to make you proud of me. But no matter what I did, Tom, Rick, Connor, or Jack were always the ones you boasted about, telling everyone how they pitched a no-hitter or scored a winning touchdown. Even when I got chosen for the All-State softball team, you didn't make a big deal about it; you just told me we were going to have to work on my pitch selection. There are lots of other examples I could bring up, but my point is, all my life, nothing I've done has ever been good enough for you."

"That's not true!" her dad argued quietly, sitting up straighter in his chair. "I've always loved you, more than you can possibly know." His voice faltered, and he paused to clear the growing thickness in his throat. When he continued, he sounded a little sheepish. "I guess I have been harder on you than your brothers, but that's only because of the tremendous amount of potential I've always seen in you. Even from a young age, you always seemed to know what you wanted and where you were going. And boy, were you stubborn. No one could ever tell you something couldn't be done." He chuckled softly and shook his head.

"Remember that camping trip when you were ten? You insisted on going with your brothers and me on that hike to the mountain summit, but we said you were too little. You sure proved us wrong. Even back then you had a special determination that not even your brothers had. And then there was the year you started playing softball."

He smiled softly at the memory. "I'll never forget the first time you pitched for your team. You were a natural. Not even your brothers had that kind of raw talent. I admit that I may have pushed you a little harder than I probably should have, but I saw it as a way to develop your confidence, to give you a chance to grow as an athlete and as a person. But you weren't just gifted at athletics, Lauren, you excelled at everything you did, and you still do."

He looked down at his hands for a moment. When he looked back up, she saw the unshed tears shimmering in his eyes. "If you felt like I was hard on you, I'm sorry. I never meant for it to come off that way. It hurts me to think you've been carrying this around for so many years. I guess I've just always pushed you so hard and expected so much from you because of everything I knew you had in you. I've always known you'd go on to do great things in your life, and so far, you have. Maybe I haven't said it often enough, but... I am proud of you, Lauren. No father could be prouder. Your head's on straight, you've embraced the gospel, you're a righteous daughter of your Heavenly Father...."

He paused, and when he spoke again, his voice was thick with emotion. "You know... you said you never felt like you measured up to your brothers. Well, in many ways, your brothers could never measure up to you."

Tears filled Lauren's eyes, and on an impulse, she fell forward into her father's arms. Never in a million years would she have guessed he thought so highly of her, saw so much in her that he'd taken it upon himself to see she fulfilled her potential. Now that she knew, her heart felt a hundred pounds lighter. "Thanks, Dad," she whispered tearfully.

When they finally pulled apart, her father's teary gaze met her own. "Next time you have something bothering you, just talk to me about it, okay? Whatever it is, I'd like to have the chance to fix it."

Lauren nodded. "I will."

With one last smile, her dad reached out to tweak her nose the way he used to do when she was little, then he stood up from his chair. "I'm glad we had this talk," he said sincerely as he picked up his plate and deposited it in the sink. "I guess I'll head to bed. Don't stay up too late, okay?"

"I won't. Goodnight, Dad."

"Goodnight, honey. I love you."

"I love you, too, Dad."

As he disappeared up the stairs, Lauren shook her head in disbelief. *To think that all these years, I thought he didn't love me as much as my brothers, that I was a disappointment to him.*

Feeling happier than she'd been in months, she got up from her chair and glanced toward the fridge. After only a moment's deliberation, she decided she wasn't hungry anymore. She walked over to switch off the light, then made her way through the darkened kitchen. She'd just reached the bottom of the stairs when a slight movement from the living room caused her to jump. Straining her eyes in the darkness, she spotted a lone figure getting up off the couch and walking toward her.

"Ben?" she whispered. "Is that you? You nearly scared me half to death. What are you doing down here?"

"I couldn't sleep, so when I heard voices down here, I came to investigate," he whispered back, his face slowly creasing into a smile. "You decided to talk to your dad, I see."

Lauren looked both surprised and startled. "How did you…?"

"Don't worry, I wasn't eavesdropping or anything, I promise," he quickly reassured her. "I was on my way into the kitchen when I heard you two talking, and I stopped when I realized what you were talking about."

"Did you hear what he said?"

"About being proud of you?" A slow smile spread across his face. "Yeah, I did. I told you so."

Lauren smiled back and stepped into Ben's embrace. "You did tell me so, and you were right. It turns out I've been worrying all these years for nothing."

"I'm really happy for you," Ben whispered sincerely as he tightened his arms around her.

But even as he told her so, he couldn't help feeling a momentary stab of remorse. More than anything he longed to have a similar conversation with his own father, to hear his father's assurances that he loved him and was proud of him. Sadly, he knew it was a conversation that would probably never take place.

Ben forced himself to push his own feelings aside as he pulled back and met Lauren's gaze. Smiling tenderly, he reached up to trail a finger gently along her cheek, wiping away the happy tears that lingered there. "It's late," he whispered, glancing over at the grandfather clock in the corner. "We should probably get some sleep or we'll be too exhausted to stay awake during Thanksgiving dinner tomorrow."

Lauren laughed quietly as they started up the stairs. "Not a chance. After talking to my dad tonight, I'll be on an emotional high all week."

Thanksgiving Day arrived with a splendor that matched Lauren's mood. The sun was shining brightly in a cloudless, blue sky, and reflected off the snow with such brilliance that it made the landscape appear to be woven from a tapestry of white sequins. But with the pre-Thanksgiving excitement came chaos as Lauren's brothers and their wives and children descended upon the Holt home. Most of the adults spent the morning and mid-day hours helping in the kitchen while the children played in the snow in the backyard.

Just as Ben had done with Connor, he also hit it off with Tom and Rick, Lauren's oldest brothers. They all talked and laughed during the meal preparations, making the atmosphere fun and festive.

Lauren soon discovered that her brothers and sisters-in-law weren't the only ones enjoying Ben's company, however. Her nieces and nephews clearly thought Ben was the greatest thing since pepperoni pizza. He spent a good hour in the backyard playing in the snow and riding toboggans with them. Lauren watched from the kitchen window, grinning, as he ran across the yard with four kids doing their best to chase after him, squealing and giggling uncontrollably as they tried to hit him with their hastily made snowballs.

When he and the kids finally came in, laughing and cold and brushing snow off their clothes, she walked to the doorway that separated the kitchen from the family room to greet them. Folding her arms across her chest, she leaned her shoulder against the doorway, unable to take her eyes off Ben as he pulled off his snow-covered boots. His brown hair was damp and rumpled, his jeans were soaked from being down on his knees with the kids in the snow, and his cheeks were flushed from the cold air. And to Lauren, he'd never looked more amazing than he did right at that moment.

She watched with a warm heart as he flashed his megawatt smile at her nieces and nephews and joked with them, and when he looked up and caught her watching him, he gave her a wonderful wink that made her heart flutter.

Thanksgiving dinner started promptly at two. Lauren's father offered a heartfelt prayer of thanksgiving over the food, then more happy chaos ensued. Dishes were passed around, plates were filled, and everyone talked and laughed as they enjoyed the wonderful meal. Afterward, when the dishes were washed and the food was put away, the kids went down for naps, and the adults relaxed and talked.

Lauren had volunteered to unload the dishwasher and was enjoying the quiet of the abandoned kitchen when a pair of strong arms suddenly slipped around her waist.

"Hi there," a husky voice murmured in her ear. "What are you doing in here all by yourself?"

"Are you kidding?" she joked, leaning back against the strong wall of Ben's chest. "After all that excitement I needed a quiet place to recharge. You're not feeling overwhelmed by everything, are you? The kids, the chaos…?"

With his cheek pressed against hers, she felt rather than saw him smile. "I like it, actually. It's fun having all these people around. I have to say, though, I wish I had half the energy your nieces and nephews have."

She laughed. "I know what you mean." She turned around in his arms and looked up into his beautiful brown eyes. Then, smiling at him mischievously, she prompted, "But admit it—you were having just as much fun out there in the snow as the kids were."

"Okay, I was," he admitted with a sheepish grin. "What can I say? I'm a kid at heart."

Her smile softened as she continued to look up into the handsome face she'd come to know so well. "I like that about you."

"You do, huh?" he asked, his eyes twinkling. "I'll have to remember that."

Lauren giggled softly at his response, and when he lowered his face to hers, she felt the world around her disappear. She closed her eyes dreamily as he gently touched his lips to hers in an intoxicating kiss that made her tingle clear down to her toes.

"A-hem!"

A sudden voice from the kitchen doorway made them jump apart guiltily. Lauren looked over to see Jack standing there staring at them, his arms folded across his chest and a broad grin spreading across his face.

"It appears I'm interrupting something," he declared, his Cheshire cat grin broadening even further as he sauntered over to them. "Laur, I thought you said you guys were just friends. Well, I think you should know, your definition of 'just friends' is a little over the top."

Lauren felt her cheeks turn crimson. She glanced nervously at Ben, but he was grinning and taking Jack's teasing in stride. Still, she felt the need to explain, and started to stammer, "Well, um, we were just... um...."

Jack waved her attempted explanation aside. "Hey, I think it's cool, my little sister falling for the guy I baptized. I'd say you owe me one, sis." He winked at her, then turned to Ben. "I don't suppose I need to give you the third degree and threaten to break your arm if you hurt her, like I used to do with the other guys she went out with."

Ben laughed. "Sorry, I'm not that easily intimidated."

Jack clapped Ben on the shoulder. "Glad to hear it. Well," he said, letting out a breath, "I just came in here for a piece of pie, but I'll get it later. You two... carry on." He winked again, then disappeared from the kitchen.

Lauren groaned softly and let her forehead fall forward against Ben's chest. "Oh, I can't believe he saw that."

Ben chuckled and tightened his arms around her. "Well, it would have happened sooner or later. You're not ashamed we got caught kissing, are you?"

Lauren looked up at him and shook her head. "No, it's not that. I just... I guess I'm still getting used to the idea of 'us' myself—and I wasn't quite ready to announce it to the world."

Ben's expression softened. "I understand. Do you want me to talk to Jack? Tell him not to say anything?"

"No, that's okay," Lauren replied slowly. "I'm sure my family all suspects something anyway. I mean, when was the last time I brought a guy home? Besides bringing you home for Jack's homecoming, of course." When he looked at her questioningly, she rolled her eyes impatiently. "Try *never*, Morrison. So just kiss me already. If someone else walks in, they'll have proof of what they already suspect."

Ben's mouth quirked into a grin. "Sounds good to me."

Chapter Eighteen

As the next two weeks went by, Lauren was amazed to discover how easy it was to be in love with Ben. He was absolutely everything she could have ever wanted in a boyfriend, and every minute she spent with him made her love him all the more. She loved that he was always thinking about her, about what she might need or how she was feeling. He was always there for her, and that sense of warmth and security she got whenever they were together made her feel like she was right where she was supposed to be.

She'd almost convinced herself that finding that "special man" was something that would never happen to her, that something as "fairy tale" as finding the man of her dreams and falling head over heels in love was only something that happened to other people, or to fictional characters in the movies. But being with Ben convinced her that it was possible, and having him love her—a fact that was evident in his softly spoken words, his tender touch, and his considerate actions—was a gift she'd never thought she'd have.

Allison was also thrilled with Lauren and Ben's developing relationship—and she delighted in teasing her friend about the vast amounts of time she was spending with him. But Lauren couldn't help herself; being with Ben every spare minute of every day was exactly what she wanted to do, and as long as she got her schoolwork done, she felt justified in indulging herself with his company.

Schoolwork began taking more and more of her time, however, and with Christmas approaching, the last minute push to get ready for finals reached a frenzied high. Lauren found herself buckling down and studying hard, but it was difficult to work as hard as she had in the past with Ben occupying so much of her mind. But after a poor performance on the practice anatomy/physiology test she'd just taken, she found herself walking out of class on Friday in a daze. She had just started walking down the building's steps when a deep voice sounded in her ear.

"Don't I know you?"

Spinning around, she found herself staring into Ben's smiling brown eyes. "Hey, what are you doing here?" she exclaimed happily. "I thought you had a tutoring session."

He shook his head. "Nope. Cancelled. Instead, I figured I'd head over here and see my best girl."

"Best?" she echoed, scowling at him playfully. "You mean there are more?"

The sound of his deep laughter made her heart melt. "No way," he insisted, draping an arm around her shoulders and pulling her close. "All I need is you."

She grinned and smacked his arm lightly. "Trying to score points? If so, it's working."

"Good." He gave her one last squeeze and smiled at her, but then his brows furrowed as he studied her face carefully. "Uh-oh. The corners of your eyes are crinkling. Let me guess. You're stressing over finals."

She sighed. "Yeah, a little. I didn't do so great on the practice final I just had. I think that locking myself in my room for the weekend and studying is the best course of action."

He frowned. "Darn. I was hoping to see you this weekend."

"I know, me too, but I need to do well on my finals. You understand, don't you?"

He nodded and gave her a reluctant smile. "Yeah, I do. That doesn't mean I have to like it, though." They walked in silence for several moments, then Ben's eyes lit up. "You know, with all the studying you're planning on doing, you need at least a little break. How about going to see Christmas Tree Lane with me tonight?"

Christmas Tree Lane was an annual tradition where the second floor of the Manwaring Center was transformed into a winter wonderland with dozens of Christmas trees beautifully decorated by community businesses, local and student wards, campus clubs, and other organizations.

"I'd love to!" she exclaimed as they entered Manwaring Center and stopped in front of the bookstore. "I haven't been up to see it yet, but I hear it's fabulous. I'm game if you are."

Ben's brilliant smile flashed across his face. "Great! What if I come by your apartment for you at, say, seven o'clock?"

"Perfect," Lauren agreed. "See you then?"

He nodded, then leaned in to give her a quick kiss. "Have fun at work."

Lauren watched him until he disappeared out of the building's doors, then finally forced herself to move. She turned to go clock in, but instead bumped into a solid wall of human flesh. Startled, she looked up and found herself looking into Dan's amused face.

"Things getting pretty hot and heavy between you two, huh?" he asked, a mischievous smile playing across his lips. "Who would've known. Ms. Sensible. In love." He shook his head in mock disbelief.

Lauren laughed. "You're only jealous because I chose him over you," she joked as he walked with her toward the employees' room. "But don't feel bad. You have what, two dates planned for tonight?"

"Three, but who's counting?"

Lauren chuckled and shook her head. "Come on, Casanova. Let's get to work."

At seven o'clock sharp, Ben was standing in Lauren's living room to pick her up for their date. He helped her on with her coat, and together they walked through the wintry evening to the Manwaring Center. When they reached the second floor of the building where the display was, Lauren gasped. With the dozens of beautifully lit and decorated trees lining the walls and foyers, it looked exactly like a winter wonderland. Ben and Lauren walked hand in hand as they admired each tree, appreciating the talents of the people who'd decorated the trees so creatively and beautifully.

"I think I like this one best," Lauren decided as they stopped in front of a ten-foot tree decorated completely in white with everything from silk ribbon and doves, to sparkling white, glass ornaments and peaceful, twinkling white lights. "It just seems so peaceful, so pure. It kind of reminds me of what the holiday is supposed to be all about."

When Ben didn't say anything for a long time, Lauren turned to him and saw that he had an unreadable, almost guarded expression on his face as he stared up at the tree. Suddenly concerned, she gave his hand a squeeze. "What's wrong? Don't you like it?"

"Oh, I think it's beautiful," he quickly replied. "What you said just kind of struck me... you know, about the holiday being about peace. But that's not the only thing Christmas is about; it's about love, and being with family." His expression became one of sadness. "And that only serves to remind me that...."

"That yours is no longer available to you," she finished for him.

He nodded, and she thought she caught a glimmer of tears in his brown eyes. "It's not like we really got along," he admitted solemnly. "But I still loved them *because* they were my family. My Christmases weren't like yours, I'm sure. Instead of sitting around a tree in the early morning hours and opening presents in your pajamas, we spent Christmas in other countries with friends and relatives. When my parents were off with their friends, my sister and I would have so much fun together. I have a lot of fond memories of spending Christmas with her."

"And this year you won't be spending it with her," she said quietly. He nodded sadly, and Lauren felt a sudden rush of tenderness toward him. He looked so lost and vulnerable that it tugged at her heartstrings. She resisted the urge to reach up and smooth away the worry lines that appeared at the corners of his eyes.

After a long moment, she stepped toward him and hugged him comfortingly. "I'm sorry," she whispered. "I wish things could be different for you."

"So do I." His arms tightened around her and he sighed deeply. "Thank you, Lauren. I don't know how I'd get through any of this without you."

She gave him one last squeeze, then pulled back to look into his eyes. "Well, I have an idea about how you can get through this," she said, her eyes twinkling mischievously. "You can spend Christmas with *my* family. You already know them, so it's not like they're going to scare you off." She grinned. "Besides, it'll give you a chance to see one of those old-fashioned Christmases first hand. You'll totally love it, I promise. We string popcorn, make sugar cookies to take to all the neighbors.... Oh, and the best thing—my brothers and I always have a snow sculpting contest... you know, snowmen, and stuff."

"It sounds great," he admitted with a smile. "I'd love to come, if it's not too much trouble for your family."

She rolled her eyes. "What, are you kidding? You saw what Thanksgiving was like—one chaotic moment after another. Christmas is twice as bad, with wrapping paper everywhere and all my brother's kids on sugar highs after eating everything in their stockings. You'd be one more adult to help with damage control."

He laughed, a hint of his old self returning. "Then I accept."

Lauren grinned. "Good. Then it's settled."

They finished walking through the display, then headed outside. Lauren tightened her coat around her against the cold December air, and without hesitation, Ben slipped his arm around her shoulders and pulled her close. Lauren nestled into his side and sighed contentedly. It felt so right to be walking with Ben like this. It was an amazing feeling she hoped she'd never have to be without.

They reached the edge of campus and Lauren pulled Ben to a stop. "Ben, you don't have to walk me all the way to my apartment. It's cold. I can get home fine."

Looking doubtful, he let his arm fall from her shoulders. "Are you sure? I don't mind walking with you; it's not that far."

She looked up into his concerned gaze and lifted her hand to his overcoat lapel. "Exactly. It's not far. I'll be fine."

He still hesitated. "Are you sure?"

She smiled reassuringly. "Positive." Then, before he could argue further, she stepped into his arms for another hug. She nestled her face against his chest, breathing in deeply and savoring the lingering smell of his cologne. After a long moment, she pulled away and looked up into his face. "Thanks for the time away from studying. You're a life saver."

He smiled tenderly as he reached out to tuck a few wisps of hair behind her ear. "You're welcome, Lauren. I'd do anything for you, you know that."

Touched by his words, Lauren felt tears spring to her eyes and she said softly, "I love you, Ben." A few months ago it would have been all but impossible for her to say, but now it felt as natural as breathing.

Feeling his heart warm at her sincerely spoken words, Ben cupped her face in his hands, then leaned down to give her a long, sweet kiss. "I love you, too," he whispered. "When you take a break from studying tomorrow, call me, okay?"

When she nodded, he gave her one last lingering smile, then turned and disappeared into the night. Lauren stared after him for several long moments before finally moving off toward home. She shook her head in disbelief. Everything with Ben was so perfect.

But as she walked, a little voice in the back of her head wondered just how long such perfection could last. She quickly pushed the thought aside, reprimanding herself for ever thinking such a thing. Ben loved her. She knew that beyond a shadow of a doubt. And she loved him. What could possibly go wrong?

Forcing her mind to more pleasant things, she turned the corner and walked toward her apartment, concentrating instead on being in love.

Chapter Nineteen

Craig looked up from his scavenging in the kitchen for a late night snack and saw Ben walking in the front door. "Hey," Craig greeted him before turning back to his search. "How'd your date go with Lauren?"

"It was awesome. *She's* awesome. I don't know how I lived without her for so long."

Craig shook his head while looking through the fridge. "You guys are so much in love, it's disgusting." He finally pulled out a half eaten hoagie and sat down at the table. As he unwrapped the sandwich, he cocked an eyebrow at Ben. "You guys seem pretty serious. Is this thing going anywhere?"

"If by 'thing' you mean our relationship," Ben said with a smile as he sat down in the chair across from Craig, "as a matter of fact, it is. I'm thinking about asking her to marry me."

Craig froze. His mouth hung open, and the sandwich, suddenly forgotten, hovered in front of his lips. "Are you serious?" he asked, wide-eyed.

Ben nodded, then rushed on when Craig remained speechless. "Craig, you have no idea how much I love her. She's the most amazing girl I've ever met. She's sweet and funny and so full of life… and when I'm around her, she makes me *feel* amazing. In fact," he continued, "I'm thinking about giving her a ring at Christmas. I've got a little money saved up. It should be enough for a down payment on something nice."

Craig set his sandwich down and studied Ben seriously. "That's great, man, really, it is," he said finally. "But… don't you think this might be a little soon? You've only been going out a few weeks."

"Going out, yes," Ben agreed, "but we've spent practically every spare minute together since September. I feel like we've been going out a lot longer than we have. And I love her, Craig. I can't imagine life without her."

After a moment, Craig shrugged and picked up his sandwich. "Well, if you're sure...."

Ben smiled and nodded. "I've never been more sure of anything in my life."

Feeling inspired by their talk, Ben borrowed Craig's old truck after breakfast the next morning and followed a map one of his roommates had drawn up for him to the Idaho Falls mall. The traffic was unexpectedly light for a Saturday morning with Christmas so near, and Ben had no trouble finding his way.

Once inside, he found several jewelry stores and started his search. He was amazed by the prices when compared to those in Boston, and realized he could afford more ring than he'd thought. He'd never talked to Lauren about her tastes in jewelry, but the only jewelry he'd ever seen her wear was a CTR ring on her right hand. It made him suspect that her tastes in jewelry were rather simple and unpretentious, so he looked for engagement rings accordingly.

He saw several that he suspected Lauren would like, but it wasn't until he stepped into the fourth and final jewelry store that he saw it. It was perfect. The gleaming, fourteen carat gold band held three brilliant, emerald-cut diamonds, the one in the middle being larger than the ones on either side of it. It was beautiful and elegant without being ostentatious. He knew Lauren was going to love it.

He was able to dicker over the price, and with some luck, was able to get the ring for what he considered a terrific price. What he thought was going to be his down payment turned out to be almost the entire price of the ring, and he had them wrap it up for her. He hoped it would be the best Christmas gift he could possibly give to her.

As he walked out of the mall and climbed into Craig's old truck, he found himself whistling happily along with the Christmas music playing on the radio. The idea of asking Lauren to marry him seemed so right. Every time he'd prayed over the last couple of weeks, asking if she was really the one for him, a warm, comforting feeling had come over him, telling him that she was indeed the one he was supposed to spend eternity with.

Not that he could believe she wasn't. The more time he spent with her, the more he realized he couldn't live without her. She was the other piece of him he'd never realized was missing, and now that he'd found her, he couldn't imagine not being with her for the rest of his life, and throughout the eternities to come. Maybe it was selfish, especially since he knew she deserved so much better, but he wanted to be with her. If she would have him.

"I'll be so glad when my last final is over tomorrow," Lauren sighed as she smothered a french fry in ketchup and put it into her mouth. "At this point, I'm just so sick of school."

She and Ben were sitting together at the Nordic, the little student café next to the bookstore in the Manwaring center, watching the snow falling gently outside as they relaxed and grabbed a quick bite to eat before Lauren went to work. Almost a week had passed since Ben had made his trip to the jewelry store, and he found himself on an emotional high. He could hardly wait for Christmas so he could give the ring to her. In the meantime, he was enjoying simply being with her and in love.

He nodded. "Yeah, I know what you mean. But I'm already done with my finals," he boasted. "It was nice to have them early. Do you want me to come by tonight and help you study for your chemistry final? I don't have anything else I need to do."

Lauren grinned, happy at the prospect of being with him, even if it was only a study date. "Sure, that'd be great."

They ate in comfortable silence for several minutes, then Ben asked, "Are you sure your mom said it was okay that I come for Christmas?"

Lauren rolled her eyes and let out an aggravated growl. "For the hundredth time, yes! She was thrilled when I told her you were coming. You're practically part of the family, you know."

Ben's heart leapt at her words, and he couldn't help thinking about that dark blue velvet ring box he had hidden in his top dresser drawer. Hopefully, his little gift would officially make him part of the family. He loved her family, and being a part of it was something he'd definitely consider a special gift.

"I haven't gotten to all of my Christmas shopping yet," Lauren admitted sheepishly. "I've been too busy studying for finals. Allison promised to spend the couple of days we'll have left before Christmas shopping with me. You're welcome to come with us, especially since I already got *your* gift." Her eyes twinkled secretively.

"Hey, don't feel obligated to buy me anything," he quickly spoke up. "Just spending Christmas with you and your family is gift enough."

"Oh, brother," she drawled, rolling her eyes again. "You're my boyfriend. Like I'm not going to get you a gift."

He laughed. "Well, I'm not going to say you can't, but I just want you to know I'm not expecting anything. I already have everything in the world I could possibly want." And with that, he leaned over and kissed her tenderly.

She grinned against his lips. "You're a real sweet talker, you know that?"

"Yes, I know." He gave her another quick kiss, then pulled back and looked at his watch. "Your shift starts in five minutes. You'd better get going."

She sighed. "Yeah, I guess I'd better." She started to gather up the tray, but Ben quickly took it from her and waved her off.

"I'll take care of this. You go on ahead."

"Thanks." She smiled her appreciation. "I'll see you later?"

He nodded. "I'll come by your apartment later tonight to help you study."

She started to walk away, but then came back and gave him a sweet, lingering kiss. When she stepped back, she smiled at the surprised and pleased look on his face. She backed away, gave him a little half wave, then hurried on.

Ben stared after her in amazement, shaking his head. She was incredible. And he could hardly wait for Christmas day when hopefully she would agree to be his for eternity.

Lauren sat at her kitchen table hunched over her chemistry book, and Ben sat beside her, playing tutor as she tried to prepare for her next day's final. "Ugh, why can't I get this?" she complained as she tossed her pencil onto the textbook and leaned back in her chair. "Maybe I'm dumb or something."

"You are *not* dumb," Ben insisted, looking at her sternly. "You're just stressing out about it and that's making it harder to grasp. Now come on, I'll explain it again."

She sighed heavily and leaned forward, trying to make herself relax. Just then the phone rang and Lauren leaped up from her seat. "Saved by the bell," she quipped, giving Ben a smile and ignoring the playful, reprimanding look he shot her way. She picked up the phone. "Hello?"

She seemed momentarily disappointed as she held the phone out to Ben. "It's for you. It's Craig."

Ben reached for the phone. "Hey, Craig. What's up?"

Lauren noticed the smile disappear from his face, and he was frowning when he hung up a few moments later. "What was that all about?" she asked curiously.

"Craig said Emily just phoned my apartment, looking for me."

Lauren's eyebrows shot up. "Emily, your sister?"

He nodded slowly, his brows furrowed in concern. "Yeah. Craig gave her your number here and wanted to give me a heads-up that she was going to be calling."

"That's weird," Lauren said, knowing that Ben and his sister emailing each other periodically was risky enough. "Did Craig say what she wanted?"

"No, just that she sounded upset." He pushed his hand roughly through his dark hair and stared at the phone, a mixture of emotions running through him. He was excited at the prospect of talking to his sister, but he knew how adamant his father had been about cutting off all contact between him and his family. A phone call from Emily could only mean that something was wrong.

Before he could think about it further, the phone rang and Ben jumped. His heart was in his throat when he answered it. "Hello?" His face immediately lit up when he heard his sister's voice. "Emily! Yeah, Craig told me you were trying to get hold of me. What's wrong?"

Lauren watched as Ben's initial excitement vanished and his face paled. His responses to whatever his sister was saying were mostly single-syllable words, so Lauren couldn't determine what was being said. When Ben finally said a solemn goodbye and hung up the phone, Lauren looked at him expectantly. "So?"

Ben looked numb as he responded, "My father had a heart attack."

Lauren gasped. "Is he all right?"

"They don't know yet," he answered solemnly. "He's in the ICU and they're running a bunch of tests. She wants me to come."

Lauren's eyes were sympathetic as she reached for his hand. "Ben, I'm so sorry. What can I do to help?"

He looked up at her, and when their eyes met, Ben felt in them a strength he wasn't sure he had himself. "Well, if it's not too much to ask," he began hesitantly, "I could use a ride to the airport in the morning. Emily booked a flight for me that leaves at eight-thirty. Oh, wait—that won't work," he quickly amended. "Your chemistry final's in the morning."

"No, it's fine," she hurried to reassure him. "I can take my final whenever because it's up at the testing center. I'll just take it after I get back from driving you to the airport."

"But your studying," he persisted, his eyes filled with concern. "Won't this mess up your cramming plans for the morning?"

Lauren shook her head firmly. "It'll be fine, I promise."

The muscles in his face visibly relaxed, and he gave her hand a grateful squeeze. "Thank you, Lauren." He leaned forward to press a gentle kiss to her lips. Then he stood up and sighed. "As much as I hate to, I need to get home and pack. Are you going to be okay studying tonight without me?"

"Absolutely." She stood and walked him to the door. Once there, she asked him quietly, "Do your parents know you're coming?"

He shook his head. "No, not yet. Emily said she'd tell them before picking me up at the airport."

"That's good, right?" she asked gently. "If your father's in bad health, I'm sure it wouldn't be a good idea to just show up out of the blue after everything that's happened."

"You're probably right," he admitted. Then something else struck him and his heart sank. "I guess this screws up our plans for Christmas," he said sadly. "I was looking forward to spending Christmas with you."

Lauren felt a tug at her heart as she remembered the plans they'd made, but she forced herself to be strong. He needed her to be. She smiled a little sadly and reached for his hand. "That's okay. This is a chance for you to be with your family... and Emily. Maybe you two can have one of your special Christmases together."

He nodded, but Lauren suspected that was only a small consolation. She knew how hard this must be on him, having to go home to face a father who'd disowned him almost a year ago. Now he was being forced to revisit a past he'd tried so valiantly to overcome. She only wished she could be there with him when he did.

Knowing this had to be his battle, she sighed as she stepped into his arms and hugged him tightly. "At least get some good sleep tonight, okay?" she whispered gently. "You'll need it for the trip."

Ben lay in bed late that night, staring up at the darkened ceiling as his mind mulled over what was to come. Christmas with his family in Boston. He would've jumped at the chance for a possible reconciliation only a few short months ago, but now... now everything was different. Not that he didn't want to be welcomed back into his family, but he'd spent the greater part of a year trying to put his past behind him and get on with his life. Now he had to face it all over again.

He sighed. *Just when you think life is going smoothly, that everything is right, that everything is perfect, something like this happens. It doesn't seem fair.*

He sat up quietly and slid open his top dresser drawer, being careful not to awaken Craig. He moved aside several pairs of socks and carefully removed the tiny, blue velvet-covered box. Slowly, almost reverently, he opened the lid.

The sparkle of the brilliant diamond ring nestled within caught the light shining in from the hallway and reflected it back, sparkling and gleaming as Ben tilted the box one way and then the other.

An almost overwhelming sadness crept into his heart. He'd wanted everything to be perfect when he proposed: the time of day, their surroundings... the circumstances under which he asked her to be his eternal companion. He wanted it to be the most incredible and memorable event in their lives. But now that was going to have to wait.

With another heavy sigh, he snapped the lid shut and tucked the ring box back into its hiding place, then he closed the drawer and lay back down on his bed. He wished more than anything that he didn't have to wait to ask Lauren to marry him, but he had no choice.

He shook his head sadly. He couldn't help thinking that being without Lauren for Christmas was only going to be the beginning of many hard things to come.

Chapter Twenty

As Ben's plane began its final approach, his hands unconsciously tightened around the large book in his hands. He glanced down at it. Immediately, a feeling of tenderness filled his heart.

His mind flashed back to when he and Lauren had stood in the Idaho Falls airport that morning saying goodbye to each other.

Lauren smiled sadly as she handed him a beautifully wrapped package and instructed him to open it. Inside was a black leather quad—a beautifully bound set of scriptures with his name engraved in gold on the lower right hand corner. Ben was utterly speechless as he reverently traced the elegant lettering with his fingertips.

"Craig told me you couldn't afford your own scriptures, and that's why you have an old, used set," she explained, a pleased smile spreading across her face when she saw the tears of appreciation in his eyes. "But I thought you deserved to have your very own."

A lump gathered in his throat as he hugged her tightly and whispered an emotional, "Thank you," in her ear. When they pulled apart, a rush of sadness encompassed him as he realized that he didn't have a gift to give her in exchange.

"Lauren, I have something for you, but—" he began, but she quickly cut him off, reassuring him that he could give her whatever it was when he got back. Then he boarded his plane and flew east, feeling like he was leaving the biggest part of his heart behind.

The sudden bump of the plane's wheels against the runway brought him back to the present. Boston. He shook his head. He had such mixed emotions about being back: he was scared for his father's health, nervous about what his family's reaction would be to his arrival, and excited to see his sister. But there was also the familiar knotting of his stomach as he thought about growing up in a home that, in comparison with Lauren's, held very little love.

Most of his memories involving his father were unpleasant. More than once, Ben could remember being glad his father was away from home as much as he was. He was definitely not an easy person to be around, and their home life was nothing like the cheery chaos he'd experienced—and loved—at Lauren's home. He'd spent most of his life walking on eggshells in an attempt to keep from upsetting his father, as had the other members of his family.

Not that his father was abusive. Not physically, anyway. But the times he spent yelling and raging like a bull came all too frequently. Ben could remember locking himself in his room for long periods of time, just hoping to stay out of his father's way. The times he'd been unlucky enough to be the cause of one of his father's infamous tantrums, however—whether it was for a grade less than perfect or for not making the right impression on one of his father's prestigious colleagues—had been miserable.

Ben had learned to cope with the hard times by shutting down emotionally, by withdrawing, often for days at a time. He'd learned it was simply easier to do that than to try to fight his father. Fighting his father had always been a losing battle.

Before long, his coping mechanism became second nature, and he started doing it whenever things got rough, whether it was at school or at home. His sister quickly learned that it was just his way of dealing with whatever was troubling him, of working through his problems and trying to find a solution—whether it was dealing with his father or with anything else that became a trial in his life.

He could remember doing it when he'd made the decision to be baptized—and as a result, to leave his family. His sister, being familiar with his coping mechanism, knew he was fighting to make some major decision, so had wisely left him alone, knowing he would tell her what was bothering him when he was ready. His explanation had come in the form of an email at her work, telling her he'd joined the Church and wouldn't be coming home ever again.

Until now, Ben thought as the plane taxied to the terminal and finally came to a stop.

Trying to push his past aside and simply focus on what the immediate future held, he left the plane with the other passengers and made his way to the baggage claim area where he knew his sister would be waiting.

When he got there, he searched eagerly for Emily's familiar face. Finally, he caught a glimpse of someone with short brown hair and warm brown eyes very much like his own, and his heart leapt. She looked exactly like he remembered her.

She spotted him at the same time he'd spotted her, and she let out a loud squeal and nearly knocked him over as she rushed to hug him. Laughing and crying at the same time, he hugged her back and spun her around, which elicited another squeal. When he finally put her down, he saw she was crying, too.

"Ben, you have no idea how much I've missed you!" she cried, wiping at the happy tears on her cheeks. "You look incredible."

"So do you," Ben answered, taking in her stylish wardrobe and her perfectly cut and styled hair. "You look like a real lady."

She glared at him playfully. "Don't you believe it. I can still beat you in arm wrestling any day of the week."

Ben laughed, suddenly recognizing how similar in spirit his sister and Lauren were. "I'll bet you could," he agreed diplomatically.

They walked to the luggage claim to get his bags, then climbed into Emily's red BMW convertible and headed for home.

Ben settled deeper into his seat and smiled. "I'd forgotten how much I love BMWs."

Emily glanced over at him and tried to smile back, but it didn't quite reach her eyes. "Yeah, Dad sold yours shortly after...." Her voice drifted off, and she turned back to the road.

"It's okay, Em," he assured her quietly. "It was a little hard going from having everything to having nothing, but I'm over it. I like my life now. School's good, I have good roommates... and I'm in love."

This time Emily's smile was genuine. "Oh, that's right! So, tell me about this Lauren. It sounds like she's really swept you off your feet."

"She has," he admitted happily. He spent the next few minutes filling her in on everything from how they met, to how she'd finally admitted she loved him. When he finished, he looked at Emily carefully. "And I'm going to ask her to marry me."

Emily cringed. "Ooh, Dad's not going to like that."

Ben stiffened. "Who cares what he thinks? He threw me out of the house like some stray dog," he said bitterly. "I don't need his permission to live my life. He made it very clear he didn't *want* to be a part of my life."

"I know," Emily said quietly, glancing over at him sympathetically. "For what it's worth, though, I'm happy for you about Lauren. She sounds really terrific."

He softened a little and nodded. "She is. You'd like her, Em. It didn't dawn on me until I saw you at the airport, but you two are a lot alike. I wish you could meet her."

"Someday I will," she said, her voice taking on a stubbornness Ben hardly recognized. "I'll be eighteen next year, and then I can do whatever I want. Dad's money and approval aren't everything, as I see you've come to learn." She was quiet for a moment as she navigated through traffic. Finally, she continued, her voice tender. "Ben, I never did tell you, but... I was proud of you when you refused to let Dad bully you into changing your mind about joining your church. It took a lot of guts. You set an example for me about how to do what I think is right, no matter how unpopular it may be."

Ben's heart swelled. He put a hand on her arm and gave it a squeeze. "Thanks, Em. That means a lot to me." Their eyes met momentarily, and he felt the bond they'd always had come rushing back, making him realize just how much he'd missed her over the past year.

Before long, Emily was pulling into the long, circular drive of their house so Ben could drop off his bags before going to the hospital, and Ben decided that the huge, three-story brick mansion with its tall white columns and ivy-covered walls looked just as he remembered it. When they went in, he noticed that his old bedroom hadn't changed much either. His posters and belongings weren't there, but his comforter was still on the bed, and he even found a couple of his framed posters tucked neatly away in a closet.

Putting his nostalgia aside, he quickly stowed his bags in a corner of the room before they ran back and climbed into Emily's BMW. Without saying a word, she immediately spun out of the driveway and headed for the hospital and a short time later, they were walking down the hall of the ICU.

"So, how's he doing?" Ben asked quietly.

"A little better today," she admitted. "It turns out his heart attack wasn't as severe as the doctors originally thought, and they're expecting to release him in another day or so. I knew he was feeling better when I stopped by this morning and heard him yelling into the phone at his secretary for canceling his meetings and court dates for the next couple of weeks." She grimaced. "Same old Dad."

"Great," Ben muttered as he followed Emily into a private room off to the left. His heart lifted when he heard his mother's voice coming from the room, and he realized just how much he'd missed her. But then he heard his father's deep voice arguing with her about not wanting to take some particular kind of medication, and his stomach knotted.

When he stepped around the drawn curtain, the room suddenly went deathly quiet. His mother froze when her pretty hazel eyes looked his direction, and his father's already pale complexion paled ever further.

After a long, painful silence, his father's eyes narrowed and he turned accusing eyes toward Emily. "What is *he* doing here?"

Ben bit back his sarcastic reply and took another step into the room. "I'm here because she told me you were sick."

"I'm not sick," his father shot back gruffly, pushing himself up a little straighter in bed. "And even if I were, I wouldn't want you here. Get out before I throw you out myself!"

"Now, William, don't go getting yourself all worked up," Ben's mom soothed, taking the cup of ice chips from her husband's hand. "We were all worried about you. You had a heart attack. I think Emily did the right thing to call your son."

"He's not my son," he whispered harshly, turning away from them and looking pointedly out the window. "Now if you don't mind, I'd like to get some sleep."

Ben stared at his father in stunned silence, then looked at his mother and sister in disbelief. They hadn't even told his father he was coming! They hadn't even told him they'd contacted him. Feeling suddenly betrayed, Ben searched for something—anything—to say that might help the situation, but his mind was a complete blank. Of course his father was going to lash out, since he'd had no warning at all that Ben was coming.

As Ben opened his mouth, praying for the right words to come to him, his father glanced over in his direction, eyes blazing.

"I said get out," he hissed from between gritted teeth, his face growing redder by the second. When Ben stood frozen in place, he yelled, *"Get out!"*

Angrily, Ben spun around and walked rapidly out of the room, his hands clenched tightly. *I knew coming here was a mistake!* he thought furiously. *What was I even thinking?* He was halfway down the hall when he heard Emily calling his name as she ran to catch up with him. Reluctantly, he slowed his steps and turned.

Emily was out of breath when she stopped next to him. "Ben, please, don't go," she pleaded, her eyes soulful and sad. "You know Dad doesn't mean it. It was just a shock for him to see you, that's all."

Ben's eyes flashed. "I thought you were going to tell him I was coming!"

She took a step back when she saw the anger in his eyes. "I—I'm sorry, but there just didn't seem to be the right time."

"Yeah, well, there never was a right time to talk to him about anything," he shot back. He glanced at his watch. "Maybe if I catch the next plane out of here, I can still spend Christmas with someone who *does* want to be with me." His tone sounded bitter, even to his own ears, but he couldn't help it. It was how he felt.

"Please, stay through Christmas," Emily begged, putting a hand on his arm. "I want you to, and Mom wants you to."

He looked in the direction she gestured and saw his mom down the hall by his dad's hospital room, watching them tearfully. His resolve wavered. "Okay," he finally conceded. "I'll stay for a couple of days."

When Emily turned to their mom and nodded, a look of relief washed over his mother's face. She walked up to Ben and hugged him tenderly. Ben closed his eyes and savored the feeling of being in his mother's arms. They'd never been as close as Lauren and her own mother were, but it had been a long time, and he realized he'd missed her more than he'd let himself admit.

For now at least, it was good to be home.

The attitude of Ben's father slowly softened as the next two days passed. First, there'd been reluctant eye contact, then a softly spoken sentence, then short, impersonal conversations. It wasn't anything monumental, but Ben knew it was a start. By Christmas Eve, after his father had been released from the hospital and was being cared for by private nurses at home, Ben felt a little more hopeful about the possibility of mending some fences.

His mother managed to pull some strings and arrange for a catered Christmas Eve dinner on short notice, and as they sat around the long, elegant, cherry dining room table to eat, Ben felt almost glad he'd come. That is, until his father resorted to his age-old habits of trying to run his life.

"You've been away for so long that you're out of the loop," Ben's father told him in his gruff voice. "But I know just what you need. You remember James Winchester? He's now a partner in the firm, and his daughter is back from Switzerland where she's been studying. Why don't you call her while you're here? She'd be good for you. She's from the right family, and she knows a lot of people from the right social circles...."

Ben groaned inwardly. Nothing ever changed. "Dad, I'm afraid that's out of the question."

His father dismissed his objection with a wave of his hand. "Now, don't give me that. You've been dodging these things for years, and this time I won't take no for an answer. You'll really like Caitlin. She's pretty, intelligent, and one of these days she's going to take over for her dad at the law firm. Pete says that she—"

Ben couldn't take it anymore. "Dad," he interrupted. But when that didn't do the trick, and his father kept rambling on, he tried again, this time louder. "Dad!"

His father's words stilled, and Ben found that he'd effectively—if not intentionally—captured everybody's attention. He said a quick, silent prayer, then reached deep inside for a strength that he wasn't sure he had. He caught his sister's eyes briefly before saying, "Dad, I don't want to go out with anybody because, well... I met somebody at school."

His dad seemed surprised by the announcement, but then his smile returned and he continued on. "Fine, fine, but that doesn't mean you can't take Caitlin out and see if things work out better between you two than this girl you met at school. You never know."

Ben shook his head. "That's not going to work, Dad, because, you see..." He paused, searching for the right words. "This girl and I are... well...." He looked around the table, taking in each intent face. "We're serious. I'm going to ask her to marry me."

For several moments, nobody said anything. It was so quiet he could hear the grandfather clock ticking out in the front hall. Finally, the sound of his father's fork clattering to his plate broke the silence, and his father bellowed, "You're *what?!*"

Ben cringed. *Let the games begin*, he thought dismally.

"You can't marry this girl!" his dad shouted, his face turning bright red in anger. "She's all wrong for you!"

"Dad, you don't know anything about her," Ben began, trying to keep his voice calm and reasonable. "She's the person I've been waiting for my entire life. She's kind, and thoughtful, and beautiful...."

"And she's probably one of those..." he paused, fumbling with his speech, "...one of those *Mormons!*" He spat the word out as if it tasted rotten.

"Dad, *I'm* one of those *Mormons*," Ben reminded him with what little patience he had left. "And yes, as a matter of fact, she's Mormon, too. It's wonderful to be in love with someone who has the same goals and beliefs, and wants the same things out of life that I do, but that's not the only reason I love her."

His father eyed him angrily. "And I suppose that if you marry her, you'll want to do it in that confounded Mormon temple of yours. I've heard about that place. Unless you're Mormon, they won't even let you in to see your child get married! Is that what you want? To shut your mother and me out of your life? Out of your marriage?"

Ben leaped to his feet, pushing his chair back so abruptly it almost tipped over. "I didn't shut you out of my life, you shut me out of yours!" he yelled, finally losing what little control he had left. "Do you have any idea how hard it's been, knowing that my own father was so set on manipulating my life that when he found he could no longer control me, he simply disowned me and refused to acknowledge that I was even his son? Do you know how much it hurt to be cast aside like that? It was hard for me to come back here, knowing I wasn't welcome, but I did it because I heard you were sick, and for some strange reason, I cared. I thought this might finally give me the opportunity to prove to you that just because I made a choice you didn't agree with, I still wanted to be a part of this family. But if you can't accept that, then I guess I'm wasting my time!" And with that, he turned and stormed out of the room.

Ben stomped up to his bedroom and fell back across the bed in defeat. *Why did I bother to come back if I'm only going to get the same abuse my father's dished out for years?* he thought angrily. *I've grown up, I'm on my own, I can make my own decisions! Why do I have to be continually punished for that?*

A short time later, a soft knock sounded on the door. "Come in," he called dejectedly.

The door opened and Emily appeared. She came over and sat down beside him. "You left a few very shocked, silent people behind when you stormed out like that."

Ben's lips tightened into a hard, thin line. "Good. What I said needed to be said."

"You've got guts, I'll give you that." She chuckled, shaking her head. "Of everybody I know, you're the only one who's not afraid to speak your mind to Dad. I wish I had your courage."

He sat up and sighed. "Yeah, well, courage isn't always what it's cracked up to be."

Emily nodded, and the mood was solemn for a moment. Then a smile appeared on her face as she pulled her hands out from behind her back and set a wrapped gift on his lap. "Merry Christmas."

Ben looked down at the present in surprise. "Oh, Em, this is so nice of you, but I didn't...."

She squeezed his arm understandingly. "I know. You had no idea we'd be together at Christmas. Anyway, it's nothing big, but I didn't want to give it to you tomorrow morning when Mom and Dad might see. They wouldn't understand." When he looked confused, she said, "Go ahead, open it."

Slowly, he started to work the paper loose from the tape. As the gift emerged from the colorful wrappings, his eyes widened. It was a book entitled, *Standing for Something*, by Gordon B. Hinckley. It took him several moments to recover from the shock of his sister buying him an LDS church book. When he finally did, he enthused, "Oh, Em, this is so great! I haven't had a chance to read this yet. This was so thoughtful of you." He opened the book and started to thumb through it.

"Well, the clerk at the Mormon bookstore said it was a good one, so I thought...."

Ben suddenly noticed that several of the pages were dog-eared and he looked up at her questioningly. A blush spread across her cheeks. "Okay, maybe I read some of it," she admitted sheepishly. "I'm sorry. I know it's tacky to buy someone a book and then read it before giving it to them, but I was curious, you know? I wanted to know what was so important about this religion of yours that would make you choose it over your family."

His heart swelled, and he smiled at her softly. "I love that you read it. Did it answer your questions?"

"Some," she responded hesitantly.

"What else do you want to know?" he asked eagerly. "I'd be happy to answer any questions you have."

Now that the subject had been broached, Emily's questions came one after another. They talked about the basics of the gospel long into the night, and when they finally said goodnight and Emily left for her bedroom, Ben felt as if he could fly.

Emily was actually asking questions about the Church. He shook his head. Never in a million years had he thought that would happen. Not that she was about to rush out and take the missionary discussions, but asking questions and being open-minded was an incredible start. It was undoubtedly one of the best Christmas presents he'd ever received.

After changing for bed, he climbed beneath the cool sheets and sighed happily. For the first time since he'd arrived, he thought that maybe there was a reason for him to be in Boston after all.

Chapter Twenty-One

"Hey, Lauren, this is great!" Jack exclaimed, holding up a burgundy tie with dozens of little prints of Moroni on the front. "It'll be perfect for church. Thanks."

Lauren looked at him uncertainly. "So, you really like it? You're not just saying that?" she asked, hoping he could hear her above the din. With her nieces and nephews running around crazily, playing with their new toys, and her mom and dad talking and laughing with her brothers and their wives, she wondered how anybody could hear themselves even think.

Jack laughed at her look of doubt. "Of course not! Being a missionary for two years, I'm a little sick of all my old ties. This will be perfect."

She breathed a sigh of relief. "Whew. I was a little worried." When he turned to help gather the last of the wrapping paper around the Christmas tree, Lauren glanced up at the clock on the wall.

Why hasn't Ben called yet? she wondered anxiously. *It's been three days since he left, and I haven't heard a thing from him. If anything, I thought I would've heard from him this morning.*

Stop worrying, the rational part of her mind argued. *He's probably up at the hospital with his dad.*

Just then she felt an arm on her elbow and she turned to see Jack smiling kindly at her. "He'll call," he whispered reassuringly. "Stop worrying."

Lauren smiled gratefully. "Thanks," she whispered back.

He patted her shoulder sympathetically, then turned and began picking up wrapping paper.

When the cordless phone rang an hour later, Lauren practically dove for it. "Hello?" she asked breathlessly, hurrying into the other room to try to hear over the racket in the front room.

"Hey, gorgeous," came Ben's husky voice, making her skin tingle and her heartbeat quicken. "Merry Christmas."

"Merry Christmas to you, too!" she replied cheerfully. "How's your dad?"

She heard Ben sigh over the phone. "He's home, so his health's improving. That's the best I can say now, though."

Lauren grimaced. "That bad, huh?"

"At least he's gotten over the shock of me being here and hasn't thrown me out, so I guess that's a start," Ben admitted, a hint of sarcasm in his voice. "I don't know, Lauren. Things here are just so awkward."

"I bet," she sympathized. "How's your sister?"

His tone brightened and she could hear the smile in his voice as he responded. "It's been so great to see her again." Then his voice lowered to a whisper, as if he was trying not to be overheard. "You'll never guess what, though. She read *Standing for Something* and had all these questions to ask about the Church. We stayed up for hours last night talking about the gospel. I couldn't believe it."

"Ben, that's awesome!" Lauren exclaimed. "I'm so glad things are going well between you two, at least."

"Yeah, they are. That's the only good thing about being here right now," he admitted, and Lauren could tell he was trying to hide how depressed he was feeling. "All my old friends are vacationing in Europe or the Bahamas or wherever, so there's really nothing to do here. At least Emily has the week off, so we're going to hang out. Just like old times."

"Glad to hear it," Lauren told him sincerely.

"So, tell me all about what's going on there," he said, changing the subject. "Is everybody having a good time?"

Lauren told him about the chaotic but fun day they were having—including Allison's latest escapade. She'd managed to talk Lauren into toilet papering an old boyfriend's house two nights before, and they'd had to hide in a ditch filled with snow for twenty minutes to avoid being caught. Ben laughed, and the rich, deep sound of his laughter made her realize just how much she missed him.

They chatted for a few more minutes, then Ben sighed. "I guess I'd better go. My family's going to be wondering where I disappeared to. I'm going to stay for a few more days, but I'll be home in time for classes to start."

"Do you know what day you're flying in? I'll pick you up."

"I don't want to make you go to any trouble—"

"Oh, brother," she quickly cut him off. "Of course I'll be there! Just tell me when."

He gave her the flight information, and she wrote it down carefully. "Great, I'll see you then. In the meantime, please try to have a little fun. I'll feel miserable if I know you're there feeling miserable."

He laughed softly. "Oh, I've missed you," he said, a hint of his usual spirit returning. "You have no idea how much."

"Probably as much as I've missed you," she told him sincerely. "Promise me you'll try to have fun?"

"I'll do my best. And Lauren?"

"Yes?"

"I love you."

Lauren felt a warm tingle start at her heart and spread out from there. "I love you, too."

"I'll see you in a few days."

Lauren smiled dreamily. "I can't wait."

They said goodbye, and Lauren set the phone back in its cradle, unable to erase the sadness she felt at hearing how distracted and unhappy Ben sounded. She knew the situation had to be hard on him, but she could only hope that the closeness he shared with his sister would get him through the next few days.

A week without Ben, she thought. How was she going to handle it? Three days had already seemed like a lifetime. She sighed as she headed back into the living room. With any luck, the chaos filling the house would last for a few more days and make the time go faster.

Ben hung up the phone and stared at it wistfully. More than anything, he wanted to be there with Lauren, sharing Christmas with her. But here he was, 2,000 miles away, in a place so far removed from his life that he could hardly believe it ever *was* his life.

A knock on the door drew him out of his thoughts, and he looked up to see his Mom tentatively pushing open the door. "Your father wants to see you."

Ben sighed. "He probably thinks he hasn't done a good enough job of ruining my Christmas."

He started to walk past his mom into the hall, but she put a hand on his shoulder to stop him. When he looked at her questioningly, she said quietly, "Please, Ben, give him a chance. He won't admit it, but... he's missed you."

Ben blinked. "Wh—what?"

His mom nodded. "You know your father—he wants everything to go his way, and when it doesn't, he starts throwing his weight around and making threats. That's what happened when you joined that church of yours. But after you were gone...." She shook her head sadly. "Just go talk to him. He's waiting for you in the den."

Ben nodded, then made his way to the den. When he reached the doorway, he spotted his father sitting in the leather armchair in the corner, staring out the window. For the first time ever, Ben thought he saw a look of vulnerability on his father's face, and he couldn't help noticing how old and tired he looked. His heart softened as he stepped into the room, and his father looked up at his approach.

"Ben," he said quietly. He gestured to the leather couch across from him. "Sit down."

Ben did as he was told, and a heavy silence filled the room. Finally, his father spoke. His voice was so quiet that Ben had to strain to hear him. "I'm sorry about last night."

Ben stared at his father in shock. He'd never heard his father apologize. For anything. Still stunned by the words, Ben found himself asking, "You are?"

His father nodded wearily. "You've always been strong willed and independent, and always went your own way—even if it wasn't in the direction I wanted you to go." The hint of a smile crossed his weary features. "Even as a little boy, you were like that. I guess I sometimes forget that you're grown up now, and free to make your own choices."

Ben sat in shocked silence. Was he really hearing what he thought he was hearing? Or was this a new way his father had found to manipulate him into doing what he wanted him to do? But as he continued to search his father's expression and body language, he saw no hint of malice—only a humbleness that came from life's adversities.

"I guess what I'm saying is," his father continued, his voice momentarily quivering with emotion, "I'm sorry that I've been so hard on you. I never meant to drive you away. I just… I thought I knew what was best for you and I wanted you to be happy." He finally met Ben's gaze, and Ben saw the hint of tears in his father's eyes.

Trying to swallow past the sudden lump in his throat, Ben leaned forward on the couch, resting his elbows on his knees. "I am happy," he insisted gently. "If I've learned anything this past year, it's that I don't need money or prestige or high society associations to make me happy. I found the best kind of happiness in other, more important things."

His father nodded slowly. "If you have, then I'm happy for you. It's just… the way we left things last year… I'm sorry. I didn't mean…." He paused. Then, in a hoarse, emotional whisper, he said, "I've missed you, son."

Ben felt tears gather in his eyes; he pushed himself off the couch and knelt before his father. He hesitated, but when his father met his gaze, a look of love and understanding passed between them. Then they were in each other's arms, and tears began to flow. For the first time, Ben felt a connection with his father and saw a glimmer of hope for their future as a family.

The rest of Ben's week went by in a dream-like blur. He'd spent not only a good deal of time with Emily, but a surprising amount of time with his father. They'd played cards and talked, and Ben found himself even getting excited about law again as his father went on about everything that was happening at the firm. More than once, Ben found himself down on his knees in the privacy of his bedroom, thanking his Father in Heaven for the incredible blessings he was receiving, for the chance to be with his family again and start rebuilding what they might have had.

He was surprised to discover that he actually felt a little sad to leave on Thursday night as he stood in his room packing. It was wonderful, feeling the bonds with his family starting to form again. It wasn't that he wasn't excited to see Lauren—thrilled was more like it—but having the chance to be with his family again had been incredible.

He was just setting out a pair of jeans and a light sweater to wear on the flight home the next morning when he heard a knock on his door. Turning, he saw his mom standing in the doorway.

"Looks like you're almost done," she observed with a smile.

"Almost. I can't believe I'm actually going back tomorrow. This has all been so weird," he admitted, turning to put a pair of his socks in his suitcase. "I came here expecting a really rough time, but it turned out much better than I could have imagined."

"I know," his mom answered, coming to sit on the bed by his open suitcase. "It's been great to have you back. That smile and enthusiasm of yours always did brighten up this place." A moment later, a look of concern passed over her features and she said hesitantly, "Ben, I wanted to talk to you about something."

Ben looked up at her curiously. "About what?"

"This girlfriend of yours... Lauren, is it?" When he nodded warily, she continued. "I think it's great you've met somebody you love. It's just...."

"What?" Ben prompted.

"Well, I think it's wonderful that you and your father are making amends. I hope this continues, but I worry about how your relationship with this girl is going to affect your relationship with your father."

Ben's brow furrowed in confusion. "What do you mean?"

"Your relationship with your father is on delicate ground right now," she told him seriously. "He's finally willing to accept the path you've taken with your life, but you know how he's always been against that church of yours. If you decide to get married in your church's temple, how do you think he's going to feel, not being able to see his only son get married? It's going to push him away again... maybe permanently this time. Is that what you want?"

Ben felt his chest tighten painfully. "Mom, I can't stop seeing Lauren."

"I'm not asking you to," she quickly amended. "Maybe just postpone your plans for a while. Your relationship with your father is at stake. *All* our relationships are at stake. Besides, isn't that what your church preaches? The importance of families?" When he didn't speak, his mom reached out and patted his arm. "Just think about it, that's all I'm asking." And with that, she stood up and left.

A moment later, he caught movement out of the corner of his eye and looked up to see Emily hovering outside his door. He could tell from the look on her face that she'd overheard their conversation. "You heard that, huh?" he asked.

She nodded and came in to stand beside him. "Maybe she's right, Ben," she began hesitantly. "Look, I know how much you love Lauren, but I just barely got you back in my life. I can't tell you how lonely it's been without you, how I've struggled without being able to talk to you or ask you for advice, or even have your stupid jokes to cheer me up when I'm having a bad day. Maybe this isn't the right time to go through with this. Please, Ben. I don't want to lose you again. Not now. I couldn't." Tears filled her eyes, and she continued, "Just... I don't know... wait a while. That's not too much to ask, is it?"

Ben sighed. "No, it's not too much to ask. I just... I don't know. I'm going to have to think about this."

Emily nodded. "I understand." She gave him a half smile, then backed toward the door. "I'll see you in the morning, bright and early. I'm driving you to the airport."

When she was gone, Ben sank down onto his bed, his mind numb. What was he supposed to do? His mom was right. Families *were* the focal point of the gospel. But what about his plans to form a family with Lauren? He loved her with all his heart. He couldn't live without her. Did this mean he had to make a choice between her and his own family? He'd already made a choice between his family and something else once. Did he have the strength to do it again? Did he *want* to do it again?

Surely, he didn't have to. He could just do as his mom and sister asked, and postpone things between him and Lauren for a while in order to make peace with his family. But if he postponed things, could he really be around Lauren every day, knowing he couldn't be with her the way he wanted to be? He was ready to take the next step with her, and he suspected she was with him. But if they couldn't take that step without destroying his newly established relationship with his family, what was the point of pretending that his and Lauren's relationship was going somewhere when it couldn't? At least, not in the near future.

He spent a sleepless night mulling over his options, and by morning he still hadn't come to any conclusions. Things only got more complicated when, just before he left for the airport, his father pulled him aside.

"Son, I want to talk to you about something before you leave," he said carefully. They went to sit in the quiet of the living room. "I know you hate it when I meddle, so please don't think I'm doing so, but hear me out. Do you remember John Zimmerman?"

Ben nodded. The man had been his first bishop shortly after he was baptized. He was a good man and a successful attorney, and they'd spent many long hours talking about life, and almost as many talking about law. Ben had learned a lot from him, and was very fond of the man.

His dad continued, "Well, I don't know him all that well because our firms are after different things, but his wife and your mother have worked on some charity committees together. I never knew until last night when I talked to John on the phone that he'd been your pastor."

"Bishop," Ben corrected.

"Whatever." His father waved his hand dismissively. "Anyway, John wanted to know if you'd be interested in interning at his firm. They have an opening coming up this spring and from what he told me, it's the opportunity of a lifetime." He went on to explain everything John had told him about the internship, and Ben had to admit, it did sound like something he couldn't pass up.

"But what about school?" Ben asked. "I'm enrolled in spring semester, plus there's—" He'd been about to say "Lauren," but quickly stopped himself when thoughts of his talk with Emily and his mother resurfaced. "Well, my life is back in Idaho right now."

"I don't see why you can't finish your spring courses, then fly back here after since the internship won't start until then anyway." Seeing his son was unconvinced, he rushed on. "Ben, you do what you feel is right, but I can't imagine you passing this up. I know from talking to you how much you love law, and this would give you a chance to be on the front lines, to see law in action and be a part of it. Personally, I think you'd be crazy not to take advantage of John's offer."

"It does sound like something I've always wanted to do," Ben said, feeling himself wavering. But then an image of Lauren jumped into his mind, and he knew it would be impossible. How could he take an internship in Boston when Lauren would be back in Idaho? He couldn't leave her behind, but he also knew he couldn't marry her and bring her with him—not yet—not with his relationship with his father still so precariously balanced.

Understanding that his son needed some time, his father patted him gently on the knee. "Think about it a while, and then let me or John know. He's waiting for an answer."

Ben nodded numbly, then spent the next half hour saying his goodbyes before boarding the plane for the long flight back to

Idaho. During the flight, he mulled his options over and over in his mind, but even the solitude of his first class accommodations didn't help him find a solution.

Taking the internship would mean choosing it over Lauren, he thought. *But how can I do that?* He loved her so much that the idea of not being with her actually hurt. They'd been through so much together over the past few months that he felt like he'd already spent a lifetime with her—a wonderfully happy lifetime. And that was exactly how he wanted to feel for the rest of his life.

So it's settled, he thought. *I won't take the internship.*

But even that didn't feel right. Law had always been his passion, and he was beginning to see that his love for law hadn't dwindled—it had merely been put on the back burner as his life had taken a drastic turn. Yet here it was again, the opportunity to get back into the field he loved.

He sighed. *If only my parents would accept Lauren, and we could get married before going to Boston,* he thought. But as quickly as the thought came to him, he brought it to an abrupt halt. How did he know if she even *wanted* to go to Boston? Her life was here. Her family was here. Her friends were here.

Okay, let's think about this. What if she doesn't want to go to Boston? he asked himself. *Would you ask her to wait for you?*

He shook his head in disgust. That wasn't fair, either. She was just so amazing, and she deserved so much better than to have their relationship placed on hold indefinitely. He had no idea how long it would take for his father to come around to his way of thinking so he could marry Lauren in the temple without alienating his family again.

It isn't fair to force Lauren to wait when she could be getting on with her life with someone who deserves her more than I do, he reasoned, his thoughts taking a turn toward self-pity. *She deserves someone who's served a mission and been raised in the Church. Someone who's had years to build a testimony and develop faith strong enough to get them through the tough times. I'm certainly not that person. I still have so much to learn. It isn't fair to hold Lauren back, to keep her from marrying someone who's as good and as wonderful and as deserving as she is.*

Ben knew he had barely been a member long enough to struggle by on his own. How on earth was he supposed to hold a family together?

The stewardess appeared at his side, but it took her three attempts before she could get his attention, and Ben realized he'd been doing it yet again—withdrawing. He was pulling inside himself and unintentionally pushing the rest of the world away while he tried to make up his mind about something important.

He apologized to the stewardess, then turned down her offered snacks. He simply had too much on his mind right now to concentrate on anything else. For a moment, he even wondered if he should call Lauren to tell her not to bother meeting his plane. He knew he was going to be poor company. His sister knew not to be offended by his tendency to withdraw when something was weighing heavily on his mind, but he doubted Lauren would understand. He'd probably only end up hurting her.

As he deliberated, he glanced at his watch and frowned. It was too late to call. His plane would be landing in just under an hour, and she was likely already on her way to the airport to wait for him.

He sighed. If only he could make a decision before then....

Shaking his head miserably, he turned and stared out the plane window at the puffy white clouds moving past. But, disappointingly, even that awe-inspiring sight couldn't help him find any answers.

Chapter Twenty-Two

"Ben!" Lauren exclaimed as she spotted him coming through the terminal on Friday afternoon. She ran toward him and threw herself into his arms, feeling all the tension of a week without him instantly draining away.

He hugged her back, but she sensed something different about him. She stepped back and looked up into his face, and for the first time, she noticed how completely exhausted he looked. His face was tired and drawn, and he looked as if he had the weight of the world on his shoulders.

"Ben, are you okay?" she asked with concern, trying to read the veiled expression in his eyes.

He nodded cautiously. "Yeah, I'm okay. I just have a lot on my mind, that's all."

"Things didn't go well in Boston?"

"Actually, they went better than I expected," he told her, pushing a hand through his travel-rumpled hair. "My father and I talked, and I think we might be able to work things out."

Lauren's eyes lit up. "Oh, Ben, that's so great! I was praying that things would work out for you there."

In some ways they did, but not in others, he thought miserably. He forced a smile onto his face for her sake and glanced toward the baggage claim terminal. "I guess I should get my luggage."

Lauren looked at him strangely. "Are you sure you're okay? You don't look... I don't know, happy, I guess. Did something else happen?"

"No, no," he said quickly, "everything's fine. I guess I'm just tired from all the traveling, that's all."

Lauren continued to study his expression for a long moment, noting how carefully he was managing to avoid her gaze. Something was wrong. Very wrong. But she knew if he wasn't ready to talk about it, there was no way she was going to be able to force it out of him.

"Well, come on," she said, slipping her arm through his and guiding him toward the baggage claim area. "Let's get your bags and go home."

Half an hour later, they were on the highway heading back to Rexburg, and Lauren found herself stealing glimpses of him out of the corner of her eye. He remained eerily quiet as he stared unseeingly out the passenger window, and no matter how many times she tried to start up a conversation, her attempts failed miserably. She'd come to know him well enough over the past few months to know this sullen silence wasn't like him. He seemed distant, distracted. Whatever was eating at him had to be pretty serious, and she had no idea what to do or say to make it better.

She sighed and turned her attention back to the road. Whatever it was, he would tell her when he was ready. At least, she hoped so.

Ben spent the next several days in intensive prayer and fasting, searching for the answers that continued to elude him. He felt lost and insecure as doubts started to creep in about what he was doing with his life, and whether or not coming to BYU-Idaho had been the right thing to do. Coming to Idaho had helped give him the faith and self-reliance he needed at a very dark time in his life, but now he found himself at the precipice of another life-altering decision. Did he give his life back to his family, or did he refuse to look back and follow his heart by marrying the only girl he'd ever loved?

He felt Satan working on him day and night, and he finally turned to Bishop Warner for a Priesthood blessing. It did help him feel more at peace when he was told that if he followed the Spirit, his answers would be given to him, but it didn't help him know exactly what he was supposed to do. He had some hard choices to make, and he knew there weren't going to be any simple answers.

He did his best to maintain a semblance of his relationship with Lauren, occasionally going out with her to a campus movie or dropping by her apartment to see her, but he knew she could tell something was wrong. He'd see the pained look in her eyes when he refused to open up, and his heart wrenched when it became apparent that his standoffish, distant behavior was hurting her.

But he didn't know what else to do. He couldn't talk to her about the decisions he was facing. What was he supposed to say? That he couldn't marry her because his father wouldn't approve? Yeah, that would go over well. And he was sure it would go over just as well if he told her that he was thinking about taking an internship in Boston, but because he wasn't in a position to marry her yet, he'd drop her a few postcards from time to time.

So, where did that leave him? He found himself growing more and more withdrawn with each passing day as his mind churned over the decisions he had to make, and he could tell Lauren was quickly losing patience.

Things with Lauren finally came to a head the last Saturday night in January when he opened his apartment door at the sound of insistent knocking and saw her standing there with a rather determined expression on her face.

"May I come in?" she asked coolly.

He nodded and stepped back, letting her into the room. He shut the door behind her, then walked over to the couch and sat down. "What's up?" he asked, his anxiety growing as he noticed the careful distance she kept between them.

"Okay, I'm just going to say this before I lose my nerve," she began, trying not to the let the familiar warm, brown eyes detract her from giving her prepared speech. "Ever since you got back from Boston, you've been different. You keep insisting nothing's wrong, but I know you too well to believe that. I'm sure you have your reasons for keeping whatever it is to yourself, so I've tried to be supportive and give you your space. But enough is enough."

She took a deep breath, then forged on. "I'm worried about us, Ben," she confessed, an emotional hitch in her voice. "Whatever this is you're trying to work through, it's driving a stake between us. I'm not going to just sit by and watch our relationship fall to pieces. I love you too much for that."

Ben saw her lower lip start to quiver, and his heart clenched painfully. He fought the urge to rush over and gather her into his arms, knowing that what he needed was to maintain his objectivity until he could figure out what he was supposed to do.

Pushing himself up off the couch, he shoved his hands into his jeans pockets and crossed over to the window. "I'm sorry I've been distant," he said quietly. "And you're right, I am trying to work through some things. I haven't said anything to you or anyone else about it because this is something I have to figure out myself, you know?"

He turned back to find her staring sadly at him, and he felt his resolve to maintain his emotional distance weaken. But it was that look of sadness that proved to him that it wasn't fair to let his own twisted emotions affect her like this. She deserved so much better.

"Lauren, look," he tried again, unable to meet her gaze. "I've got so many things going on in my head right now that I just... I don't know." He sighed sadly. "I know I haven't been much of a boyfriend lately, and I'm sorry. But I've got some hard decisions to make, and I need to make them on my own." He swallowed past the lump in his throat, then forced out the words he hated to say. "So, um... maybe it's better if we just take a little break."

The instant the words were out of his mouth, he took one look at the shocked and pained expression on Lauren's face and wished he could take them right back.

"A break?" she asked in a hoarse whisper. "Are you saying you want to break up?"

"No!" Ben blurted, his eyes widening. "No, I don't want us to break up. I just need a little time to think about things, so maybe some time apart would be a good idea—"

Lauren laughed humorlessly as her expression became a mixture of pain and anger. "Come on, Ben, don't play me! Either you want to be with me or you don't. You can't have it both ways."

"I do want to be with you," he insisted, taking an urgent step toward her. "But things are just so complicated right now—"

"What things?" she yelled in frustration. "Why can't you tell me what's wrong?"

His eyes reflected his sadness as he shook his head slowly. "Lauren, I can't. Please, what I'm dealing with is just too hard...."

Lauren folded her arms across her chest and glared at him defiantly, trying to ignore the tears stinging her eyes. "So, things get hard and you bail? Is that it? I thought two people who loved each other as much as we do were supposed to stick together through everything, no matter how hard things got. Just tell me what's wrong and we'll fix it. Don't I mean enough to you to even do that?"

He flinched. For a moment, he couldn't say anything. Finally, his expression turned determined and steely. "I'm sorry, Laur. I just can't."

When Lauren saw his determined stance and the unwavering look in his eyes, she felt as if he'd just ripped out her heart and sent it through the grinder. "So that's it? You don't care enough about our relationship to try to make things work?" She waited for a response, but when she didn't get one, her jaw tightened and she nodded abruptly. "Fine."

She whirled around and stalked to the door, yanking it open angrily. Before she went out, she turned back to him and was surprised to see what appeared to be a momentary look of panic flash into his dark eyes. But the pain in her heart was too intense to let it affect her and she simply brushed it aside.

"You know," she said bitterly, "all this time I thought you were different. I thought I'd finally found a guy who was mature enough to handle an adult relationship, someone who

I could trust not to hurt me, someone to give my heart to and be loved in return. But I guess I was wrong. You're nothing like I thought you were, Ben. You're just like all the rest of them." And with that, she turned and left, slamming the door behind her.

Telling herself not to look back, Lauren was across the parking lot and halfway down the street before she finally stopped running. Tears blurred her vision, and her breath came in short, labored gasps. She kept hoping to hear the sound of footsteps behind her, to hear Ben calling out to her, telling her that he'd made a terrible mistake and that he was sorry for being such a jerk. But she didn't. All she heard was the sound of her own crying.

And the sound of her heart breaking.

What went wrong? she asked herself in bewilderment. She'd planned out exactly what she was going to say when she went over to Ben's apartment to talk to him, and had every intention of walking out of there with things right between them and their relationship back on solid ground. But things had escalated and completely unraveled before her eyes, and before she knew it, it was over.

When she finally reached her apartment, she rushed into her darkened bedroom and threw herself down on her bed, sobbing uncontrollably. *You don't need him,* she told herself fiercely. *You were fine before Ben Morrison walked into your life, and you'll be just fine without him. In fact, you'll probably be better off without him wreaking havoc with your emotions and monopolizing your time. In no time at all, you'll be over him and will have forgotten all about him. Just you wait and see.*

But as she continued to sob into her pillow, she knew she was fooling herself. As hard as she tried to convince herself to the contrary, she doubted her life was ever going to be the same again.

Chapter Twenty-Three

Ben watched her go a hundred times over in his mind by the time he climbed into bed that night, feeling utterly despondent and dejected. Never in a million years had he expected things to end like this. Lauren was the love of his life, yet in one awful moment, it was over between them. He didn't even know what had happened. One minute she was pleading with him to open up, and the next, she was storming out of his apartment.

His heart lurched when he remembered the look of devastation on her face before she'd left. He wanted more than anything to stop her from leaving, to bare his soul to her, and tell her everything he was going through. But he couldn't. Not when he didn't have any answers to give her for the questions she'd be sure to ask.

Maybe it's better this way, the little voice of reason consoled. *Doesn't this make your decisions easier?*

He shook his head. Maybe, but this wasn't the way he wanted it to be. He'd wanted to find a way to be with her and appease his family at the same time, but he was beginning to think that was impossible.

Letting his head fall back onto his pillow, he sighed sadly. Nothing seemed to have an easy answer anymore.

"Lauren, wake up, you're going to be late for church."

Feeling the gentle shake on her arm, Lauren rolled over and opened her eyes to see Allison standing over her, dressed for church. She blinked a couple of times, trying to figure out why her eyes felt so scratchy and painful. Then it all came back to her in a heart-wrenching rush.

A few leftover tears threatened to spill down her cheeks, and she shook her head miserably. "Allison, please, just go without me."

The look of sympathy on Allison's face made Lauren feel even worse. She'd told Allison everything that had happened when her friend had come home the night before, and Allison had stayed up with her late into the night talking to her and trying to make her feel better. It felt good, knowing she had her friend's support, but nothing came close to taking the pain away.

"As much as I'd like to let you wallow in your misery, we told Anne next door that we'd help her set up for her Relief Society lesson, remember?"

Lauren groaned. "I can't go to church. Everyone there will take one look at me and know what happened."

"Not with some expertly applied make-up," Allison said. "Besides, you can't avoid Ben forever. What are you going to do, stop going to church completely?"

Lauren sighed. Allison was right. They were in the same ward; she couldn't hide from him indefinitely, even if she wanted to. With a feeling of resignation, she dragged herself out of bed and into the bathroom, shuddering at her reflection when she glanced in the mirror. Too much crying and not enough sleep had left her eyes red and puffy, and her skin looked pale and blotchy. Not good signs for someone pretending she hadn't been affected by the events of the night before.

She got dressed, pulled her hair up into a clip, then let Allison perform her magic. By the time they were done, Lauren wanted to award her friend a medal. She'd been able to cover the dark circles under her eyes and the blotchiness of her skin, and with the help of a few eye drops, her eyes were no longer red. The puffiness couldn't be helped, but Lauren figured she'd wear sunglasses outside and then sit somewhere in the back of her church meetings to avoid speculation.

As she finished getting ready, none of her roommates said anything about what had transpired, but it was obvious by the kindness and sympathy they showed her that Allison had told them. They never left her side as they walked to church and into the building, and they wordlessly found seats in the very back during sacrament meeting and carefully managed to seat her in the middle of them. She'd never been more grateful for friends in her life. With their support, she felt a little better about her chances of making it through the day.

As she sat waiting for sacrament meeting to start, she found herself scanning the room for Ben. When she didn't see him, she didn't know whether to be relieved or disappointed. She was finally starting to relax as Bishop Warner stood at the podium to conduct the meeting when the door at the back of the room opened. She peered over her shoulder, and when she saw Ben's tall, dark figure, her heart skipped a beat.

But when she saw he wasn't alone, her heart lurched. Elena was walking next to him with her arm threaded through his. She was making a big show of smiling up at him and tossing her long, brown hair over her shoulder.

Lauren felt as if someone had punched her in the stomach. She found it difficult to breathe, and even more difficult to watch. She realized she no longer had any claim to Ben, but seeing him with Elena—after everything they'd meant to each other—was almost too much to bear.

The twosome walked down to the front where there were empty seats, and throughout the meeting, Lauren watched Elena flirt shamelessly with Ben. When the last hymn was finally over, Ben and Elena stood up to leave, and Lauren couldn't help noticing that he seemed a little embarrassed by Elena's loud laughter and obvious attention. That made Lauren feel a little better. Not a lot, but a little.

When they started up the aisle toward her, Lauren knew she couldn't take it anymore. She couldn't sit there and watch them together even one more second. Blinking back hot tears, she stood up and rushed from the room.

• • •

When the meeting was finally over, Ben heaved a sigh of relief. Never in his life had he been so glad for a meeting to end. It had been all he could do to be polite to Elena when she'd latched onto him just before he'd come into sacrament meeting, and it continued to be a real test of his patience as she'd continued to flirt with him shamelessly throughout the meeting. Now that the meeting was over, he was eager to get out of there and away from her. He had too much on his mind to deal with her flirtatious antics—now or ever.

As he stood up to leave, he found himself glancing around the room, anxious to catch even a glimpse of Lauren, to see how she was doing. Finally, he spotted her near the back of the room, and his heart sank when he saw her crestfallen expression and her puffy eyes—a telltale sign that she'd spent a lot of time crying during the night. Before he could decide whether or not to go catch up with her and try to talk to her, she was out of her seat and rushing out of the room.

He walked dismally through the doors and into the hallway with Elena still attached to his arm. He didn't get far, however, before he found his path blocked by Allison. She stood in front of him, a smoldering look on her face, telling him in no uncertain terms how she felt about him standing there with Elena. He cringed. If Allison was mad at him, it must really be bad.

An arm tightened on his, and he turned to see Elena looking up at him with a frown. "Are we going to Sunday School or not?"

Biting his lip to keep from saying something he was sure to regret later, he made a point of slipping his arm out of hers, then said, "You go ahead."

When she saw the look of determination in his eyes, she finally nodded, turned on her heel, and disappeared down the hall. As soon as she was gone, Allison smacked his arm, causing him to jump.

"What did you think you were doing, flaunting Elena in front of Lauren like that after what you've done to her?" she exclaimed indignantly.

Ben's eyes widened. "I didn't flaunt Elena in front of her! Elena just grabbed my arm as I was walking into sacrament meeting and invited herself to sit by me. I didn't have any say in the matter!"

"Of course you had some say—you could've said no!" Allison told him angrily. "Lauren's having a hard enough time with you breaking up with her without you making it worse!"

Seeing the pained expression on Ben's face, she suddenly realized he was hurting as much as Lauren was. Her tone was softer when she continued. "Look, I don't know everything that went on between you two, but I do know that if you have any plans to work things out with Lauren, letting her think you're going out with someone else—especially Elena—isn't going to help."

"Honestly, there's nothing going on between Elena and me," Ben assured her. "Will you please tell Lauren that?"

"Why don't you tell her yourself?" Allison asked gently.

Ben sighed and shook his head. "I can't. Not yet. There are just some things I have to straighten out before I can, you know?"

Allison looked at him sadly. "No, I don't know, and neither does Lauren. But please… for Lauren's sake, figure it out fast so you can fix whatever's wrong between you. She loves you."

"I love her, too," Ben admitted with a hint of sadness.

But other than that, he didn't know what to tell Allison. He knew he wasn't ready to talk to Lauren yet; not until he had some answers.

"Lauren, there you are," Bree said with a note of relief when she walked into the apartment and found Lauren in her bedroom, changing into jeans and an oversized, grubby sweatshirt. "Allison and I were looking everywhere for you."

Lauren sniffled and wiped the tears from her cheeks. "I'm sorry, I didn't mean to make you worry. I just couldn't stay there any longer."

"I know," Bree answered sympathetically. She watched Lauren tie the laces on her sneakers, then stand up to grab her keys from the dresser. "Where are you going?"

"I've got to get out of here, at least for a little while," Lauren explained, pulling on her ski jacket. "Tell Allison I went for a drive, okay? I don't want her to worry."

Bree nodded. "Are you going to be okay?"

"Yeah," Lauren said on a sigh. "As soon as I can convince myself that Ben's a horrible person and that I deserve better, I'll be fine."

"You do deserve better than him," Bree answered firmly. "You'll see. You'll meet someone else who will love and appreciate you for who you are and for all that you have to offer. Then you'll know that Ben was just a little blip on the radar screen of life."

That caused a little smile to creep through. "A blip?"

Bree grinned sheepishly and shrugged. "Well, you know what I mean. You'll get over him. I know it's not going to be easy, but you have to get on with your life and try to forget about him."

Lauren felt a fresh ache in her heart. "That's a little easier said than done."

"I know," Bree said understandingly. When Lauren started to leave, Bree called after her, "Be careful, okay?"

Lauren nodded. "I'll be home by curfew."

When she climbed into her car and pulled out onto the snowy road, she had no idea where she was going. But then it hit her. She knew exactly where she wanted to go. Home.

She arrived at her house half an hour later, and when she walked in through the front door, her mom, still in her church dress, looked at her in surprise.

"Lauren! How nice to see—" But her voice trailed off when she saw the distraught look on her daughter's face and instantly knew something had happened. "Honey, what's wrong?"

Lauren thought she'd regained control of her shaky emotions on the drive home, but the sympathy in her mom's voice sent her spiraling over the edge again. "It's Ben—everything's over," was all she managed to say before the tears came.

Crumbling into the comforting circle of her mother's outstretched arms, she allowed herself to be steered to the couch where her mother held her tightly for several minutes until her shuddering sobs finally subsided. When she lifted her head from her mother's tear-soaked shoulder, she accepted the tissue she was handed.

"So, you want to tell me what happened?" her mother asked quietly.

Lauren poured out the whole story, about how differently Ben had been acting since he'd returned from Boston and how everything had come to a head the night before when they'd argued and broken up.

"I don't know what to do, Mom," Lauren admitted tearfully. "Ben was everything to me. What am I going to do now?" She choked back a sob, and her mom's arms immediately went around her again.

Just then the front door opened and they looked up to see Jack coming in. A look of concern clouded his features when he saw Lauren crying. "What's wrong?" he asked, his eyes shifting from Lauren to his mom, searching for an explanation.

"Jack, not now," his mom whispered tactfully, trying to wave him on.

But Jack shook his head and stubbornly remained where he was. "No, I want to know what happened."

Lauren turned and glared at her brother. "Ben broke up with me, okay? Is that what you want to hear?" Then, before he could respond, another sob escaped and she fell forward once again into her mother's arms.

Jack stood in shocked silence, staring at them in disbelief. It wasn't until his mom scowled at him and once again waved him on that he was able to force his feet to move. With one last helpless look at his sister sobbing in his mother's arms, he disappeared up the stairs to his room, reluctantly leaving them alone.

Sister Holt turned her attention back to the emotionally distraught daughter in her arms and stroked Lauren's hair lovingly. "Honey, I know your heart's breaking," she murmured quietly, "and I wish there was something I could do or say to make all the pain go away, but there just isn't. I know you loved Ben, but you are the most compassionate, sweet, loving person I know, and if Ben doesn't see that...."

Lauren sat up and wiped the tears from her cheeks with the damp tissue. "If you say he doesn't deserve me, I'm losing all faith in your ability to console me." She gave the hint of a smile, then heaved a long, shuddering sigh. "I keep telling myself that, Mom, and my friends keep telling me that, but here," she placed her hand over her heart, "it doesn't seem to make much difference."

"I'm sure it doesn't, honey," her mother answered sympathetically. "They say time heals all wounds, and it's true. I know how special Ben was to you, and it might take a very long time to get over him. But someday, you will."

Lauren's face started to crumble again and she let her hands fall dejectedly into her lap. "But why do I have to? Why couldn't things just work out this time?" she cried. "Did I do something wrong? Maybe I'm too independent and headstrong. Or maybe Heavenly Father's punishing me for something. Maybe I haven't been praying enough, or reading my scriptures as often as I should, or maybe I needed to be doing more of something—"

"Oh, honey, Heavenly Father isn't punishing you," her mother quickly interrupted. "Sometimes things just don't work out in our lives, no matter how much we want them to. But I honestly believe that everything happens for a reason. That's not much consolation to you now, I know, since it's impossible to understand Heavenly Father's reasoning, but maybe years from now you'll be able to look back on this and understand why things had to be this way."

She put a finger under Lauren's chin and tipped her face up so she would meet her gaze. "These heartaches, as horrible and sad as they feel now, are what make us strong. They teach us about ourselves and strengthen our testimonies and our faith as we rely on Heavenly Father to get us through them. So please, don't think you're being punished. Heavenly Father is still there for you. He wants to help you. Fast and pray and ask Him to help you get through this. He'll be there for you. He's promised us that much."

Lauren swallowed past the lump in her throat, then nodded wordlessly as she leaned forward to hug her mom tightly once more. "Thanks, Mom. I'm sorry to just drop in like this, but I didn't know where else to go."

"Oh, sweetie, no apology is necessary; you can always come here. I just hope something I said has helped."

Lauren nodded. "I'm sure it will eventually. I'm just kind of numb right now and can't process much at all."

"I know. So don't rush back to Rexburg," her mom suggested. "At least stay the day and let me pamper you. There's no harm in being pampered, is there?"

The first genuine smile of the day—albeit small—appeared on Lauren's face, and she shook her head. "No, there's no harm in that at all."

Chapter Twenty-Four

When Lauren returned to Rexburg late that evening, she still felt miserable and heartbroken, but at least she didn't feel so hopeless. It helped to know she had family and friends on her side who would be there for her whenever she needed them.

Allison cornered her in their bedroom shortly after she returned and told her about talking to Ben at church, and of how distraught he'd seemed over everything that had happened. She assured Lauren that Ben had seemed sincere in his contention that he wasn't the least bit interested in Elena, and that he still loved Lauren. But Lauren wasn't sure how to take that. After all, if Ben still loved her, shouldn't he be here, trying to work things out with her? But he wasn't. And that realization hurt even more.

Before going to sleep that night, Lauren made a special effort to kneel down beside her bed and pour out her heart to her Father in Heaven, asking for understanding and for help to ease her heartache as she fought to survive this latest trial. By the time she ended her prayer, she felt a little better.

But how long that feeling would last, she didn't know. She only hoped that Heavenly Father was planning on hearing from her an awful lot the next few weeks as she struggled to get on with her life. Somehow, though, she couldn't help wondering if her life without Ben would ever be the same.

For the next couple of days, Lauren tried to lose herself in her schoolwork, but it would only take one fond memory of Ben, triggered by a place on campus or a particular phrase overheard in a conversation, and the pain in her heart would threaten to overwhelm her once again. Nothing seemed to keep her mind off things for long, although her friends and family tried valiantly to cheer her up. It didn't always work, but she appreciated them for trying.

On Tuesday night, she was sitting on her bed with a textbook open in front of her, trying unsuccessfully to concentrate on the words. Finally, she gave up and closed the cover of the book with a thump. The moments seemed to come and go, but tonight was one of those nights when she found herself missing Ben so much it hurt.

Just then she heard a knock on her door. "Yeah?" she called sadly.

The door opened and Melia stuck her head into the room. "Your brother's here. He's waiting in the front room."

Lauren felt her spirits rise. "Thanks, Melia. Tell him I'll be right there."

Melia nodded, then left to relay the message as Lauren slid off her bed and gave her reflection a quick inspection in the mirror. Her face was pale and her eyes still had that glazed look from excessive crying, but she figured Jack wouldn't judge her rumpled appearance too harshly. Sweeping her fingers back through her loose hair in an attempt to smooth it, she turned and headed for the living room.

She thought she had it together until she walked into the front room and spotted Jack standing there with a foil-covered plate in his hand and a look of concern in his eyes. She blinked back fresh tears as she walked into his warm embrace.

When he released her a few moments later, he studied her intently. "How are you holding up?"

She shrugged. "As well as could be expected, considering I've just had my heart broken for the umpteenth time in my life."

"Laur, I'm so sorry," he said, his eyes filled with sympathy. "I wish there was something I could do to make you feel better."

The hint of a smile crept across her face. "You could go over there and rough Ben up a little, like you always threatened to do to those guys back in high school."

He chuckled. "The thought has crossed my mind," he admitted. Then he remembered the plate in his hand. "Here. Mom made these for you."

Taking the plate, she lifted the edge of the aluminum foil to peek at the contents. This time her smile was genuine. "Brownies. Mom must think my life is really bad if she sends you all this way with chocolate desserts."

"Well, they're not just any brownies. They're double fudge with chocolate chips on top." He grinned. "Anyway, coming here was my idea. When I told her where I was going, she made me wait while she made these."

Lauren felt tears of gratefulness filling her eyes. "Jack, what would I do without you?"

He smiled and shrugged, then jerked his thumb over his shoulder toward the front door. "Come on. Let's go somewhere and talk."

For the rest of the week, Lauren went through her schedule of classes and work in a daze. She tried to concentrate, but with everything that had happened, it seemed like it was all she could do to simply show up. She only hoped her professors, classmates, and co-workers at the bookstore couldn't tell just by looking at her what had happened. She worried that somebody might ask her what was wrong, and she didn't think she could give them an answer without bursting into tears if they did.

When her alarm clock startled her awake on Friday morning, Lauren quickly turned it off and dragged herself out of bed. She went to get clothes out of her dresser and was dismayed to find that she only had one shirt in her drawer, and no pants in sight. She groaned. She'd been so preoccupied lately that doing her laundry had been the last thing on her mind.

Glancing around the room, Lauren shook her head in disbelief at the piles of dirty clothing surrounding her bed. Why hadn't she realized how far behind she'd gotten on her laundry? She actually felt embarrassed, knowing that Allison surely had to have noticed what a slob she'd been lately, but hadn't said a thing about it.

With a sigh, Lauren decided that doing several loads of laundry was going to be her chore for the evening. She tried not to wake Allison as she rummaged around in the piles and managed to find a pair of nice jeans that appeared to be relatively clean, then slipped on her sole remaining shirt and hurried to finish getting ready for class.

Lauren dragged herself through her classes, but by the time she started her shift at the bookstore, she was very ready for the day—and the week—to be over. She couldn't seem to do anything right at work. She kept screwing up the cash register, so her boss assigned her to stock shelves. When she kept putting things in the wrong place, she was moved to stocking accessories with Dan. When she dropped the box of BYU-I buttons she was unpacking, causing them to scatter all over the floor, Dan had finally had enough.

"Lauren, what is *with* you?" he asked, looking at her strangely. "For an entire week now you've been dropping stuff, putting things in the wrong place, or knocking things over. No wonder Brother Jenks' nerves are frazzled today. You're an accident waiting to happen."

As she looked down at the dozens of buttons around her feet, Lauren felt tears gathering in her eyes for what seemed like the hundredth time that week. "Gee, thanks," she muttered, crouching down to pick up the buttons. "You really know how to flatter a girl."

Keeping her face averted so Dan wouldn't see the threatening tears, she concentrated on picking up the buttons, but the warm, gentle pressure of his hand on her arm stilled her movements. She looked up to see him crouching down in front of her, his expression unusually serious.

"Lauren, what's wrong?" he asked softly, his eyes intently searching hers.

She fought to keep her voice even as she reported, "Ben and I broke up."

She felt Dan's gaze on her bowed head for a long moment, then he nodded solemnly. "I figured as much. What happened?"

"It's a long story, and if you don't mind, I'd rather not go into it. If I do, I'll dissolve into weepy tears and you'll never think of me the same way again."

"I see," he replied gently. "What if I promise not to think any less of you if you do?"

She glanced up at him in surprise. This serious side of Dan was new to her, and it seemed strange to be talking to him and not hearing him crack a joke a minute. Finally, she tore her eyes from his and glanced around the busy store. "This isn't exactly the time or place for an emotional conversation."

He finished gathering up the last of the buttons, then stood up with the box. "Point taken. Then how about after we get off work? I'll buy you dinner and we can talk."

She cocked an eyebrow at him suspiciously. "Dinner? I don't think so. I'm not about to become one of your dating statistics."

He laughed. "No, no statistics. Come on, Lauren. We're friends, and right now I can tell you really need one. Besides, you need to give me a chance to prove to you that not all us guys are scum."

That brought a smile to her face. "So, this isn't a date? No pressure, no pretenses, no expectations?"

He shook his head. "No strings attached. Nothing but two friends getting together for something to eat and a little friendly conversation."

She studied him carefully for a moment, but when she saw nothing in his eyes to indicate he was being anything other than truthful, she nodded. "Okay."

Lauren was pleasantly surprised by what a great listener Dan turned out to be. They spent an hour and a half after their shifts eating dinner at the Nordic and talking. By the time they headed out into the snowy January night, Lauren not only felt better, but had gained a new appreciation for Dan's friendship.

As they walked down the steps of the building, Lauren tightened her coat around her and told Dan sheepishly, "I'm sorry for talking your ear off like that. I guess I had a lot more to get off my chest than I thought."

"But you feel better because of it, don't you?" he pointed out as they reached the bottom of the steps.

Lauren nodded. "Yeah, I think I do, thanks to you." But when she saw a smug smile start to work its way across his face, she stepped forward and grabbed the front of his coat in her fist playfully. "If you say, 'I told you so,' I'll rip out your tongue."

He laughed and held his hands up in a gesture of surrender. "I wasn't going to say a thing!"

She let him go and they started walking away from the building. As they turned the corner, Lauren crashed into somebody coming the other direction. She looked up to apologize and let out a little gasp.

Ben.

The same look of shock and surprise on Lauren's face was registered on his, and they stared at each other for a long moment. Then Ben's gaze shifted to her left and he saw who she was with. For a fleeting moment Lauren saw something else flash across his features. Was it jealousy? Regret?

Before she could decide, Ben dropped his gaze to the path beneath his feet and hastily mumbled something that sounded like "Excuse me," then hurried off down the path and disappeared from sight.

Lauren's heart started to ache all over again. She felt Dan's arm go around her shoulders comfortingly, and for once she didn't shrug it off. It was nice to have a friend right now.

Why can't I get over him? she asked herself miserably as Dan walked her home. *Why does something as simple as running into him make me fall to pieces? Will I ever be able to see him on campus or at church and not dissolve into a weepy mess?*

Somehow she doubted it. She didn't give her heart to just anyone, and when she gave it to Ben, he'd stomped all over it.

One thing was for sure. Love certainly wasn't all it was cracked up to be.

When they got to her apartment, Dan studied her carefully. "Are you going to be okay?"

"Yes, I'll be fine," she replied unconvincingly. "Thanks for tonight. You're a good friend, Dan."

He smiled gently. "Glad I could help. Feel better, okay?"

She nodded. "I will. Goodnight." Then, with a half-hearted smile, she went into her apartment and shut the door.

Melia looked up from the couch where she was relaxing and reading a book. "Where've you been?" she asked. "I thought your shift at the bookstore ended two hours ago."

"It did, but Dan and I decided to get some dinner and talk." When Melia raised her eyebrows in surprise, Lauren shook her head. "Just as friends, believe me."

"Oh." Melia smiled sheepishly. "Good. You needed to get out. I've been worried about you, the way you've pretty much holed yourself up in your room. Are you sure you're okay?"

"Not yet," Lauren admitted, "but it's getting better. Thanks for your concern, though. It helps to know I have good friends." She smiled gratefully at Melia, then left her roommate to her reading.

When Lauren walked into her bedroom, she flipped on the light and groaned at the sight that greeted her. Piles of dirty clothes surrounded her bed, and she remembered her plan to spend the evening catching up on her laundry.

With a sigh of resignation, she gathered up her clothes, sorted them quickly, then carried them to the laundry room at the end of the second floor walkway. She struggled with the doorknob for a moment, then pushed the door open and walked in. She took two steps inside before she saw someone sitting on the floor across from the dryer with her back against the wall, waiting for a load to finish. When the girl looked up, Lauren almost turned and ran from the room. It was Elena.

Great. That's all I need tonight—a barrage of nasty remarks about losing my boyfriend, she thought miserably.

But when she walked over to the washer, mentally preparing herself to be emotionally attacked, Elena remained silent. Surprised, Lauren turned to glance at her as she lifted the lid on the first washing machine. She was even more surprised when she saw that Elena had been crying.

Lifting her eyebrows in curiosity, she studied Elena for a moment, then asked cautiously, "Are you okay?"

Elena sniffled and swiped a tear from her cheek. "What do you care?" she retorted.

Lauren hesitated. Normally, she might have felt a certain sense of satisfaction at seeing the person who had gone out of her way for so many years to torment her upset. But it seemed so out of character for Elena that she couldn't help wondering what was wrong.

"I care," Lauren refuted quietly. "Do you... want to talk about it?"

Elena sniffled again, then looked up at her with red-rimmed eyes. "My life just royally stinks right now, okay?"

Lauren shifted from one foot to the other as she tried to decide how to take that. "Um, okay," she finally responded carefully. "So, what happened?"

Elena lifted a sheet of paper for Lauren to see. "It's a letter from my dad in Colorado. Apparently, my parents' divorce is finally official, and he wanted to let me know that he's getting married again."

"And... that's bad?" Lauren asked warily.

"Yes, that's bad!" Elena snapped, her eyes flashing dangerously. "He's marrying some woman he met in his new ward down there, and she has four kids from a previous marriage. Do you know what that means? It means he's going to be too involved with his 'new family' to have time for me now. I'll go down to visit him once a year or something, and I'll never fit in because I won't know his new wife or any of her kids, so it's pretty much guaranteed I won't feel like I belong." She paused, then looked down at the paper and fidgeted with the corner. "And as if that wasn't bad enough, I just found out my mom's taking a job in Utah, so she's going to be moving down there."

Lauren was having a hard time following. "Why should that matter?"

"Because, it does!" Elena snapped, fresh tears springing to her eyes. "I felt displaced enough in my family as I was growing up, but now my parents are taking on new lives of their own, *doing* new things of their own, and where does that leave me? When holidays come, where do I go? My parents are no longer together, which isn't entirely bad because their constant fighting made it miserable to be around them anyway. But now this means I no longer have a home to speak of. My older sister lives back east and couldn't care less about staying in touch with me, and to top everything off, I'm just horrible at this school stuff, and I probably won't pass half my classes. I'll probably be put on academic probation..." Elena's sentence trailed off, and she started to cry.

As Lauren stood there, rooted to the floor and completely at a loss for what to say, she found herself feeling sorry for Elena. Lauren couldn't imagine having her parents divorced, nor could she imagine feeling so displaced. It sounded like Elena's home life had never been that great, but now....

Finally, Lauren whispered, "I'm sorry. I had no idea...."

Elena glared back up at her. "Of course you had no idea," she shot back. "You were always too busy with your happy little life to notice. You had so many good friends, parents who loved you, brothers who stuck up for you and paid attention to you, and according to pretty much everyone in the stake, you practically walked on water, what with all your sports accomplishments, your great grades, and the callings you held at church. Do you have any idea what it was like to hear how great you were all the time, and to hear people constantly tell me I was nothing but trouble?"

Lauren's jaw dropped. She had no idea Elena had felt so threatened by her for so long, and was so jealous of everything she had. When she'd recovered enough to speak, she squeaked out, "Why didn't you say something?"

Elena snorted. "Like what? 'Lauren, the rest of us can't compete with you, so could you stop doing everything right?'"

Lauren frowned. "No, but I don't see why you had to be so mean to me instead. It's not my fault that I worked hard in school and did well in sports. And you can't blame me for having friends when you didn't. It's your fault for being so mean all the time."

"I know," Elena admitted, her tone softening a little. "It just seemed easier to take it out on you instead."

"Well, you did a good job of it," Lauren retorted a little bitterly. "It didn't exactly make you an easy person to like."

Elena nodded slowly. "I know," she repeated. "For what it's worth, I'm sorry. I know I was nasty to you, and you didn't deserve it."

Lauren's eyes widened in shock. Hearing an apology from Elena was the last thing Lauren ever expected to hear. Finally, she nodded. "Thanks. That helps more than you know."

It was quiet for a moment, then the buzzer on the dryer sounded, indicating that its load was done. Elena wiped the remaining tears from her cheeks and stood up. "Well, I guess I should get my clothes and get going. I still have a few pages of algebra to struggle through."

Lauren felt a rush of compassion for this girl whom she'd previously thought was only interested in making her life miserable. But now she realized there were some logical explanations for Elena's bitterness and her nasty attitude all these years.

Without hesitation, Lauren found herself asking, "Do you need some help with your algebra?"

Instead of getting the flippant, off-hand remark she was used to, Lauren was surprised to see Elena smile tentatively. "Thanks, but I'll be okay tonight. I might take you up on that offer later, though."

Trying not to look as shocked as she felt, Lauren simply nodded as Elena finished retrieving her clothes from the dryer and left the laundry room. When Lauren was alone, she shook her head in amazement. Never in a million years had she expected an apology from Elena.

As she started to put her clothes in the washer, she realized how much her encounter with Elena had lifted her spirits. While one part of her heart still hurt terribly, another part of her heart felt much lighter. And right then, that meant everything.

Chapter Twenty-Five

Saturday morning, Ben woke up early from a troubled sleep. It didn't take him long to realize he still felt as horrible that morning as he had when he went to bed only a few hours before.

What have I done? he asked himself for the hundredth time since seeing Lauren walking with Dan last night. *How stupid was I, to let her get away?* Seeing Lauren with another guy was an image that would most certainly haunt him for the rest of his life. And he knew he had no one to blame but himself.

He lay in his darkened bedroom, trying to go back to sleep, but his emotions were too churned up. A faint whisper crept into his mind, reminding him of what he'd done in other dark periods of his life.

Read the scriptures.

He tried to shake off the suggestion as he rolled over in bed. He wasn't in the mood to read his scriptures right now. He wanted to just lay in bed and indulge in a good old-fashioned bout of self-pity. But as he lay there, the quiet whisper came again, this time more insistent.

Read the scriptures.

Ben sighed and sat up slowly. He knew that the still, small voice wasn't going to let him rest until he obeyed. *Okay, okay,* he thought in resignation. *I'm going.*

Being careful not to wake Craig, he slipped out of bed and tiptoed over to his dresser for his scriptures. Then he tiptoed out of the room and went into the darkened living room. It was early enough that all his roommates were still asleep, and he found himself thankful for the opportunity to read without interruption. He turned on the lamp by the armchair and sat down, staring silently at the black leather quad resting in his lap. His chest tightened. Just a few short weeks ago, Lauren had given these scriptures to him as a gift. And in return, he'd broken her heart.

An almost overwhelming feeling of sadness encompassed him, and it took him a few minutes to bring himself to open the book. When he finally did, he turned to 1 Nephi and started to read. He was quickly immersed in the story of Nephi and his family, and the struggles they had to face as they followed the commandments of the Lord. When he came to chapter fifteen of 1 Nephi, the words of verse eleven jumped out at him and sent a familiar shiver down his spine.

Do ye not remember the things which the Lord hath said?—If ye will not harden your hearts, and ask me in faith, believing that ye shall receive, with diligence in keeping my commandments, surely these things shall be made known unto you.

He stared at the words of the verse until they became a blur on the page. He'd read the Book of Mormon several times since becoming a member and had read this particular verse many times before. But this time the words seemed to be providing him with the counsel he needed. They made him realize he'd been going about getting his answers the wrong way. Yes, he'd been fasting and praying, but he had to admit, he'd been asking for answers in frustration instead of in faith. The things he'd been struggling with seemed so monumentally unsurpassable in his mind that he hadn't even considered there was a solution.

Ben lifted his eyes from the page and stared unseeingly into the darkness of the room. The words hadn't necessarily given him the answers he needed, but they served to remind him that he only needed to humble himself and ask in faith, believing that Heavenly Father would give him the answers he sought, and then he would receive them.

Feeling more hopeful than he had in weeks, he closed his scriptures and slid off his chair. Then, kneeling in front of it, he folded his arms and bowed his head. This time he reminded himself to pray in faith.

Over the next few days, Ben continued to pray fervently and study the scriptures regularly in order to get more in tune with the Spirit. But while he felt the whisperings of the Holy Ghost telling him everything was going to be okay, he still hadn't been able to come to any conclusions.

As the week dragged on, he could feel Satan working on him harder than ever, and he spent most of Friday afternoon shut in his bedroom and down on his knees. His unanswered questions swirled about in his mind, and no matter how hard he tried, he just couldn't see anything clearly.

Finally, in an urgent plea, he knelt once again in prayer and begged for help. *Please, Heavenly Father, I need help. I'm miserable. I have some life-altering decisions to make, and I've tried my best to do everything thou hast told me to do. But I'm struggling, Father. I still haven't found the answers I need, and I don't know how much longer I can do this. Please… I need thy help.*

He'd no sooner closed his prayer than he heard a knock at his front door. Not in the mood to talk to one of his roommates' friends who seemed to pop by at all hours of the day and night, he sighed and made his way to the door. When he opened it and saw who was standing on the other side, his heart stopped.

It was Jack.

For several long, awkward moments, Ben found himself staring at Lauren's brother. His apprehension grew when he saw the muscle twitch in Jack's tense jaw, and for one scary moment, all the stories Lauren had told him about what her brothers had done to stick up for her flashed through his mind.

He was in trouble. Big trouble.

Finally, Jack spoke. "I should beat the crap out of you for breaking my little sister's heart," he said, a slight growl creeping into his voice.

"I know. I probably deserve it, too," Ben answered quietly, averting his gaze so he wouldn't have to see the rage in Jack's eyes.

An unsettling silence weighed heavily upon them for several moments, but then Jack spoke again, this time his tone softer. "I was on my way up here to check on Lauren, but for some reason my car just kind of steered its way over here."

Ben felt a tingle go down his spine and a lump formed in his throat. Heavenly Father had heard his prayers.

He invited Jack in, and for the next hour, Ben found himself pouring his heart out to Jack, telling him the whole story about how his dad was sick, the wonderful reconciliation they'd had, and how his mom pleaded with him to keep their newly restored peace by not marrying Lauren, at least not yet. He confided in Jack how distraught he'd been lately without Lauren, but that he hadn't been able to come up with any solid answers to his questions.

When he finished, Jack's eyes were filled with sympathy and understanding. "Look, Ben, I'm not going to tell you whether or not you should marry my sister," he began quietly. "It sounds to me like the decisions you have to make aren't going to be easy, but you've been through something like this before when you had to make the decision whether or not to join the Church. You need to do the same things you did then: you have to pray with all your heart and listen to the promptings of the Spirit."

Ben thought about that for a long time after Jack left, and while he knew Jack was right, he'd been doing all these things and it still hadn't helped him solve his problem. How *was* he supposed to follow his heart and keep his newly reunited family together at the same time?

When he woke up the next morning, Ben still hadn't come to any conclusions. He dressed in jeans and a comfortable navy blue sweatshirt, knelt beside his bed to say yet another quick prayer, then headed into the kitchen to try to force down some breakfast. His roommates were already in the process of raiding the refrigerator and cupboards, so he retreated to the couch to wait for the kitchen to clear.

As he sat on the couch, he glanced around the room, his eyes scanning the various pictures and posters on the walls. When his gaze fell on the small, framed picture of the temple sitting on top of the TV, his heart started to pound.

That was it! The temple. He had no trouble remembering the unbelievable feeling of peace he'd felt there when they'd gone as a ward to do baptisms for the dead. It was a feeling like none other, and he suddenly knew that it would be the perfect place to go to think, to hopefully be able to receive the clarity he needed to make his decisions.

He leaped up from the couch and turned to Craig, who was leaning up against the sink, eating a bowl of cereal. "Hey, Craig, can I borrow your truck?"

Craig looked up from his breakfast curiously. "Sure, yeah. Where are you off to?"

"I need to go to Idaho Falls," he answered cryptically. "I should be back in a couple of hours."

Craig shrugged. "No sweat. The engine's running a little rough lately, though, so take it easy on it."

"I will." He got the keys from Craig's dresser and headed out the door, his breakfast completely forgotten.

He managed to find the highway turnoff to Memorial Drive, then followed the statue of Moroni that he could see gleaming brilliantly atop the temple in the near distance. It wasn't long before he reached the temple grounds. He pulled in through the open wrought iron gates of the parking lot and steered the truck into a vacant parking spot.

When he climbed out of the truck, he found himself unable to tear his gaze away from the beautiful white spire pointing heavenward. A feeling of peace pervaded his soul, just as it had when he was here before. Only last time, the circumstances had been very different. Lauren had been at his side, and he'd felt a tiny piece of heaven there with her beside him. This time, he was alone.

Trying not to let the familiar feelings of despair crowd out the gentle whisperings of the Spirit, he walked slowly across the parking lot and onto the temple grounds. Even the snowy blanket of white covering the sloping grounds did not deter from their beauty; in fact, the snow seemed to add to the temple's magnificence. The brilliant morning sun reflected off the shimmering white surface, causing little pinpoints of light to sparkle and reflect everywhere around him.

He walked slowly past the visitors' center until he spotted a stone bench along the carefully shoveled path. As he sat down, he realized he wasn't alone. Several dozen young people, dressed in their Sunday best and wearing warm coats, were standing around talking and laughing, and Ben wondered if they were there to do baptisms for the dead as he had done not many months before.

He watched them for several minutes, then turned his attention back to the problems at hand. If there was any place that would help him get tuned in to the Spirit, he knew this was it. Trying to be discreet, he bowed his head humbly and said a prayer, once again asking for guidance, to know once and for all what he was supposed to do.

He had just closed his prayer when a sudden commotion reached his ears. He looked up to see a young couple coming out of the temple. The young woman was dressed in a beautiful satin and lace wedding gown, her face glowing as she held onto the arm of a beaming young man in a fitted white tux. Camera shutters clicked all around them, and it was obvious from the glow radiating from their faces that they'd just been sealed for time and all eternity. After a few dozen pictures, the gathering crowd on the temple grounds rushed up to talk with them and offer their congratulations.

Never before had Ben been so moved by such an incredible sight. He continued to watch the handsome young couple, the light of the gospel clearly evident in their eyes as they posed for picture after picture with their arms around each other, gazing at each other blissfully and smiling as if everything was right with the world.

And then it hit him. That couple coming out of the temple was supposed to be him and Lauren. *They* were supposed to be that young, newly married couple. *They* were supposed to be sealed together for time and all eternity, just as this young couple had been.

He straightened up in shocked silence. That was it. He had his answer. He was supposed to marry Lauren, even if it meant his parents weren't ready to understand his decision. Yes, his parents and his family were important to him, but he suddenly realized he couldn't go through life trying to please everybody else while making his own life miserable. And that's what he was without Lauren. Miserable.

Maybe one day his parents would come around, but if they didn't, he knew now, without a shadow of a doubt, that this was what he was supposed to do. The Holy Ghost had testified of the gospel's truthfulness to him a year ago, and now it was testifying to him again in much the same way, trying to give him an answer to his prayers.

He didn't know if he was supposed to pursue a career in law or if taking the internship was the right thing to do, but the one thing he *did* know for certain was that marrying Lauren was the right thing for him to do at this point in his life. He loved her more than life itself. She was the other half of him, the other half of his soul that he'd never known was missing. All the other decisions they could make together.

As he watched the beaming young couple before him, he suddenly couldn't wait to be in their place. He wanted to marry Lauren in the temple, where they could be sealed together for time and all eternity. He couldn't think of anything he wanted more than to have her as his eternal companion.

In that moment, everything became perfectly clear. He knew what he had to do.

Leaping to his feet, he ran across the temple grounds and jumped into the truck. He couldn't wait to talk to Lauren. He jammed the key into the ignition, turned the ignition on... and nothing happened. He stared down at the steering wheel in confusion. He turned the key again. Still nothing.

Letting out an anguished cry, he let his head fall forward against the steering wheel. *No! Not now!* he screamed silently. *This can't be happening!*

Opening the door, he leaped out of the truck and ran to find a phone.

Chapter Twenty-Six

"Are you going to stare out that window all night?" Allison asked as she walked into the bedroom. Lauren was sitting on her bed dressed in blue plaid flannel boxers and a baggy white T-shirt. She had an elbow propped up on the windowsill, and her chin rested in her hand as she stared morosely out at the dark, star-scattered sky.

"Maybe," Lauren mumbled without turning. "Last I heard there was no law against being depressed."

Allison rolled her eyes and came over to stand beside the bed. "Lauren, you're making *me* depressed. You haven't come out of this bedroom all day other than to eat and use the bathroom. Snap out of it! You can't spend the rest of your life pining away for Ben."

"Wanna bet?"

Allison sighed and shook her head. "Fine. Go ahead and sulk. But I tell you, it's not healthy. It's Saturday night, for cryin' out loud. You missed all the fun up on campus. Bree and Melia and I went to the movies, and we met the cutest guys...."

Lauren finally moved back from the window and turned to Allison. "Al, please. Right now I really don't want to hear about guys, okay?"

The smile faded from Allison's face. "I'm sorry—"

"Oh, it's okay," she sighed, waving off her friend's apology. "I'm just being a grump."

Allison studied Lauren for a moment, then said, "Laur, why don't you go out with us next Friday? Maybe I can set you up with someone like Ben—"

Tears prickled the backs of her eyes as Lauren shook her head sadly. "There *is* no one else like Ben."

A knock sounded on the front door, interrupting their conversation. Allison glanced over her shoulder toward the living room, then turned back to Lauren. "That's probably Trevor. He said he might stop by tonight." She hesitated. "Are you going to be okay?"

"Yeah, I'll be fine," Lauren assured her. "Go ahead. I'm just going to mope a while longer."

With one last sympathetic look at her friend, Allison left the bedroom and went to answer the door.

When she was alone again, Lauren flopped onto her stomach and dropped her chin into her hands. She hadn't been joking when she'd told Allison she wanted to mope. Moping seemed to be the order of the day. And she was entitled. After the disastrous relationships she'd had, she'd sworn never to do three things again: let herself be taken in by a handsome face, let her guard down, and fall in love. And in the past six months, she'd done all three.

She shook her head sadly. *This is what comes from listening to your heart instead of your head,* she chastised herself silently. *I hope you remember this the next time you're confronted by a pair of warm brown eyes and an incredible smile.*

Sighing heavily, she rolled over on her bed and stared up at the ceiling. She heard voices coming from the front room and felt like sticking her tongue out at them. Trevor was a good guy, and Allison deserved that, but right now it only made her heart ache worse to see somebody else happy in love when she wasn't.

The voices grew louder, and Lauren's brow wrinkled in confusion. It sounded like someone was having an argument. Her curiosity piqued, she sat up and strained her ears to listen. She could hear Allison's voice, and there was a quieter, yet insistent male voice as well. It sounded vaguely familiar, but she was too far away to place it.

Finally, her curiosity got the better of her, and she tiptoed out of her room and into the hall to eavesdrop. She neared the living room and was surprised to see Allison standing in the open doorway, blocking somebody from coming in. And judging by the agitation in her voice, she was telling the caller to get lost. Just then Lauren heard the fellow speak and her heart leaped into her throat. Ben!

She took a couple of steps into the living room and froze when she caught a glimpse of Ben standing in the open doorway, his entrance still blocked by Allison who remained rooted firmly in place.

"What's going on?" she asked in confusion.

Ben stopped talking abruptly at the sound of her voice. He had to peer around Allison to see her. "Lauren!" he exclaimed, sounding both excited and anxious. "Please, I've got to talk to you."

Allison glanced over her shoulder at Lauren, and when Lauren finally nodded her permission, Allison moved back to let him in. When he stepped through the door, Lauren gasped.

"What on earth happened to you?" she asked, taking in Ben's rumpled appearance. He had a long streak of grease running along his right cheekbone, his hair was tousled, and he looked more frazzled than she'd ever seen him.

"Don't ask," he grimaced, raking his fingers through his thick brown hair in an effort to look presentable. "Let's just say that Craig's truck got a series of engine repairs today, thanks to me."

Lauren stared at him in silent confusion, and Allison took that as her cue to leave. She stepped between them in passing, and when she was merely inches from Ben's face, she glowered at him and threatened, "You hurt her again and you'll wish you'd never lived." Then she disappeared into the back bedroom of the apartment.

Ben stared after her retreating figure in surprise. "Wow, you certainly don't need a bodyguard with Allison around."

Lauren crossed her arms and did her best to glare at Ben, in spite of the pounding of her heart. "Yeah, well, she's loyal. Which is more than I can say for you."

Ben flinched at her barb. He turned pleading eyes in her direction. "Lauren, I need to talk to you. Please, say you'll hear me out."

She hesitated, but when she didn't say no, he took that as a good sign and steered her over to the couch. He sat down beside her and took a deep breath to calm himself. He'd imagined this moment a hundred times over during the day as he'd fought to get back to Rexburg, but in each of those hundred times, he'd never imagined her looking so beautiful.

Lauren's oversized T-shirt and flannel boxers did nothing to detract from her slender figure and her long, reddish-brown hair that was disheveled and hanging down around her shoulders. Her face had been scrubbed clean of all makeup, leaving her skin with its natural, warm glow. He didn't think he had ever seen her look more enchanting. His excitement grew as he thought about the possibility of being able to see this side of her on a daily basis for the rest of his life.

"Lauren, the most amazing thing happened to me today. I've been fasting and praying a lot the past few weeks, trying to come up with answers to some tough questions, but no matter what I did, I couldn't get the answers I needed. Then I realized that what I was missing was a place I could go that would bring some peace into my soul and help me think more clearly. It dawned on me this morning that the perfect place was the temple. So I borrowed Craig's truck and drove down to Idaho Falls."

He tentatively reached for her hands. "When I got there, I found a quiet place on the temple grounds to sit and pray. When I did, something happened that suddenly made everything perfectly clear. I was so excited when I realized that I finally had my answer that I could hardly wait to come back here and talk to you. So I jumped into Craig's truck—and it wouldn't start."

Lauren stared at him in confusion. "What do you mean it wouldn't start?"

"I put the key in the ignition and turned it on, and nothing happened!" He shook his head and grinned. "The engine wouldn't even turn over. I thought it was just the battery, but when I finally found someone to help me, we discovered that the starter motor was bad, and a couple of other things needed to be fixed." He rolled his eyes and groaned. "Man, it was just one thing after another. But while I was stranded in Idaho Falls, getting more and more frustrated by the minute, it dawned on me that Satan knew I had the answer to my prayers and was doing everything in his power to stop me from getting here tonight."

"Ben, you've completely lost me," Lauren said impatiently. "What exactly are you trying to say?"

Ben's eyes shimmered with unshed tears as his hands tightened around hers. "Don't you see? All these years I've been struggling to find my place in this world, to know who I am and what I was supposed to be doing with my life, and then I found the gospel. But even after I was baptized I knew there was still something missing, something I couldn't quite put my finger on. Then when Craig talked to me about coming here to BYU-Idaho, I had the strongest feeling that this was what I was supposed to do. I couldn't shake the feeling that there was something here for me, something that no other college could offer. And this morning, when I was at the temple, it was as if a veil had been lifted from my eyes. Everything became perfectly clear."

Lauren stared at him, her eyes questioning.

"It was you, Lauren," he whispered, his voice becoming thick with emotion. He took her into his arms and looked deep into her eyes. "I know now that I came 2,000 miles to find *you*."

"Oh, Ben..." she managed, tears stinging her eyes.

"Heavenly Father sent me here to find you, and I did." He raised one hand to her face and tenderly brushed a stray lock of hair from her cheek, then pulled her closer. "I know I got a little confused and distant, but some things happened when I was in Boston that threw me into a tailspin. I had some big decisions to make, and I was afraid you'd misunderstand my motives if I told you what was bothering me. You've been hurt so much in the past by guys telling you one thing and doing another, and I've seen what it did to you. I thought I was shielding you from that, but instead, I've hurt you by keeping everything to myself."

Lauren pulled back from him a little as painful memories of the past few weeks flashed through her mind. "You did hurt me;

I won't deny that. But what was so terrible that you thought you couldn't tell me or let me help you work it out?"

Ben lowered his gaze and again took her hands in his before he continued in a strained whisper. "My dad and I managed to smooth things over while I was home, and I even got up enough courage to tell him I'd fallen in love with you and planned to ask you to marry me."

Lauren let out a little gasp, but he just held her hands tighter and hurried on.

"When I was in my room packing the night before I flew back to Idaho Falls, my mom and sister begged me not to go through with my plans, worrying that if I married a Mormon girl in the temple where my father couldn't watch the ceremony, it might ruin our tentative reconciliation." Ben hesitated, searching for the right words. "I... I got scared, Lauren. It was like being baptized all over again and knowing that I could be splitting my family apart for the second time. After the roller coaster I've been on this past year, I wasn't sure I could handle that."

Tears started to flow freely down Lauren's cheeks, but she made no effort to wipe them away.

Ben pressed her hands to his lips and kissed them gently. "At the same time, I knew that our relationship was ready to move to the next step, that it would be impossible for me to just be your 'friend' much longer.

"There's one more thing," Ben continued huskily, struggling to keep his own emotions under control. "I was offered an internship in Boston by my former bishop. It sounded too good to pass up, but accepting it meant I'd have to move back to Boston, and the thought of not being with you every day was too much to bear. I had so much to think about and so many critical decisions to make that I distanced myself from you—and from everyone else—trying to eliminate distractions so I could make the right decision."

It was quiet for a moment before Lauren nervously whispered, "But you said you'd finally gotten some answers?"

He nodded, then looked at her steadily. "I still don't have all the answers, but I do know that the thought of losing you was far worse than the idea of losing my family again." He drew her closer and pressed her hand over his heart. "Lauren, you mean everything to me. You're my life. Whatever decisions I still have to make, we'll make them together. I love you, Lauren. Please... please say you'll give me another chance."

For a moment, Lauren was overcome by emotion and couldn't speak. Her fears and anxieties were struggling to return, threatening to overwhelm the simple beauty of his words. She fought down a momentary urge to panic. She slowly pulled her hands from his grasp and stood, then walked a few paces away from the couch and turned away from him, wrapping her arms around her as if to shield herself from his influence. She couldn't think clearly with him so close. She loved him so much. Still....

Ben stared at her in confusion. "Lauren? What is it? What's wrong?"

She shook her head slowly, struggling to steady her voice. "Ben, half an hour ago I was resigned to the fact that we were through, and that I'd have to move on with my life. But now, here you are, wanting things the way they were. I'm not sure that's as easy as you're making it out to be."

Ben stood and rapidly closed the distance between them, then gently turned her around to face him. "Why isn't it, Lauren?" he said earnestly. "Tell me, I really want to know."

A sudden onrush of tears blurred her vision as she tried to meet his gaze. "You broke my heart once, Ben, and I managed to live through it. I'm not sure I could do it a second time."

"I messed up, Lauren, I admit that, but I promise you, there won't be a second time. I've been miserable without you, and I can only guess at what I've put you through." He winced at the pain in her eyes, but he pressed on. "All I can say is that I love you, Lauren, and I need you in my life more than you could possibly imagine."

He gently wiped the tears from her cheeks, disgusted at himself for making her cry. "Oh, Lauren," he murmured, gently pressing a kiss to her forehead, "I'm so sorry for what I've put you through these past weeks. But I'll prove to you that I'm ready to make myself a permanent fixture in your life."

Wordlessly, Ben released her and slipped his hand into his pocket. He withdrew a tiny, blue velvet box and stared down at it for a moment, fingering its soft fabric. Lauren's eyes opened wide in surprise.

"As soon as the truck was fixed," he explained, "I drove home as fast as I could and got this from my apartment before coming here." He paused, then slowly opened the lid.

Lauren's hands flew to her mouth. Nestled inside the velvet box was the most beautiful engagement ring she had ever seen. The three sparkling, emerald-cut diamonds mounted on a beautiful gold band glittered in the light and took her breath away. She looked up at Ben in shock.

He smiled a little sheepishly. "I got this for you for Christmas. I was hoping I could convince you to marry me then, but things got a little crazy and, well… you know the rest."

He glanced down briefly at the ring, then looked into her eyes, searching their depths to judge her reaction.

"I want you to know that this doesn't mean I think we should rush to set a date or anything," he quickly assured her. "If you need some time, I'm willing to wait for you. I'll wait as long as you need. It will be a few more months before I can take you to the temple, but I wouldn't think of marrying you anywhere else except in the Lord's House—I'm not settling for any, 'until death do you part' clause. When you're ready, we'll be married in the temple and be sealed for time and all eternity."

For a long moment Lauren didn't say anything. She looked from his face to the ring in his hand. "I don't know, Ben," she said, hesitating. "I wasn't expecting… I wasn't ready for this. I…."

But Ben didn't give her a chance to finish. "Lauren, listen to me. Do you remember what we talked about at Thanksgiving? You told me you were afraid our love wouldn't last beyond tomorrow. Well, I'm standing here before you right now to prove to you that you were wrong."

He slipped the ring back into his pocket, then gathered her hands in his and held them tightly. "I know you're scared, Lauren, but I learned a year ago that sometimes you have to follow your heart. Now I'm asking you to do the same. Forget what your head's been telling you, and listen to your heart."

He paused for a beat, letting his words settle in her mind, then he went on. "I know I was a real jerk to push you away when things got rough, and I know you probably deserve someone better than me, but if it takes me the rest of my life, I'll prove to you that I can make you happy." His voice dropped to a husky whisper as her tear-filled eyes met his determined ones. "Please, Lauren, say you'll marry me. I can't think of anything I'd love more than to spend the rest of eternity with you."

Lauren stared silently into his intense brown eyes, so filled with love and tenderness. Slowly, and with a conscious effort, she pushed aside the warning voices in her mind and listened instead to the gentle stirrings of her heart. What she heard there were the soft, sweet whisperings of the Spirit telling her that this man had been brought into her life for a purpose. He was someone she could love and trust, and someone who would love and trust her in return. He was, without a doubt, the man she thought she would never meet.

A warm, joyous feeling slowly spread throughout her body when she realized that the Spirit had spoken simply and sweetly to her soul, giving her the answer she sought.

Fresh tears sprang to Lauren's eyes, and a sob escaped her throat as she stepped into Ben's arms and buried her face against his shoulder, wetting it with her tears. "Ben, I don't know what I ever did to deserve you."

Her muffled words were music to his ears. He tightened his arms around her and whispered into her hair, "So, is that a yes?"

This time she laughed, and when she stepped back, she gave him a teary-eyed smile and nodded. "Yes, that's a yes."

Ben crushed her in his arms and whirled her around, causing her to squeal with surprise. Then he stopped and just held her close, savoring the incredible feeling of having the woman he loved in his arms, and reveling in the certainty that she would someday be his wife.

"Oh, Lauren," he breathed as he buried his face in her hair and closed his eyes blissfully, "you have no idea how happy this makes me."

When he finally released her, Lauren's face held a look of caution. "Ben, I hope you were serious about taking things slowly and not rushing into setting a date. There are still so many things I have to work through...."

"I know there are," he said as he took her face in his hands, "and I meant what I said about waiting until you're ready. We both have some growing to do. And who knows, maybe by the time we're ready to get married, I can turn my dad around and convince him that this is what's best for me... that it's what I want in my life. Somehow he'll just have to understand that marrying you in the temple is the most important thing in the world to me."

Without taking his eyes from her beautiful face, Ben again retrieved the velvet box from his pocket and removed the ring. He reached for her hand and took her delicate fingers in his strong ones, taking great pleasure in slipping the ring onto her finger.

Lauren's cheeks flushed with a mixture of disbelief and inexplicable joy as she stared at the sparkling diamonds adorning her left hand. She looked up into Ben's face and gently traced the dark grease streak on his cheek with her hand. He was so handsome, so perfect. And inside, she knew there was a beautiful soul to match.

Ben opened his arms, and she nestled deeply into his waiting embrace, letting herself imagine how it would feel to wake up beside him every morning, to have him there to cheer her up when she was down, to have his smile brighten her every day....

She closed her eyes and smiled softly, her musings melting away when their lips met in a tender, loving kiss that said more than mere words could ever express. And in that moment, she knew how life with Ben would feel. It would feel *wonderful*.

ABOUT THE AUTHOR

Erin Klingler is a stay-at-home mom who rarely finds herself actually staying home. When she's not shuttling her kids to their activities or fulfilling her church responsibilities, she loves to indulge herself in her two favorite pastimes: reading and writing. She rarely goes anywhere without a book in her purse and a notebook to jot down story ideas that pop into her head at the oddest times (like at red lights or while buckling kids into car seats).

Additionally, Erin loves to decorate her home, sew, design websites, ride horses, and run errands in her classic 1979 Volkswagen Beetle yellow convertible, affectionately named "Tweety." She also loves to play sports and prides herself on being able to play a mean game of tennis. She currently serves as the Relief Society secretary in her ward.

Born and raised in Milpitas, California, Erin moved to Idaho to attend Ricks College (now BYU-Idaho), where she majored in Preschool Education. There, she met her husband, Dave, a Rexburg native. They married soon thereafter and moved to nearby Idaho Falls to raise their family.

Erin and her husband still live in Idaho Falls, Idaho, with their five children. They share their busy lives with two German Shepherds, a blue and gold macaw, and a Norwegian Fjord/POA pony named "Moose."

Erin loves to hear from her readers. You can send her email at erin@erinklingler.com, or visit her website at www.erinklingler.com.